DEADLY DREAMS

John Scirica

authorHOUSE®

AuthorHouse™
1663 Liberty Drive
Bloomington, IN 47403
www.authorhouse.com
Phone: 833-262-8899

Published by AuthorHouse 08/16/2021

ISBN: 978-1-6655-3454-3 (sc)
ISBN: 978-1-6655-3452-9 (hc)
ISBN: 978-1-6655-3453-6 (e)

Library of Congress Control Number: 2021916189

DEDICATION

I dedicate this book to my wife, Marie, who has been my constant support for over fifty years. Throughout our journey through this life, she has never wavered in her belief that I would be successful. As I struggled mightily to become a public-school teacher, attending college at night after already receiving my degree in order to become certified, and sending in countless teaching job applications, there were days I thought it better to surrender and find a different career path. She never lost faith in me. I leaned on her then. I lean on her now.

CHAPTER 1

The first time it happened, he didn't even realize what had occurred. It was the beginning of a lifelong nightmare. He had just turned nine years old and had completed his training to become an altar boy. He had served as an apprentice server several times along with another newbie and two veteran servers. This was his first time as a real altar boy without the assistance of older boys and he was looking forward to not having to be their slave and do all the clean up and take all the verbal abuse that went with being several years younger.

As he walked up to the stately structure with its towering pillars on each side of the three soaring marble stairways, he was under whelmed. You see, Jimmy grew up only a few blocks from St. Basil's and, although it was an impressive sight, it was typical of the many Catholic Churches in the New York borough of Queens. It was a mild day for late fall and the Dodgers were going to play in the World Series that afternoon. Little did the faithful fans realize that next year, their beloved team would leave Brooklyn and play the 1958 season on the other side of the continent in some la-la land called Los Angeles.

Jimmy Reardon was a slight boy with dirty blond hair and blue eyes. His hair was neat and shiny and combed back with a small wave on one side. He arrived in the sacristy earlier than he needed to. The sacristy was the area in the back of the altar where the preparations for service took place. It was narrow but encircled the rear of the altar and was quite long. Since the floor was made up of small tiles and the closets were wooden, every step the young boy took echoed throughout the dark and gloomy expanse.

However, Jimmy was filled with energy and unbridled enthusiasm. He chose his black cassock, a long garment with billowing sleeves, from the closet. It was important to find one below the level of his socks but not so long that he would trip over it. You sure didn't want to trip and fall on the altar on your first time on the sacred stage. He didn't put on his surplice yet (the white, starched, short-waisted garment which went over the cassock) because he did not want to look too anxious, and all the older boys always seemed to wait until the last minute to put it on.

He walked around alone in his thoughts, looking at the cruets that would hold the wine and water, playing with the candle lighter and adjusted the wick many times. Soon it was getting late, and no one had arrived to join him. Two boys were assigned to serve the mass and they were to arrive a half hour prior to Mass to get all ready. It was now 7:35 am and only twenty-five minutes until Mass would begin and no one else had arrived. He knew what needed to be done but was nervous to begin without the senior altar boy who was to join him.

Now it was 7:45 and Father Kleinburger, the old pastor arrived. He called out loudly for an altar boy. Jimmy quickly ran toward the grumpy voice and said, "I'm here, Father." The balding old man peered over his glasses at the young man and growled, "Why aren't the candles lit? And you should have turned on the lights on the altar. Where is the other boy?" Jimmy squeaked out, "The other boy hasn't shown up yet, Father." The priest bent down and through his yellowing teeth spit out, "Do you know what you are supposed to do? I hope you can do this without messing up. How long have you been an altar boy?" The little boy stuttered out, "This is my first time as a server, Father." The old priest straightened up and made a frown. "Well, get going. And put on your surplice. And don't forget to fill the cruets with the wine. Do you know which wine is mine? Never mind, I'll do it myself. Now get dressed and light the candles on the altar."

Jimmy ran to get the brass candle lighter, adjusted the taper and ran toward the sacristy door that led to the altar. Realizing he hadn't yet put on his surplus he skidded to a stop, sliding along the tile floor as his leather soles refused to grip on the smooth and worn floor of the old room behind the church. Clutching the five-foot-long brass and wood candle lighter, he ran back to get his surplice which was on a hanger to keep the creases that his mother had proudly ironed into it. Confused and in a hurry, he didn't know where to place the long pole to free his hands, so he quickly put it on the floor and pulled his surplice from the hanger. The metal hanger bounced and fell onto the hard tile floor and made more noise than Jimmy would have liked but he pulled the white garment over his head, pushed his arms through the gigantic sleeves, grabbed the candle lighter off the floor and ran to the church entrance.

His heart was beating so hard, he could feel it thumping in his chest as he climbed the marble steps of the huge altar. He placed the taper next to the burning wick of one of the smaller candles on the altar which were kept burning and it lit. He then raised it up to the tall candles in their massive holders and waited for the candle to light. Nothing. The flame on the taper began to shrink so he brought it down and adjusted the waxy string and the glow suddenly increased and the flame came to life. Again, he brought the burning taper next to where he thought the wick on the candle was. It seemed like the candle had grown even larger, towering well over the nine-year-old's head. He moved it carefully around the top of the candle and hoped to touch the evasive wick, but it would not light. The taper almost burned out, so he again brought the pole down and pushed up the adjustment attachment and bent the taper downward as he had been shown many times by the senior altar boys. Raising the long pole again to the candle, his shoulder began to ache as the candle-lighter seemed to become heavier with time.

He knew time was now short, but he didn't realize how short. He heard Father Kleinburger's deep sigh and turned to see the priest, red-faced and looking angry at the portal to the sacristy. He came out in his elaborate vestments, carrying the cruets filled with wine and water that Jimmy was supposed to have brought out by now and placed on the small table next to the altar. Handing the cruets to the mortified child, the pastor grabbed the candle lighter and said in a voice that echoed throughout the vast church, "Are you blind? You're missing the wick completely. Give me that!" He quickly lit the candles as Jimmy hurriedly went to put the cruets in their proper place. The boy who now felt his face flush with both fear and embarrassment hastily returned to the priest. The clergyman shoved the wooden and metal pole into the boy's chest and stormed off the altar into the back room. Jimmy followed and returned the candle-lighter back on its place on the metal ladder that led to the roof of the church. He immediately heard the gruff voice of Father Kleinburger calling him to get back and get ready to start the Mass. Jimmy ran up and led the priest into the church as he pulled on the long, red cord that rang a small bell signaling to the congregation that the Mass was about to begin.

It would be six months before Sister Mary Elizabeth set up the eye chart in back of the classroom and Jimmy had to bring home a note to his parents that he failed the vision test and should be brought to an eye doctor. His parents immediately made an appointment and the doctor found that he had serious nearsightedness and would need glasses. But today, he had no thought of glasses and no idea that his vision was anything less than what it should be. He didn't know that his poor vision kept him from seeing the wick in the candle high above his head. He had studied all the Latin prayers diligently, he paid attention to the many moves he needed to do on the altar, he even listened carefully to the senior altar boys who were often brutal to the trainee youngsters because he so much wanted to be a good server, serving both the priest and the Lord. Now he felt so deeply pained. This was his first time as an altar boy, and he blew it. And, of all the priests who would celebrate the mass, it had to be the pastor. His eyes welled up with tears as the Mass progressed and Jimmy perfectly anticipated the celebrant's needs. All his training and studying had clicked in. But he was devastated. He wanted this to be perfect and the candle fiasco before the Mass even began had ruined that.

The Mass ended without another flaw and Jimmy led the priest into the sacristy. This time they exited through the door on the other side of the altar which led to the priest's dressing table. It was an elaborate wooden structure with many cabinet doors and a long counter in which the priest could place the many smaller items of his vestments. Jimmy remembered to bow his head and recite the interjection, "Praise be to you, Lord Jesus Christ." The old cleric didn't even bother to answer him as Jimmy had expected. In training, he was told that the priest would answer, "Peace be with you." Father Klineburger said nothing as he began to remove his vestments. Jimmy stood there for a few seconds, making sure the priest would not respond since he didn't want to appear rude. But when he realized that no reply was forthcoming, he walked back to the other side of the back room to begin his post-Mass duties. He first turned off the main church lights and left the altar lights burning as he had been told to do. Then he went and lifted the candle lighter from its place on the metal ladder. His heart began to beat faster again as he relived the painful memory of his futile attempt to light the candles. Now, however, he was able to extinguish them without difficulty.

After bringing in the almost empty cruets, pouring the water and the tiny amount of wine left down the drain of the small sink, and rinsing them out, he removed his surplus and carefully placed it on the hanger his mother had given him. Now dressed in only the cassock, he looked out the small, dirt covered window that looked out upon the church courtyard. He was alone – the pastor was on the other side of the sacristy – alone both in being and in thought. He was so upset and tried to tell himself that it was not a big deal. Goof ups probably happened often to new altar boys. At least the rest of his first mass went smoothly. He remembered all he needed to do and said all the Latin prayers perfectly. Still, his eyes began to fill as he breathed deeply. Suddenly, he heard a somewhat familiar voice.

The voice was from someone that he heard before, but it didn't sound normal. It was strange, kind of like listening to someone speaking through a dense, thick fog. The words had to fight their way through some sort of barrier on their way to his inner ear. And yet, he knew this voice, but he couldn't place it. For some reason, it frightened him. He felt the small hairs on the back of his neck begin to rise on their own, like a small platoon of soldiers rising to attention.

As shaken as he was, he began to move toward the eerie sound. He walked into the sacristy and what he saw caused his feet to become rooted to the tile floor. He felt an icy finger crawling down his spine and now the hairs on his arms joined the hairs on his neck rising as if they had a mind of their own. He couldn't move, couldn't speak, couldn't look away even though the sight before his eyes petrified him beyond anything that he had yet experienced in his young life.

There before him was Sister Anastasia but it wasn't really her. It looked like her, but she was faint and somewhat out of focus. He didn't realize it at the time but after recalling this event later, he saw that she was not in color but in black and white. Then he noticed, concluded without doubt that Sister had no body – just a floating head in this ghostly mist and yet, the missing torso didn't cause him more anxiety – no, he began to feel a calmness washing over him. The frigid feeling he had began to melt away.

This was probably the first time that he was in the presence of Sister Anastasia – if he was actually in her presence – that he wasn't fearful that he would be slapped across his face or, at the very least, scolded for something he did or didn't do. Sister was the school's principal and a strict and mean tempered disciplinarian. Jimmy was a good student but liked to make his classmates laugh and was quite adept at causing fellow pupils to convulse at inopportune times. Sister Mary Elizabeth, his teacher, did not find this activity as funny as Jimmy's audience and he was often sent to Sister Anastasia for discipline. That usually meant having Sister's face in his, so close that he could see his reflection in her unframed glasses. He knew at these times that an open hand would soon strike his cheek and the wait was worse than the actual blow. He would wish that the scolding would be fast so the inevitable whack would be over with quickly.

But this time, he was not anxious, not afraid, not in a rush for the nun's words to end. Her voice did not have its usual timber. Rather than harshness, it was almost soothing and gentle. That's why, although he had some recognition of the sound earlier, he couldn't quite identify it. Up to this point, he hadn't focused on what the now gentle nun was saying. He listened to the weightless head and now could understand the words that it spoke.

"Please ask Father to help me," the bobbing head pleaded. "I am in pain. I am afraid I am dying." It wheezed, "Please get Father. Tell him I need help. Now." Jimmy had hated Sister Anastasia because every interaction with her was a painful one. But now, he felt compassion for her. He wanted to help her or it or whatever this thing was. The face looked softer than it had ever looked when he faced her those times in her office or in the hallway. Rather than being superior to him, she was now begging for his help. The image began to fade and then suddenly, it was gone.

Jimmy stood there for a moment, confused and lost. His neck felt wet, and he wiped perspiration from the collar of the cassock and then mopped his brow. He became conscious that his breathing was rapid and the calmness that he had just felt only a few moments ago was now replaced by a tension that felt like a tightening cord around his chest. He gathered his thoughts and reviewed what had just taken place. Despite the ludicrousness of this vision, there was no doubt in Jimmy's mind that Sister was in desperate trouble.

He looked about and then ran into the other side of the sacristy where Father was just about ready to leave. As Jimmy slid to a stop, the old priest looked up and a scowl formed on his ruddy face.

"What do you think this is, a playground? What's your name again?"

"Jimmy Reardon, Father."

"Well, you listen to me, Mr. Reardon. If you want to continue to be an altar boy, you better get your act together. Do you understand me?"

"Yes, Father, but I have to tell you something."

"Now what?" the crusty cleric crowed.

"Uh, Father, Sister Anastasia needs your help. I think she's sick."

"What! Was she here? What are you talking about?"

"I, uh, I saw her. Here. Before."

The clergyman moved slowly toward the young man. His eyebrows began to descend as his lips curled downward. He slowly moved his head closer to the boy. "I'm asking you again, was Sister here?"

"Well, no, Father. But I saw a vision of her, and she said she was sick and needed you to come right away."

The priest pulled his head back a bit. "A vision? A vision? Now, you listen to me. I don't know what kind of game you think you are playing here. Maybe you think that you are like the story of Bernadette at Lourdes that you learned in school?" His voice began to grow louder and deeper as his anger rose. "Now you clean up in there and get back to school and I will speak to Father Krause and see if you should continue to serve on the altar. Now get going and not another word about this nonsense."

"But Father . . .," Jimmy stammered. The priest slowly turned toward the little boy; his eyes blazed behind his glasses.

"Get going!"

Jimmy turned and walked slowly back to the other side of the sacristy. He was so sure that Sister needed help, but he tried. He began to take off his church garments and looked up as Father Kleinburger left by the door that led to the side of the altar. It was hopeless. He wouldn't listen to him and trying again would only further anger the priest.

Jimmy descended the steps in the back room of the sacristy and left the church and headed toward the school which was housed in an old stone building next door to the rectory where the priests lived. He had just enough time to get to his classroom on the second floor before attendance would be called.

Soon he would find out what occurred that morning in the church would have a major impact on his life – both now and forever.

CHAPTER 2

It was close to 11:00 AM and Sister asked the class to take out their math textbooks. Math was not one of Jimmy's favorite subjects despite being one of the brightest students in the class, even though he was often (very often) in trouble for displaying his comedic abilities. His classmates looked to him to break the monotony of studies and Jimmy happily obliged. One of his favorite bits involved Madeline Kaufer when she ate breakfast in class. You see, if any students received Communion at Mass before school, they were permitted to eat breakfast in class. Madeline would always have the same so-called meal – a package of chocolate cupcakes and a small container of an orange juice drink. Jimmy would do all he could to make Madeline laugh and cough up some of her food and drink. Timing was everything and he wouldn't feel he was successful unless poor Madeline had brown glop pouring forth from her mouth while stream of orange colored liquid shot out in streams from her nostrils.

But that scenario had played out hours earlier and now it was time for math. Jimmy was filled with dread as the children all turned to the page that was written on the blackboard. Just as Sister Mary Elizabeth began to lecture about remembering how to carry over remainders in long division, the old wooden door in the back of the room opened and Sister James Marie, the fearsome 8th grade nun, motioned for Sister Mary Elizabeth to come to the rear of the room.

Now, nuns were like any other group of workers, they had their cliques, and these two nuns were seldom in each other's company. The children may have been young, but they recognized these little groupings. James Marie was feared by both the children and parents and probably some of the other nuns. Mary Elizabeth was a young and usually kind person who liked to laugh. Jimmy often got her to laugh in spite of herself when he pulled off some of his shenanigans.

James Marie was short and stout. She was shaped somewhat like a square and even with her starched headpiece that rose about 6 inches on top of her wrapped up head, she barely reached Mary Elizabeth's shoulders. Her usual ruddy complexion was even more flushed as her cheeks took on a deep scarlet hue.

Her body language suggested that she was quite agitated, as she made frequent and rapid gestures with her hands. Mary Elizabeth occasionally looked back in the direction of the front of the room where Jimmy was sitting. This was not unusual since this interaction between the two nuns was an ideal time for him to find some way to cause hysteria to break out in his area of the room. But not this time. Something told Jimmy that this was serious, and he didn't know why, but he felt he was intimately involved.

He watched intently as Mary Elizabeth suddenly raised both her hands over her mouth as if in horror. Keeping her hands in their place she nodded slowly and then turned and called for Jimmy to come to the back of the room.

His classmates watched as the boy got up and began walking to the rear of the room, his leather soles producing a clap with each step. The other children had seen this before. Jimmy was in trouble, but this time made the mistake of doing some mischief that involved James Marie. This was a serious mistake. James was quick with her hands and often used her fists rather than the open hand preferred by the other nuns. Jimmy stood before the two women dressed in layers of black and white, giving the appearance of clothed penguins. He had tried to think about what he had done that he hadn't yet been punished for as he walked up to them. Nothing had come to mind, but he knew that innocence meant little when dealing with the supreme authority of these purveyors of pain.

Mary Elizabeth spoke first. "James, Father Kleinburger wants to see you."

Jimmy was confused. What did he screw up this morning that wasn't already dealt with? His mouth was dry, and his eyes welled up in spite of himself. "Sister, there was no other altar boy this morning. I was alone and tried to light the candles, but I had trouble finding the wick. I didn't . . ."

Sister James Marie interrupted his stammering, "Never mind all that, mister. Father needs to see you. Now!"

Turning abruptly, she started to walk quickly toward the stairway. Jimmy turned to his teacher with pleading eyes, but she responded to his forlorn look by saying, "Go with Sister, James. You must go see Father. It will be alright."

But Jimmy sensed that it would not be alright. He saw tears in Sister Mary Elizabeth's eyes and a look that frightened him.

"Well, mister, did you hear me? Let's go!" Sister James Marie commanded.

Jimmy knew there was no option. He turned from the nun at the door to his classroom and reluctantly followed the broad, hulking woman whose arms swung in opposite cadence with the long string of rosary beads that hung from her belt.

She moved rapidly, faster than Jimmy thought this portly nun could travel. He had to almost trot to keep up with her. Soon they arrived at the principal's office. There seemed to be much activity going on and there were two policemen standing just outside the doorway speaking to Father Krause who was the young priest in charge of the altar boys.

"Sit down, there," Sister James Marie barked out to Jimmy as she pointed to a long wooden bench opposite the door to Sister Anastasia's office.

He plodded over to the hard bench where he had sat many times waiting to see the principal when he was in trouble for some perceived misdeed. While he shuffled to the long pew, he looked up at the two men in uniform with wide eyes. Something was up and it wasn't something good.

He sat there until it was almost lunchtime and knew that if he weren't allowed to go to lunch soon, he would miss lunch time which was strictly held to schedule. The police officers had left, and Father Krause had gone into the office and closed the door. He could hear voices but didn't recognize them through the door and was unable to understand what they were saying. Finally, Father Krause came out and approached Jimmy. He was a young man of about 27 or 28, with dark hair slicked back on both sides. The girls in school thought he was handsome and cool, and Father Krause often stood outside smoking a cigarette and talking to the kids, mostly giggling girls. He was the priest in charge of the altar boys and Jimmy had learned the Latin needed to be said at Mass and all the moves necessary to serve as an altar boy from Father Krause.

He smiled at Jimmy and said, "Father Kleinburger wants to talk to you, Jimmy."

"But Father, I tried my best this morning. The other kid didn't show up and I was all alone, and I had trouble lighting the candles and I did everything else right. I think I did."

"Jimmy, relax," the genial cleric soothed. "I don't know what it's about, but Father isn't mad at you. He said he wanted to just talk to you about this morning's Mass. I think it's something about the cassock or something. Nothing to worry about."

His cassock? He didn't understand. He thought he picked one out that was long enough, and he was sure he closed all the snaps.

Jimmy rose from the bench and accompanied Father Krause to the door. He entered and turned to see the priest smile and close the door without entering himself. Jimmy would face the pastor alone.

CHAPTER 3

Father Kleinburger was seated at Sister Anastasia's desk. He sat facing one of the giant windows that had huge roll-up shades that were partially opened. He was deep in thought and appeared to not have noticed Jimmy entering the room. The small boy stood near the entrance to the office, fearing to take any steps toward the priest until told to do so. Slowly, the old priest turned toward the child and a forced smile slowly emerged on his face. Rather than making Jimmy feel comfortable, this attempt at warmth brought a chill to the boy's entire being. He wasn't sure if it were the fact that he had no recollection of ever seeing this crusty man in black smile or whether he could sense that this effort to make Jimmy relax was false. Whatever the cause, it was having an opposite effect. The little boy was frightened. He wasn't sure why but the fear he felt deep within him kept him frozen in place. A syrupy voice bid the intimidated and suspicious boy to approach him.

"Come over here, Jimmy. Sit down," the now grinning cleric said, pointing to a chair on the opposite side of the desk.

The youngster moved slowly toward the sizable wooden chair that enveloped him as he sat down, his feet well above the floor.

Jimmy tried not to squirm as he shrunk and appeared even smaller than he was. He noticed that he was swinging his legs slightly as he uncomfortably waited for the aged preacher to begin speaking. He could feel his heart beating in the middle of his chest and his mouth felt so dry that he didn't think he could make an intelligible sound if asked a question. The smile now appeared more like a sneer that deepened the feeling of dread. The grizzled man leaned forward, and the now pale and paralyzed child could see specks of gray stubble on the cheeks and chin surrounding the yellow stained teeth that were contained in a sardonic countenance. The depth of his fear reached into his soul.

What had he done? He knew instinctively that this was not a friendly encounter but rather a confrontation and he had no idea what the cause nor the result would be. This man of the cloth whom he always respected and somewhat feared, now seemed only malevolent. The frightened child began a silent prayer to deliver him from this villainous character who was peering at him with a false smile.

The priest sat back and brought his chin down toward his chest. His lips moved from the phony grin to a mild scowl.

"You know what happened to Sister?"

"No, Father, but I saw two policemen here. Did someone get arrested?"

"No one was arrested," came the reply with a sense of exasperation. "Sister is dead."

This last statement was said without feeling and took the boy by surprise. His eyes widened and his mouth opened but no sound emerged.

"It seems that she had a heart attack this morning and lay right here on the floor for about an hour or so. When she was found a little while ago, her body was still warm, so the doctor thinks she died just a few minutes before she was found."

Jimmy didn't know if the priest expected him to speak but words were not possible. He could neither think of what to say nor make any sounds that resembled speech.

"You remember that happened this morning in the sacristy?"

The overwhelmed child nodded.

"I don't know what you were thinking or what was going on there, but I want you to forget about it. Completely forget about it."

His face now changed from a serious look to one filled with wrath. His eyes opened wider as he leaned forward and looked right into the boy's innocent eyes.

"People will think you are crazy if you start telling anyone about this vision you had. Anyone would have thought so if they were in my place. There is no way I am responsible for sister's death. Sure, if I had sent someone immediately to her office, she might have been saved. But who would have done that when a stupid kid says he saw a vision? Hah?

"Now you listen to me. Keep your mouth shut. If you tell anyone about this, you will be committing a mortal sin. It was the devil that brought this to your head, and you will give the devil power if you spread this around. Do you want to go to hell?"

The old man had a droplet of thick white saliva in one corner of his mouth. Jimmy focused upon it and felt repulsed by the sight of the pastor who was now just a degree above ranting. All he could do is nod in agreement. All he wanted was to be free to leave this office prison.

Father Kleinburger sat back, and the weird, unnatural smile returned. Tobacco-stained teeth appeared again.

"Good boy! I know you are a good boy and don't want to be a servant of the devil. Sister is gone and with God now in heaven. She is smiling now because she knows you will keep quiet about this."

Jimmy couldn't think or move. He stared at the man who was the leader of St. Basil's and no longer felt fear as much as sorrow. He didn't realize it yet, but the sorrow was, not for Father Kleinburger or Sister Anastasia, but for his faith which was dealt a blow. A jolt that would change his beliefs forever.

CHAPTER 4

Jimmy continued to serve as an altar boy for the next several years. However, he never felt the same as he did on that first day. Due to the powerful events of that day, he lost some of his innocence, some of his youth, some of his faith. He had become more introspective, more mature, as it were. Even his classmates noticed a change. Jimmy was still a comedian who could cause raucous laughter almost at will but now there was something different about the boy.

There were periods of serious thoughtfulness. He often appeared to have his mind in another arena, a place far away where no one else had gone. A glassy look would appear, and he was no longer in the midst of his playmates. Sometimes a friend would call his name and bring him back from wherever it was that he was escaping to. As quickly as he had left, he returned – usually with a wisecrack or a joke that would make light of the fact that something was now interrupting his childhood.

The vision that he had experienced that fateful day had not returned. Neither did he "see" Sister Anastasia again nor did he encounter other phantasms of any type. No, these mental excursions were difficult to explain. They were like daydreams yet, different. He still daydreamed as all people of every age do. But these wanderings were more. He actually lived, if only for a few moments, in another place, another world.

During these short spans of time, Jimmy found himself lost in another plane. He would "zone out" and appear as if asleep but with his eyes open. His breathing would be steady but slow and deep. Many thoughts and scenes would evolve within his mind even though these sessions would last only seconds on a clock.

He was unable to cause these dream-like events to occur at will. They would just happen and would vanish just as unpredictably as they began. Often it was someone who was with him who would arouse him from this clairvoyant slumber but even when alone, these spells would not seem to last more than several moments in real time.

His friends didn't seem to make much of his daydreaming. Boys at a preteen age were mostly tolerant of each other's idiosyncrasies. This may be because they didn't really know what was considered "normal." To point out someone else's differences when you were not sure if it truly were different, could turn everyone's attention to you. Of course, once puberty struck, the rules changed drastically. An inherent part of the right to passage for a boy to a man was to make sure every particle of peculiarity was expressed, properly teased and ridiculed.

Adults, too, were somewhat oblivious to anything that made a child stand out in a negative manner. For one thing, adults often paid little attention to what children around them were doing, as long as they didn't interfere with adult activities. In addition, parents had a blind spot, a rather large one, when it came to what they saw when they did take the time to notice their own children.

No one, neither friends, parents, teachers, no one really, paid much attention to Jimmy's somnolent display. Whether it was accepted or ignored is a moot point. Whatever it was, Jimmy got a pass at this point of his life. This state of ambivalence was not to last, however. Another apparition, this time one that was more personal, would alter his life forever.

CHAPTER 5

Jimmy was now in eighth grade. In parochial school in the '50's and '60's, the grades went from kindergarten to eighth grade. From there, the students went to high school, either to gender specific Catholic High School or the gender mixed public school. Now, *"Public School,"* was frowned upon by the nuns at St. Basil's. It was meant (according to them) for those poor students who were not bright enough to go to Catholic School or for those whose parents didn't care enough to spend the pittance (in their view) for the tuition. Of course, neither child nor parent understood that this was nonsense and was another ruse to keep the Church's coffers full. Entrance tests were administered in the winter of eighth grade and the results would arrive by mail at the students' homes all on the same day. This was the first time that tests of some type would move children into categories and separate them from each other. Most of these children were together now for almost nine years. They had grown up together, learned their lessons together, went to church together and, in many cases, sinned together. Now, some scores on an IBM card that they had filled out months before would determine which school they would go to and who they would spend the next four years with.

The children, at the ripe old age of twelve, had to make choices that would decide where they would go to high school. For some, it was just a matter of the nearest Catholic High School. But some of these schools were occupationally specialized. That is, there were some commercial high schools for the girls, for those who would decide to be secretaries or office clerks. There were technical high schools for boys who would commit to a trade in the technical fields. There were no counselors or guidance for these pre-teenagers who had to choose a possible lifetime occupation at this tender age.

For Jimmy, it was even more complicated. He couldn't quite remember how it had happened but somewhere around sixth grade, it was decided that he would be a priest. Since this vocation was met with much clamor and respect, he had accepted it. Indeed, since Jimmy loved the spotlight and this made him stand out amongst his classmates, he embraced it. It was somewhat of an ambiguity since he was still the class comedian and always in trouble with his teacher and, yet he would be going to a seminary high school – if he made the entrance requirements.

Sister James Marie was the toughest and hardest hitting of all the nuns in St. Basil's. Jimmy had felt her fist often on the side of his head or the sting of a wooden ruler on his knuckles. But nothing deterred him from being the center of attention with his quips and sense of humor. He would often risk a beating to get several students laughing at his antics. Sometimes he was able to look like an innocent bystander when hysterical laughter broke out near him, and he would escape punishment. But if he were caught, he would take whatever Sister James Marie would dish out. This seemed to infuriate the nun and would often mean that Jimmy would get more than the usual amount of pain inflicted upon him. But crying or even showing fear was not going to happen.

Now the children had waited anxiously for the day to arrive when the mail would contain the acceptances or rejections of the chosen high schools. This week the word was out that the notices had been mailed and would be received any day. Each passing day heightened the excitement and when Monday turned into Tuesday and Tuesday became Wednesday, the excitation reached a fever pitch. When the calendar changed its page to Friday, it became impossible for the students or their teacher to think of anything else but the incoming mail.

Sister James Marie had a strategy set up with one of the parish priests. Father Mark often visited the classroom. He was a dedicated and sincere cleric who enjoyed spending time with the children. Sister James Marie would get all flushed and hyper when Father Mark entered the room. It was easy for this class of 12-year-olds to see that she had a crush on him, although it was just as clear that it was not mutual. She would run up to him when he appeared at the door of the classroom and act like a teenager. Of course, although she was stout and almost as wide as she was tall, it was difficult to ascertain a nun's age under all those black and white garments. She might not have been much beyond a teenager, herself. Father Mark would smile and then start to speak to the students at their desks.

During this week, sister had set up a routine with Father Mark to signal the class if the results were in today's mail. He had arranged to receive a phone call from one of the parents when the mail was delivered and, if the awaited responses were in today's mail, he would pull down the shade on a particular window in his rectory room which faced the eighth-grade room from across the courtyard. Each day of the week, the shade did not move but today, around 10am, Father appeared at his window and slowly pulled the shade down. Sister turned to the class to announce the long-awaited signal but one of the boys in the row near the window stood up and saw the shade coming down and yelled out, "They're in!" All hell broke loose. Rather than her usual stern look, the nun smiled as she held her hands up to try to quell the raucous reaction of her pupils.

Soon the nun from across the hall who taught the other eighth grade class came to the door after hearing the explosion of sound. All Sister James Marie could do is nod and the other nun ran back to her class to let them in on the news. Now the class had to wait for two hours until lunch dismissal. In these schools, the children went home for lunch since most of the youngsters lived within a few blocks of the school. Additionally, the nuns had to have their lunch and there would be no one to supervise a lunchroom.

These two hours were the longest two hours any of these children had experienced. However, for those few who had not taken the entrance exams and knew they were "doomed" to the public school, this whole event was anti-climactic. It was easy for an outsider to pick out those who were in this category since they slouched in their seats with sullen looks upon their faces while most of the students were bouncing in their chairs.

No one seemed to be cognizant of the pressure that was placed upon these youngsters. You could almost feel the intense heartbeats and rapid breathing that was taking place within each little body. Everyone was chattering and sister was allowing it! This was certainly not a usual event. A few faces were neither angry, sad or bursting with excitement. These few sat with eyes wide and mouths slightly open as they sucked in air. They appeared frightened and apprehensive. These were the children who had believed that they must go to Catholic High School to succeed in life but might not have the ability to score high enough to be accepted.

CHAPTER 6

One of these boys was Bobby Imperioli who was Jimmy's best friend. Jimmy and Bobby were just about inseparable, and it had been this way since kindergarten. During the second day of kindergarten, Bobby suddenly came down with a complete fear of school and the kindly, old nun who taught this beginning grade. Bobby spent the entire day crying and the sister made a cursory attempt to console him but when he continued to wail, she went on with her lessons and just ignored him. The other children were upset with their new classmate's heaving sobs and stuttering breathing.

This went on for hours and around 11 am, the class was given a 15-minute break to have a snack and talk quietly. During this time, the children took out their cupcakes, fruit and candy bars and spent the time eating and talking with new friends. Jimmy, however, went over to this boy who he didn't know and offered him one of his cream filled cupcakes. Bobby had his head buried in his arms and his shoulders were bouncing up and down as he continued to blubber. However, Jimmy noticed that his new friend very slightly raised his head and peeked to see if anyone was watching. The rest of the class was too busy eating and chatting to notice Bobby and seemed to have gotten so used to his whimpering that they no longer paid any attention to it. Finally, he lifted his head up and looked at

Jimmy with swollen eyes as red as the apple on the little girl's desk who sat next to Bobby. His sputtering breathing began to slowly return to normal.

Jimmy held out a chocolate cupcake with brown icing and a swirling line of sugary white frosting. Bobby hesitantly reached for the cupcake and moved his eyes from the treat to Jimmy and back to the snack. He accepted the goody and took a small bite. A smile began to emerge on his face and his eyes told Jimmy that this boy was filled with gratitude and that a strong friendship was about to begin.

This friendship had now lasted for eight years and had only grown stronger. Bobby was even smaller boned than Jimmy but both boys participated in just about every street sport – stick ball, punch ball, handball, tag football and hockey on roller skates. Whenever possible, they made sure they were on the same team and, when it happened that they were on opposing teams, they attempted to keep from making the other look bad.

One day when the boys were about 10 years-old, Jimmy, Bobby and two other younger boys were playing a form of hand ball against a wall of the corner knitting mill. Knitting mills were as common as cemeteries and taverns in this town. They were incredibly noisy places where women stood at giant automated machines and made sweaters of all colors and textures. These garment factories were brutally hot in the summer and the windows and doors were kept open to allow some of the heat to dissipate. The brick exterior made for an excellent court for a type of mini handball called Ace/King/Queen. Since the noise inside was deafening, seldom did someone come out and chase the kids away. They only had to watch for Kenny, the somewhat dimwitted young laborer, the only male in the sweatshop, who would occasionally come outside for a quick cigarette.

On this day, however, a group of older boys from another part of the neighborhood came walking through. When these boys stopped to watch the foursome play, an air of apprehension permeated the scene.

When young boys felt their territory invaded by another tribe, the adrenaline would begin to flow, and they could almost feel their blood flow speeding up within their veins. Something was about to occur, and they knew it was not something good. After a few minutes of watching the game, the four teens slowly strutted over and one of them grabbed the pink rubber ball as it rebounded off the brick wall.

"Hey!" exploded from Jimmy's mouth. He was generally the leader of his pack of buddies who lived within a three-block radius and hung out together.

"What are you going to do about it?" said the smallest but meanest looking of the invading gang of punks.

Jimmy swallowed but felt that his mouth was already dry from the hormone coursing through his body. "Give us the ball back!"

The biggest of the group appeared somewhat slow of mind and had been standing there with his mouth slightly open. He sauntered up close to Jimmy, placed his hand in the middle of the boy's chest and shoved him. Jimmy lost his footing and stumbled a few steps back but regained his balance and walked right back up to the future hoodlum.

"Give us the ball back!"

The big lug smiled as he looked back at his cohorts and then turned and sent a right-handed fist into Jimmy's face. The other three adversaries moved in front of the younger boys and dared them to enter the fray without speaking a word.

The husky aggressor was on top of Jimmy in an instant and began to punch him again and again as he pressed his knees into the younger boy's shoulders. Jimmy was helpless to defend himself and could feel the awful sting of the raining blows. Tears filled his eyes but there was no way the overwhelmed child would cry or give in.

His friends stood motionless as they faced these intruders who were four to five years their senior and significantly superior in size and much more belligerent in attitude.

Suddenly, little Bobby went berserk and, screaming, he dove past the three goons and jumped on the back of the hulking boy who was pummeling his friend. The little boy scratched and punched and gouged at the enemy's face.

The three accomplices were at first startled by the diminutive fellow's actions but now ran to their comrade's aide. They tugged and pulled at Bobby's shirt and, finally, were able to extract him from the overwhelmed assailant. Bobby continued to swing his fists and kick his feet at anything and anyone as he yelled as if he was in mortal danger.

The combination of flailing arms and legs and an almost frightening sound that seemed to be more than one could expect from so little a creature, caused the ruffians to back off with a feeling that was something between fear and awe. One of them picked up the ball which had been the booty they originally fought over and threw it down the block.

"Next time you'll know better than to mess with us," bragged the brute who was beating on Jimmy. But he was the one who looked beaten as his face was covered with bleeding scratches and he was huffing and puffing.

"C'mon, let's get out of here," he gasped. He and his cronies were all too willing to leave the battlefield.

As they walked away, the other boys went over to Jimmy whose face was now red and swelling rapidly. His left eye was almost shut and was sure to turn black and blue within the hour. But Jimmy smiled and through a fattened lip, looked at Bobby and said, "Thanks, you saved my butt."

The two buddies walked off with their arms over each other's shoulders and headed to Jimmy's house for some ice for a black eye and a glass of soda for a parched throat. Although it hurt to do so, Jimmy started to laugh out loud as the two boys knew in their heart of hearts that they were the best of friends and would remain so forever.

Chapter 7

The minute hand of the clock moved slower than usual. The children who were waiting for weeks for the results of these tests had never experienced how the passage of time could be slowed down so drastically when one is anxious for time to pass. Finally, it was 11:40 AM and it was time to get ready to go home for lunch. They would be dismissed at 11:45 and be expected back in line outside the school at 12:50 PM.

Walking slowly in a double file was brutal when your heart wanted your legs to move as fast as they could. They were not permitted to run until they got to the corner and crossed the first street. Once they were across the street, they were beyond the authority of the nuns and the race was on. Jimmy ran so fast that he feared he would fall on his face as he leaned forward and pumped each leg in front of the other, faster and faster. It wasn't until he was almost three blocks from school and only one block away from home when he realized that Bobby wasn't right behind him. In fact, he turned and could not see him as he tried to look above the charging crowd of eighth graders who were about to find out if their future was going to be successful or if they were doomed to a life of a street cleaner which is what the nuns had indoctrinated into them for years. This was as close to being damned as one could get, even though the sisters had failed to explain that street cleaners were unionized and made more money than college educated teachers.

Where was Bobby? Jimmy wanted so badly to continue speeding home and each second that he waited was a slow tick of the clock within his brain. But he had to wait for his best friend and make sure he was alright. Finally, as the crowd passed him, he could see Jimmy now about a block away walking at a leisurely pace. Jimmy was too anxious to just stand there and wait for his buddy to catch up, so he now ran toward him to see why he was meandering when this was one of the most important days of their lives so far.

"Hey, what are you doing," Jimmy panted as he pulled in deep breaths to try to regain normal respiration? "Why are you such a slow poke?"

Bobby looked strange or at least not what Jimmy would expect as everyone was excited about the mail that was waiting for them at home. His face did not show the flush that others had from both the running and the hubbub. In fact, he appeared kind of pale and gaunt.

"Are you, OK?" Jimmy went from inquisitiveness to concern.

Bobby looked into Jimmy's face with eyes that were deep with a sadness that Jimmy had never seen before from his usual jovial friend.

"I don't care if I make it into Catholic High School. What's the big deal? Public school is okay. You're going to go to a different Catholic School anyway. We wouldn't be in the same school even if I made it."

Jimmy had never really thought about not having scores high enough to make at least one school. He never really understood that Bobby was deeply afraid that he wouldn't score well enough and would be left behind – doomed to a broom and shovel while his friend went on to better things.

"C'mon, are you kidding? You'll have your pick of schools. Cut the crap and let's get home and check out the mail."

He put his arm around the shoulders of his longtime friend, and they walked the last couple of blocks at Bobby's pace.

As they parted ways at Bobby's house which was around the corner from Jimmy's home, a strange and unusual feeling suddenly washed over Jimmy. He felt the little hairs on the back of his neck begin to rise and a cold shuddering began at the top of his spine and continued straight down his back.

Bobby stopped at the top of the concrete stairs that lead to door of the four-family house. He looked down at his schoolmate and pal and waved. It was not a gesture of joy but one of a sad farewell.

Jimmy thought, "He's acting like a baby. He'll be back to his old self after lunch." He waved back, feeling kind of foolish since they never waved off when they went home for lunch.

After taking a few steps, Jimmy began to trot and then after a few strides more, broke into a full gallop as the neared his own home. He leaped up the stairs two at a time and burst into the vestibule and pushed the bell with his dad's name above it. He had been told numerous times to only ring the bell once and wait for the buzzer to open the inner door. But this time, his finger had a mind of its own and he pumped the pushbutton over and over and over again. The buzzer started before he removed his finger from the little black button, and he charged through the door. His mother, wearing a plain house dress with a flowered apron over it, opened the door to their apartment.

"I told you not to ring that bell more than once. I can only move so fast, you know."

"Ma, ma, did you get the mail?"

"Of course, and there is something for you," she said with a smile as she stood with her hands on her hips.

Mrs. Reardon was an attractive, middle aged woman who had a no-nonsense attitude. She was fast with her hands when it came to disciplining her only son. Jimmy's sister, three years younger, had not come home yet. When her son came home, he was full of animated chatter while his sister, Ann, was quiet and mostly listened to her older brother's detailed account of the morning's activities in school.

Mrs. Reardon pushed back her brown hair and looked into Jimmy's blue eyes with her own light blue orbs. Her usual severe countenance was missing as she handed the boy a large brown envelope. It was unusual for Jimmy to receive any mail but they both knew what this was.

He carefully opened the flap at the top, being sure not to tear anything contained within. Slowly, he pulled out the contents and held his breath. There was a cover letter that he pushed aside and immediately began looking at the four pages behind it. Each was from one of the four schools he had applied to. His eyes quickly scanned the page and were drawn to the place where a check mark was made.

There were three choices that could be checked. Each was preceded by a small box in which a check could be placed. The first had "Accepted" printed after the box. The second - "Not Accepted." The third - "Waiting List."

The first page he looked at was his first choice - Sacred Heart Seminary. There it was – a check mark next to "Accepted." Jimmy yelped and jumped up. His mother's eyes teared with pride as she realized what his exuberant reaction meant.

Now the 12-year-old boy was dancing like a Native American Warrior before he went off to battle. While Jimmy was hooting and hopping all around the kitchen, the doorbell rang again, and Mrs. Reardon pressed the button which released the inner hallway door. That would be Ann who had arrived home for lunch.

Ann came in the door to the apartment and stopped as she watched her brother looking like he was in the midst of a tribal celebration. As was her usual manner, Ann said nothing but smiled as she slowly and deliberately took a seat at the kitchen table, keeping her eyes fixed on her brother. His mother was laughing at Jimmy's antics but told him to look at the rest of the results.

He sat back down and with hands that were now shaking, he struggled to separate the papers. The second paper was from St. Peter's High School. "Accepted" was again checked!

Moving to the third choice – Bishop McHenry - "Accepted!"

The last paper was this fourth choice. The children were told that seldom was a student accepted at their last choice since schools realized that as the last pick they would not be chosen and wanted to give the opportunity to someone who would probably attend.

Holy Name High School was Jimmy's final choice. His gaze moved down the page and his eyes focused on the checked box next to "Accepted."

"Hey ma, I hit a grand slam!"

Jimmy's mother had no idea what a "grand slam" was, but she was beyond proud of her son. It was now worth all those trips up to school after lunch to meet with his teacher because of some incident that had occurred in school in the morning. It seemed like Mrs. Reardon was asked to come up and meet with her son's teacher at least once a week since first grade. Some nuns were pleasant to this respectful, church going woman. They would try to lessen the blow that her son was causing a disturbance due to his mischief and high jinks. But some of these so-called religious women were downright nasty and would insult his mother by saying her son was no good and would probably be incarcerated someday.

Mrs. Reardon hugged her boy as tears welled up in her eyes. But she quickly regained her composure and told Jimmy to eat his soup and sandwich because time was going by and being late to school was not tolerated.

Jimmy put the papers down and started to eat his canned vegetable soup. But his mind was elsewhere. He did it! He made it! A smile was forming on his face, and it grew with each spoonful of potatoes and carrots that were swimming in a red broth.

Now his life was set.

CHAPTER 8

After finishing his lunch, Jimmy went into the bathroom before leaving for school. While he was washing his hands, that strange feeling came to him. He hadn't felt it for a long time but there was no mistaking it. He looked in the mirror and saw that his face seemed to be slightly out of focus. Strangely, it frightened him and yet, he didn't want it to go away.

As his eyes glazed over, he started to hear a familiar voice. At first, he couldn't make it out but then he realized that it was Mrs. Imperioli, Bobby's mom. Soon her voice became clearer and she was asking Bobby to come out of his room. "Bobby, you can't stay in there all day. I know that you didn't want to go back to school this afternoon but it's time you got out of your room. Your brothers and sisters will be home soon, and I've had enough of this."

There was several moments of silence and then Bobby's mom again said, "Do you hear me, young man? It's not the end of the world. I'm sure many of your friends will be going to Jefferson High School, too."

Still there was no reply.

"Your dad is on the day shift today and if you are not over this foolishness by the time he gets home, you're gonna get it. Do you hear me?" This tactic always worked in the past since Bobby's dad was a sergeant in the New York City Police Department and was not real patient with his kids. There usually was only one warning before he used his hands or his belt.

There was another few moments of silence but this time the lack of sound was deafening. It sounded like when one is under water, and everything is still. Suddenly, there was a tremendous crack, exploding through the dead air. Jimmy's head jerked back as if the explosion was in this bathroom, and he was recoiling from the percussion.

He didn't realize that he was sweating profusely, and the shock of the sound stalled his reverie momentarily. But now, he re-focused and saw Bobby's mother – her eyes bulging, her mouth gaping open as she slammed into the door to her son's room with all the force that her slight body could bring. Again and again, Mrs. Imperioli threw herself at the door with her arms bent at the elbows and kept pressed against her chest. She started to scream Bobby's name - "Bobby, Bobby! What have you done?"

Finally, the door gave in to her relentless pounding and burst open, rebounding off the wall and hitting the woman as she charged through the opening. She steadied herself and then a scream came forth – a scream that was filled with excruciating pain. A scream that brought icy cold fingers down Jimmy's neck and back. He shivered in response to the tiny pimples that were rising on his neck and face.

Then, he saw. There covered in blood was his best friend. There was the boy who was always there for him, a small hole in his forehead with thick red fluid oozing out. There was the youngster who he was playing ball with yesterday, who he had just walked home for lunch with – there was Bobby with the back of his head blown away and the wall behind him splattered with his blood.

Jimmy felt lightheaded and had to grab hold of the sink in order not to fall. The scene played before him had ended and now he saw himself, pale and wet, looking back in the medicine cabinet mirror. What did this mean? When he saw Sister Anastasia talking to him in the sacristy those few years ago, it turned out to be a premonition. Father Kleinburger has told him never to speak of it and he didn't. But he never forgot. Now, it happened again but this time it involved his friend. Bobby was the brother he never had. Should he keep this to himself? Could he?

"Hey, mister, it's late. What are you doing in there?" his mother called.

"I'll be right out, ma," Jimmy choked out.

He wiped his face and neck with a towel and opened the door. His mother looked at him with a quizzical expression. "Are you OK?"

She put her hand on his forehead and felt for his temperature.

"Your hair is all wet. Do you feel sick?"

She got a face cloth and wet it with cold water and wiped his face. She looked into Jimmy's eyes with concern.

"I'm . . . I'm OK, ma. I saw something . . ."

"Comb your hair. It's a mess and get to school. You have no fever. You got too excited about this whole school thing. Everything will be fine. Go comb your hair. You can't go to school looking like you just got out of bed."

Jimmy wanted so badly to tell his mother about his vision of Bobby, but he was confused. Father Kleinburger had told him to forget about these things. His mother was a no-nonsense woman, and she would never accept that her son was seeing future events.

"C'mon, get going. If you get to school late, Sister will get mad and might call Sacred Heart and tell them not to take you."

Jimmy knew that this was his mother's way of getting him to leave on time. There was no way being late once would keep him from the high school of his choice but, as he usually did, he obeyed his mother. He went back into the bathroom and now saw his face clearly in the mirror. His hair was truly soaked, and his forehead had again begun to perspire. He combed his hair and wiped his face with the towel. He looked at this face one more time and decided that he wouldn't say anything at this time to his mother.

He kissed his mother on her cheek and left for school.

CHAPTER 9

Jimmy's sister, Ann, had already started out for school. Often Jimmy would walk back after lunch with his little sister but today he was a bit behind schedule, and she didn't want to wait for him. Lining up outside school before the afternoon session began was a chance to interact with classmates and the girls, in particular, looked forward to some time to gossip about who liked who and which classmate had a new haircut that could be mocked. Both Jimmy and his sister usually arrived at St. Basil's well before the first bell which signaled it was time to line up and be quiet.

As he walked around the corner, Jimmy could feel the air as it entered his lungs and it refreshed him. His mood was elevated from the wonderful news he found at home but as he passed by Bobby's house, that same air became thick and heavy as cream. His breathing was no longer light and deep but labored and forced. He slowed as he passed the wrought iron fence encircling the cement steps leading up to the outside door to Bobby's apartment. He always went straight to school without stopping at his buddy's house and met him outside of school as the children all got ready to line up for the afternoon session.

This time, however, he hesitated, lingering a bit, thinking, thinking. Should he go inside and check on his friend? The memory of the vision he endured in his bathroom reappeared – not clearly as the phantasm he suffered – but as a thought he consciously brought forth. He tried to tell himself that it was just a daydream but deep within his heart, he knew it was more. He stopped and looked up at the second story windows hoping to see some signs of movement, of life. Looking down the street to see if anyone was watching him. Maybe he would see another classmate who he could ask to go with him up those steps which now seemed higher, longer. He knew it was futile since most of his friends from school lived around the block and walked up the parallel avenue.

Certainly, there was nothing happening in Bobby's apartment or there would be activity. Yet, he felt obligated, compelled to climb those stairs and be sure, be sure his best friend was alive and well. Forcing a deep breath and conscious that his hands were suddenly sweating, he walked through the gate and started up the steps. As he grabbed the black iron railing, he could feel the chill of the painted metal as it touched his hot, damp palms. The change in temperature on his hands caused him to study the iron pipe and for the first time he noticed the chipping of the paint and a red underlying color beneath ultra-shiny ebony exterior. He gently rubbed the spaces between the chipping paint with his thumb as he deliberately rose step-by-step.

Reaching the large wooden double door, he took hold of the burnished brass doorknob and slowly turned it clockwise. The door latch released, and Jimmy walked into the vestibule. He looked at the considerable brass plate that contained the individual apartment doorbells and mailboxes. It had long ago turned almost black from oxidation and each little bell button was housed in a small indentation. The rubbery nubs were old and worn and turned slightly in different directions, like small black orbs all askew. He knew which bell belonged to Bobby without having to look at the nameplate. It was the moment of truth. Would Mrs. Imperioli answer the bell with sobs and screams that would bestow veracity upon his vision? He couldn't bring himself to gather the strength to press that tiny knob that he feared would bring about an explosion of terror. If something horrible has occurred but you don't know about it yet, then it hasn't really happened in your sphere of existence.

Forcing a breath and holding it in, he pointed his right index finger and moved it to the tiny projection that sagged toward 5 o'clock. He pressed it. He held it in – longer than he usually would and waited.

The loud electric buzz startled him, although he heard it hundreds of times. He pushed the inner door to the hallway, and it opened. Entering the dark hall of the four-family apartment house, he immediately identified the scent that he always noticed as he entered anyone's hallway. Everyone's house seemed to have its own unique aroma, not an unpleasant odor nor a sweet scent but rather an identifiable smell that he could attach to a particular abode in his memory bank. Sometimes the smell in the hallway was different from the scent in an individual apartment. He knew if someone had blindfolded him and brought him to one of his friend's homes, he could immediately report whose house he was in. Bobby's hallway was dark and today seemed even dimmer and the usual scent troubled him unlike any other time he entered here. There was a sinister atmosphere that caused his heartbeat to increase and his mouth to suddenly feel dry as if he had a wad of cotton jammed within the orifice.

He started to feel frightened and wished he hadn't given in to his urge to call for his buddy. Then the door on the second landing opened and Mrs. Imperioli yelled down, "Who is it?" Jimmy tried to swallow to relieve an overwhelming dryness. There seemed to be no saliva available to quench his parched throat and this attempt at swallowing only made matters worse as his throat seemed to close and his smallish Adam's apple pushed inward and upward, almost choking him. With no immediate response, Bobby's mom walked to the head of the stairs and looked down upon the slight boy who felt smaller and smaller by the moment. Jimmy looked at the woman who had often walked into the living room as they watched a horror movie on their 14-inch black and white television and offered the boys some chocolate chip cookies. She didn't appear upset as she kindly waited for words to come from her son's best friend. She was wearing a blue-print dress with a white apron that hung below her waist. Finally, words squeaked out from Jimmy's sandpaper throat.

"Did Bobby leave for school yet?"

"No, Jimmy, and I don't think he'll be in school this afternoon. He isn't feeling well but I'm sure he'll be OK tomorrow. Please ask Sister for his homework assignment and could you bring his books home this afternoon? If he thinks he's getting out of doing his homework, he has another thing coming."

"Mrs. Imperioli, is Bobby OK?"

"Sure, he'll be fine. He's just a little upset. He didn't make any of the Catholic Schools, but he'll get over it."

"Are you sure he's OK? I mean, uh, he's not hurt or anything, is he?"

Mrs. Imperioli smiled, and snickering said, "No, he's not hurt, Jimmy. Well, maybe inside his heart hurts a little but he'll live."

Jimmy felt calmer but he was not completely relieved. He wanted to ask the smiling woman who stood before him with her head cocked to one side and her eyebrows raised if she could just check to be sure but he knew that would result in a quizzical and negative response. He stood there longer than normal and, although only a couple of seconds passed, they appeared as if they were frozen in place, made into statues in a wax museum scene.

Mrs. Imperioli broke the stare down. "You better get to school. Don't forget to ask Sister for Bobby's homework."

"OK, Mrs. Imperioli, I won't forget. See you this afternoon."

Jimmy quickly turned and opened the hall door and almost ran out of the house and down the outside steps onto the sidewalk. He was about two houses down the street when he allowed his mind to return to the scene that had just taken place. He was glad it was over, but something was not right. Something was just not right.

Chapter 10

Jimmy arrived at school later than he usually did but he was still in time to get on line before the bell rang. His parents were sticklers for punctuality and this trait was even stronger in Jimmy. He was almost never late for anything even if it was just a time set by his friends to meet for a game of punch ball. He couldn't think of one day in those almost 9 years when he appeared at school after lunch and missed hearing the first warning bell. That first bell would signal the children to stop talking and immediately get on line. The power of that resonant clanging was awesome as the several hundred children momentarily froze and then, zombie-like, moved to their designated places and stood quietly. The second harsh bellowing of the bell signaled for the lines to begin moving in an orderly fashion. Students all dressed in navy blue and white walked trance-like in total silence with even spaces between them. That is, all except those few who were whispering as they attempted to get the last few sentences completed in their conversation. The unfortunate ones were seen by their nun teacher who quickly strode over to the misbehaved and delivered a hard slap to the rear of the guilty one's head while glaring with countenance that could melt a block of stone. Thus, was the power behind the bell.

As Jimmy's class entered the classroom, there was more talking and noise than usual and after a minute of this unusual chatter, Sister James

Marie shouted out, "OK, that's enough! You all got your mail. Now sit down and shut your mouths!"

The boys and girls immediately obeyed the female Drill Sergeant and quietly moved to their wooden desks and sat down.

Although the children all were dying to share their news with each other, the nun wouldn't allow it. However, she was more than curious herself and announced that the class was to write down the answers to six essay questions at the end of the chapter in their history books or do it for homework that night. While they were looking up the answers and writing their responses, she would call each one up to her desk and ask them what was in their mail.

The first one she called to her desk was her pet, Robert Hermann. Robert was the younger brother of a former student of hers whom she apparently adored and made every effort to assist little Robert in succeeding. Robert, himself, appeared embarrassed by the constant attention of this stout relative of an Antarctic bird. She would often waddle over to his desk and check on the slight boy's work, gently offering suggestions to improve upon his answers.

One time, after grading a test, she announced that the class did not do well, and the test would be given again the next day. It turned out that several students scored well – Jimmy and a few others had received high nineties – but they all had to re-take the exam. It was discovered that Robert only scored a seventy-eight and, therefore, the whole class had to be re-tested.

Jimmy and another boy, Dennis Van Houten, who was often Jimmy's partner in his humorous escapades, spoke up. Although they knew this could result in a painful reaction from the Gestapo agent dressed in black and white, they were incensed and could not hold their voices back. The result was a chilling stare from the monochromed monarch. They were sure they had caused a reverse curve in their grade, but it was worth it, as their classmates looked upon them with awe. Few spoke up when they felt they were unjustly dealt with by their teacher for fear of reprisals, physical or otherwise.

The room was quiet as the nun spoke in whispered tones to her little pet. A smile spread across her wide face as Robert apparently told her that he was accepted by one or more of the Catholic High Schools. It turned out that he was only on the waiting list for his first choice - Holy Name High School. His father would have to contact the school and use his influence (that meant check book) to get Robert accepted.

The children worked quietly on their assignment while keeping an eye on the conference that took place at the front of the room. Soon she called up another child and then another. Some children were spoken to with expeditiousness and quickly dismissed; others were spoken to in a manner not often seen – at times she almost appeared human. But before this character change could take hold, a youngster would begin to cry as she berated him or her and her voice rose for all to hear.

"If you paid attention in class, you might have been accepted by at least one of your choices!" These admonitions were bellowed out for all to hear in order that everyone would know the weeping juvenile had failed to score well enough. Rather than consoling these tender psyches, she felt a perverse enjoyment by causing further pain in the hearts and minds of these pre-pubescent charges.

Jimmy's attention began to shift from the interactions at the sister's desk to the assignment at hand and back again as one of the girls in his class began to sob uncontrollably. Soon, however, his vision started to blur. As focus was lost, his mind left the classroom and soon was traveling, floating to another dimension. When these "spells" occurred, an emotion would rise up. The mood could be soothing; it could be excited; it could be fearful. This time the mood was horrifying.

No actual event or person was yet presented to Jimmy. But he felt great anxiety and almost tried to end the reverie. However, he knew he must let it go on. He drifted, floated on some unseen river of premonition, allowing the tide of thought to take his mind on its predetermined journey. This time the destination was one that he would rather have avoided. The horrific climate that he felt as this voyage had commenced was only a hint of the terror he would soon face.

CHAPTER 11

He found himself in a bathroom. It was strange yet somehow familiar. It was cold – not chilly cold but damp and evoked a sense that brought chills down to the marrow of his bones. He wanted out, out of this terrifying toilet and he wanted out now. Then he saw – perceived - a face in a mirror. He was in someone's else's eyes and viewed the reflection of Bobby's face - the countenance of his best friend. Bobby's eyes were red and swollen. A thick stream of clear liquid oozed from one nostril. He was sobbing. But who was sobbing? Was it Bobby or was it Jimmy himself? He was confused because he could feel the grief as his own chest heaved and felt heavy. He realized he somehow had become Bobby.

Now he opened the bathroom door and saw Bobby's mother standing at the kitchen sink with her back to him. Now he ran, ran for the sanctuary of his room but as he approached his room, a sudden urge caused him to change direction. He went into another room. He quickly realized that it was Bobby's parents' bedroom. He turned and locked the door. What made him enter this room?

His heart began to beat faster and harder, so hard that he knew it would burst from his chest. He was now panting through his mouth as his nose no longer brought enough air to his pulsating lungs. He was in front of a door, a closet door and he opened it. He now ran for a small stool that had a pair of women's shoes in front of it and he almost fell as he tripped over them. He grabbed the stool and brought it over to the closet. Climbing up he could now reach the shelf above and moved a cardboard box to the side and, standing on his tip toes, felt his fingers reach another, smaller box but this one was made of wood. He slowly scratched at it and got the box to slide inch by inch until it was within his grasp.

He climbed down from the stool with the box in his hands. His breath was now exploding in and out of his mouth, feeling as if he had been running for a mile as fast as he could. He lifted off a small padlock that wasn't locked, twisting the hasp away from the body of the lock and opened the box. There, nestled in a bed of foam rubber, was his father's old service revolver.

He grabbed the pistol and opened the cylinder as he had seen his father do many times before he left the house when he was still in uniform. It was loaded.

He threw the box down and ran with gun in hand into his own room. Jimmy felt a deadly dread deep within his soul. Now he could see a hand turning a small lock below the doorknob on Bobby's room. Suddenly, everything started to move faster and faster. The room seemed to lose equilibrium and his head felt light and unfocused.

Bobby's mother began to shout from outside the door. He couldn't completely make out the words she was saying but now he heard Bobby's voice.

"Oh my God, I am heartily sorry for having offended thee. . ." Bobby was praying, the prayer of forgiveness for a past sin or one about to be committed.

His mother's voice became louder, but the volume didn't make it any clearer. All Jimmy could hear was the continuing prayer and as it was recited, a calmness began to fall upon Bobby. Jimmy felt the cold that had froze the blood within his veins begin to dissipate. In its place was a new and comforting warmth. He looked up through his best friend's eyes and saw a bright light.

The light was intense yet did not cause him to shrink from it or look away. Rather, it brought a peaceful awareness of a powerful, yet loving and comforting force.

Bobby raised the gun to his head. ". . . to amend my life. Amen."

He pulled the trigger.

CHAPTER 12

"I'm speaking to you Mister Reardon! Are you deaf?"

Jimmy's eyes focused upon the visage of his teacher's rotund and rubicund countenance. A scowl was present on her mouth, that is, a grimace more pronounced than her usual appearance. It quickly brought him out of his reverie and back into the present reality.

Sister was standing behind her desk waiting for Jimmy to come up and have his tete a tete with her. Apparently, she had reached his name in the alphabet. Once the nun had finished with her favorite, Robert Hermann, she went to the "A's" on her class roster and went down the list. It seems like Jimmy must have been out of it for some time because she was nearing the end of the alphabet with his last name.

Jimmy quickly recovered his bearings and rose shakily to his feet. He lifted the hinged seat as he was taught to do beginning in kindergarten and slid out from behind his desk which was anchored to the floor.

As he walked up to the teacher's desk, he revisited the final scene of his daydream and saw his friend lying dead with his blood splattered on a wall. Just as he reached the nun's desk, an intense nausea overcame him. Sister James Marie stared at him with disdain and said, "Will you hurry up and get up here and sit down? I don't have all day for you, you know."

Jimmy arrived at the chair facing his teacher's desk. But instead of sitting down, he stood in front of the chair and just looked at her. It seemed like time stood still as seconds ticked. Neither moved or said anything further. He leaned forward over her desk as if to wish to whisper a secret that only she should hear. Sister moved in closer, waiting for this child to bear his soul to her.

Then, he threw up.

CHAPTER 13

Chaos had engulfed the classroom. Girls screamed in disgust. Boys were laughing – both at Jimmy and at their teacher who stood in shock with the front of her habit covered with peas and carrots from the boy's recently eaten lunch. Jimmy stood confused and looked down to see if there was any regurgitation on his clothes. Fortunately for Jimmy and unfortunately for the nun, he had projectile vomited all over her desk, the papers on it and on the teacher's black and white garb. They both didn't move for several moments while the background sounds of squealing girls and cackling boys filled the room. Finally, Sister James Marie's eyes swelled, and she slowly mouthed the words, "Go down to the health office. Now!"

Jimmy walked quickly to the rear of the room as the other students who were standing in the aisles parted as if a leper was in their midst. He felt his face flush as he passed the faces of girls who had distorted frowns of disgust and of boys who were teary with laughter. He burst out the door to the classroom and ran down the stairs to the door with the frosted glass that read, "Health Office."

The health office was empty as it usually was. There was no nurse on duty in this small Catholic School. A nurse from the city's health department would come to administer polio vaccine injections once a year and seemed to be there on rare other occasions when she did some sort of paperwork. Now, it was a cold room with a desk and little furniture. The sound of Jimmy's footsteps echoed as he walked up to the bare metal desk.

He stood for a while not knowing what to do. Finally, he sat down on a metal folding chair that was facing the desk. He put his folded hands between his knees and slouched over. His mind began to slowly unravel the events that had taken place. He went back in reverse order and pictured his teacher standing before him, covered with his lunch as they looked at each other in surprise. Then the scene that caused his sickness rebound.

He began to shiver as he thought about the visage that he now had twice in a few hours. Was his buddy alright? Was he alive? Why did he have this horrible, terrifying daydream? What was wrong with him? Normal kids don't think about their friends dying. Maybe he was crazy. Maybe he needed to see Dr. LaBiancho, his family doctor. Was there medicine for this disease?

He looked around the stark room. There were a few old and yellowing posters promoting hygiene and nutrition. He had seen the same posters in the same spot on those walls for all these years at St. Basil's. There was nothing else but a large, white electric clock with a black cord hanging down to the outlet near the baseboard. He watched the second hand pulsate, second by second, and read the time which was now 2:53 PM. Dismissal would be signaled by the ringing of a large, hand-held bell that was rung in the hallway on each floor by a student in the other eight grade. It would ring at approximately 3 PM and announce that the school day was ending.

The seconds moved by slowly. What should he do? He wasn't sick. He needed his books for his homework that night. Did the nun forget about him? Should he wait until someone came for him? Seconds took minutes as he watched the long, thin second-hand jerk from one mark to the next. The minute hand now read 54 and after what seemed like an eternity – 55. He finally made up his mind that when the minute hand got to 56, he would head back to class.

He would rather have permission to go back to his room but was concerned that no one would come from him. He began to fantasize what would happen if he were forgotten and was locked into the school. It would get dark. His mother would be looking for him. They would find him sitting in his empty classroom, surviving on the remains of snacks that were stuck to wrappers in the waste basket.

Of course, he would be in trouble. It would be his fault that the nuns had forgotten him and locked him inside this ancient building that now was his prison. Actually, it was like a jail with the nuns as the cruel jailers with keys attached to the hanging rosary beads which swayed from their belts. They were like those evil guards in those "B" movies in women's prisons. He would never be allowed to see one of those movies. They were listed in the Catholic newspaper as "Morally objectionable in part for all." He wasn't sure exactly what that meant but he thought it must be due to the sweaty women with large breasts that were beaten by the guards in those movies. He caught only glimpses of these scenes in coming attractions. Now, he was concocting one of these films as he sat waiting to be freed from the cell of the health office.

He glanced up at the clock again. It was 2:58! That's it! He would wait no longer. He already went past his own deadline. He got up from the hard, brown metal chair and ran to the door. He was sprung!

He quickly walked down the hall and up the stairs to the second floor where his classroom was. He would not run because that was forbidden but he was often caught moving as fast as he could without technically running. This would cause one of the nuns who always seemed to have an eye on the corridor to yell, "Slow down there, mister!" But it rarely resulted in a reprimand more than that. If you were actually running, look out! There was a subtle but very real difference between walking fast and running. He thought he might have to do with always having one foot in contact with the floor.

He reached the door to his classroom just as he was jarred by the sharp timbre of the dismissal bell. He had no time to think about the possibilities – would Sister be there waiting to yell at him? Would his classmates all stare and laugh at him? He grabbed the doorknob and entered the room. As was the usual case after the bell rung, everyone was standing and throwing books into their school bag and talking about where they would meet after school.

No one seemed to pay him any attention. Jimmy went up to his desk and started packing his books. He glanced up and saw that there was no nun present. There were two girls from the other eighth grade at the front of the room looking official as they stood watching the class. Behind them were several names – all boys – that they had apparently written on the blackboard.

If a nun had the rare occasion to leave a room unattended for any length of time, eighth graders were sent to keep order. They always used girls and never from the class that had to be covered. This was because girls would snitch on others must more readily and, if girls were chosen from their own class, they would be somewhat reluctant to write down names or, conversely, might report those they had a recent squabble with. It was a method that was rife with difficulties but there were no other adults available, so they utilized the resources they had.

Jimmy went about packing his books and was thrilled that no one gave him a second look. Soon the second bell rang, and everyone sat down and was relatively quiet on cue. The nun from the other class appeared at the door and announced that they should line up and follow her class out of the building. The two female agents at the front of the room strutted out to their classroom with a smug and condescending expression.

Soon the class lined up in its usual manner. They were so regimented that each student moved as if they were programmed robots. The last two rows were first at the door and, as the last of the pupils from the class across the hall left, they began to file out, following in pairs.

CHAPTER 14

Jimmy was soon out in the afternoon sunshine, walking briskly. After reaching the first cross street, it suddenly dawned on him that he forgot completely about getting Bobby's books for his homework assignments. He stopped and looked back toward the school. Should he run back to school? He realized that his classroom would be empty and maybe locked. He thought about the possibility that Sister James Marie would be sitting at her desk, cleaning up the mess he had left. That horrific thought was more than enough to cause him to turn around and continue his trip home. There was no way he wanted to run into his teacher at this point in time. Better to allow some time to pass and maybe she would have a small portion of pity on him for vomiting all over her and her papers.

He would have to explain to Bobby's mother that he had gotten sick and had just enough time to get his own books together. She was always a kind woman who never seemed to get angry or upset, even though their household usually seemed loud and chaotic. They were a boisterous family – they yelled and laughed with raucous abandon. There was a love of family that always shone in their eyes and they made everyone feel welcomed as if they were adopted into their clan.

Now his mind returned to Bobby and his stomach tightened as he once again pictured his buddy lying all covered in blood. He must be insane. Why else would he continue to picture this terrible scene? Was there some

49

perverse, deep-seated reason for him to keep conjuring up this vile display? He didn't even realize that his feet were moving faster and faster as he approached his friend's home.

Then he saw a sight that stopped him cold.

He was at the beginning of the block of his best friend's home and as he gazed down to the corner where Bobby's house was, there was a crowd gathered. He stopped, frozen in his tracks. Saw more and more people gathering. Unintentionally, he feet again began to move. He found himself on the outer edge of the growing crowd. He felt lightheaded as his eyes fell upon two black and white police cars parked haphazardly at the curb.

There were uniformed policemen telling mumbling neighbors to stay back. Then there was a sudden silence. Never before did Jimmy feel the force of such a lack of sound. He felt like a cosmic push had taken his breath away. All eyes were on the top of the concrete stairs as the tall wooden door opened. Jimmy's eyes widened as Bobby's father emerged holding onto his wife as they slowly took steps as if they were an elderly couple tentatively feeling their way step by step.

As they reached the mid-way point down the stairs, Jimmy saw Mrs. Imperioli had extensive dark reddish stains on her housedress. He knew what they were. His eyes filled with tears. There was no doubt in his mind. His reveries had again come true. Bobby, his best friend – was dead.

Chapter 15

The days and weeks that followed were surreal for Jimmy. There were times that he was able to take himself away from the reality that his best friend had died. But these respites from the searing pain in his heart were few and far between. For most of his waking hours (and indeed, in his sleep as well), Jimmy pictured his diminutive pal, at times playing ball with him, laughing foolishly as they often had done and at other times, covered with blood with part of his head missing. Neither the ghoulish reverie nor the happier times brought anything but deep sadness to this little boy.

After the initial shock and utter melancholy that took hold of his heart, Jimmy began to feel a sense of guilt. He knew, he knew this would happen. And he didn't stop it. He went to his buddy's house and asked Bobby's mom if he was alright, but he didn't push it. He didn't insist to her that there was danger ahead. He knew she would have dismissed his words, but that knowledge did little at assuage his mounting guilt.

The wake and funeral were beyond anything this 12-year-old had ever felt. He knew that he would be scarred forever. The first day of the wake was the worse.

His mother and father told him he didn't have to go but he knew he really had no choice. Indeed, he wanted to see his friend, see him as much as he could before he would be laid into a cold, dark grave. He needed every moment to somehow connect with him and being in the same room as his now soulless body somehow made him feel closer.

He will remember every aspect of that first trip to the wake. School was closed for his class and the other 8th grade. He woke up early in the morning covered with perspiration, the result of another frightening dream.

He dreamed that he and Bobby were both getting buried, however, only Bobby was dead. His friend was missing the back of his head, but he was talking to him. They were walking in the cemetery toward an open grave where dirt was piled high on one side. Inside the grave lay a coffin that was open and empty. Bobby climbed down and got into the coffin, squirreling around as if to get comfortable. Then with soulful eyes, he reached his hand up toward Jimmy and beckoned him to join him.

Bobby was afraid. He wasn't dead. But he felt obligated to go along with his buddy. After all, it was his fault that Bobby was dead. Slowly, he forced himself into the grave. The dirt felt cold and damp. Then Bobby's hand touched his and it was icy and lifeless. He body shivered and he hesitated. But he looked into Bobby's pleading eyes and he knew he had no option. He had to join his friend in the confines of the coffin. It was filled to overflowing with white, shiny, puffy fabric. He climbed in.

They snuggled in together and then Bobby smiled. The lid of the coffin slowly creeped closed. The limited light began to fade. Then, blackness. Total blackness. Jimmy began to feel as if he couldn't breathe. The air was quickly disappearing. His mouth opened and his chest began to heave, and his mouth opened like a fish that had just been brought up out of the water and was sucking for oxygen but finding none to be had.

Bobby no longer spoke, and he couldn't see his friend in the pitch darkness that enveloped them. His heart raced and fear caused his entire body to stiffen. His back arched upward and his face felt the coolness of the glossy fabric which now could no longer be seen in the utter darkness of his deathbed.

He was going to die. Join Bobby in the great beyond. He wanted to be with his friend, but this was more than he had wished for.

One last breath. His body sunk back down, exhausted. It was done.

And then he woke.

The day began.

CHAPTER 16

Jimmy went back to school and strangely, or maybe not so strangely, no one spoke to him about Bobby. It was like he never existed but there was an underlying feeling when he spoke to a classmate as if the other student was looking for some sort of reaction from him. But there was nothing to say. Nothing to do. There was a pain inside him that he couldn't explain or truly deal with.

Father Mark had come to the classroom the first day back and said that if anyone needed to talk about what happened, they should ask Sister that they wish to come and speak to him. Of course, no one would take him up on his offer. For one thing, going to James Marie and saying they wanted to see Father Mark would probably mean dealing with a grilling of questions from the portly nun. Facing any one-on-one meetings with this rotund, cherry-cheeked woman in a penguin costume was not something you would do voluntarily. Secondly, although Father Mark was a young and pleasant priest, Jimmy knew there was little he could say that would remove or even lessen the emptiness and sadness he felt in his heart. Father Mark would say that Bobby was in a better place. That he was now happy and with God. Bull! Bobby would be happy playing stick ball or punch ball or drinking a Pepsi as they sat on the sidewalk together.

So, Jimmy dealt with his pain in the only way he knew. He would spend time alone with Corky.

Corky was his dog – a mix of a yellow Labrador Retriever and a German Shepherd, although he looked mostly like a lab. He was a large dog, weighing around 90 pounds. He and Jimmy were awfully close friends and, now that Bobby was gone, Corky was certainly his best friend.

After school, rather than going to the playground and finding some guys to choose sides with for a game of stick ball or touch football or whatever, as he usually would do, now he took Corky to the cemetery that was about a block away. This was where Jimmy would go to think and be alone – alone except for his canine buddy.

It was so quiet at the cemetery, and no one would notice him talking to his dog. Corky was a good listener. He was wise because he never gave bad advice. He never gave any advice. But Jimmy could often come to good decisions when he talked things over with Corky.

He spent hours these days after the funeral talking to Corky, first about Bobby, then slowly, about other things. He first asked his dog if he thought there was a heaven. If he thought that Bobby could see and hear him. If his friend knew how much he missed him. Slowly over some days, however, the one-way conversation moved to which baseball team was the best, what high school would be like, if the blonde girl, Ingrid, in the third row in his class liked him.

Something was happening to him – he started to look at girls in a different way. He had never liked any of the girls in his neighborhood or class. They were noisy, silly and, basically, useless. They couldn't play ball. All they did was talk and giggle – a lot. But he now noticed that he didn't think they were so bad any longer. In fact, he now found himself thinking about them more often and sometimes, looking at them for longer times than was necessary.

There was no way he could talk to anyone about these feelings – not his other friends, not his parents, not Father Mark – certainly not Sister James Marie! He started to laugh about that thought. God, she must have been a girl once. What did she look like with hair and wearing normal clothes? Yuch! She must have been as ugly as a girl as she was as a nun. That's probably why she became a nun. No one thought of them as real people – certainly not as a human woman. She was . . . well, a nun.

But he could talk to Corky about these strange but kind of pleasant feelings he had when he thought about the girl in the third row, or when he caught a glimpse of Susan's underwear when they had to crawl under their desks during an air raid drill. She caught him looking up her skirt that was hiked up high on her legs as she sat with her knees up under the desk. Susan quickly pulled her skirt down and gave Jimmy a look, but she didn't seem angry. Right after the drill, Jimmy saw her talking to Anna who sat behind her and they both looked at Jimmy and started laughing. He wasn't sure if they were laughing at him since girls seemed to laugh a lot. He could feel his face burning but he knew he would do it again if the opportunity came about.

Corky would listen intently to everything Jimmy would tell him. Even though he didn't answer his questions, Jimmy knew that his dog understood and was wise. He never laughed at him or yelled at him. He just looked deeply into his master's eyes and wagged his big tail. When he talked to his dad about something - not girls, of course – his dad's attention would wander. He could tell because his dad would either get a look in his eyes that appeared like they were out of focus, or his dad would ask him to repeat a question. But Corky never let his attention wander, except maybe when a squirrel would climb a nearby tree, or somebody would walk by.

"Corky, do you think Ingrid likes me? What about Susan? When I think about the time I saw her underpants, my breathing gets faster. Is something wrong with me? Do you think I should tell Father Mark in confession? No, I don't think so. He might yell. I told him that I sometimes had impure thoughts and he told me to keep busy. Maybe take music lessons. I tried it. It doesn't work. And I hate the piano. I never learn any good songs. They're all songs that my parents would sing. You don't think I'm weird, do you?"

Corky wagged his tail and licked Jimmy's face. All was right with the world.

CHAPTER 17

The following months went by – slowly at first and then when school ended, and summer began – the time began to speed up. Thoughts about Bobby never went away completely but the loss of his dear friend became somewhat less intrusive into his consciousness. He did, however, have the occasional dream. Some were pleasant, formed by memories of good times together. Some were frightening, causing Jimmy to wake up crying out, sweating and breathing hard. They seemed to have a central theme – Bobby is dead but able to communicate with Jimmy. Often Bobby takes Jimmy's hand or otherwise invites him to join him in death. They usually take place in a cemetery with Bobby leading Jimmy to his grave.

One such nightmare particularly petrified Jimmy. They were playing punch ball in the street. This game usually had 3 or 4 players on a side. This time it was just the two friends playing against each other. Although it seemed natural, Bobby had the back of his head missing and his brain was exposed. This trait was frequently seen in these dreams and the horrific appearance had no effect on the game or the way they interacted.

But after the game, which Jimmy won, Bobby took Jimmy's hand and silently guided his friend down the street and toward the cemetery that was Jimmy's tranquil retreat. Just the walk down there with his trusty Corky at his side, brought a peacefulness to his soul. This time, however, Jimmy could feel his breath quickening with each step. He felt an anxiousness that began to wash over him. By the time they reached the gate, Jimmy hesitated and pulled back on his buddy's lead. But Bobby was persistent and pulled his reluctant friend past the open gate and onto the cemetery roadway.

Jimmy could see the concrete path, cracked and broken, by the years of traffic and large trucks that were often entering to move dirt or open an area for the addition of new graves. He wanted to stop, desperately wanted to go back and leave this place that had so often been his place of meditation and calm. But he knew it was fruitless. In a dream, one often wants to stop or change direction, but the reverie has its own agenda and there is no deterring where it will take you unless you awaken. But this night, the dream would persist.

Bobby continued to direct their march wordlessly. Jimmy's trepidation increased step by step. He was sweating profusely, longing to leave this dwelling of the dead but, at the same time, knowing he must persevere. As the two boys passed tall, gray statues of cement, they appeared to take on animation. Heads of angels with enormous wings, turned as the Jimmy stumbled by. A huge male figure with a staff and a hefty beard, lifted the curved pole and pointed in the direction they were headed.

Bobby then jerked Jimmy onto the grass and before a row of head stones. The drab, somber markers contrasted deeply with the dark green grass they stood upon. They all looked identical until they came to a place where the earth had been removed. Bobby pointed to the grave next to the open pit and there was his gravestone. Unlike the others, it was not gray, but a deep maroon color and his name was etched in white. Then he smiled and pointed to the stone at the head of the open grave and there was the name – Jimmy Reardon. Jimmy felt a chilling cold whip through his body from the back of his neck and down his spine, like a shock of electricity, causing him to straighten up and stiffen.

He peered into the face of his dead friend and could discern his smile was growing but it was becoming less and less pleasant. Indeed, it grew and grew until the grin was literally from ear to ear with his teeth garishly exposed and appeared to grow larger and larger until they were the fangs of some yet to be conceived species.

Then suddenly, the friend turned fiend, jerked his hand and Jimmy plummeted into the gaping hole. He could feel the cold and damp dirt which he squeezed into small clumps in his fists as his lie face down in what would become his tomb. Propping himself up on his still tightly clenched fists, he turned to face the opening. There stood his best buddy, his closest boyhood friend, with bulging eyes and saliva frothing and slowly hanging in wet threads from his still growing teeth. This monster began to push the dirt that was piled high into the crypt and onto his face and into his eyes and mouth. He choked and his eyes burned.

He woke up. Sweat was dripping into his eyes causing them to sting. Even though he was perspiring, he felt frigid and began to shake uncontrollably. He looked to find Corky who was sleeping, curled up at the side of his bed as he always was.

He jumped down and buried his wet face into his dog's neck as the sleepy dog slowly raised his head wondering what was wrong. "Bobby, Bobby! I'm sorry I didn't save you. I knew what you were going to do, and I didn't do anything to stop you." He sobbed himself to sleep, still embracing his companion. "Bobby! Bobby!"

CHAPTER 18

Summer continued. Soon Jimmy began to meet with his many neighborhood buddies and get involved in games of punch ball, slap ball and stick ball. Each day brought a bit more peace to his soul as the event of his best friend's death moved further into the recesses of his brain. Bobby would never be forgotten but he was becoming more of a good memory than an evil and frightening one.

As September approached, thoughts of high school began to enter the minds of the kids. Some were headed to Lincoln High School, the local public school. Many were headed to different Catholic Schools which meant long bus or train rides on public transportation and most often, into foreign and, many times, dangerous neighborhoods.

It was ironic that parents who would never, under any circumstances, allow their children to travel to these low-income areas would now pay tuition to have their precious offspring ride a bus through some of the more menacing neighborhoods in the city.

It was also curious that the youngsters didn't let that danger enter their minds. They had more to think and worry about. For instance, how difficult would high school be? Would they meet and make new friends? Would they lose their old friends who were either going to public high school or a different Catholic School? What about the street games they love so and played every day? Would they get home in time to play, or would the public-school kids get started so far ahead of them that they would be left out by the time they got home? These and other questions began to take up much of the thought process now that summer was almost over.

As the first day of school approached, Jimmy had a different problem that none of the other kids were dealing with - his vocation or lack thereof. Jimmy was going to a high school for those who had decided - at the ripe old age of thirteen - to become a priest. Now, as the beginning of school approached and the other boys and girls were wondering about what second language to learn and what clothes they would wear, Jimmy thought about whether or not he wanted to pursue this calling. After all, this meant he would have to essentially be separated from his friends. This school had the insane schedule of having a day off on Thursday and going to school on Saturday. They never explained the reasoning for this, but most thought it was to force a wedge between the seminarians and the rest of the teenage population. Maybe it was so the priest/teachers could play golf on Thursdays. Who knows?

More basically, Jimmy wasn't even sure he wanted to be a priest anymore. He tried to trace back to why he even had this idea originally. The best he could come up with was that in sixth grade he led the boys in hating the girls and when people said that he would change his mind in time, he came up with a plan to shut them up and show them he meant business. He would become a priest! See, now they would believe him. However, something happened that he didn't plan - his attitude toward the opposite sex was changing. It didn't happen overnight, but he started to notice a pleasurable feeling he would have when he thought about some girl in class or one he saw on the street. Spending his entire life without female companionship, well, it wasn't so attractive any longer. Now he began to wish he weren't so adamant about his dislike for girls.

Additionally, being an altar boy for years had brought him closer to priests than the majority of parishioners had the opportunity to be. This was not necessarily a plus. He witnessed Father Kleinburger's nastiness; Father Schmidt's alcohol problem; and Father Krause being a bit too friendly with the girls who were ahead of others in physical development. He seemed to often have his hands touching them or hugging them. All of this confused Jimmy. Now he was planning to study to become one of them. He wasn't so sure anymore.

CHAPTER 19

The grass was damp after the misty rain earlier in the day. It was a humid day in the town of Poughkeepsie in upstate New York. Benjamin peered through his thick glasses and squinted at the locust that was perched upon the leaf of a weed. He carefully squatted down until the bottom of his pants touched the wet turf. Slowly his experienced hand moved closer and closer to the unsuspecting insect. Then with a sudden swing of his open hand, he grabbed the bug and clasped it firmly in his fist but not so tight as to injure it in any way. No, he needed the insect to be completely unharmed, in no way damaged, so that it would feel every exquisite step toward its demise.

He brought his closed fist closeup to his face, right up to the lens covering his right eye. Looking through a tiny opening that was formed by his curled index finger he peered in to see his captive. It was too dark, so he slowly began to open a breech between his index and middle fingers- enough to allow light in but not enough to provide an avenue for his hostage to escape. It was still too dark, so his fingers moved ever so slightly apart. A bit more. A bit more. He violently pulled his hand from his face as the long feelers from the locust seemed to suddenly emerge and appeared to be reaching out to grab him. He could feel a tickling sensation as the imprisoned insect began to move its many legs in a desperate attempt to escape his grasp.

The little boy with the brown slicked down hair smiled as he regained his composure. "Do you think you are going to get away?'

"Now we are going to have some fun."

With his left hand he picked up the string that he had placed on the ground between the clumps of weeds that made up his backyard. With great care, he allowed the trapped grasshopper to climb by lessening the tension of his fingers. Now the locust had emerged sufficiently to expose his antennae and head.

Benjamin deftly took the string and, with only one hand, looped the center of the string around the insect's head. He held one end of the string in his left hand and clutched the other end in his front teeth. This meant bringing his face awfully close to the frantic bug which was now scrambling for all its worth. It was as if he realized that his fate was nearing its climax.

The bespectacled boy smiled presenting surprisingly yellow teeth for a child of eight. He took one more close examination of the small creature wondering if it felt fear. Actually, hoping that it could understand that it was about to suffer and die.

Through clenched teeth he said, "Die bug, die."

With that he let the insect escape his hand and immediately grabbed hold of the end of the string held within his tarnished teeth. The locust extended his wings and tried to fly away from his captor but to no avail. The child had the fluttering grasshopper tied up in his noose of string.

Then with a flourish, Benjamin pulled the ends of the string and made it as taut as a banjo string.

The locust's head popped off and it began to fly in a haphazard pattern but headless.

The boy jumped and laughed and clapped his hands as the helpless bug flew right above him-up, down, then left, then up again and finally stopped trying and sailed downward until it landed on a clump of crabgrass.

Benjamin looked down at the insect which was now making jerking movements but was probably mercifully dead. The boy opened his mouth and crinkled his nose as he studied the animal whose suffering was at an end. He had to get close enough to focus as his vision was poor even with glasses as thick as a deck of cards.

"How did that feel? Did it hurt? Couldn't see where you were going, huh?"

He laughed at his joke - a laugh that didn't sound natural. It sounded like someone who was trying to laugh on cue. Someone who was not comfortable with laughter. Someone who had experienced pain himself. Maybe more pain than a child of eight should have known.

CHAPTER 20

"Where the hell is that stupid kid? I'll kick his ass if he is playing with those fuckin' toy soldiers again." Benjamin's father, unshaven, a burning cigarette squeezed in between yellow fingers of his right hand, snarled at his wife. Mrs. McGrath, cowering near the old stove with stains of dried food encrusted around the knobs, mumbled, "Please, Kevin, please don't hit him. He's sensitive. He's a good boy. Please . . ."

Mr. McGrath, dressed in a baggy and dingy t-shirt that couldn't hide his protruding belly, looked up at his wife from his wooden chair. "If I want to kick his ass, I'll kick his ass and you'll shut your trap, dammit."

His wife looked away from her husband, fearing that his wrath would turn from her son to her, as it often did. She had put herself between the boy and his father many times and had the scars to show for it. Today she did not feel strong enough. She just couldn't take a beating today. Not today.

The man picked up his can of beer from the kitchen table. Droplets of water dripped onto the faded Formica from the sweating can in the hot and humid air. Air conditioners were not within the budget of a family whose main source of income was whatever occasional odd jobs the man of the house could find, that is, when he even wanted to work or was sober enough.

He drained the remaining liquid from the now warm container. He crushed the can in his fist and tossed it back onto the table. Bringing the tiny butt of the cigarette up to his mouth, he sucked hard and pulled the last bit of smoke past yellow teeth and deep into his lungs. A smile formed on his fat lips as he extinguished the smoke that now had no tobacco left on the side of the disposed of can.

"So, you gonna stop me, woman? Got nothin' to say?" A laugh that only brought fear to those who would hear it poured forth from his mouth. He leaned his head back and began to bellow but his laughter soon turned to a nasty, phlegm-filled cough. His face turned dark crimson as he tried to get control of his breath.

Kevin McGrath was one of those men who had basically no redeeming qualities. He was ugly, gross, fat and lazy. He drank too much, smoked too much and smelled like stale tobacco and acid body odor. In other words, he took up space and used up oxygen and the world would be a better place if he had never been born.

But he was born. Born to a father not unlike himself who died when Kevin was 14. Tears were not forthcoming when he had to attend his father's funeral. Why would the teen weep for a man who spent his days cursing at him and beating him with his belt? Kevin's mother was slightly overweight but not unattractive and she used this to her advantage by inviting men to visit their trailer home and giving her money for an hour of her time.

She had begun this method of making money before Kevin's father died but once he was gone, it became an almost daily activity. The town they lived in was a small farming community and there was an endless parade of migrant farm workers who would stop by the trailer park for some paid for affection from Mrs. McGrath.

Kevin often had to sit in the living room right next to his mother's bedroom and listen to the laughter and moans from her room. Finally, one day when he was 16, a wiry farm worker knocked at the trailer door. Kevin opened the door which signaled by squeaking loudly. He just burst into the small living quarters, brushing Kevin aside.

"Hey!" Kevin said as he stumbled and almost fell. The visitor slapped the boy with the back of his hand and leaned down to bring his face, grizzled with stubble, close to the boy. At that moment, Alice McGrath came out of the bedroom wearing a loosely tied robe.

"Now, boys, what's goin' on here? C'mon, Charlie, let's go inside and have some fun. No need to wrestle around with my boy there."

She reached out and took Charlie's hand. The tanned and wrinkled man smiled at Kevin and turned to walk off into the bedroom with Alice.

Suddenly and without thought, Kevin leaped to the kitchen counter, grabbed a knife that was lying next to a partially sliced watermelon and plunged it into the back of his mother's customer. The blade snapped off at the handle and Charlie screamed like a dog whose tail was stepped on.

Kevin ran from the trailer and never looked back. He had $34 in his pocket that he had stolen from his mother's dresser drawer. Alcohol often kept her brain a bit fuzzy, and he had been skimming money from her prostitution business for some time without her knowledge. Now it would be time to use his savings.

CHAPTER 21

In town he got on a Greyhound bus and went as far as $20 could take him. He used the remaining money to buy food and he got a job cleaning out barns on a farm and was allowed to sleep in one of the barns. Since Charlie was only slightly wounded, no charges were filed, especially since he didn't want to tell authorities why he was visiting Alice.

Kevin found odd jobs and eventually married Helen Neely who was extremely shy and very plain. Kevin didn't care how she looked but he wanted a wife who wouldn't be attractive to other men and who would give him complete control.

Eleven months after they were married, Helen gave birth to a nine-pound baby boy who she wanted to name Benjamin. She felt this was a name that had class and would help her son rise above living in trailer parks and spending his life sitting in a webbed chair, drinking beer out of cans.

Kevin was furious when Helen told him she was pregnant. He didn't want any kids. It would be another mouth to feed and would assuredly take up too much of Helen's time. Of course, he refused to have any part in wearing a condom and Helen had to be ready for sex whenever he pleased which was often, at least when he was not too drunk and would pass out before he could complete the act.

Now he had a kid. Well, sure enough, the damn thing took most of Helen's time and she wanted to pamper him with new clothes and treats and candy. Shit, he was never treated that way. Maybe if that damn kid hadn't come along, he would be treated like the king he deserved to be.

As Benjamin grew, he became chubby with rounded cheeks and his own little pot belly. This was due to both his genes and to his mother's constant offers of treats. He was tested in school when he was eight and found that his vision was seriously myopic, and he would need glasses. Kevin refused to pay for glasses for the little twerp. So, Helen went into town and asked the local pastor for help.

Although the McGraths were never seen at church on Sundays, the pastor knew of them and was a kindly man. He referred her to the local Lions Club who were known to assist those with vision problems.

An old man sat at a reception table in the clubhouse in the old Lions Club building and, after listening to Helen's pleading, he went into a back room and came out with a cardboard box filled with old, discarded glasses. Helen looked through them and found a pair that, although were too large, appeared the smallest in the box. They had large, round lenses with an amber, plastic frame. She thanked the man and put the glasses in her pocketbook.

She then went to the school to pick up Benjamin and when the class was dismissed, she ran up to Benjamin's teacher. "Miss Ahern, I'm Benjamin's mother and I wanted to ask you something."

"Mrs. McGrath! It's good to finally meet you."

"I know we haven't been up to see you for open house or for the meeting you asked for, but my husband is very busy and we haven't had the time to make an appointment."

The tall, thin, middle-aged woman forced a smile. "We really need to talk about your son. He is having some difficulty with his social skills. I'm afraid he doesn't mix well with the other children."

"I promise we'll come up to discuss it with you soon, but I wanted to ask for a favor. You see, I received your note about Benjamin's vision problems, and I got a pair of frames for him, but I can't afford new glasses and was wondering if you could suggest someplace, I could go to for help."

The teacher's eyes looked down, knowing full well that the thought of Benjamin's father coming up for a meeting was highly unlikely, as well as not something she would look forward to, having heard gossip about his drinking and behavior. Then she looked up and saw the desperate look in a mother's eyes and felt compassion for her.

"Well, Mrs. McGrath, I happen to know that the principal has a small fund for assisting families in need. Why don't you give me the frames and I'll see what I can do?"

Helen's eyes filled with tears as she thanked her son's teacher. "Thank you, Miss Ahern. Thank you, so much."

She reached into her pocketbook and pulled out the glasses she had just received. The teacher took them and saw the large, round frame and smiled as she nodded at this sad woman. She couldn't bear to tell her that they were much too large and old fashioned for a boy of eight. She just took them from her and then they wordlessly said goodbye.

Benjamin was standing off about 20 feet away. He was unable to hear the conversation as children were gleefully yelling as they ran to their mothers at dismissal time. He was squinting, trying to see what his mother's reaction was to her conversation with his teacher.

Then his mother turned toward him and waved. He was not in trouble. His teacher didn't tell his mother what had happened in school today.

CHAPTER 22

Recess for the children was a time for freedom from their lessons and an opportunity to interact with the other boys and girls in their 3rd grade class. It was a fun time for all-well, almost everyone. For Benjamin McGrath it was not a time he looked forward to. He felt awkward and separate from the other boys and girls. They had their cliques. There were the popular and pretty girls. There were the girls who were quiet but bright. There were the plain girls, some who were overweight and some who were thin and pale. There were the boys who were athletes. The boys who were cool and popular. There were the nerdy types who seemed to spend time just walking and talking.

Then there was Benjamin. He was one of the "loners." He didn't seem to fit in with any group. He often sat by himself, thinking about things or sometimes even talking to himself out loud. Of course, this habit made him even more separate from his classmates.

He was called, "Bengie" or "Skank" by most of the kids. But they didn't tease him too often. They seemed to almost be fearful of him for some reason. There would be times that he felt a need for some attention, but he didn't know how to attain it without some form of self-depreciation which could involve making a face or pulling a green snot from his nose. This would have girls scream or the boys yell, "Gross!" But Benjamin didn't care, or at least, he didn't appear to on the outside. In reality, his soul was tormented. He really wanted to be accepted, to be part of some clan. But he knew deep inside, that was not to be - ever.

So, he would be his own companion. He would spend his time at home playing with his toy soldiers in his scrubby yard where there was more dirt than green. But something happened on this particular recess period. He made one of his last attempts to be social. At the age of eight, he would make a decision deep within his psyche that other people were not going to be his friends. That he was alone and would be by himself for the rest of his miserable life.

He was sitting under the old oak tree where he often sat. His knees were pulled up under his chin and his index finger was making lines in the dirt next to him. Then he looked up to see three boys from his class standing in front of him. These kids were always together and were extremely popular with both the other boys in the class and the girls who seemed to want to be noticed by this trio.

They were smiling and Matt, probably the most popular boy in the class, said, "Hey, Skank, what're you doing?"

John, another of the "cool" guys, said, "We thought you might want to hang out with us."

Benjamin felt uneasy. These boys never even spoke to him before. But he felt excited that they walked over and made overtures to include him in their recess time. The sun was shining in his eyes causing him to squint and make a grimace which showed his yellowed teeth.

"Sure, if you want to," the chubby boy replied.

By now a few girls had wandered over, maybe wondering what was going on with this appealing threesome and the gawky, grungy boy.

"Hey," called out Dennis, the tallest and biggest of the boys, "Show us how you pick your nose."

With that, the three boys all started laughing and the girls who had just arrived all let out a chorus of "Eeeeuuww!"

Benjamin immediately realized that friendship was not on the group's agenda. Rather they were there to make fun of him. Not knowing how to handle this situation, he did what he would normally do to gain some form of attention - he made fun of himself.

He stuck his index finger which had previously been drawing outlines in the dirt into his nose. Still squinting from the glare of the sun, he looked up approvingly at his tormentors, hoping for some form of acceptance. It was not to come.

One of the girls yelled, "You're disgusting!"

The boys all were laughing hysterically and started to walk away.

Dennis stopped and turned back to face the little boy with the finger still jammed into his nose. Besides being popular, he was also the most feared boy since he was the largest guy in the class and had an attitude of bravado that caused all others to back down.

"Hey, geek, do you know everyone in the class thinks you are fat, stupid and ugly?"

With that, the girls started covering their mouths while they giggled.

Benjamin's eyes filled with tears, but his finger remained in his nose as if it was glued in it. But these tears were mixed, some caused by pain and humiliation; some caused by an inner fury that was rising in a crescendo of rage.

He had felt anger before but never at this level of enmity. It energized him. He felt a rush of strength that he never sensed before and it felt incredibly good.

He removed his finger from his nostril and rose from the ground. By now the boys had already turned and began walking away, bumping each other as they talked and laughed. The girls, too, were returning to their usual recess hangout.

Benjamin walked quickly but steadily toward his tormentors. With no thought or plan, he grabbed Dennis who was at least a head taller than him. Pulling the surprised youth around, he reached for his face with fingernails filled with black dirt. A growl that didn't seem human emerged from his scowling lips as he pulled and scratched at the face of the shocked punk.

The much bigger lad, taken completely by surprise, fell hard on his back as Benjamin clawed and teared at his skin. The other boys stood and watched, frozen in both surprise and fear as they watched their leader get his face lacerated. Blood came oozing out of deep scratches as the pudgy child dug his fingernails deeper and deeper into this bully. Animal sounds continued to rise from deep in this throat and drool hung down and dripped onto the now vanquished enemy.

Benjamin was in another world and only focused on his harasser until he heard the yells of Mrs. Mancone, a portly teacher aide who supervised recess while the teachers ate their lunch. She grabbed at Benjamin and tried to pull him off the now crying tough.

Suddenly, Benjamin became aware of his surroundings. He had somehow left and gone into another world - a world where he was strong and powerful and respected and . . . feared. It was a world that made him feel wonderful and he would visit this world again and again.

CHAPTER 23

Jimmy began his freshman year in high school feeling fear and confusion. He had to take two city buses to get to the school which was in an area that was considered run down and dangerous. He arrived after bus rides that took almost an hour and a half and walked into the huge courtyard where 100's of boys were standing around wearing white shirts and ties. Knowing no one, Jimmy walked around hoping to catch someone's eye and see a welcoming look. It didn't happen. His stomach felt queasy, and he really wanted to cry. He felt like he didn't belong here and missed his friends back in his own neighborhood.

Then a priest spoke on a loudspeaker and called out for everyone but freshman to begin entering the school and to go directly to the homeroom listed on the letter that was sent home. Of course, there were some who had lost the letter and didn't know where to go. They went up to the priest who appeared in charge. He was a thin, short man wearing rimless glasses and had a sour look on his face. It turned out he was the assistant principal, Father McCormick.

He loudly chastised each and every boy who said they didn't know their homeroom. It was obvious that none of them were too happy to approach this dour priest. He told them to stand aside and wait until he had the time to look up their homerooms. Soon about fifteen boys were standing around him looking quite miserable.

Then the priest again spoke into the microphone and said that only freshman should be remaining in the courtyard, and they must pay strict attention as he would begin calling out names and homerooms. Once a name was called, the boy must go to where he was directed and once a homeroom was completed, they would be led inside the building to the room.

The upper classmen who forgot their assigned rooms stood around looking down and scraping their shoes on the concrete. They would have to wait until Father McCormick was done with calling every freshman and getting them all situated before he would find out where they had to go. It was a long, uncomfortable wait.

Little by little the size of the crowd dwindled. Jimmy tried hard to hear his name. He knew there was no way he wanted to miss hearing his name called out and have to go up to this man who seemed so powerful, although small in stature.

Finally, "James Reardon" was called out. He walked over to the group of boys who had lined up in front of a pleasant looking young priest. Since the names were called alphabetically, there were already about 20 boys in two rows waiting for instructions.

Soon, "Carl Zoeller" was called, and his homeroom was complete. The priest at the front of the group turned and began walking and the young boys behind him followed like lemmings. Doing whatever a priest told them to do, Jimmy soon saw was the way it was. And not always for the betterment of these young lads.

CHAPTER 24

That first day of high school was an anxious day of meeting new people and new teachers. There were also new smells - of books, old classrooms and cleaning materials. The custodial staff must have worked hard to make this old building look somewhat shiny and clean. The paint on the walls was old and scraped in a few places. Every room was painted the same light green. There must have been a sale on that color decades ago when it was purchased.

Jimmy's first class after homeroom was Latin and the priest who taught it was a young, handsome guy named Father Loudin. He had dark, slicked back hair - a bit long for a priest. He smiled easily and spoke in a gentle and friendly manner. He said they would be learning vocabulary and conjugations of verbs. The words in Latin seemed to change form to express how they were used in a sentence. It sure seemed complicated and confusing, but Father Loudin's kind manner made it seem like the boys would all learn it without too much difficulty.

His second class was history and Father Michaels was the teacher. He had short, dark hair and glasses.

He was a tall and stern young priest, not quite as young as Father Loudin but much more serious and he didn't smile once during the period.

Then came music with Father Simmons as the teacher. He was older than the first two priests and smiled often. His personality was not unlike the music he sang. He sang a few religious songs that Jimmy had sung in church while in elementary school. He also sang some old-time tunes such as, "Dixieland" and "Jubilation T. Cornpone." None of the students had ever even heard of these songs.

Father Simmons seemed to stretch his smile as he sang, and his eyebrows almost left his forehead as they rose in concert with his voice. His hands made exceptionally soft, fluid movements as if he were directing himself as he sang. Some of the other boys looked knowingly at each other and made faces which caused a bit of quiet laughter. Jimmy thought it was funny as well but really didn't know why. He would come to find out.

His last class of the morning was math. This was probably going to be Jimmy's worse subject. He just didn't like math. It was dry and boring and had to be perfect to be acceptable. There was no middle ground with math. His teacher was Father Weiss. He was the biggest man Jimmy had ever seen. It wasn't his height. He was probably about 5'10" but it was his girth that made him so large. He was enormous.

Father Weiss was without a doubt in excess of 350 pounds. He looked fairly young, although with his weight it was hard to be sure. He had wisps of shocking red hair that were strung over his bald crown. His billowing black cassock which was kind of a shapeless black gown was stretched to reveal his almost female chest and protruding stomach.

Although Jimmy went into the classroom almost dreading it due to his dislike of math, he soon was enjoying the big man's friendly, easy manner. Father Weiss seemed to look into Jimmy's eyes several times and it made the boy feel like he was being talked to personally. Maybe math wasn't going to be so bad after all.

Next came lunch and recess. The cafeteria was a huge open area in the basement that had ugly metal lights handing down from a dirty ceiling that had a myriad of large pipes painted white although now they had so much black dirt on top of them that the white color was mostly a memory. It looks like the custodians didn't look up as they cleaned the school during the summer months.

Inside the hall were table after table set up with folding chairs on each side. A priest who Jimmy had not yet seen was at a microphone yelling to classes as they came in, directing them to certain tables. They were told that these were their assigned tables, and they were not, under any circumstances, to sit elsewhere for the rest of the year.

Jimmy sat down at the table he was placed at and the boys next to him had sat near him in math class. He didn't know who they were, so he introduced himself.

"Hi, I'm Jimmy Reardon."

The boy to his left said, "I'm Anthony Viscone" and shook his hand.

The boy to his right said, "I'm Ralph Thompson." Ralph had dark rimmed glasses and looked like he was about to throw up. He didn't shake Jimmy's hand but quickly looked straight ahead.

"Hey, are you okay?" said Jimmy.

"Yeah," replied Ralph. "I just feel a little nervous in my stomach. I don't think I'll ever find this cafeteria on my own."

"Don't worry," said Jimmy. "We'll all be coming down each day together after math."

"Hey, Jimmy," said Anthony. "Did you have music yet?"

"Yeah, I had it third period," said Jimmy.

"I had it second period and wow, that Simmons is a queer!" said Anthony.

"What do you mean, Anthony?"

"Hey, call me Tony, okay? Around here I always say Anthony because they don't like nicknames, but no one calls me Anthony except my mom and that's when she's mad."

Jimmy said, "What do you mean, Tony, about Father Simmons being queer?"

Tony said, "You know-a fairy. He's one of those."

"What's 'one of those'"?

"You know . . . he likes boys," said Tony.

"Oh, yeah," said Jimmy but he really didn't know for sure what Tony was talking about.

Jimmy turned to Ralph. "Hey, it's almost time for us to go up and buy lunch."

Ralph turned to Jimmy and vomited all over the table. Jimmy and Tony leaped up, but it was too late. Some of the spew rebounded off the table and hit both Jimmy and Tony on their shirts and pants.

"Shit!" blurted Tony just as he looked up and saw Father Loudin who was supervising lunch standing there.

Father Loudin went right over to Ralph and helped him to the lavatory to get cleaned up.

"Watch your mouth," Father Loudin whispered to Tony as passed by carefully holding up Ralph so he wouldn't get any upchuck on himself. Father Loudin smiled and winked at Tony as he said it.

"Gross!" said Tony.

"Now what do we do?" said Jimmy.

Just then their table was called to go up to buy lunch.

"I guess we eat," said Tony.

CHAPTER 25

After eating their lunch, Jimmy and Tony asked for permission to go to the bathroom to clean up the bits of Ralph's breakfast that was now dried onto their clothing. Jimmy almost felt like throwing up himself due to the odor and look of the hardening vomit on his pants and shirt. As the boys approached the boys' room in the corridor, they saw Father Loudin and Ralph coming out of the bathroom.

Upon reaching the pair, Jimmy noticed that Ralph's clothing was wet where apparently Father Loudin had cleaned him up. Ralph looked kind of weird with a confused look on his face. Jimmy guessed it was from being sick all over himself.

Father Loudin said, "All cleaned up guys. Your buddy here is going to be all right."

Tony said, "We're going in to wash off this dried-up puke on us."

With that Ralph looked like he was about to cry.

"Hey, don't worry about it, Ralph," said Jimmy. "I hope you're feeling better."

Ralph's mouth opened but no words came out. His eyes welled up and he looked up at Father Loudin. The priest just smiled and patted the young boy on his shoulder.

Inside the bathroom, the boys ran over to the sinks and began splashing water onto their shirts and pants' legs.

"Oh, man! This is so gross," said Tony. "How am I going to sit in class this afternoon? I smell like puke, and it looks like I wet my pants."

Jimmy said, "Hey, you know what? We are wetting our pants. And our shirts, too."

Tony looked at Jimmy for a moment and then both boys started laughing until their stomachs hurt.

Suddenly, the door to the lavatory burst open and Father McCormick stood there with his hands on his hips and at first said nothing. He stood and glared at the two youngsters who also were silent.

Finally, words came forth from the priest, but they were slow in leaving his thin lips and it seemed as if he was weighing each syllable before sending it over his tongue and into the air. "Well? What's going on here? Lunch is over and you are both supposed to be in your homeroom."

Jimmy tried to respond but no words came out of his mouth. He knew this made him appear guilty for some trespass that he wasn't quite sure he did.

Tony, however, spoke up with strength and clarity.

"The guy sitting next to us in cafeteria puked on us and we were sent here to get cleaned up."

Father McCormick scowled, "You mean he became ill. We do not use words like "puked" in our school." The word "puked" was said like the black robed man was about to, well, puke, himself.

"Are you sufficiently cleaned up?"

"Yes, Father," said Tony. Jimmy was still unable to utter anything more than some grunting noises.

Father McCormick looked down at Jimmy as if to say that the sounds he was making were irritating him.

"Then get going to your room!"

"Yes, Father," Tony repeated, and the boys quickly stepped by the priest and into the hallway.

They said nothing until they were sure they were far from hearing distance from the assistant principal.

"Man, what a jerk!" said Tony.

"Shhhh!" said Jimmy. Not sure his vocal abilities had returned; he was glad to hear that he could at least make a sound that communicated a notion.

"Don't worry, he can't hear us from here," said Tony as he took the stairs up two at a time.

Jimmy was going upstairs slower, thinking as he went. He was feeling more and more uncomfortable here and the first day was only half over. He tried to tell himself that it was first day jitters. He tried to tell himself that this afternoon would be better. He tried to tell himself that tomorrow things would fall into place and it would just be school like always. But something wasn't right about this place. No matter how hard he tried to persuade himself that nagging feeling would not let go. Something was wrong here. He didn't yet know how right he was.

The afternoon progressed without further incident. The afternoon classes were English and Science. In English, the priest was Father Hunter who was tall and athletic looking with slicked back brown hair and spoke real fast. They would read several books and learn some writing skills. Since English was Jimmy's favorite subject, he felt at ease in this class. They all received a copy of "Great Expectations" by Charles Dickens and were told to read the first 20 pages tonight for homework. Although he liked English, the book looked real boring.

Finally, he went to science class. It was called general science and the teacher was Father Stockman. He was a small, red faced man with glasses and quick mannerisms. His movements were fast and sharp and so was his voice. He seemed to often embarrass himself as he spoke because his red face changed from red to crimson at different times. He spoke without stopping for the entire 40-minute period. He said they would learn about weather, properties of matter and living organisms. By this time, Jimmy was tired and just thinking of the bus rides home. His mind could not concentrate on Father Stockman who droned on and on about how science was important.

Often during this last class, Jimmy kept picturing Ralph leaving the boys' room and was trying to read his face. Ralph must have been sent home because his name was called in both of Jimmy's afternoon classes. The mention of his name brought a few giggles to the boys in the class as they recalled the lunch period.

Jimmy did not join in the laughter. Something disturbed him about that look on his new friend's face. Something disturbed him about this school. Now he only wanted to hear the bell and get his books and go home.

CHAPTER 26

School became more mundane as each day passed. The routine of trying to sleep early enough was difficult for Jimmy. He always had trouble falling asleep and often had strange thoughts and feelings just as he was about to fall asleep. During this pre-sleep state, his mind seemed to open up to reveries that seemed real and precognitive. Occasionally, he would remember something from these premonitions and when they proved to be true the following day, he decided that he didn't really dream the event but just thought he did.

One time he had an illusion that caused a tickle that crawled up his neck and made the tiny hairs on the back of his neck stand up. He opened his eyes wide and sat up in bed. His hands were shaking, and his mouth felt like he had chewed a spoonful of sand. A man whose head was turned away so that Jimmy could only see the back of his head was waving to crowds of people from the back seat of a convertible car. Slowly he turned and Jimmy still couldn't see his face because there was none-it was totally blank. But there was a feeling of fear and anxiety even though the scene seemed like a happy occasion. Then suddenly the man fell forward, and the car raced off.

Jimmy didn't know what it meant but he had a great deal of trouble going back to sleep. After what seemed like hours, Jimmy thought about getting up and having a drink of water or milk but then finally fell asleep.

The next morning, the music on his clock radio played but the music didn't wake him, it just entered a dream he was having. He was dancing with a girl from the neighborhood. She was one of the few girls he knew who wore a bra who actually needed one. They were dancing apart and then he took her hand and pulled her closer to him. He felt her breasts push against his chest. His breathing started to increase. His body temperature started to rise, and he moved his mouth closer to her and . . .

"Jimmy! Wake up! You're going to be late for school!" It was his mother. Nothing can take a boy away from thoughts of girls faster than a mother's voice.

Jimmy jumped out of bed and raced into the bathroom. It took a bit of time to urinate since the excitement of his dream hadn't completely left his organ. He dressed quickly, putting on the clothes that his mother had always laid out for him the night before.

Breakfast was usually a small bowl of boxed cereal and today it was Cheerios. His dad said nothing as he had his roll and coffee and read the Daily News that his wife had picked up at the candy store early this morning.

Jimmy gobbled down the little circles of oats that were floating in milk, drinking down the last bit of milk by picking up the bowl and sipping from the edge. His mom would tell him that was not good manners, but she was at the sink and his dad had not looked up from the paper.

He quickly stopped by the bathroom to brush his teeth and then went back into the kitchen to pick up his brown paper bag containing his sandwich for lunch. He kissed his mother on the cheek, said goodbye to his father who looked up and returned the farewell and pushed his sister's shoulder as a sign of sibling recognition.

"Hey, cut it out," said his sister as the Rice Krispies she was eating splashed up on her chin.

It was a Friday and next week would be Thanksgiving and a four-day weekend. The weather was not bad for a November day and the thought of a short week next week brought a bounce to his stride as he walked briskly to the bus stop.

The day seemed to go quickly and soon it was science class and the dismissal bell was only minutes away. Suddenly, a priest that Jimmy recognized but did not know came into the room and spoke to Father

Stockman. He seemed upset and spoke in hushed tones. Father Stockman's red face paled for the first time, and he took off his glasses and wiped his eyes with a handkerchief.

The diminutive man stood in front of the class and seemed to be waiting to find words. This had never been a problem for Father Stockman who usually spoke non-stop from beginning to end of class. He then took a breath and said that our president has been shot in Dallas, Texas.

The boys began to whisper back and forth, and one boy called out, "Is he dead?"

Father Stockman said he didn't know at this time but said that school would be dismissed as soon as possible.

The boys were sent to homerooms and were told to pack their bags and be ready for dismissal. One boy, Matthew Ward, said, "Couldn't he have been shot this morning so we could have gotten out earlier?" The other boys just looked at him and he quickly regretted his remark. Within a few minutes, the boys were dismissed and headed to buses and trains.

No one said much, walking like they were in a trance. The bus came just as Jimmy got to the bus stop and he boarded a bus that wasn't as jammed as usual but still had no available seats. He moved toward the back since he had a long ride and didn't want to deal with people entering at each stop and shoving their way through the bus.

He got to the rear of the bus and put his book bag on the floor and grabbed onto a silver metal pole. It was the first time he had a moment to consider the events that had taken place in the past half hour. The president of the United States was shot! Who could have done this? It must have been a Russian spy. Did they catch the shooter? Is the president in a hospital? Will we be going to war?

When Jimmy got home, he found the street empty. Usually, a few kids from the public high school were around as they got home earlier. There might be a woman washing the stoop in front of the house as these steps were always kept spotless. But today, no one. Not a soul was to be found.

Jimmy walked up the steps to his house and opened the hallway door with the skeleton key that he carried. He moved through the darkened hallway to his apartment door. There he used the house key to unlock the door and could immediately feel a somber atmosphere that permeated the air. Then he heard a muffled sound. He couldn't identify it until he walked into the living room where his mother and sister were standing in front of the black and white TV and his mother was sobbing into a tissue.

"They shot the president!" his mother choked out.

Although he wanted to know if he were alive, he remembered the kid in class and how he felt that it was a question that should not be asked as if the very asking would make it happen. So, he stood next to his sister and watched Walter Cronkite as he spoke in his powerful and deep voice. He spoke about the president as if he were dead. Finally, Jimmy asked the question. His mother sobbed into her tissue which could no longer hold the sound back. His sister said, "They; said it before you got home. He's dead."

It was a few days before a film of the assassination was shown on TV. Jimmy watched it and saw the president as he dropped forward when he was shot. Then he watched a film that was taken before the shot. He saw the back of the president's head and he slowly turned. Only now the face wasn't blank. It was President Kennedy and then he was shot and fell forward.

Cold chills came up from his spine. The hairs on his forearms rose and his whole body shook as if a cold wind had blown into the living room. He remembered his dream or was it a premonition? He saw the assassination the night before it happened. But who would believe him? He decided that he would not tell anyone about his dream, but it would not be the last.

CHAPTER 27

School for Benjamin was the same, yet different, after that day in the school yard when he responded to the nasty teasing of his classmates by tearing at the class bully's face and plummeting him. Dennis, the ruffian and tormentor of most of the boys, gave Benjamin a wide berth from that day forward. In truth, he lost much of his intimidation ability after that day. It seemed like the other boys in class gained some strength and courage from Benjamin's physical reaction. But there was no outward sign of gratefulness. Both the boys and girls kept their distance from Benjamin. He was still alone.

There was no sanctuary from loneliness at home either. Benjamin would come home to find his mother cleaning or cooking and often his father would be home and drunk. Sometimes he found his mom crying quietly. He noticed bruises on her arms quite a number of times and once she winced when he hugged her after he came home from school.

His father's mood, which was never pleasant, would be frightening when he had been drinking. Benjamin would watch television shows where someone had too much to drink, and there was much laughter as the inebriated man (it always was a man) stumbled around and would sing and act like a clown. He knew this was fictional. Drinking made his father angry - no, mad as a rabid dog. He would be demanding and yell vulgarities at both his son and his wife.

At night Benjamin had trouble sleeping. He often would lie in bed and be in an almost sleep state and have these strange dreams that were not really dreams since he was awake. In these states he would often see short one act plays that involved his parents, his classmates, himself and most of the time they were disturbing.

The most frightening ones would end in someone hurt or killed and, for some reason, the painful or terminal ending brought peace to Benjamin, and he would finally drift off to sleep. He hardly remembered real dreams that happened while he was asleep. However, he vividly remembered the reveries he had prior to actual slumber.

After moving onto high school, Benjamin's solitude seemed to become his regular way of life. As a young teenager, he had normal feelings toward the opposite sex, but the chubby and unattractive young man knew deep inside that he would not have any kind of normal relationship with a girl. Although it was incredibly painful to understand that, it was even more difficult to accept it. He saw boys and girls holding hands in the hallways of school, girls giggling and boys strutting. He hated them.

One day during his sophomore year in high school, a pretty girl who apparently was popular since she would eat and hang out with the "in" crowd, dropped her books in the corridor as she passed Benjamin's locker. He stood there for a moment and looked down at this adolescent female. Her hair was light brown and not one strand was out of position in her ponytail. There was a red ribbon holding her unbraided shiny hair. She looked up at Benjamin with huge, wet brown eyes that were accented by a light application of makeup. Benjamin was in a trance.

"Well, are you going to help me?"

Benjamin tried to answer but no words came out and his mouth became instantly as dry as a chalk covered blackboard.

Finally, he just bent over and started to help her gather her books. He glanced at her as she bent over, and his eyes drifted to her blouse, and he could see the top of her bra which held two perfectly shaped and budding breasts. He stopped cold.

"Hey, you pervert!" she cried out. "I see you looking at my chest!"

Benjamin's voice was nowhere to be found and he just looked at those moist eyes and froze.

"Hey, you little shit head," was the next sound Benjamin heard. It was Billy Handel, one of the football players on the varsity team.

Billy slapped the tubby 15-year-old boy on the back of his head.

"What'cha lookin' at, huh?"

"Na, na, nothing."

"Na, na, na," mocked the athletic teen. "What's wrong with you, man? Can't talk?"

Not knowing what to say or how to get out of this, Benjamin stood up and tried to go over to his locker.

"Hey, I'm talkin' to you, buddy," Billy said as he moved in front of the now red-faced boy. As he said this, he pushed the bespectacled boy in his chest and Benjamin fell back into the lockers with a loud, metal crash.

By now a crowd was gathering and it was growing by the second. This only made Benjamin more nervous. He looked at the girl he was trying to help and saw a wide, jeering smile.

"Sorry," the frightened boy said as his eyes looked down at the tile floor.

"You know, I should kick your ass for lookin' at my girl that way, you piece of trailer shit," said the boy who was looking larger and more muscular by the minute.

"Okay, break it up!" It was one of the teachers who was walking by and saw a crowd gathering. "Let's go everyone. Get to class - now!"

Another quick shove and Billy leaned over and whispered into Benjamin's ear, "This isn't over, punk."

No, it wasn't.

CHAPTER 28

The dismissal bell rang, and the portly boy walked quickly to the school bus. Actually, his walk was more of a fast waddle as his excess weight shifted from side to side with every step. The day seemed longer than usual, and his stomach was queasy after the altercation in the hallway. For the rest of the day, he kept wondering if Billy Handell would confront him again.

As he walked up to his assigned bus, he couldn't help but notice Billy, Annie, Billy's girlfriend, and another couple standing around the other guy's car and looking directly at Benjamin. His restless stomach felt like it began to churn, and a wave of nausea washed over him like a sickening stormy surf.

He got on line to enter the bus and he wobbled to the sanctuary of the rear of the bus. His bus was always less than half full and the back of the bus was usually unpopulated. There other misfits sat in seats by themselves. A few were similar to Benjamin - loners who seemed to have no one to share the day's events with.

There were also a few toughs who also sat by themselves, picking at pimples with feet on the empty seat next to them. Occasionally, one of these troublemakers would light up a cigarette even though there was a no smoking sign prominently displayed above the windshield of the bus. The driver had no intention of enforcing this rule, however. Inciting a fracas was not something the driver wanted any part of. Driving this bus which went to the town trailer park was enough of a difficult job. He sure didn't want to deal with any of those parents.

Benjamin plopped down in the long bench at the very rear of the bus. He then slid on his butt little by little to the side window. Now he was safe and alone with himself. He looked out the side window at the gray and overcast day. The pallid sky seemed appropriate to his mood. Soon he would be home, although that was not necessarily a retreat from fear and trepidation.

He could only hope his father would not be home. Maybe he would be out buying beer or cheap wine and give him some time alone with his mother. Maybe she would have baked some of those chocolate chip cookies he liked so much. Maybe they would sit and talk over milk and cookies and his gentle mother would empathize with his sadness.

Then he saw the car. The two couples who were glaring at him as he entered the bus were following him. His stomach which had calmed a bit was now in full and complete turbulence. He looked around the proximity of the bus and saw several bored teenaged boys staring into space. No help there. The other outcasts would certainly run for home if there was a fight of any sort. The two toughs wouldn't shy away from a scrap but were not ones to expect any assistance from. In fact, they both had beat up Benjamin themselves more than once.

After a few other stops the bus pulled up to the trailer park. The car stopped a few lengths away from the back of the bus at each previous stop. They were waiting for Benjamin to exit. He waited for a moment not sure what course of action to take. He really had no choice but to get off the bus and maybe try to run for his trailer. It wasn't too far from the street. Maybe he could make it before they caught up to him.

As he slid out from the corner of the bench seat, he glanced out the rear window. He saw the four youths getting out of the car and slowly walking toward the bus. Knowing he had to get off and try to make it home before they caught up with him, he changed his gait and moved as fast as he could. But speed was not his forte. He had yet to find his talent.

"Hey, shit face," came the now familiar voice of Billy.

Benjamin didn't look up but started to run. To no avail. Quickly, Billy and his cohorts caught up with the frightened boy and grabbed his flannel shirt from behind. Two buttons popped off and a somewhat dingy white tee shirt became visible. Not releasing his grip on the shirt, Billy grabbed Benjamin by the neck and pushed his head back - hard.

Tears filled his eyes - not so much from fear or pain but from trouble breathing. He began to wheeze as the air made a whistling sound in his throat. Often an asthma attack would be brought on by stress and this sure as hell was stressful.

In one swift motion, Billy kicked behind the leg of the now almost paralyzed youngster as he pushed even harder under his chin. Instantly, Benjamin lost all balance as his legs flew out and his head struck the hard ground that had only a smattering of weeds to soften the blow.

His glasses shot off his face like they were propelled with tiny jets in the frames. His vision was blurred both from his lack of spectacles and the burning tears welling up under his lower eyelids.

Billy leaned down close to Benjamin's face.

"Man, you have bad breath! Your breath smells like shit. Look at this kid's teeth. They're green and brown and look like a box of crayons.

With that, all four of the teens laughed hysterically.

Then Billy stood up over the fallen boy and kicked him in the side. The other boy, who Benjamin recognized from school as another player on the football team, kicked him in the other side. Soon they both kicked and kicked again.

The two girls laughed and appeared to be enjoying the scene before them.

Benjamin began to wheeze louder. He tried to catch his breath and, as much as the pain from the beating was severe, he only thought about getting air to keep from suffocating. The sounds of his attempts to pull air into his lungs was horrifying but Billy kept on kicking - harder and faster.

Steve Reith, the partner in the attack, stopped and stared down at the fallen boy. Nancy, his girlfriend, stopped laughing but Annie was clapping and laughing and jumping up and down.

"That's enough, man. Okay, Billy. Hey, that's enough," said Steve.

"Stop it! Stop it! Stop it!" cried Nancy repeatedly. "You going to kill him!"

Finally, Steve grabbed Billy who responded with a hard shove into Steve's face.

"Hey, c'mon, man. You paid him back. That's enough."

Billy was flushed and breathing hard. His eyes were wide and wild. His mouth was open, and a bit of saliva was dripping from one corner of his mouth.

A full minute passed as his chest heaved up and down and he stared at his buddy. Then he bent over the fallen boy and leaned down. He spit in his face.

Annie grabbed Billy and kissed him. "I love you."

Benjamin looked up at the two of them as they embraced. Breathing now was his only concern. He felt as if he might black out. He was alone. No one would help him. He would never have an Annie. He was ugly and discarded by everyone. He closed his eyes and wished he would die.

Then he felt air entering his lungs. His struggling breath was easing. He patted the ground to find his glasses and, finding them, placed them uneven on his squat nose. He raised his head to see the two couples walking to their car, holding hands.

Benjamin sat up and only now began to feel the pain from the beating. But the pain from his heart was much worse than the pain from his sides.

He began to cry.

CHAPTER 29

Benjamin slowly got to his feet. His clothes were covered with dry, sandy soil. He wiped the tears from his cheeks with his shirt sleeve and began to slowly walk toward his home. Before he walked up the concrete blocks which made up the steps leading to his home, he tried to dust off his clothes as best he could. Since he only had one pair of jeans, he wore them every day of the week. His mother would wash them on Sunday, and he would wear a worn and tattered pair of brown slacks on Sunday. He tried to make the jeans somewhat presentable since he would have to wear them tomorrow for school.

Also, he didn't want his parents to know about the fight. His mother would try to console him, but he didn't want her pity. His father would react differently, especially if he had been drinking. Then, you could never know how he might respond but it would not be good.

Sure enough, the moment he walked in his mother said, "What happened to you?"

He wasn't sure if it was the dirt on his clothes or the redness in his eyes or his sad expression, but his mother always seemed to be able to read her son's mind.

She quickly put both her hands on either side of her child's face and looked directly into his eyes. Benjamin tried to look away, but it was impossible to avoid his mother's stare. As much as he tried not to, he immediately began to shake, and sobs forced their way out of his tightly closed mouth. Soon, he was crying, and the tears poured down his cheeks like streams of salty water.

His mother removed his glasses and buried his face in her bosom. Now Benjamin was sobbing uncontrollably.

"What happened, Benjie? What happened?"

As she hugged her chubby boy, her hands reached down to his sides and she felt him wince.

"Are you hurt? What happened?", she asked again.

Benjamin tried to speak but only one word would alternate with a sob.

"I . . . got . . .off. . .the. . .bus. These. . . kids. . . from. . . school. . . They. . . Oh, mommy."

His mother sat him down and unbuttoned his shirt, noticing that a few buttons were missing. She removed his undershirt and saw that his sides were bright red from where the toughs kicked him.

"Oh, Benjamin, you're hurt."

By now the stout boy was beyond grief. The pain of the beating combined with the embarrassment of crying and not being able to defend himself was more than he could bear. He was inconsolable.

His mother rubbed some alcohol on his sides and told him to take a shower and change into his pajamas and to lie down in his bed.

In the shower he seemed to begin to find control of his sobbing and, after changing into his night clothes, he climbed into his bed and almost immediately fell asleep.

He soon found himself in a dream. It was one of those dreams that felt so real that you could feel your surroundings, not just see them. He dreamed of Billy and Steve. It was nighttime and the air seemed cold and damp. There was some type of horn blowing in the distance. Then he saw a water tower and there were tracks - many railroad tracks woven like some intricate but haphazard non-pattern. The two boys were smoking cigarettes and the exhaled smoke shot out of both their mouths and nostrils.

Billy nervously flicked his thumb on the filter as if he were trying to keep ash from forming on the glowing tip. In his left hand was a small bottle of some type of liquor which he occasionally sipped from. Steve said, "Hey, give me a hit on that bottle, huh? I paid for half of it and I want my share." With that, Billy took another gulp and passed the bottle to his friend.

Steve took a long pull on the bottle and began coughing violently. His eyes teared and his nose ran. Billy started laughing hysterically and soon joined his buddy in a duet of alternately coughing and laughing. They appeared to be quite high. Finally, the gagging fit ended, and they took turns emptying the bottle. It was apparent that they were both drunk as they staggered over to one of the tracks and stood between the two rails. Steve tried to balance himself on one of the wooden planks joining the metal rails. His arms flapped as he tried to stay on the board, but he kept falling off onto the gravel between the planks. Billy howled with laughter and shoved Steve off the track.

"Man, watch me," Billy said.

As he stepped up onto the beam, he immediately began to wobble and stumble off the timber. Now it was Steve's turn to crack up.

"You're so cool, man. You look like an asshole. You're flapping your wings like a drunk bird, man."

Billy responded, "Oh yeah? Well, let's see who can stay on the track the longest when a train comes into the yard."

Steve said, "You're on, man."

The horn that seemed so distant earlier was now more pronounced. Both boys stood one behind the other in the middle of the track. After a short time, a solitary light appeared in the distance. The horn grew louder and more urgent. Billy's head began to bounce forward and back as his body swayed in nervous anticipation of the oncoming train. A smile that hid the fear within him was glued to his face as he took a final drag of his cigarette and flicked it away with his middle finger.

Steve was not smiling. He was frozen in fear. The light was now much larger and somewhat blinding as the hulking steam engine roared closer and closer. The horn exploded the air and overwhelmed the booming sound of the now visible, black locomotive as it was bearing down on the two boys.

Steve felt wetness in his pants and couldn't wait any longer. He jumped to the side and safety. Billy saw him peripherally and turned to his buddy and smiled triumphantly. His phony grin turned into a satisfying smirk as he slowly stepped out of the track. He head was bobbing like a rooster walking with anticipation into the hen house. He had won.

The colossal metal Cyclops now blinded them completely. No sound could be heard above the ear-splitting roar. The ground below their feet went from vibrating to shaking so severely that their feet seemed to leave the ground. They both stayed close to the track knowing that the train was forced to stay on the rails and couldn't touch them where they stood. There was a power that was beyond anything they had felt before.

The mammoth monster was now only a few feet away. Suddenly, without hesitation, both boys seemed to leap from their safe haven right in front of the charging, fire breathing behemoth. Their screams made no sound as the blast from the train's whistle and the roar of the steam engine drowned out any possible noise.

Both boys were immediately pulled under the apron of the engine. Skin was torn from their bodies. Bones crushed like fragile eggshells. The freight train had thirty-eight cars not counting the caboose. Each car with its enormous steel wheels and oily metal undercarriage brought further damage to the adolescent bodies that no longer resembled a human form.

When the caboose ended the journey for what was once living organisms and were now merely pieces of bone and tissue, an arm and two heads bounced up and off the tracks. Amazingly, both heads, while brutally damaged, still were somewhat recognizable as human appendages. Both had their eyes intact and they were open and staring. Although no longer seeing they projected the extreme terror that was experienced in that last moment of life. A strange and eerie sound began to fill the air. It was a kind of laughter but yet, not. It was not cheerful or jovial but terrifying and somehow confident.

Benjamin woke up covered with sweat. His pajamas were damp and clung to his arms and legs. The memory of the bashing he took from those boys was now flooding back into his memory. His eyes welled with tears, but he didn't cry. He turned his head to one side and stared at the wall of his small room. Cool air brushed aside the thin curtains by his open window. There was a full moon on this rural New York night, and it cast a light in his room that made everything look black and white.

Then he revisited his dream and it made him feel better. Then he heard himself laughing. Not a giggle. Not a smirk. Not a laugh that was familiar.

No, it was familiar. It was the same chilling, sneering cackle he heard in his dream. But this time it didn't frighten him. Each click of sound gave him relief and solace.

He didn't know who he had become but it was someone new. For a change he was the one witnessing someone else's pain. And he liked the way it made him feel.

CHAPTER 30

The assassination of the president was still on everyone's mind as Jimmy headed back to school on Monday. In his homeroom class, it was announced that there would be a memorial mass for the slain president later this morning before lunch. There was a different atmosphere at school that Jimmy couldn't quite put his finger on, but things were just not the same.

Jimmy, Tony and Ralph hung out together whenever the opportunity arose. Mostly, they sat together for lunch and stood together in the courtyard during recess. The school was built in a circle and the courtyard was a huge cement area surrounded by the gray stone school building.

Indeed, gray was the predominant hue of the school. The building was gray, the ground was gray, the hallway walls were painted gray a shade darker than the exterior of the building. The priests were all dressed in black cassocks with white collars. It seemed like there was little color anywhere once you entered the building.

During recess there were about a hundred boys dressed in suits standing in clusters of two, three or four. There were no uniforms like there were in Catholic grammar school, but everyone had to wear a sport coat or suit and tie.

Occasionally, Ralph would be called away during recess and not seen again until later in class. When asked where he went, Ralph would just say that he had to go to the office. He didn't seem to want to explain it and both Jimmy and Tony never pressed him on it. If he didn't want to talk about it, they didn't want to pressure him. Maybe he had to have some counseling or something and didn't want to talk about it.

Whatever it was, Ralph seemed even more quiet and distant than he did those first few days. Since they were all recently acquainted, neither Jimmy nor Tony knew if this was just Ralph's normal personality. But there was an underlying sadness in Ralph that was more felt than recognized by his friends.

Before mass as they assembled in the chapel, Father Simmons, the music teacher, began to explain what songs they would be singing during the mass. As he spoke, his arms waved excessively, and his hands seemed to be loosely attached to his wrists. Jimmy had never seen someone quite like him. There were more than a few chuckles among the boys but Father Simmons either didn't hear them or just ignored them and went on with his exuberant detailing of the songs they were to sing.

The entrance bell jingled gently, and everyone rose as two upperclassman who were the altar servers led Father Ireland, the principal, to the altar. The mass seemed longer than usual and the songs that Father Simmons had gone over earlier were led by the juniors and seniors who knew the lyrics better. Most of the freshmen were lip syncing since not many knew all the words.

After mass, the freshmen went to lunch. Jimmy went up to get his milk and dessert since he always brought his own sandwich. The sandwiches available at the lunch counter looked awful. They were obviously not made on site, but we brought in from somewhere and those that weren't sold would be out again tomorrow. Once, Jimmy forgot the sandwich at home that his mother made him, and he had to buy one at school. The bread was stale, and the ham was dry and crumbly. He never forgot his lunch at home again.

When he got to their usual table, Tony was already there and heartily eating his overstuffed hero that his mother had made him. Tony's lunches were large and often unusual. They often contained foods that Jimmy had never seen nor even heard of but they always smelled great. Ralph was not there yet. Jimmy sat next to Tony and began to unwrap his roast beef sandwich with nothing else on it but a bit of ketchup - just the way he liked it.

"Where's Ralph?" said Jimmy as a bit of chewed white bread oozed out of the side of his mouth.

"Don't know," choked Tony as some salami and provolone cheese appeared in his mouth. His sandwich today had some kind of yellow-green vegetable mash as well as the meat and cheese. In his mouth it sure looked gross but man, it smelled good.

Lunch was more than half over when Ralph appeared. He sat down and didn't even greet his friends. He looked kind of pale and weak. Jimmy said, "Where were you, Ralph?"

The bespectacled boy slowly turned to look at him and paused a moment before saying," I had to go to the office." The way he said it gave the distinct impression that he didn't want to discuss it and his buddies seemed to understand and didn't pursue it further. Ralph never opened his lunch bag and declined sharing Jimmy's chocolate cupcakes.

The bell soon rang announcing the end of the lunch period. Tony still had some apple pie to finish and to speed things up, he put down the plastic fork and picked up the remaining pie with his hands and forced it into his mouth.

"Okay, all done." At least that's what it sounded like he said as his mouth was jammed with pie. The boys carried their garbage to the pail at the end of the table. All the students were well trained in cleaning up the table and following procedures for dismissal from the cafeteria. Once that bell rang it was if robots were going about their assigned tasks. Soon they were all lined up and heading to their afternoon classes.

Jimmy was bothered by Ralph's demeanor, but he didn't feel comfortable questioning him about it. Later he would wish he had.

CHAPTER 31

After arriving home from school. Jimmy raced into the house, sort of greeted his sister with a quick "Hi," downed a glass of milk and grabbed his roller skates and hockey stick to go meet his friends in the park for several games of hockey. His mother worked now to help pay for his tuition to Catholic High School and be prepared for his sister's eventual high school days. His grandmother lived in the apartment next door, and he always ran over to her apartment before running out to tell her he was home safe and was going out for a couple of hours.

"Hi, Nana, I'm home," Jimmy said as his matronly grandmother answered the door. "Where are you going?" his grandmother asked. "Are you hungry? Do you want something to eat?"

"No, Nana, I have to hurry to the park and meet my friends. I had some milk."

"You're going to get even skinnier if you don't eat something. Have a peanut butter sandwich. I'll make it for you."

"I can't Nana. I have to go. My friends are already there. I'll miss the next game."

"Always in a hurry. You must slow down. I don't like that hockey you play. You're going to get hurt. C'mon, you can be a little late. Have a sandwich."

"Nana, I'm fine. Got to go," Jimmy said as he kissed her cheek and ran out before she could try again to entice him to stop and have something to eat. It seemed like his grandmother's main goal in life was to fatten him up. She was always trying to get him to eat more.

"Be careful with those sticks!" Jimmy's Nana called out as he ran to the door at the end of the hallway corridor.

Jimmy waved without turning back. He had to hurry to the park which was about three blocks away. His friends were either in the public high school in the neighborhood or still in St. Basil's. They would always start the games without him because they didn't have a long ride home on two buses. The skates banged up and down on his back as they were slung over his shoulder, and he ran the entire way to the park.

Once he got to the park, he could see about eight or nine boys of varying heights playing street hockey and yelling loudly. Several called out greetings to Jimmy as he sat on the asphalt puffing and putting on his skates.

None of the boys had those kinds of skates that were shoes with wheels incorporated into them. These were strapped onto their sneakers and there were clamps in the front which were tightened near the toes with a skate key. This meant that sometimes a skate would come loose just as you might be skating hard on a breakaway and that would mean a serious tumble once the skate less shoe hit the ground. Getting a little bloody or bruised was just part of the game and scabs and black and blue marks were badges of play.

After about 2 hours of hard, spirited play, it was about five-thirty and starting to get dark. That was the signal for Jimmy to stop and get home and walk his dog before his parents would arrive from work at six and dinner would be prepared. Jimmy would be in trouble if he were not home, and the dog wasn't already walked by the time his parents got home. He always tried to be sitting down and looking at a schoolbook when his parents walked in the door.

Fortunately, he could hear his dad's key in the door and would quickly turn off the small black and white TV set that would be showing a "Three Stooges" short. At this first sound of the key, he would jump up, turn off the television and pick up a book that he had left already opened and give the appearance that he was hard at work.

For some reason, along with needing to do his schoolwork, his father had this hatred for "The Three Stooges." Jimmy had tried in the past to explain to his father that they were funny, but his dad would just say, "Turn off that crap. I don't like you watching that junk." So, it was best to keep his enjoyment of Moe, Larry and Curly to himself. He wouldn't even do his "Curly finger snapping" in front of his father, although his mother would smile when he did it for her.

After supper and spending about an hour and a half on Latin, math and history homework. Jimmy was permitted to watch a half hour of TV and then wash up for bed. Tonight, he seemed especially tired. He often had trouble going to sleep. He felt he was forced to go to bed too early and he tried to explain to his parents that he would sleep faster if he was sleepy when he went to bed but to no avail.

This night, however, he was into his pre-sleep mode quickly. These were often the times that he would start to imagine all sorts of strange thoughts. Sometimes he wasn't sure how much of the time he was actually awake and how many times he was already dreaming. It was kind of an in-between state of consciousness. Tonight would be one of those strange and disturbing times.

CHAPTER 32

Although he was feeling tired, Jimmy had a difficult time going to sleep. His mind seemed to be like a movie projector that was on a repeating loop. He thought about the President's death and then his mind switched to his friend, Ralph, and then started over with reverie about the shooting of President Kennedy. Both scenarios disturbed him. He could understand why replaying the assassination would be upsetting but he was confused as to why picturing Ralph sitting at their lunch table and staring out into space bothered him so much, but it did. Indeed, he seemed more agitated visualizing his friend than he did envisioning the gunning down of the leader of the United States.

He could see the man sitting in the car and waving. Then he slowly turned, and Jimmy could see the face this time, not the blank countenance he first saw in his daydream but President Kennedy's smiling face. Then he was jolted forward, and a piece of his skull was ripped from the back of his head and flew toward the front of the car in slow motion like a replay of a football going through the uprights. He slowly turned and faced Jimmy again, smiling but with blood gushing down his face.

As horrible as this sight was, Jimmy's stomach tightened each time that assassination loop ended, and Ralph appeared in his mind's eye. There were no gory details. No blood or brains being spilled. Just a pathetic boy whose sadness was so overwhelming that Jimmy wanted to cry each time the young boy sat at the cafeteria table and looked straight ahead. His eyes were cold and empty like he was in a semi-conscious state - breathing but not truly alive.

Finally, after countless replays of these two scenes, Jimmy fell into a restless sleep. But sleep did not bring him peace. For, as soon as he entered a REM state, he began to dream - dream of his friend and it was not pleasant.

This time Ralph was not sitting at their lunch table. He was in a room or more like an office. There was a wooden desk and a bookcase. Then he saw a single bed, so it was not an office but a bedroom. Ralph was sitting on the bed, motionless. His hands were on his thighs, and he was looking up at something or someone. Then another figure entered the dream.

A hand extended and moved slowly toward the boy's crotch. Carefully, the youngster's belt was unfastened. The button on his pants was released. Then his fly was opened so slowly that you could almost hear each tooth separating from its opposite partner. Ralph's eyes remained fixed on the person whose hand was now reaching into his open pants.

The view of the scene now became a closeup of his buddy's face. Fluid welled up in his blue eyes and when he finally blinked, two enormous tears overflowed from his eyes and cascaded quickly down his cheeks like two speeding waves.

Jimmy awoke and found himself crying. He wasn't sobbing but the tears on Ralph's face in the dream were now flowing down Jimmy's face. He could feel a tickle on his chin as they hug suspended before he wiped them away with the sleeve of his pajamas. He quickly sat up. The tightness that he felt in his stomach before falling asleep had given way to nausea. His breathing was elevated, and he felt light-headed.

He jumped up from his bed and ran out of his room and into the bathroom which was situated off the kitchen in the apartment. He burst into the bathroom and immediately bent over the toilet bowl and threw up.

The first heave brought up nothing. The second heave again did not empty the contents of his stomach, but it felt like his insides were going to come through his mouth. Finally, the third attempt brought relief as his dinner, now a brown and foul-smelling liquid, rushed forth and exploded in a torrent, splashing both water and vomit up and onto his pajama top.

He then sat back on the cold, tile floor, his eyes wet and glassy, his stomach aching from the regurgitation activity but feeling somewhat relieved. He began to review his dream. He did not fully comprehend what he saw but he thought of Ralph and remembered the boy's blank expression and those tears rolling down his face and Jimmy began to weep, at first quietly and contained then more forcefully until his sobs were uncontrollable.

CHAPTER 33

The next morning Jimmy's mother came into his room before he awoke.

"Are you sick?" she asked. "I found a few spots of throw up on the floor and on the toilet bowl."

"I'm okay," said Jimmy. "I guess it was something I ate."

Jimmy didn't want to share his dream with his mother. He still was reluctant to talk about his dreams with anyone else. He wasn't sure if it was the admonition from the priest years earlier or that he just felt others, even his mother, might think he was weird.

"Let me feel your head and see if you have a fever," said his mother. This was standard procedure to diagnose an illness and decide whether or not Jimmy should go to school. A thermometer was only used if he felt hot.

"You don't feel hot. Better get dressed for school."

If you're not burning up, you're well enough to go to school. Often Jimmy wished his mother were a bit more sensitive to his health. There were many times he would rather stay home but not today. Although he wasn't sure how he would feel when he saw Ralph, he did not want to stay home and spend the day alone with his thoughts.

So, Jimmy got up, brushed his teeth and rinsed his mouth several times with water. He had an awful, bitter taste in his mouth from his vomiting last night. The water didn't help much but he thought that he would feel better after having some breakfast.

Soon he was on the city bus heading to school. Although the bus was so crowded that people entering on stops after Jimmy had to stand, he felt so alone. He was not able to get a window seat but stared past the woman's head next to him, viewing the passing buildings and kept replaying his dream. He tried stopping several times, even so far as forcing his mind to think of sports or girls or anything but nothing kept his mind from returning to that scene of Ralph and the hand.

He then heard a voice. It was like it was from outside his daydream. He could not understand what it was saying but it kept repeating. Finally, he snapped out of his almost trance-like state and blinked to see the black woman sitting next to him. She was saying something.

"Son, I need to get off here. Hey, boy, wake up. I need to get out."

Jimmy looked at her confused at first. Then he realized where he was and looked straight at the lady with the round face and small red hat, the color of which matched her red lipstick.

"Oh, I'm sorry," Jimmy said.

He immediately jumped up from his seat and bumped into an older teenaged boy who was standing next to the seat.

"Hey, man, watch it, huh?" said the tall and gangly youth.

"Sorry," Jimmy said. He was apologizing left and right.

He stood in the crowded aisle and allowed the lady to squeeze past. She mumbled something unintelligible and pushed her way to the rear door of the bus.

Jimmy slid in on the seat and sat next to the window. He grabbed his school bag which was under the seat in front of where he was sitting and shoved it under the seat where he now sat. The lanky boy jumped into the seat next to him before anyone else could grab it. Seats at this point in the trip were at a premium.

Neither boy spoke to each other during the remainder of the ride. Soon the bus started to slowly empty out and, by the time Jimmy was getting off, there were no standees and there were a few empty seats. The boy next to him rather than getting up to let Jimmy exit when it was his time, merely turned a quarter turn to his right and put his legs in the aisle not leaving his seat.

Jimmy squeezed past him, his school bag in his hand and left the bus by the back door. As he walked the three blocks to his school, the thoughts of his dream again entered his mind. Ralph's teary face, the hand reaching for his friend - somehow, he needed to eradicate these painful thoughts from his mind.

Ahead he could see the school building, tall and majestic but cold and gray. His spine shook from his neck to his lower back. His eyes began to fill with fluid which the boy fought with all his might. He didn't want to enter the school with tears streaming down his cheeks. Finally, he stopped at the corner before he got to the school and, as other boys walked quickly past him, he took out a handkerchief to dab at his eyes. His mother always made sure he had a clean handkerchief, even though he rarely used one.

He had to get control of himself. He put the cloth away and took a deep breath. It was time to enter the school. Time to face Ralph. He had no idea what he would say to Ralph or if he would say anything at all about what he dreamed. Somehow, he knew, he absolutely knew, that this was not just a simple nightmare. This was real. It was something that happened or was about to happen and he must decide what course of action he will take.

CHAPTER 34

Class that day was mundane or at least it was to Jimmy since his mind was occupied on other thoughts rather than math, history, and Latin. No matter how hard he tried to concentrate on algebra, the American Revolution or the conjugation of a Latin verb, Jimmy's mind again and again went back to his dream of Ralph and the reaching hand. At one point, he tried to concentrate on the hand to see if there was any clue as to whose hand it could be. But there was nothing unique about it, nothing that made it stand out.

Soon it was time for lunch. Usually, near the end of math class, Jimmy's stomach was growling with hunger since he hardly ate breakfast this morning. But today, he wished that lunch and recess could be skipped. Facing Ralph was not something he was looking forward to.

As he walked up to his usual table, there was Tony taking huge bites of his sandwich which was made on a half loaf of Italian bread. All sorts of different colored mashed foods could be seen oozing from the sides of the bread as Jimmy approached the table.

Tony spilled out a muffled, "Hi," as his tongue competed for space with meat, cheese, tomatoes and that green, thick liquid that seemed to be a regular addition to his sandwich.

"Have you seen Ralph?" Jimmy asked.

What sounded like a "No" pushed from Tony's mouth along with some provolone cheese.

It was obvious that Tony's concern was his hero sandwich, not Ralph.

Jimmy sat down and started looking toward the door as he began to unwrap his roast beef sandwich on two pieces of white bread with a touch of ketchup. His sandwich appeared diminutive compared to Tony's but, then again, a three-course meal probably contained less food than the huge hoagie sandwich that Tony could barely hold with his two hands.

Jimmy took a bite as he continued to watch for his friend. A glop of ketchup dropped onto the table and Jimmy used the napkin that his mother always packed to clean it up. As he did so, he could hear the metal of the chair legs scraping along the floor next to him.

He looked up and saw Ralph had appeared suddenly from out of nowhere and was slowly and deliberately sitting next to him.

"Hi, Ralph. How're doing?" Jimmy asked.

"Okay," was Ralph's only answer.

Jimmy took a breath. "Anything new with you?"

"Nah," said Ralph as he began to open his lunch bag.

The table the boys were sitting at was called to go up and buy lunch, get drinks or dessert. Tony put down his behemoth sandwich which was now more than half eaten. Both Tony and Jimmy got up to get something to drink but Ralph didn't make a move.

"Aren't you getting anything to drink?" asked Jimmy.

"Nah, not today." said Ralph.

As the two boys got on the line to purchase something to drink, Jimmy turned to Tony and said, "Ralph seems quiet today."

"He's always quiet. He's just kind of there, you know?" Tony said.

"I don't know. I think something's wrong with him."

"You mean he's sick? Shit, he better not puke again," said Tony.

"Nah, I mean he seems upset, you know?" Jimmy said.

"As long as he doesn't puke on us again." Tony said with a grin.

Jimmy realized that either he was imagining something, or Tony was just not aware of their friend's state of mind.

After buying a chocolate milk, Jimmy headed back toward the table. As he slowly walked back, he could see Tony was already there, again attacking his lunch with a vengeance. Then he saw Ralph. Standing behind him was a priest in his black cassock. Jimmy's heart started beating uncontrollably as he noticed the cleric's hand was resting on Ralph's shoulder.

When he got to the table, he saw that it was the music teacher, Father Simmons. The priest was now leaning down and talking to Ralph, almost whispering into his ear.

"Good afternoon, Father," said Jimmy as he looked curiously at the smiling priest.

"Good afternoon, son," said Father Simmons with a smile that did not seem genuine but forced and stretched across his face.

"Just checking up on your buddy here." Father Simmons replied in his usual sing-song voice. Even when he wasn't singing a religious song or an old tune, he sounded like he was about to break out in song.

With that, Father Simmons tapped his hand several times on Ralph's shoulder and walked away.

"Are you okay?" Jimmy asked his friend.

"I'm fine," said Ralph. Turning his head to face Jimmy, Ralph again repeated, "I'm fine."

But his eyes said something different.

CHAPTER 35

That night, Jimmy had trouble falling asleep. Although he felt exhausted, mentally and physically, his mind was too occupied for sleep. His thoughts went from Ralph to his dream, to Father Simmons and back again to Ralph. After hours of tossing and turning in his bed, sleep finally arrived. But rest was not going to be part of his night. Instead, his dream would bring him more disturbance. In fact, it would both confuse and terrorize him.

He found himself in what appeared to be a train yard. Not one that was at all familiar to him. There were two teenaged boys who he had never seen before and they seemed to be drunk. They were loud and laughing. Occasionally, a loud train whistle would disturb the air, but no train could be seen in the darkness.

The boys walked along a track - one of several that could be seen - and drank continually from a bottle in a paper bag they took turns holding. Suddenly, there was another whistle, this one louder than any other and a huge train engine appeared nearing the place where the two boys were standing. They both walked onto the track of the approaching train. They seemed oblivious to its approach as it moved closer and closer to them. Then, with time to spare, they leaped off the track, first one, then the other.

Suddenly, without any warning, both youths seemed to jump into the air and land right in front of the oncoming train. No, they didn't land. They seemed almost suspended in air, backs to the approaching train as movement in his dream went into slow motion mode. Jimmy could feel his voice trying to force out a scream, but he could do no more than moan. His fearful cry was muffled as his mouth would not open. But a scream would do no good.

He saw the distorted faces of the two unfamiliar boys that revealed fear, a deep panic and horror, that caused Jimmy's back to rise up from the bed so only his head and legs were in contact with the mattress. More futile attempts to cry out did no good as both boys were hit by the massive black train engine. Their bodies exploded into a mass of crushed body parts - muscles, bones, blood everywhere.

The pieces of what had been two young men were now dragged under the train and were further pounded and pulverized into a mash of tissue and sinew, no longer distinguishable as human. The train continued traveling onward, clicking and clacking with no regard for the lives it had just destroyed.

Jimmy woke up covered with sweat and he was shaking violently. He felt cold and light-headed. The darkness of the room was invaded by the white light of a full moon. Then it happened. The two boys from the dream, no, not the two boys but only their bodiless heads, suddenly appeared and seemed to dangle and bob in front of him. Hovering above his blanketed feet, they stared at him, voiceless. But their eyes spoke. They begged for salvation and pity. Their countenance was that of absolute dread and Jimmy could feel their fright which made him cringe and shake even more so.

He threw off his covers and stumbled into the bathroom. He turned on the light which burned into his eyes as he squinted as much as possible to relieve some of the discomfort from the brightness. Placing his hands on the counter to keep from falling over, he looked into the mirror and found himself breathing rapidly with open mouth and tearing eyes.

He thought that he might dream again of Ralph and the hand of the priest but instead he had a nightmare of two strangers who he had never seen before. He had never experienced the absolute terror that was communicated by the looks of those two boys. Try as he might, he could not erase the memory of the appearance of those two heads, floating over his bed when he awoke.

It was not part of the dream nor merely a remembrance of the nightmare but a phantasm or a hallucination that appeared so real, he felt he could touch them if he dared. However, it was not something he had ever experienced before. He saw a similar apparition years ago in the sacristy of St. Basil's. It had the same reality as the time that Sister Anastasia appeared to him to ask him for help.

And that time, the event came true.

CHAPTER 36

Today was a Catholic holiday. There was no school and Jimmy had plans to go into the city to a pet store that he had wanted to visit for a long time. He had seen a catalog sent by this store that had tropical fish that his local pet shop never had. He had two fish tanks with the usual mixture of fish - guppies, swordtails, platys and catfish but nothing like the exotic fish contained in that catalog.

There were albino catfish, angelfish with colors and patterns that he had never seen before and blind cave fish. They interested him the most. He researched and read about them. Apparently, they had lived their entire lives in total darkness in caves and, as a result, no longer had the need for eyes or any pigment in their skin. Therefore, they were born without eyes and were pink albinos. They were able to navigate and find food with some type of sonar like a bat used to find its prey. Jimmy just had to get a pair of these fish for his collection.

He had taken the subway many times before and was sure he could find his way to the address in Manhattan listed in the catalog. He had breakfast and told his mother that he was going to the store and would be taking the train. Since he rode the public bus well into Brooklyn each day for school, his mother was alright with him riding a train into the city.

After the usual cautions from his mother, he left for the train. Although she was giving him permission to travel on the train, he did lie a bit, telling his mother that a friend was going with him. He knew this was necessary to get permission because, for some reason, she wouldn't allow him to travel by himself. He walked the five blocks to the subway station and went down into the cool and damp underground station. When he bought the tokens for the roundtrip ride, he asked the clerk which train he would need to transfer to in order to reach his destination.

The clerk explained that he needed to take the elevator train a few blocks away rather than the subway because the underground train did not go to that area of the city. This was a major problem for Jimmy.

Jimmy had a fear of heights. He had had this phobia ever since he could remember. It sometimes caused embarrassment when he was unable to climb a ladder or a fence or stand on any type of precipice. His friends didn't seem to understand why Jimmy would completely freeze when they climbed a tree or went over a fence to get a ball that had gone into someone's yard.

But his terror when facing any kind of height, although unexplainable, was very real and paralyzing. He remembered when his father took him up on the roof of their two-story house. There were four families living in his apartment house. It was owned by his grandmother who occupied one apartment on the first floor. His family lived in the other first floor apartment. There were two tenants on the second floor.

On the second floor in the hallway near the stairs, was a black metal ladder that went straight up to a hatchway. There had been a jam in an air vent on the roof that had to be cleared and his father felt the need to have Jimmy go with him onto the roof. His father was aware of his fear of heights and maybe he was trying to help him deal with it.

"Just follow me up the ladder and don't look down," his father said.

His dad went up the ladder and unlocked the hatch and flung it open so that it landed with a thud. His father climbed up the rest of the way and told Jimmy to follow him. Jimmy took two steps up the ladder and froze.

"C'mon, Jimmy, just go up one step at a time and don't look down," his father said.

This was not possible. He tried hard to force his leg to go to the next rung of the ladder, but it would not move. He glanced down and could see, not the floor beneath the ladder, but all the way down the hallway stairs to the floor below. He could not move.

After several pleadings, his father came down, leaving the door open. "Okay, I'll stand below you and you go up."

His father positioned himself below his son and Jimmy tried again. He wanted so badly not to disappoint his father and be a coward. Again, he looked down when he reached the second step of the ladder but now, he could only see his father's smiling face.

He willed his leg to go to the third step and took a deep breath. He brought his other leg up to the third rung but no further.

"Go ahead. Don't worry. I am right here. Just keep going and don't look down."

Again, Jimmy took a deep breath expanding his chest and started up the ladder. He could feel the cold metal in his hands, and it felt like it was icy. He had to do this. The fourth rung was followed by the fifth and soon he just kept going up and up until he reached the top. There was no way he could now look down because he knew he would fall. There was no turning back. He grabbed the raised edges of the opening and pulled with all his might and crawled onto the roof.

His dad was right behind him and climbed up, grinning.

"See, you did it. Now come here and look at the view."

His father walked to the edge of the building and looked out at the neighborhood. Jimmy walked gingerly toward his father but once his eyes could see the ground, he froze and quickly moved back a few steps. Now he was shaking with fear. His father tried to take his hand and bring him closer, but Jimmy screamed out.

"No dad, I can't! Please! I can't. I can't."

His father let him be but the disappointment on his face hurt the boy. He let his father down and Jimmy felt ashamed. He only wanted to get down from the roof and the horror was increasing by the minute. His father went over to the vent and took a wire he had rolled up in his pocket and forced it down the pipe and turned it around and around.

Jimmy stood in the middle of the roof as far from any edge of the roof that might give him a view of the height of the building. But his fear continued to multiply and soon he felt like the edge was moving closer to him. Closer and closer. Then his mind began to picture him falling, falling. Gravity pulling him, flying down toward the cement sidewalk below. He tried to stop the movie in his mind but to no avail, for as soon as he tried to end it, it began again. He would peer over the edge and begin to fall, and the ground would race up to meet him and he would be smashed and squashed. As soon as he hit the earth, the photoplay would rewind, and he would begin his descent again and again.

His legs buckled and he soon was on his hands and knees. For some reason, this gave him a small amount of relief and the scene of this demise stopped its continuing loop. His breathing was rapid, and his heart was racing. His eyes were tearing as he looked up to see his father standing over him with a look of concern on his face.

"C'mon, let's go down," his father said.

This was easier said than done. For now, he had to go to the hole in the roof and lean over and step onto the ladder. He tried but he immediately could see all the way down, down to the first floor of the hallway. He shuddered and his head violently pulled back.

"Just climb over the door and step on the first step, Jimmy. C'mon, just put your feet on the first step."

"Oh, God," Jimmy thought. "I can't do it. I can't."

He wanted to cry but that would only make things worse and his humiliation in front of his father would only escalate. He was both petrified and mortified but he knew he had to get off that roof and there was only one way down. Well, there were two ways, but he had visualized the other way over and over and that was not an option.

His hands were shaking and cold, yet the ladder felt colder when he reached for it. He closed his eyes because there was no way he could look down and see the drop that he would experience if he missed a step. His foot waved around in the air and couldn't find that first rung. His head was leaning out over the roof and he could smell the acrid odor of the tar paper which filled his nostrils. Finally, his foot felt the top bar of the ladder. He stamped down on it with his right foot and then brought his left leg over and stepped next to his right foot.

He quickly stepped down, rung after rung, never looking down but straight ahead. He reached the floor of the landing and moved to a wall away from the stairs and leaned back, feeling damp under his arms and between his legs.

He could hear his father slam the hatch door closed and pull the hasp tight. Then he saw his father's legs as he descended the ladder with ease.

No words were said between the two of them. His father just walked to the stairway and started down. Jimmy followed feeling sad, mostly because he felt he let his father down. The incident was never spoken about again, but Jimmy would never forget it.

After replaying the whole scenario of the episode of the roof, Jimmy arrived at the stairway entrance to the elevated train. He could feel his heart begin to pump in his chest. He looked up the long metal stairway, took a deep breath and began to climb.

CHAPTER 37

The metal steps of the elevated train station seemed to clank with every step Jimmy made. But since the stairway was somewhat enclosed, he felt secure, and the climb was not as frightening as Jimmy had thought it would be. He still had the tokens from the subway booth, and they were interchangeable between the subway and the elevated trains since they were all part of the New York City Transit Authority. So, he just walked over to the turnstile and after dropping the small brass colored token into the slot, he pushed through the large wooden spoke of the turnstile and entered the boarding area.

He walked down the cement walkway about half-way so he would be near the middle of the track in case the train wasn't long enough to fill the entire station. Now he would wait for the train that would bring him to the area of the city where the pet store was. However, now he had time to realize that he was several stories up and his mind forced his eyes to look through the tracks and peer at the street below.

That awful fear began to slowly creep into him. It never came upon him all at once. It was like a wave of anxiety that would build and build to an overwhelming agitation. No matter how hard he would try to reason with his fear, it would continue to rise-up and overtake him. He would try so hard not to think about it but it was to no avail. No matter how hard he tried, his eyes would drift to the tracks and the street below.

It was as if his brain had a mind of its own. He knew, oh, how he knew, that looking down would cause paralyzing panic. Yet, his crystal blue orbs would focus upon the road below time and time again. He saw cars and trucks and buses roaring by, horns honking. Litter seemed to take flight after each vehicle raced by. Jimmy began to watch a brown paper bag float up and up and then slowly descend before being popped by the windshield of a speeding car.

Jimmy sucked in a hard breath. He began to sway, and he knew that he must move further back from the track so he could be out of the sight line of the tracks and the street below. Behind him was a black metal barrier with giant advertisements on them. Past the metal wall he could see the roofs of nearby apartment houses.

Now the view of the houses affected him. He put his hand on an ad for cigarettes with a picture of a couple who were smiling as they smoked. A giant red box of the brand of cigarettes dominated the huge photo and Jimmy's hand rested on the young woman's smiling face. No matter how hard he tried his eyes kept peering over at the rooftops and he began to sweat.

On one side was the black iron rampart and on the other side was the drop down to the tracks and the street below. He had nowhere to turn. Panic began to rise-up in his throat and his breathing became rapid and labored. If he could have ran back down the stairs to the safety of the ground, he would have but that was no longer an option. Now the thought of going down the steps to the street below was not even possible. He was frozen in this terrifying place.

At that moment, he heard the loud clacking of the approaching train. At first, he was totally relieved. Now he could board the train and be safe. However, the entire station began to sway. At first, he was a slight movement. Jimmy wasn't even sure if it was real or his imagination. Then it increased and rocked back and forth.

Several commuters moved to the edge of the platform and leaned out over the tracks to watch as the train come around the bend and into the station. Jimmy had to quickly turn away because he couldn't bear to see these people brazenly bow and jut out over the track. He slowly walked to the middle of the cement platform and place his legs wide apart in order to balance himself against the swaying station.

Finally, the train arrived and blocked the view of the street. The people began to move toward the train as it slowed down with screeching brakes. Jimmy waited until it totally stopped and walked behind the small crowd that had formed in front of the double doors. He waited his turn and entered the car and sat down on one of the empty benches. He let out an emphatic breath of air through his pursed lips.

His heart rate began to return to normal. Once inside the train he would be fine. As long as he is enclosed, his fear is non-existent. Now he could continue his journey to buy the tropical fish he had hoped to. Then a thought entered his mind. He would have to return home on this same train! He would have to live through this ordeal again.

It didn't seem like a pair of albino blind cave fish were worth the suffering he had endured.

CHAPTER 38

School was hell for Benjamin. Each day brought pain and embarrassment, real or imagined, for the youngster. Other boys mostly ignored him, girls often stood in groups, looked at him and giggled. Their laughter was as if a sharp dagger plunged into his heart. He would fight it but his eyes would tear up and it took all his strength not to cry right in the school hallway.

There were two boys, however, that did not ignore him, and he wished they would. Just the sight of Billy and Steve would cause Benjamin's stomach to jump, and his breathing would escalate as his chest would rise and fall with each rapid breath.

They could not pass him in the hall, spot him in the cafeteria or see him in the school parking lot, without calling out to him and making some nasty remarks. It had become one of their games, a game that many mindless bullies play on their victims. And if there was an audience, especially some girls they were trying to impress, the banter became much worse.

"Hey fat boy," yelled Steve as Benjamin headed toward the school bus on this Friday afternoon. He peeked over to his right and spotted both Steve and Billy leaning on their car with grins on their faces. There were three girls - a bit younger than the two roughs - who were chewing and cracking gum and laughing.

Benjamin dared not look directly over at them. He just wanted to go home and get away without further interaction. But that was not to be.

"Hey, I'm talking to you, you fat piece of shit." Steve now moved off the car and started to approach him. Benjamin knew that running was not an answer and would only make things worse. No teachers were around. On Fridays, they left as fast as they could after the second bell signaling dismissal.

Benjamin stopped and turned to face his tormentors with a forced smile, hoping against hope that somehow, they would just let him go to his bus. Of course, that was not meant to be.

"C'mere, kid," chimed in Billy. "We're not gonna hurt you. We just want to invite you out tonight."

Benjamin stopped and Steve walked up to him and put his arm around his neck and squeezed. It looked like they were buddies, but friends don't hurt when they hug. He pulled Benjamin toward the group and the chubby boy's eyes began to well up. Through teary eyes he could see the three girls snickering, their gum cracking faster and faster.

Steve said, "Listen Bengie, why don't you join us tonight by the train tracks in the old train yard? We'll have some good stuff to drink, and we can all party. The girls will come, too so they'll be three of us and three of them. What do you say?"

"We can't go, Steve," said the shortest of the girls. She had a full face and dark red lipstick. Her chest was the largest of the three and stretched out her white, tight sweater. It made her look older than her actual age of fourteen.

"Yeah, our parents won't let us stay out past nine at night. My father would hit the ceiling if I stayed out late. He would really go nuts if he knew we were with you guys," said a taller and thinner girl whose braces dominated her narrow face.

"Well, Bengie old pal, it looks like it will only be the three of us. What do you say, huh?" Steve's face was no more than a few inches from Benjamin's. Then his smile left his face.

"Man, you stink. You have breath worse than my old dog. Hey, look at his teeth! Didn't you ever hear of a toothbrush, man?"

With that, the five teens laughed hysterically. In his desperate hope not to be beat up, Benjamin tried to smile at this insult. All he wanted was to go home.

"I . . . I can't go either. I have to . ."

"I was kidding, you jerk. You think we want an asshole like you hanging out with us?"

With that, Steve let go of Benjamin and kicked him in his rear. The boy stumbled a few steps and then fell. His hands scraped on the concrete as he braced his fall. The palms of his hands were red and burned with the irritation of the gravel embedded in the cement. But the pain was far less than he felt deep inside.

He turned and looked up at the tall teenage boy who stood laughing at him. Slowly, Benjamin's eyes widened, his lips curled, his nostrils flared. It was the same look that enveloped his countenance when he defended himself once against some other bullies.

Steve was taken aback by the look on his victim's face and the smile immediately vanished. He took a step back as the rotund boy struggled to get back on his feet. All five of the harassers stopped laughing. Indeed, none were still smiling.

Benjamin stood for a moment staring at Steve. There were no sounds to be heard as time seemed to stand still. Then, he turned and began to walk again toward his bus. The once audacious group remained still, faces frozen, chewing gum silenced. No one said a word until the boy was well beyond earshot.

"He's a weirdo, isn't he?" Steve said to his pack. The smile returned to his face, but it was not natural. All could see that his bravado had been melted by the look of his prey.

Steve and Billy looked at each other and, although no words were spoken, their eyes spoke volumes. For some reason, they were afraid of this pudgy target of their scorn. They didn't realize at that moment what the reason for their fear was. They would soon find out.

CHAPTER 39

That night supper was as usual. Benjamin sat down at the old wooden table that was painted white or at least, it was white at one time. Now it looked dull and dingy and had many lost chips of paint on its edge. His mother dished out some home-made beef soup and gave her son a couple of pieces of white bread. The soup smelled delicious. It may not have contained much meat, but it had a good portion of vegetables and was thick and hardy.

His father was not home yet from his daily visit to the local tavern where he would brag about his useless life and get relatively intoxicated before he would stumble to his old blue sedan and drive home in a cloud of smoke billowing out from his hanging exhaust pipe.

Benjamin preferred the times when he and his mother could get through supper without his father appearing, although his father's anger often rose when he got home and realized that his wife and son had not waited for him to come home before eating. But you could never know what time he would find his way home and sometimes it was well after dark when this grim and somber man might arrive home. Often an argument would occur, no, rather a one-way yelling episode as his wife would usually quiver and take a verbal beating. Benjamin preferred to hear the raucous shouting through his bedroom door in order that it would be somewhat muffled.

That is what happened this evening. Benjamin and his mother had finished dinner. He brought the dishes to the sink for his mother to wash them. He then said he would go to his room to finish his homework and go to bed. There was only one television, and it was in the living room. Benjamin preferred the solitude of his own room rather than having to see his drunken father even if it meant that he would skip watching television on a Friday night. Homework was certainly not going to be done since it was a weekend and homework was hardly assigned on Fridays. His mother knew this, of course, but she also understood that her boy would be better off not being available to suffer his father's wrath. She always preferred to be a buffer to protect her child from his father's mindless rage.

Benjamin sat in his room and looked out the window of the double-wide trailer. He would have liked to open the window on this cool autumn night, but it was off its track and would not budge. He told his father about it, but he could only hope it might be fixed by summer when the heat would be unbearable. There was no air conditioning and without a window, summer would be true torture.

The youngster daydreamed about living somewhere else and having a group of good friends. He pictured having a girl who held his hand as they walked in a field and smiled each time they looked at each other. She was pretty but not in a glamorous manner. She was sweet and her eyes twinkled whenever she looked at him. He took a deep breath, and a loud sigh left his throat. The sky was dark now, but the moon was full and the scrubby yard behind the trailer took on colors that were so different than they were in sunlight. The leaves of a tree that were now turning red in daylight appeared almost black and there was a near yellow glow to the ground as the moonlight played tricks with eyes. For some reason, it made Benjamin feel relaxed and he pictured the girl's red dress now changing into black and white. Even though the colors were leaving her countenance, her face became even prettier in this achromatic hue.

Suddenly, a loud slam of the front door jolted Benjamin from his reverie. His father was home. Immediately, he could hear the somewhat muffled gruff voice. It was difficult to understand the exact words due both to his door being closed and his father's intoxicated state. The words were slurred but the volume was loud, and he was not happy.

Soon he heard a pot or a pan bang on the floor. He forced himself to go to the door and put his face close to the frame so he could hear what was going on without going into the kitchen. He heard another door slam closed and then slam again. He slowly opened his door to peek out. There was no one in the kitchen. His mother must have gone into the bedroom and his father must have followed her. He slowly moved into the kitchen.

His assumption was accurate as he could now hear yelling coming from inside his parents' bedroom. Then there was an unmistakable sound of a vicious slap. Again. Again. Each time the sound of a hand hitting skin, the boy flinched as if he, himself, was struck. Then the yelling was replaced by crying and begging.

"Please, Kevin! You're hurting me! Please stop! I'm sorry. I'm sorry."

But the slapping sounds increased in both intensity and speed. Then there was a small respite.

"No, Kevin, don't. Please!"

The report changed in tone. It no longer sounded like skin on skin. There was a sharp cracking sound as if something else was being used to inflict pain. Indeed, his father had removed his wide, leather belt and was beating his wife on her shoulders, side and buttocks with it.

After a dozen or so of these horrific whacking sounds, it finally stopped.

After a few moments of quiet, Benjamin could hear his mother's sobbing. He quickly ran into his room and closed the door, not knowing if his father was going to come out of the bedroom and make him his next target.

He sat in the semi-dark with only the light of the full moon giving a now eerie tint to his room. Gone was the warming and pleasant feeling that the moonlight had bestowed upon him. Now his stomach was knotted up. He sat sweating and in desperate fear that his door would open at any moment and his father's distorted face with wide and wild eyes would enter looking for his next victim.

But he soon heard some dishes banging in the kitchen and he deduced that his father was preparing to eat his late supper. He began to allow his breathing to return to almost normal. Now his fear was being replaced by anger. He hated his father. He hated himself for not going to his mother's aid. She was always there to protect him, but his cowardice blocked him from attempting to stop his mother's terrible beating.

His eyes welled up but not from sadness. He was furious and filled with violent rage toward this man who said he was his father. His father? His mother's husband? How could a man bring about so much pain on those he should love and cherish?

Then it happened again. Benjamin's features began to change. It was as if a metamorphosis took place. He was . . . transforming. His eyes widened. His breathing quickened. His lips began to stretch into an almost sardonic grin. He felt powerful - filled with an explosive madness.

Someday, somehow, he would be rid of his father. He would kill him. He would kill his father.

CHAPTER 40

The young boy awoke in confusion. It took a few moments for him to realize that he was in his bed, in his room. Apparently, he had fallen asleep in his clothes. As his mind began to clear, he remembered his mother's cries, his father's angry voice, his inability to come to his mother's aid. When his mind reviewed what had happened earlier that evening, he felt like he should cry but he couldn't. This, too, upset him.

He rose from his bed and squinted to try to read the clock on his night table. He couldn't read the time, so he felt for his glasses and pulled the spectacles onto his face. The clock read 11:45. He felt that his mouth was dry and there seemed to be a paste over his tongue. It tasted bitter and he thought about Steve and what he said about his bad breath. Anger began to rise in his belly.

He quietly walked over to his bedroom door and listened to try to hear if his father was still up and about. Hearing nothing, he walked back to his window and looked out into the moon lit yard. His thoughts went back to Billy and Steve and thought about their bogus invitation to join them to drink in the nearby train yard.

His breathing increased, his eyes began to bulge, anger was replaced by a feeling of strength and power. He made a decision. He again moved to his bedroom door and this time slowly opened it and stuck his head out and looked around. No one was in the kitchen or living room. He slowly stepped out and was careful not to bang into anything as he moved. Each step in his worn and dirty black sneakers was deliberate. Each step was planned and placed gingerly. Then he heard a noise.

He stopped, frozen in his tracks. He turned his head, so his right ear was facing the source which was his parent's bedroom. Then it became familiar. It was his father's snoring - a loud roar, followed by a few moments of silence. Then the blast exploded again. Benjamin stood still, stiff and fearful. Then he became calmer as he pictured his father in bed, laying on his back, belly swollen, mouth open and a roar blasting from his throat.

He then continued his move toward the front door. He deliberately and gently unfastened the lock on the door and when it snapped into the open position, his hand moved to the doorknob and millimeter by millimeter he turned it clockwise until the door was free. Pulling the door open caused a mild squeaking sound that in the normal everyday use of the door was never even noticed. His father's snoring was now his signal that all was clear, however. As long as he heard this father, he knew he was safe.

Benjamin carefully closed the door behind him and then felt a feeling of freedom that he had not experienced before. The night air felt cool and sweet as he drew it deeply into his lungs. The colorless trees and mobile homes in the trailer park had an eerie look yet it seemed to sooth him. He still walked with light steps as if the sound of the gravel crunching beneath his feet might wake his father. But by the time he reached the entrance to the trailer park, his steps became regular and brisk.

He walked along the paved road. No cars passed and the only sound was that of insects' mating calls. The serenity washed over him but then the faces of his two tormentors appeared in his mind's eye. He pictured them walking by train tracks, drinking and laughing. Laughing - probably at him. Hatred and anger began to build. His steps became quicker as he moved with determination.

CHAPTER 41

The night seemed a bit cooler than usual. Billy and Steve were out enjoying the night. What was not to like? It was a Friday night; their parents didn't want them home until around 1 AM and they had some good stuff to drink.

Even though they were not of age to buy liquor, it was so easy to acquire. Earlier they hung out in the parking lot of the strip mall where the neighborhood liquor store was. They would wait until someone just over 21 showed up and then ask the guy to buy them a bottle of bourbon. Sometimes they had to sweeten the deal with a few bucks but often the guy would do it for free because he probably did the same thing himself a few years ago.

Tonight, it was even easier. After only about 15 minutes, Zach Johnson drove up in his '55 Chevy with glass pack mufflers that you could hear several blocks away. Zach was cool and his younger brother was in some of Steve and Billy's classes, so they knew each other. He was more than willing to buy a bottle of Jack Daniels for the boys.

Now they were drinking and walking in the train yard which was a regular hang out for the "in" group at school. It was a place where you could drink, smoke, make out and no one would bother you. There was a security guard but as long as you didn't do any damage other than throwing trash or painting your initials on rail cars, he didn't care. He basically stayed in his little hut and listened to his portable radio and looked at dirty magazines. You could see him through the window, smoking and drinking coffee with his feet on the desk. Even if he saw some kids, he preferred leaving them be rather than confronting them.

"I wish our girlfriends could have made it tonight," said Billy.

"Man, too bad those freshman girls couldn't come tonight either," said Steve.

"Yeah, that Linda got big tits. I'd like to grab a hold of those babies," said Billy.

Steve said, "Yeah and Barbara knows how to make out, man. But you've got to watch out for those braces. I hurt my tongue on them last week."

With that, both boys started laughing until Steve started to cough violently. That made Billy laugh even harder. The combination of hysteria and the bourbon made both boys light-headed and they staggered a bit before catching their footing.

Steve, recovered from his coughing fit, now took a long drag on his cigarette and then coughed some more. His eyes were red and watering, and it made it tough for him to see clearly. This was a great Friday night for these two.

Soon they heard a train moving in their direction. Billy looked up and saw a huge locomotive heading in their direction as they stood next to one of the many tracks. It was time to play a game that they often did in the train yard.

"Hey, man," said Billy. "Let's see who jumps off the track last when that freight comes down here."

"Yeah," said Steve. "Last time you punked out before me. I'll beat your ass again."

"Bullshit!" said Billy. "You chickened out last time."

"No way! You jumped off before me," said Steve.

"C'mon, chicken," said Billy as he walked to the middle of the track. The train was approaching at a slow but steady pace.

"I'll bet you a buck I will stay on longer than you," said Steve as he, too, moved to stand behind his buddy.

They both took drags on their cigarettes and then took long swigs from their shared bottle, the dark brown liquid burning their throats as it passed down into their stomachs.

The train continued in their direction but was moving slowly but picking up speed. The two punks knew that there was plenty of time to jump off the tracks before the train reached them. Indeed, although they thought they were demonstrating great courage, they always jumped well before the plodding engine reached them. Then they would congratulate each other on their pseudo bravery.

The engineer could now see the two hooligans as the light on his engine began to light up the area where they were standing. This was a somewhat regular occurrence at the train yard and stopping the train was not going to happen. First of all, it took a long time to get it going again since he was pulling almost forty cars. In addition, although he was traveling at only a few miles per hour, stopping quickly was impossible. With all that weight, he needed over 100 feet to stop even at this reduced speed.

The engineers dealt with this often and if they stopped every time, they would disrupt their schedule and there is nothing on earth that is more concerning for trains than schedules. So, he did what he always did, blew his horn. These idiots would jump well in advance of the oncoming train. They always did.

Sure enough, after several blasts of his horn, the troublemakers jumped clear. They were now out of his vision and clear of the illumination of his light beam. He could proceed as usual.

Billy and Steve were now again laughing and pounding each other on the shoulders and back.

"You jumped first, you chicken shit," said Steve.

"No way, man," said Billy, "You jumped first."

The roar of the engine was now drowning out their protests as to who leaped first. The noise was deafening but they both kept yelling louder and louder. Neither could hear the other nor could they hear or see a figure rising from the ground near them.

A dark, but short and portly form was moving toward them. It began slowly but then suddenly moved with a quickness that belied its shape. Both delinquents were facing the oncoming train and unaware of what was going to occur.

Just as the gigantic, black iron horse was almost upon them, a hand pushed at the back of each drunken youth. Both seemed to become airborne as they flew over the rail of the track and right in front of the oncoming train.

The engineer suddenly saw these two boys seemingly suspended in air in front of him. Billy held onto the bottle of liquor as if to save it from destruction. But their eyes. Their eyes. The operator of this massive metal machine would never, ever forget those eyes.

Immediately, he grabbed the emergency brake and heard the wheels screaming and screeching as metal slid against metal and tried desperately to grab hold. The impact was vicious. Fortunately for the train engineer he didn't see the effect that this rampaging 150-ton steel monster would have upon the young and tender bodies of these teens.

They were dragged beneath the apron of the engine and crunched and brutally torn apart. Arms, legs, torso were ripped as tendons and ligaments were as useless as worn-out rubber bands that had no strength left to do their job of holding bones and muscles together. Death did not come as instantly as one would imagine.

The pain of an arm being torn from the shoulder was excruciating. When legs were crushed before finally being amputated, the wheels and undercarriage of the train each took its turn plowing, twisting and dismembering. Finally, both young men were decapitated.

Their heads were spit out from the side of one of the cars. They rolled right up to a figure standing there in the moonlight. Benjamin looked down at the two faces that were at his feet. Unseeing eyes were open and looking up at him. Or did they see their executioner?

He bent over to get a closer look. A smile displayed his brown and yellow teeth. He knelt down and moved close to the heads and alternately looked into eyes that appeared to look back.

"Can you smell my breath, now? Take a sniff. Oh, yeah, you have no lungs so you can't breathe, can you?" said Benjamin.

A strange and frightful sound came from deep within his throat. It didn't sound human. Didn't sound like anything living. It was the sound of evil. A powerful yet muffled voice of evil. And Benjamin liked the way it sounded.

The chubby boy rose to his feet and began to walk away as the train continued to brake and screech.

Two lives ended and one was reborn. No, not reborn as much as transformed and this transformation would affect the lives of many.

CHAPTER 42

Although the academics of school were not much of a problem for Jimmy, there were other aspects of his high school experience that were very troubling. For one thing, his faith was not as strong as he believed. Indeed, he began to question whether he belonged in a high school for future priests. A major obstacle was his increasing interest in the opposite gender. The girls in his neighborhood began to have a new and strangely pleasant affect upon him. He was always the chief "girl hater" among his friends. But now, he found these same girls attractive, and he liked talking to them. The idea of never getting married, as a life in the priesthood would necessitate, felt less and less attractive.

Another area that was both confusing and disturbing was his suspicion that something was wrong with his friend, Ralph. Ralph was a quiet kid who didn't talk easily. He never seemed to start conversations but would rather respond to other's remarks. But more and more, Ralph's replies were becoming shorter and with no emotion. He seemed distant and often appeared to be in a dream world of his own.

Sure, Jimmy also found himself in a dream world many times during the day, particularly during Latin class but he would be either thinking about playing street hockey or picturing Linda, Nancy or one of the other girls in his neighborhood sitting on a stoop in front of his house and listening to a transistor radio. He felt certain that Ralph was neither daydreaming about sports nor girls but rather something unpleasant. His countenance was blank but appeared pained.

Also, he noticed that Ralph seemed to have lost his appetite and hardly ate his lunch. He often took a bite or two from his sandwich and would sit and stare until the bell rang and then quietly get up and throw most of his lunch in the garbage. His other lunch mate, Tony, was the polar opposite. Tony would eat enormous lunches and would continually talk, mostly with his mouth full and food spilling out onto his shirt, the table and even Jimmy if he got too exuberant. Tony didn't seem to share Jimmy's concerns about Ralph but, then again, Tony was mostly concerned with having enough time to ingest his daily massive sandwich.

One day, Ralph was home sick, and Jimmy again asked Tony if he shared any of his notions that their friend was upset and not himself.

"Tony, do you think there's something wrong with Ralph?" Jimmy asked.

"Whatta ya mean?" Tony responded as a mixture of salami, tomatoes and some yellow-green goop oozed out of his mouth and plopped on the table.

"I think he's scared or sick or something. He hardly talks anymore," Jimmy said.

"Ah, he never talks much. He's kind of a dork, ya know? I mean, he's a nice guy and all but, c'mon, he's not too cool, ya know?" Tony said.

Jimmy had to agree with Tony. Ralph was not an interesting conversationalist. But he hadn't been this quiet and inward. He couldn't help but feel that something was not right with him. However, it was obvious that Tony was not one to discuss this with. He would be of no help in figuring out if there really was something upsetting Ralph.

But he couldn't help but feel that he needed to discover what was wrong. He still had a recurring dream that Ralph would be sitting in a small room and a hand would slowly descend toward his pants. Jimmy could only see the left hand of the man and not his face. He would, however, see Ralph's face and, although his features were without expression, there was a deep sadness that Jimmy could perceive.

Why did he keep having this dream? And was this image merely a delusion that was influencing his mind and making him think there was a problem with Ralph when he was just being himself - a quiet, shy kid?

After all, he didn't know him so well. They only met a few months ago and outside of lunch and sharing a class, they didn't spend time together. It must be just this stupid dream that is causing all this angst.

Too many things were going on in his mind. His brain was going in all sorts of directions. School, religion, girls, sports, Ralph. He had a headache. He looked over at Tony. His friend pushed the last remnant of his sandwich into his mouth. How could he eat so much? Jimmy started to laugh to himself. Tony seemed to be trouble free. He was only concerned with his lunch and trying to pass Latin and math. He was flunking both and when there were a few minutes left after swallowing enough food for a family of four, he would ask Jimmy for some help with his homework assignment. But even though there was a good chance that his report card would have some red marks on it, Tony didn't seem to have a care in the world.

Jimmy began to realize that maybe he needed to slow down his thoughts and try to concentrate on sports. This was a suggestion that Father Loudin had given him in confession when he told him that girls were on his mind more than often. He thought about telling the priest his fears concerning Ralph, but he hesitated and held back. The priest would probably think he was crazy to hold dreams to such importance. Father Loudin was one of the younger priests and was someone he felt was closer to his age and more understanding. But he didn't want to have someone he admired think he was foolish. So, he didn't speak of it in confession.

Jimmy again looked at Tony who was wiping his mouth on his sleeve. Yes, he would try to relax and become more like his buddy. A smile came across his lips.

Tony looked at him with a quizzical expression on his face. "What?"

Jimmy grinned and said, "Nothing."

CHAPTER 43

It was late that night and Jimmy was up watching the Tonight Show with Johnny Carson on the TV in his room. He was a night owl and his parents let him stay up and watch television as long as he got up on time in the morning. Tonight, Johnny and his side kick, Ed McMahon, were really clicking and Ed's hardy laugh brought on laughter for Jimmy.

It was good medicine. He realized he was laughing out loud, and it felt good. He started to think that he was getting too serious in his private thoughts and needed to relax a bit and enjoy life more. At that point, Johnny, wearing a turban, held an envelope up to his head and predicted what it contained. The punch line caused the studio audience, Ed and Jimmy to roar with laughter.

He caught himself and realized he better not get too loud, or his father would come in and tell him to turn off the TV. His mother was probably sleeping and his dad, like him, would stay up late. It was understood that Jimmy was up watching TV but if he got noisy, his dad would come in and tell him to go to bed.

Soon, the program was over, and Jimmy went to the bathroom to brush his teeth and wash up. The apartment had only one bathroom and it was off the kitchen. He quietly walked through the rooms to the bathroom. After brushing his teeth, he looked into the mirror and studied his face. There were some new pimples, so he took a tube of acne cream that was kind of brown in color. He guessed it was to cover it up, but the color didn't match his complexion and only made the zits more obvious. Teenage years were tough.

Then he checked out his teeth and made several attempts to smile. Some were with his mouth open. Some with his mouth closed. He wanted to see which made him look more mature. He settled upon a closed mouth with a slight smile. He would use this one the next time he ran into a girl and try it out.

He returned to his room, removed his slippers and turned out his night table light. He punched his pillow a couple of times and turned his head around on it to make an indent. He didn't like the new pillow his mother had gotten him. It was foam rubber and didn't leave an impression for his head to fit into. It just rebounded right back. It just didn't feel comfortable.

Soon his eyes became heavy, and he began to float in that state between waking and sleeping. Then it happened - again.

He pictured his friend, Ralph, sitting quietly in a straight-backed chair. Although he was expressionless, Jimmy felt an air of anxiousness that was extremely uncomfortable. The room he was in seemed to be some kind of office. After a few moments, a hand come into view. It moved to Ralph's leg and seemed to just rest there. Ralph's breathing became more rapid, and his eyes welled up with tears. There was no sound other than this buddy's inhaling and exhaling. The hand began to move up his thigh and began to open his fly. Then Jimmy saw the sleeve - a white shirt appearing from under a shiny black oversleeve.

Jimmy recognized that he wasn't asleep but in a twilight zone between the states of waking and sleeping. Suddenly, the images left his mind's eye and actually appeared in his room, right before him in front of his bed. These were not thoughts or phantasms, but Ralph was physically present. However, the only part of the adult he could see was the hand and arm. The rest of the man was blocked out in a kind of fog.

The hand entered the boy's pants and Jimmy tried to yell out. But he could only open his mouth and try and try to make a sound. Finally, a deep grunt came out and then another and another. The hand suddenly pulled out as if the person attached to the appendage heard him. The arm slowly dissolved but Ralph was still there.

He slowly turned to look at Jimmy. A tear began to descend from the lower lid of one eye, leaving a wet trail on his cheek. Although no voice was heard, Jimmy could feel his friend's terrible anguish. And then he was gone.

CHAPTER 44

Jimmy woke up after a restless night of sleep. When he had these disturbing dreams, he awoke still tired, even if he slept his usual number of hours. He wanted so badly to turn over and go back to sleep but he knew he had to get up and ready himself for school.

He guessed he looked as tired as he felt when his mother recognized his sleepy state.

"You are staying up too late watching television. Your face looks swollen, and your eyes are all red."

"Oh, ma, I'm fine. I didn't stay up any later than I always do," replied Jimmy.

"That's what I mean. You stay up too late every night. You need more sleep," scolded his mother.

Jimmy's dad didn't look up from his newspaper. He picked up his buttered roll and took another bite without saying a word. Conversation with his father was minimal most times but especially during breakfast. His father concentrated on the Daily News and his roll and coffee. At the rare times that Jimmy actually got into the kitchen before his dad, he would very carefully turn the pages of the paper to the back sports pages. He had to return the paper to its pristine condition before his father entered the kitchen because he wasn't allowed to touch the paper before his dad read it.

Jimmy sat at the kitchen table and drank a glass of orange juice. Although his mother had a fresh roll for him that she bought early that morning from the nearby deli, he hardly ever ate any breakfast. He just wasn't hungry in the morning.

As soon as he drank his juice, he went into the bathroom and brushed his teeth, retrieved his book bag from his room and said his good-byes. He then walked the several blocks to the bus stop for his ride to school. It took two city buses and about an hour to travel to school each day. It was kind of strange that so many Catholic kids traveled to what was considered "bad areas" to go to their schools. On the way there, Jimmy would see old brownstone houses with boards on some windows and black men sitting on sidewalks drinking from paper bags.

Everything looked brown and gray as he looked out the window of the bus. It was as if the scene changed from color to sepia as he traveled from his neighborhood to the depressed area where his school was. Even with having to travel on two buses, he still had to walk several city blocks to school. The walk from his house to the bus was always uneventful but the five-block walk from the last bus stop to the school filled him with anxiety, especially after he was the victim of two attempted muggings, once going to school and once on his way home.

The first one was only mildly upsetting. A black boy about his age, who was apparently mentally disabled, came up to him and started kicking him. He was slight, even smaller than Jimmy, and said he wanted money. Jimmy kept walking while the kid continued to kick his leg and his book bag. After almost an entire block, the kid just stopped and cursed at him as Jimmy kept on walking. Ignoring the angry boy whose facial appearance manifested Down's Syndrome, seemed like the best tactic and it worked. Once Jimmy was a block away, he turned around and could still see the boy standing in the same spot. He appeared to be talking, probably still cursing at Jimmy from afar.

Once Jimmy got close enough to see his school his hands began to shake uncontrollably. He felt light-headed and his empty stomach seemed to be jumping around inside him. He arrived at his home room and sat down trembling. But once Father Loudin entered and called out for quiet and told the class to rise for prayer and the Pledge of Allegiance, his body calmed down and he was back to normal.

This event was followed a few months later when he was accosted on his way home from school. This time the situation was much more frightening. He was about two blocks from reaching the first bus stop when a bunch of teenage boys, five of them to be exact, ran up to him.

"Hey, boy, you gotta dime?"

"Gimme a dime, boy," another one said.

Jimmy knew that once he took out money, they would take it all. He needed a nickel for the bus fare that was five cents with his school bus pass. Losing his money meant he would have no way to get home.

Jimmy tried the same tactic as last time. He would just keep walking. He made it about half a block. Then suddenly one of the bigger kids grabbed him and pushed him against a building.

"Hey, you deaf, man? He said, 'you gotta dime?'"

Jimmy said nothing but attempted to walk again. But this time the thug pulled a knife and held it to Jimmy's throat.

"Maybe you don't hear too good. Now give us some money, man."

The knife was pushed against Jimmy's throat, and he could feel the coldness of the metal as the knife began to indent the skin above his Adam's apple. Jimmy stood frozen and said nothing. Then, suddenly, another black teenager but older than the others, came running out of one of the brownstone houses and down the long, high set of steps. He raced toward them. Jimmy thought he was doomed as an even bigger young man was going to join in the attack. But instead, the group scattered and ran.

The older teen came up to Jimmy. "They botherin' you?"

"They wanted my money," said Jimmy.

With that, he turned and ran after them. Jimmy continued to head toward the bus stop. As he waited for the bus to arrive, the boy who held the knife returned. He brandished the knife and said, "We weren't botherin' you, man. Why did you tell him that?"

Jimmy looked around and didn't see his defender anywhere in sight. However, now there was only one attacker and even with though he had a knife, Jimmy felt he had a chance to defend himself. Just as the kid moved closer, the bus began to pull into the stop.

Seeing the bus, the assailant put the knife in his pocket and started to walk away.

Jimmy got on the bus and, like the last time, his hands began to shake after a few minutes. At this point he already didn't want to stay in this school and now he wondered if he would even live through his high school years.

He awoke from his daydream to see that the bus was about to arrive at his stop. After getting off the bus, he began his walk to school, and he had a bad feeling that he might be accosted again. Why did he allow himself to review those two incidents? Why couldn't he predict when things like this happened? Why couldn't he control when he saw a vision of a future event? The orange juice in his stomach was churning as he spotted the spires of the high school rising into the sky. He made it safely to school.

But he didn't really feel comfortable. School was not a sanctuary. The schoolwork was difficult, his faith, the very reason he was attending this school, was weakening. And then there was the whole circumstance with Ralph. Maybe it was time for a change.

CHAPTER 45

Benjamin awoke the day after the late-night murders in the train yard. He opened his eyes and looked up at the peeling paint on the ceiling above his bed. He began to remember the night before and could envision the two decapitated heads of his victims. As he pictured the two young men who had been torturing him for months, a smile came across his face. He took a deep breath and felt, not any guilt, but rather relief that he would no longer have to face these toughs when he went to school.

His lips tightened and he began to nod with satisfaction. He was a murderer, but he was surprised that he didn't feel remorse but instead felt empowered. Because of his own actions, these vile delinquents would never bother him or anyone else again. His actions not only solved his problem, but he probably saved others from having to deal with these lowlifes. He wasn't a murderer. He was a hero. Yes, a hero and he felt proud of himself, maybe for the first time.

He got up, got dressed and went into the kitchen. His mother was at the sink and turned as she heard him enter. Her face was swollen and bruised. There were black and blue marks on her upper arms where they were exposed in her short-sleeved house dress. She forced a smile.

"What would you like for breakfast, Benjie?"

Benjamin could only glance at his mother and feel the terrible guilt that was the result of his inability to help her when she was attacked by her husband. His eyes quickly looked away.

"How about some Cheerios or some Fruit Loops, honey?"

Benjamin usually ate two to three bowls of packaged cereal each morning but suddenly his appetite was lost.

Still not looking up from his gaze at the floor, he replied, "No, momma, I'm not hungry this morning. Is father still here?"

"No," his mother said. "He left a little while ago while you were still asleep. You should eat. C'mon, have at least one bowl of Cheerios."

"No momma, I'm not hungry," he said as he slowly raised his eyes to look into his mother's face.

There was deep sadness in her eyes, and they made his heart heavy with both regret and humiliation. How could he allow his father to brutalize his mother? He promised himself that he would never permit anyone to hurt his mother again.

"Benjamin, if you don't eat now, you won't have anything until lunchtime. You know how hungry you get even when you eat breakfast. C'mon, have a bowl of cereal."

Benjamin looked up at this woman who was the only person on this earth who cared about him. "Okay, momma, I'll have some Fruit Loops."

"That's my boy!" said his mother as she reached for a white bowl from the cabinet and proceeded to fill it to overflowing with the multicolored sweet cereal.

Benjamin poured in some milk and started to spoon the crunchy morsels into his mouth. Two full bowls later, he wiped his mouth with a napkin and went into his bedroom to get his book bag.

When he returned to the kitchen to say good-bye to his mother, he saw that a tear had run down her cheek. She smiled at him and bent over to kiss him.

"Benjie, you are getting so big! I hardly have to bend over to reach you anymore," his mother smiled belying her tear-filled eyes.

Benjamin smiled back, although his true feelings were of sorrow rather than happiness. "Bye, momma. See you later."

Benjamin walked out the door and headed for the bus stop. As the bus approached, his mind left his mother in the trailer and traveled to his school. This time, however, he did not get the usual knot in his stomach as he thought about walking up to school after leaving the bus. Today there would be no Steve and Billy to harass him or beat him up. Those days were gone - forever. A smile again appeared on the chubby boy's face but this time, true pleasure was the reason behind it.

CHAPTER 46

As the school bus approached the school, Benjamin noticed something was different in the school parking lot. At first, he didn't know what it was but after the bus pulled into the stop and everyone was standing waiting to exit, he realized that there were many more students standing around outside and no one seemed to be moving toward the school entrance.

As usual, Benjamin was one of the last to leave the bus since others often pushed him aside and got off ahead of him. So, the portly boy waited by his seat until no one was behind him before going into the aisle. It was better to just wait rather than be shoved aside. There were groups of kids who were all looking serious and talking in hushed tones.

Benjamin had no friends, and he had no group he could join so he stood near a small group of three boys and two girls and tried to find out what was going on. They were talking in whispered voices, so he started to move a bit closer without looking too obvious.

As he slowly shuffled within ear shot while trying not to look conspicuous, he spotted the three girls who were with Steve and Billy on Friday. They were not laughing this time. Indeed, they were crying. The girl with the large chest seemed to be on the verge of hysteria as her cries got louder and louder. Other kids began to look their way, and this only seemed to make her wail even louder. Benjamin felt the anguish she was demonstrating was more for drawing attention than it was for actual grief.

Benjamin continued to deliberately move closer to the group until he could begin to make out their conversation.

"I still can't believe it."

"They must have been drunk."

"I wonder if they felt anything."

"I heard they had to use a shovel to pick up all the parts."

"I heard their heads were lying by the side of the tracks and their eyes were open!"

"Gross!"

Now Benjamin knew what was going on. For some reason, he wasn't expecting any big deal after the end of Steve and Billy. As he thought about it, he came to the realization that all these students, all the kids who either didn't know he even existed or pushed and teased him repeatedly, all these many classmates, they were outside discussing, venting, crying about an occurrence that he, Benjamin, the boy scorned by everyone, had accomplished. He didn't feel sad. He didn't feel guilty. He didn't feel upset in any manner. He felt proud. Yes, shoved, beaten, despised, mocked but now empowered. A new and wonderful sensation surged through his body.

The whole school, every student and teacher, was affected by the actions of this ridiculed youth. He no longer would be frightened or feel powerless. Truly, he would no longer be the object of actions, but he would be the initiator. Afraid no longer but soon to be feared.

CHAPTER 47

Benjamin, not having a clique to hang out with, continued to walk toward the school front doors. The front of the school had two huge double doors in the center of the entrance and a single large door on each side of the entry. As he approached the entrance, one of the side doors opened and the assistant principal, Mr. Berman, appeared, carrying a red and white bullhorn.

"All right everyone, listen up," Mr. Berman's amplified voice bellowed from the megaphone. "I want everyone to enter school slowly and quietly and go directly to the auditorium for an assembly. And I said slowly AND quietly. Let's go. Move it!"

With that, the students began to move toward the front of the school. Benjamin was already close to the front doors, so he was one of the first ones to enter the building. He walked down the corridor to the auditorium with a spring in his step and when he walked into the assembly hall, he started to go into a row in the back but Mrs. McManus, another assistant principal, was at the microphone and shouted, "All the way down to the front. Let's go. No picking seats. Come down to the first open row and move ALL the way down and sit in the first available seat. Let's go, Mr. McGrath. That means you."

Mrs. McManus may not have known everyone's name, but she knew Benjamin's. He had to see her on a number of occasions when he was the recipient of some name calling or a beating. One time three boys cornered him in the boys' room and began shoving him around, calling him names and finally spitting on his face. Another student saw what was happening and told a teacher who was sitting at a desk in the hall monitoring passes and keeping some type of order.

Benjamin was sent to Mrs. McManus and, instead of consoling him and punishing the other boys, she got into his face and yelled at him to stop being a patsy and to stand up for himself. He hated her more than he did the three boys. The memory of the event upset him, and he looked at the assistant principal with eyes filled with fury as he slowly entered the second row of seats. However, instead of his usual self-loathing, he began to grin. After all, he was now licensed to act rather than to abstain from action.

The portly boy shuffled down to the first empty seat which was next to a girl. She looked over at him to see who was going to sit next to her and scowled with a look of disgust. Then she turned to the two girls sitting next to her and whispered something. They both looked over at Benjamin and giggled. He knew they were talking about him and making fun of him. But, for some reason, it didn't bother him as much as it usually did.

Mr. Loughlin, the school principal, walked up to the microphone and stood watching as the entire student body was getting seated. He waited until they had all found seats and, although there were voices to be heard, the large amphitheater was much quieter than usual. When everyone was seated, the gray-haired man in his blue blazer addressed the student body.

"Boys and girls, I come before you today with terrible and disturbing news. You may have already heard but this past weekend we lost two of our students to a tragedy. Steve Reith and Billy Handel, two young men who had their lives ahead of them were killed when they were hit by a freight train just outside the train yard. You know them as classmates, friends and football players. They were fine, young men."

The last statement by the principal made more than a few students look at each other and snicker. Young, yes, but fine young men? They were known throughout the school as poor students and bullies. In fact, if they hadn't been top players on the football squad, they might have been expelled for fights, smoking and drinking.

"We will have our counselors set up in their offices today and will have several social workers from the county here as well if anyone has a need to talk to an adult about this awful tragedy. Please take advantage of talking to any of them or any of your teachers if you are feeling upset and need to see someone."

Again, students looked at each other and chuckled as they thought of the three school counselors - two overweight men and a tall, lanky woman with glasses. The two men did not seem to do much but sit at their desks and snack on soda and donuts. The woman, on the other hand, was never seen not moving about frantically but none of them ever seemed to spend time counseling. It was doubtful that many students would seek their advice or comfort.

Mr. Loughlin said, "If you have no need for counseling, you may leave school. Regular classes will be suspended today. You will take your usual means of transportation home. Normal dismissal buses are now ready for loading. If you are staying to meet with a counselor, there will be after school buses to take you home. You may now leave in a quiet and orderly manner."

"You heard Mr. Loughlin. He said to leave in a QUIET AND ORDERLY MANNER," Mrs. McManus yelled into the microphone.

Benjamin felt a new and strange sensation as he sat and heard the principal speak. Many of the other students had already heard the news in the parking lot before entering the school but everyone seemed to be in some state of surprise and shock. All that is, except Benjamin. He not only knew about the events personally but intimately. He smiled with pride as he thought back to the night outside the train yard and how it was he, Benjamin, who killed those two bastards.

He leaned his head back and a wide smile of satisfaction spread across his face. He breathed in slowly and deeply and felt a deep gratification that he took care of business and those who had made him suffer would no longer escape retaliation. No, from now on they will pay - dearly.

CHAPTER 48

Benjamin left school with the hordes of students who seemed to have recovered quickly from their grief over their lost classmates. There were some small groups talking in somewhat hushed tones but, for the most part, it was an unexpected holiday. Cars were revving up and laughter began to infiltrate the atmosphere. The smell of diesel exhaust from the school buses filled the air and the youngsters who didn't drive began to enter the buses for an early ride home. Benjamin walked to his bus with a spring in his step. He had not felt so alive since . . . well, never. Although the temperature wasn't really warm, he could feel the sun caressing his face bringing a pleasant flush to his cheeks.

The death of these two tormentors brought life to the boy. It was as if he absorbed their life force and was exhilarated by their demise. There was a new and exciting force pulsing through his body. He no longer felt weak and afraid. He was more confident and assured.

As he entered his bus, he almost jumped up each of the three steps and walked briskly to a seat. In his enthusiasm, he bumped into another boy who immediately turned to face him. This interaction would have normally caused Benjamin to look away and apologize. Without thinking, he looked directly into the boy's eyes and waited for a response. Amazingly, the other boy turned away.

"Sorry," said the other youth.

The little exchange may have been insignificant to almost anyone but to Benjamin it was a rebirth - a metamorphosis. The flush in his cheeks was now a glow that he felt from his head down to his groin. He slid into the seat and sat next to the window.

He stared out at the mid-morning sun and wondered what new world he was about to enter. He was leaving his old, timid self and his soul was entering a new being. Those two idiots who tried to make his life miserable were his magical elixir. When he pushed them to their deaths, he seemed to have absorbed their bravado.

When the bus arrived at the trailer park where he lived, Benjamin got out of his seat, pushed past the boy sitting in the seat by the aisle and exited the bus. He bounded down the steps of the bus and jumped from the last step to the gravel below. His entire gait was different. Rather than walking with a shuffling stride, he now walked with confidence. Rather than bowing his head with his gaze on the ground, he held his head high and looked up into the cloudless sky.

As he thought about it, he wondered if this was just a dose of a potion of power. Was this a temporary change or was it just the beginning of a new and bold Benjamin? He wasn't sure but this much was certain. It was a sensation that he would not easily give up and he wanted more - much more.

CHAPTER 49

As Jimmy entered school, he saw his friend, Ralph, talking to Father Simmons, the quite effeminate music teacher. Jimmy walked past the two who were huddled close together on the side of a row of lockers. Since they seemed to be in serious discussion. Jimmy didn't try to greet his buddy but, as he passed the pair, he noticed Ralph appeared to have tears in his eyes and a somber expression on his face.

Jimmy breathed a sign of concern as he entered his home room and took his seat. The boys were all talking casually but the noise level which was relatively substantial had no effect on him. He shut out the sound of all the excited voices and thought about Ralph. There was something about Father Simmons that disturbed him, but he couldn't quite get his concern into focus.

Soon, homeroom was called to order. The class rose for the Pledge of Allegiance and a prayer to start the day. Attendance was taken. Two students were reprimanded for whispering during the call for attendance. There was to be no talking at all during this time.

Jimmy's mind went back to the scene in the corridor. Something about Ralph's demeanor was troublesome. After several minutes of concern, Jimmy realized that he had to dismiss these thoughts and start to think about his own life. This constant worrying about Ralph was interfering with his personal existence. It's time to move on.

Morning classes went smoothly, and thoughts of Ralph were successfully pushed aside. That is until lunch. Jimmy found his usual seat and his two buddies, Tony and Ralph, were not yet seated. However, there was a large, brown paper bag with grease spots seeping through, hinting at the huge sandwich contained inside. It was a sure sign that Tony was already here and was getting something to drink at the lunch counter.

Sure enough, Tony soon appeared with not one, not two, but three containers of milk. Man, could this guy eat! Plopping down in the seat in front of the stained paper bag, Tony began tearing open one of the milk containers and proceeded to drink the entire contents with one long gulp.

"Hey, Tony." said Jimmy.

Wiping the residue milk mustache from his upper lip, Tony replied, "Hey man, how's it goin'?"

"Good. This morning's classes dragged but that's par for the course. How's your day so far?"

Tony had already jammed a large chunk of his overflowing sandwich in his mouth and had to wave for a short time out before he could answer.

"No sweat, man," Tony answered with a mass of meat, bread and who knows what else slowly working its way down his throat.

"Have you seen Ralph?" Jimmy asked.

Tony held the sandwich right before his open mouth and before chomping down, he said, "He's gone home. I saw him coming out of the office and he told me he was sick and was going home."

The sandwich was now mercilessly torn with Tony's teeth as he turned his head to add torque in order to rip another giant piece into his mouth. Jimmy smiled a bit as the sight reminded him of his dog tearing the ears off a dog toy.

Jimmy began to open his own lunch bag and as he removed his white bread sandwich wrapped in wax covered paper, his mind drifted back to the school hallway at the beginning of the day. He allowed himself to picture Ralph talking to Father Simmons and appearing so upset. Something about that sight wasn't right. He had kept his mind away from that scene all day but now it seemed important to revisit it.

What had caused Ralph to be sick and go home early? Was he talking to Father Simmons because he was already ill and was asking to go home?

Or was his conversation with the priest the reason for his early departure from school?

The two boys spent most of the lunch period in silence - Tony busy with his enormous lunch and Jimmy busy with thoughts of his pal who was obviously having some kind of continuing difficulty. By the time the period bell sounded, Jimmy knew he would have to find out the basis of Ralph's troubles.

CHAPTER 50

Later that night, Jimmy, having finished his Latin homework, which was a major hassle, brushed his teeth, checked out two new pimples that had erupted on his face and spent a few minutes looking for a hint of a whisker or two. He wondered how he would look with a mustache. Maybe a beard? Would he ever need to shave? It sure took a long time for adolescence to kick in. But he did occasionally hear a crack in his voice. He was told that was the beginning, but it sounded so goofy. Some stubble would sure be a much cooler sign.

As he lay in bed, he began to think about poor Ralph. Jimmy didn't believe the reason he went home was that he was physically sick. He thought it had something to do with that scene in the hallway with Father Simmons.

Now, maybe for the first time, he hoped one of his dreams which seemed to forecast events would occur and he would "see" Ralph and receive a clue as to what was going on with his friend. Maybe he would learn why Ralph had gone deeper into himself and appeared upset all the time. Maybe if he kept thinking about Ralph as he drifted off to sleep, a dream involving his buddy would ensue and he would come to the bottom of this. Then what? What if it involved Father Simmons? What would he do? What could he do?

Soon his eyelids became heavy, his breathing became rhythmic, and slumber washed over him. He began to dream. Usually, these phantasms materialized while he was not quite asleep but in that state between the worlds of conscious and unconscious thoughts. He wasn't sure if they were dreams or trances because he would not be asleep. This time, however, he was deeply asleep.

He saw a man - overweight, unattractive and loud - yelling words that were not discernible. He appeared to be bellowing at a round faced boy wearing thick glasses. He recognized neither but they seemed so real. Then the man stumbled out of what appeared to be a messy kitchen and into another room and slammed the door shut.

His reverie then focused on the boy, possibly not much older than Jimmy, whose eyes seemed to widen. His nostrils flared outward, and a powerful mood of uncontrollable anger filled the vision Jimmy was experiencing. It scared him. He wanted to exit the dream, to run from the scene but he had no way out.

The boy then moved to the kitchen sink and lifted a long, pointed knife from the drain board. As he turned, Jimmy could see a thick froth beginning to form on the corners of his mouth. Jimmy felt a fear that seemed to paralyze him. He tried to move, to rise up from his bed and run. No matter how hard he tried, he felt imprisoned in his own body. He was frozen and would be forced to witness whatever was about to happen.

The boy moved slowly and deliberately to the door where the man had exited. He opened the door slowly and there was the man, face down on his bed. Suddenly, he jumped up as if he felt the boy's presence. Seeing the knife, he began to laugh.

"Do you think I am afraid of you, you little bastard?" said the powerful looking man.

The boy said nothing but kept moving slowly toward the now sneering brute.

"C'mon, come closer. I am going to take that knife and shove it up your ass," the man snarled.

A low growling sound began to emerge from the young boy. First it was almost too low to hear but it began to gain volume and sent vibrations of fury outward.

The hulking man upon absorbing the effect of the youngster's animal eruption seemed to lose a bit of his bravado. The smirk on his face began to change and soften.

"Okay, Benjie, just give me the knife. I promise I won't hit you. I know you're just upset. Tell you what. I'll even split a beer with you. Father and son. Man to man." He hesitated a moment to see what affect his words had. The boy did not appear moved.

"Give me the fucking knife!"

The eerie and frightening sound coming from deep inside the boy's chest grew louder, louder. It was a sound of total fury.

Jimmy shook with a start. Sitting up in his bed with an involuntary, "Uh!" he looked around the room for the chubby boy with the knife in his hand. There was no one there. He sat up in bed for a few long minutes huffing and trying to catch his breath. He was sweating but felt cold. He began to shiver. His pajama top clung to his body with a wetness that made him feel uncomfortable.

He slowly got up and went to the bathroom all the while looking around his room for the boy and listening for that unearthly growl. There was no boy and no sound except for the ticking of his old wind-up alarm clock which glowed with the time.

After splashing cold water on his face and wiping down his chest and arms with a dampened face cloth, he climbed back into bed. He wondered what it all meant. Why didn't he dream about Ralph? Who was this kid? Was he real or some kind of memory of an old movie or character in a book he read? He tried to remember his name, but he couldn't. But he would not forget his face or that animal-like sound - not ever.

CHAPTER 51

As spring began to affect a welcome change in the weather and the first balmy days brought the scent of early blooms and fresher smelling air, the school year also began to wind down. Thoughts were mixed between the excited anticipation of summer vacation and the dread of final exams. There was a heightened feeling in the air and students all seemed to be ready for the upcoming end of the school year.

Tony and Jimmy were feeling the euphoria of spring as they sat down for lunch. Easter vacation would soon set them free of school for a bit over a week and the respite from school and homework would be most welcomed. It became hard to keep one's mind on class as their thoughts were on many things other than Latin, math and history.

As Jimmy sat down at their usual table, the soft, warm breeze coming in through the open cafeteria window felt like a caress that gently touched his face. While waiting for Tony to return from the lunch line, Jimmy closed his eyes for a moment and let his mind wander. He first pictured an attractive girl he saw this morning on the bus ride to school. He had no idea who she was, but she was pretty and actually smiled at him. Maybe she felt the rush of spring as well.

Then his mind moved onto Ralph who had not yet arrived at their lunch table. Jimmy's mood took a turn for the worse as he pictured his somber friend. However, thoughts of Ralph left quickly and were replaced by an unusual vision. As he closed his eyes, his mind brought him to a scene in which he saw a boy standing with his back facing Jimmy. Slowly, the boy began to turn, and he recognized the face of the boy in his dream last night. He had no idea who he was, but he was sure it was the same kid.

The fantasy appeared as if it was a movie as the camera of his mind began to zoom in slowly until the boy's face took up the entire screen. A smile no, more like an evil grin, began to emerge on his face. Then he heard it. The same horrible sound he heard last night. The same sound that frightened him so much that made his spine shiver. A low tone that was both powerful and depraved. Part growl, part cackle.

Jimmy wanted to escape this daydream. He tried to force his eyes to open. But his eyelids seemed locked down. He pushed his eyebrows upward and could feel his entire face contorting with the effort. But he was trapped. The head, which was close began to move even closer, closer. Soon he could feel the boy's breath upon his own face. He leaned his head back to try to avoid any impact but to no avail. This strange boy was almost touching him. There was no escape.

"Hey! What the hell is wrong with you, man?"

A voice that sounded familiar interrupted the advance of the head just before it seemed that there would be contact between them.

"Hey! Are you okay?"

The spell was broken and the seal that had cemented his eyes shut was broken and Jimmy was able to finally open his eyes. The light was powerful and blinding and caused Jimmy to squint. When his eyes adjusted to the florescent lights, the worried face of Tony began to come into focus.

"Shit, man, what's going on with you?" Tony looked worried.

Jimmy took a minute to get his bearings and then looked straight at Tony. He wanted to hug him and tell him how he saved him from the chilling sight he had just witnessed. But he held back, knowing that Tony would never understand.

"Yeah, I'm fine. Just felt a little sick," Jimmy said.

"A little sick? You looked like you were seeing Frankenstein's ghost. I never saw anybody look so scared, man," Tony said.

"No, it's okay. I just felt like I might get sick and was holding it back."

Jimmy could see that Tony wasn't completely buying his explanation. He still looked like he was questioning his buddy's sanity.

"I'm fine now. Nothing to worry about."

Then Jimmy looked right into Tony's eyes and said, "Thanks."

Tony took it to mean that Jimmy was thanking him for his concern but in reality, Jimmy was thanking him for saving him from a fate that was . . . well, he didn't know what it was. But it sure terrified him.

Tony began to prepare his daily assault on his lunch, but he wasn't his usual talkative self. He kept glancing up at Jimmy as he gorged on his hero sandwich. Few words were spoken between them when Ralph joined the two friends. He was late and the period was almost over. Having Ralph join them broke the tension that seemed to be building.

"How come you're late, Ralphie boy?" Tony said.

Ralph looked at Tony and just shrugged his shoulders as he began to unwrap his sandwich. Conversation among the three boys was strained and seemed contrived. But Jimmy welcomed any diversion from his earlier episode. Soon the bell sounded signaling the end of lunch. Ralph had hardly eaten anything but that was the norm lately.

The three got up robotically as most of the boys in the cafeteria did when the bell rang. They cleaned up their trash and walked over to the line by the nearest garbage can. After dumping the rubbish, they slowly moved to the exit where a crowd had formed heading toward the stairs to the classrooms above.

None of them said anything until they got to the main floor and parted ways. They awkwardly wished each other a good afternoon and started for their first class.

CHAPTER 52

That night, Jimmy watched the monologue on the Tonight Show with Johnny Carson before going to bed. He wasn't tired, but he knew he had to get up early for school tomorrow. Jimmy was a night owl and going to bed early just didn't work. If he tried to hit the sack any earlier, he would just lie there awake for hours. He would get less sleep than if he went to bed later and was sleepy when his head hit the pillow.

As he tossed and turned in bed, he thought about that strange boy he saw today at school in his daydream. His breathing became quicker, and he felt fear - fear that he would dream of him again. It took well over a half an hour for Jimmy to finally begin to doze.

As his eyelids became heavy and the skin on his face began to relax and droop, his breath slowed and soon he was dreaming of playing stick ball with his neighborhood buddies. His friend, Pete, who he often played with, was pitching the small, pink rubber ball as he stood waiting with a broom stick in his hands which they used as a bat. Pete threw one of his slow, blooper pitches and Jimmy swung hard and missed and suddenly, they both burst into hysterical laughter. Jimmy and Pete fell to the ground and laughed until their stomachs were cramping.

Then Jimmy heard a voice. He recognized it immediately and stopped his laughter. He looked up and it was Ralph. Pete was no longer there, in fact, they were now in the corridor at school. Ralph was crying and was standing alone with no pants on. He was calling out for Jimmy as he sobbed standing in the middle of the hallway wearing his white shirt and tie but only his boxer underwear and socks below his waist.

"What's the matter, Ralph?"

Ralph sobbed louder. Each syllable seemed to erupt from his mouth in a breathless mournful cry.

"Jim . . . my. Help. . . me," Ralph repeated over and over.

Then Jimmy saw a figure in the distance. It seemed further away than the end of the corridor would naturally be. The man was in darkness and was dressed in black. He slowly lifted his arm and it appeared as if he was beckoning to Ralph to come toward him. Jimmy listened for a voice but there was none.

Ralph turned and looked at the dark figure and then turned back and looked at his friend. His face was contorted into a painful expression. Jimmy felt helpless and he tried to speak but, although he could open his mouth, try as he might, no sound would come out. He could feel himself straining to tell Ralph not to go back to the figure in black, but it was impossible.

Ralph gave Jimmy one more look without words, but he communicated that he was begging for help. Then he turned and began walking toward the man in black. Jimmy could feel himself leaning forward, pulled toward his friend but to no avail. Ralph continued toward the sinister image.

When he reached the gloomy entity, Ralph turned once more to look back at his chum. But this time, as if he knew there was no escape, he took the black robed man's hand and they walked off into the darkness.

Jimmy awoke with a start. He sucked in a gasp of air and sat up quickly in his bed. He knew he had been dreaming but in his confused state, he looked around the room for Ralph and the man in black. The full moon cast a white light on the many shelves of model cars that Jimmy had on one of the walls of his room. His window was open because the night air of spring was cool and sweet with the scent of the new beginnings.

When he caught his breath and his heartbeat returned to normal, he allowed himself to plop down on his bed. His head hit his pillow which was damp with perspiration. He thought about getting up and going to the bathroom to dry his head and face but was too exhausted to leave his bed.

He finally turned his head to one side and made a nodding motion with his head to bury the side of his face into the pillow. He closed his eyes but before going back to sleep, he made a vow to himself. Tomorrow he would see someone at school he trusted. He would talk to Father Loudin and tell him that something was wrong with Ralph and that he suspected Father Simmons had something to do with it.

CHAPTER 53

The alarm clock rang out with its shrill and most unpleasant racket. He would often wonder if a soft and sweet chime would be a better choice for an alarm. However, he realized that without that blaring, ugly and loud ring, he would probably remain asleep, and the bell would just become part of his dream.

He arose from his bed and immediately remembered his vow to himself last night right before going back to sleep. Today he would speak to Father Loudin about Ralph and Father Simmons. Anxiety overcame him and he began to wonder if he might postpone the fulfillment of his promise. No, it had to be done and it had to be done today. He couldn't stand another nightmare about Ralph. He was positive something was seriously wrong.

He began to get dressed and knew he would skip breakfast this morning. He was never much for eating breakfast as it was but today, he really had no appetite. That would cause a problem with his mother. His mother was constantly harping on his eating habits. Cookies, cake, chips and such were never seen in the house unless company was expected. It was eat well or not at all. Jimmy was a picky eater and breakfast was just not something he enjoyed. Still his mother was the forever optimist and would make many attempts each morning to find something nutritious for Jimmy to eat.

Today he really didn't want to deal with his mom offering rolls, eggs, hot cereal, pancakes. He just wanted to tell her he didn't feel like eating and be done with it. After dressing, except for his tie which was the last thing he put on so he wouldn't get it stained, he walked into the kitchen. His dad was already reading the newspaper and his sister was eating a bowl of corn flakes.

His mother was at the sink and asked, "What would you like this morning, Jimmy?"

"Ma, I'm really not hungry at all this morning. I just want some juice, please."

Jimmy was shocked when his mother poured a glass of orange juice for him and went back to the sink without another word. She had the radio on above the sink and was listening to her favorite program which was both talk and music - mostly talk. She seemed engrossed in what was being said about the actors on some afternoon soap opera that she watched on television.

Jimmy downed the juice, realizing that he was quite thirsty. He could have had another glass but his mother had put the container back in the refrigerator and he didn't want to take a chance in getting her started about eating something substantial for breakfast, so he left the table and went back to the bathroom to brush his teeth and comb his hair. Finishing those tasks, he went back to his room and grabbed his tie and book bag. His tie was a clip on. He never mastered the art of tying a tie and it seemed like there was no need. The clip on was quick and easy. So easy in fact, that he put it on with one hand as he walked back to the kitchen with his book bag in his other hand.

There was his lunch ready made in its little brown paper bag. He knew it contained a sandwich that he liked and a piece of fruit with a napkin, of course. There were napkins available in the cafeteria, but Mrs. Reardon wanted Jimmy to have one from home just in case there were none available. There was no sense discussing it. He had tried to explain that there were many napkin dispensers in the school cafeteria, but his mother would not relent. There certainly were more important things to try to persuade his mother to his way of thinking. So, he always had a napkin from home.

He kissed his mother goodbye. She was still involved with the story about some actor who apparently was arrested the night before. So, he was free to skip his meal this morning. He said goodbye to his father who looked up from his paper and nodded a farewell.

"Bye," he said to his sister.

She replied, "Bye."

They had to be civil to each other or receive the wrath of their father. Of course, Jimmy always got the worse of that, so it was best to just acknowledge the existence of the other.

He was out the door and headed to the public bus. He made it without having to testify about why he had no appetite this morning. As he waited for the bus, he began to visualize his meeting with Father Loudin and think about how he would approach this exceedingly difficult discussion. He began to weaken and wonder if he might just forget the whole thing.

The bus arrived, he paid his nickel while showing his bus pass and went to the back of the bus. His friends who went to the public school could walk to the local high school and be there in 10 minutes. He had to take two public buses and travel over an hour to get to school. But it often gave him time to think and today he needed every minute.

He found a seat near the rear of the bus by the window and as he looked out, he began again to picture meeting with the priest and the different scenarios that he could imagine. This would not be easy - not at all. He wished he could avoid the whole thing, but he knew that was impossible. Even if he could ignore his friend's pain, he couldn't deal with another night of distressing dreams. They would not end unless he actively got involved.

How would Father Loudin react? He would soon find out.

CHAPTER 54

Jimmy made it through his morning classes. His first class was Latin, and he would see Father Loudin, his teacher. He knew he couldn't bring up the subject of Ralph before class, but he felt he had to force the issue on himself by seeing the priest after class and asking to speak with him later in the day.

When the bell rang signaling the end of Latin class, Jimmy waited for the other boys to race off to their next class. When the teacher and he were left alone in the room, he approached the desk.

"Father, can I see you later today? I have something I need to talk to you about," said Jimmy.

As a few students began to enter the room before the next class would start, the priest looked up at Jimmy.

Smiling he said, "Sure Jimmy. I have my lunch at the same time as you do. Do you want to talk then?"

His kind smile and reassuring manner immediately made Jimmy feel more relaxed. He began to feel like he was doing the right thing by speaking to his teacher. Of all the priests at his school, Father Loudin was the easiest to talk to and the one the boys could best relate to. He kept his hair a bit longer and slicked back. He wasn't pompous like so many of his other teachers.

"That would be great Father," Jimmy replied enthusiastically.

Father Loudin said, "Bring your lunch back to this classroom. I'll give you a note to give to the teacher on duty. We can eat while we talk, okay?"

There was little doubt now that this was the right move. Jimmy took the note from the priest and shook his hand. The priest's grip was firm but not overpowering. Jimmy felt the large ring that Father Loudin had on his right hand. It looked like a high school or college ring and had a large, light blue stone. It just added to his feeling that this man was a regular guy.

The rest of the morning went well, and Jimmy no longer was dreading his meeting. He still went over what he would say but no longer was frightened about what the reaction would be. Soon it was lunch time.

Jimmy went down to the cafeteria and bought a container of milk. He glanced over at the table where he always sat with Tony and Ralph. Neither were there yet so he wouldn't be able to tell them where he was going. He then walked over to Father Weiss who was his math teacher and who was on lunch duty today.

"Father, I have a meeting with Father Loudin," Jimmy said as he gave the note to the priest. Father Weiss was a huge but friendly man. He was the stereotypical overweight but happy fellow who laughed readily. He smiled as he took the note and read it to himself.

"Didn't do your Latin homework, eh?" Father Weiss said.

"No, I just need to have a talk with Father Loudin," replied Jimmy.

Father Weiss' face broke out in a big smile. Jimmy wasn't sure if it was because the priest had so much skin on his round face or not, but his countenance lit up like the sun whenever he smiled. Math was Jimmy's least favorite subject, but he liked his teacher.

The priest handed the note back to Jimmy and the boy walked briskly out of the cafeteria and to the classroom. All the trepidation he had been feeling was now gone due to the comfort zone that both Father Loudin and Father Weiss had put him in.

The door to the classroom was open and Jimmy walked in and saw the priest sitting at his desk, eating a sandwich and reading a newspaper.

"You can close the door, Jimmy," Father Loudin said as he looked up from the paper.

Jimmy closed the door and sat down at one of the student desks in front of the teacher's desk.

"Start eating your lunch," the priest said. "You will have to get to your class after lunch period ends. So, what's up?"

Jimmy began to unravel the waxed paper that his sandwich was wrapped in. His apple fell out of the bag and rolled off the desk onto the floor. He leaned over to pick it up and almost fell out of the seat. He grabbed the apple and straightened himself out. He looked at the priest as he felt his face begin to redden.

"Ha, ha, relax, Jimmy. Tell me what's on your mind."

Jimmy began, "Father, my friend, Ralph is in trouble."

Father Loudin's expression immediately changed, "What do you mean? What's wrong with him?"

"Well, Father, Ralph has been acting sad and weird. Then I started having these dreams about him. I have had these kinds of dreams before and they sometimes come true. I thought about going to Father McCormick about it," Jimmy spilled out. He was talking too fast. The nervousness he thought he had under control was surfacing.

"Now hold on, Jimmy!" Father Loudin's expression was stern but then melted into his warm smile.

"You have to be careful about telling everyone about dreams you are having. They might think you are a bit strange; you know what I mean?" Father Loudin's face was now comforting.

But Jimmy was on a roll, and he couldn't hold back now that he got this far.

"I think it has something to do with Father Simmons," Jimmy said.

"Father Simmons! Is he in your dreams, too?" Father Loudin said.

"No, but I have seen him talking with Ralph a lot and sometimes Ralph looks upset when he is talking to him," Jimmy said.

"Hmmm, that's interesting. But Jimmy you need to promise me that you won't talk to Father McCormick or anyone about this. I am afraid they would think you were losing your mind and you could get in trouble."

Father Loudin's expression hardened a bit. "You do understand me, don't you? Let's just keep this between us for now. I will investigate your concerns, I promise you, but you can't tell anyone about this. I don't want you to get in trouble."

Jimmy took a deep breath through his mouth and exhaled slowly. He looked at the priest's warm eyes and felt better.

"Okay, Father. I won't say anything until you tell me what to do," Jimmy said.

"That a boy! I won't let you down. Let me check around and we'll meet again soon," Father Loudin said.

He extended his hand for a handshake that meant as much as a seal of a promise as it did as a goodbye.

Jimmy suddenly realized that he didn't even take one bite of his sandwich. He gathered up the waxed paper and tried to wrap it around his lunch. He didn't do a good job, but he stuffed it into the bag and put the apple in as well.

"I guess we didn't have much time to eat, eh?" Father Loudin said with a smile.

"No, but it's okay, I'm not hungry anyway," Jimmy said.

Jimmy stood up and didn't know if he should leave or not. It was an awkward moment.

"You better get going, Jimmy. Lunch period is almost over. And don't forget our deal," the priest said as he cocked his head to one side.

"I won't Father and thanks," Jimmy said.

The boy left the classroom and started to head toward the lunchroom, but the bell sounded ending the period and immediately the halls were filled with young men heading off to their next assignment. Jimmy stood still for a moment trying to get his bearings and think about where he was going next. English was his next class, so he began to head in the direction of the room.

He had only two more classes and then the school day would end. Once he got to English class and sat in his seat, he began to feel better about what had occurred. He trusted Father Loudin and felt that he would do some investigating. It would be a good idea to keep his thoughts to himself until he got the word from his Latin teacher. He didn't want to get in trouble, and he began to feel a bit foolish about his dreams.

Yes, they had come true too often but maybe that was just a coincidence. He will keep it to himself - for now.

CHAPTER 55

Life at school had changed for Benjamin. The death of those two punks seemed to have brought about a sense of confidence and even power. He now felt less like a victim and more like someone who could control his destiny. That was the "new" Benjamin at school but his life at home had not altered. His father continued to come home drunk and abuse both him and his mother.

He feared his father under the best of circumstances but when his father was drunk, he was absolutely terrified of him. He appeared out of control and there was no sense of any limitations on the physical and emotional pain he might inflict on both Benjamin and his mother.

Since Benjamin had no friends to speak of, he spent most of his time alone or with his mother. She seemed to always be supportive and affectionate to her boy. This, however, only added to his suffering because he felt he should not just stand by when his mother was being abused by her husband.

But standing up to his father was impossible. Not only was his father a large and physical man but his drunken moods were unrestrained and boundless. Anything could occur during one of these events and they seemed to be becoming more and more frequent. It was ironic that school was now a hiatus from fear.

As the school year began to wind down and summer was approaching,

Benjamin began to despise the thought of being home all day with the potential of almost daily interactions with his father. There were no positive times spent together. When his father wasn't drunk and out of control, he was basically uncommunicative and would sit smoking and drinking a beer out of a can.

The boy knew that the upcoming summer would be hell and the thought of it made him feel sick to his stomach. Even his mother didn't say much when her husband was home because she feared any talk might set him off. So, the three of them would just exist in the same house with little to no interaction. Two months of that was more than Benjamin could bear the thought of.

The balmy spring weather was refreshing, however. There was something special about warm, gentle breezes on a Friday afternoon after school let out. The air seemed to be filled with promise and excitement for the students of the high school. All of them except for Benjamin.

As the other students raced to the buses and their cars at dismissal time. Benjamin trudged slowly toward his bus. While the others were looking forward to a weekend away from school, hanging out with friends, parties and just freedom from schoolwork, the chubby teen had only a weekend of dealing with an abusive father in a double wide trailer with nowhere to hide.

As he exited the bus, he hesitated in front of the door, eyes squinting in the afternoon sun behind thick glasses. The door of the bus slammed shut and the bus roared off leaving a cloud of dust from the dirt road. He bowed his head and slowly dragged his feet, moving in the direction of his home. He was probably the only boy from his school who wished it were already Monday.

Benjamin passed several pre-school children who were playing in the dirt just off the path that went down the middle of the trailer park community. He could hear their laughter - the boys roughhousing and the girls giggling and squealing. Their sounds of joy only brought him sadness as it reminded him that he never had the opportunity to interact with other children, even when he was their age.

Arriving at his trailer, he deliberately climbed the three steps and grabbed the handle of the screen door. Since the weather had warmed up, his mother often kept the door open with just an old wooden screen door separating the living area from the outside. Part of the screen was torn so its effectiveness at keeping insects out was seriously impaired. His mother had told her husband that the screen had ripped but he did nothing about it and one thing both she and Benjamin had learned was that you didn't ask his father for something more than once.

The door creaked open and then slammed shut, bouncing twice before settling in. The sound of the screeching and subsequent smack of the door into the jam announced his arrival to his mother. Without looking up from the kitchen sink, she welcomed her son home from school.

"Benjie! You're home! How was school?" His mother always greeting her son with enthusiasm regardless of how depressing her day may have been.

"How about a glass of chocolate milk and some cookies?"

Benjamin dropped his book bag on the floor at the kitchen table and plopped down in one of the metal chairs with red, plastic covered cushions, each with a tear or two in the seat or the back of the chair.

"Sure, Mom. I'm hungry and thirsty," said Benjamin.

His mother quickly poured a glass of milk and squirted some chocolate syrup into the glass and stirred it until it turned a dark brown. She dropped a bag of chocolate chip cookies on the table and put the glass of milk in front of her son.

Benjamin looked up to thank her and he immediately noticed her face. She had several bruises on her cheek and her lip was drooping and swollen on one side. On the other side, her eye appeared partially closed and there was a black and yellow mark underneath and above the eye.

Realizing that Benjamin was staring at her face, she quickly took her hand to cover what she could and turned back to the sink. After several seconds she broke the silence.

"So, you didn't say how school was today," she said with false sweetness.

Benjamin could not answer right away. An anger began to rise from the boy's belly. His breathing became more and more rapid. He pictured his father standing in the kitchen with a scowl on his face. Although the man did not speak, the look that the boy was imagining was taunting him. A strange growling sound began to erupt from the boy and was soon followed by a clipping laugh that seemed to come from deep inside him.

"Benjamin! Benjamin! What's wrong?" his mother cried out.

Saliva began to form on one side of his mouth and oozed between his lips to drip down onto the table.

"Benjamin! You're scaring me," his mother yelled.

The boy seemed to wake from a trance-like state and blinked at his mother. He wiped the wetness from the corner of his mouth with the back of his hand and grabbed a paper napkin from the holder and mopped up the small puddle that was next to the bag of cookies.

"It's nothing, Mom. Nothing. I was just thinking, that's all," said Benjamin.

He picked up the glass of milk and drank it down without stopping. He snatched a couple of cookies, picked up his school bag and headed for his room.

"Thanks, Mom. I'll eat these inside," said Benjamin.

He went into his room and closed the door and fell back onto his bed. He stared at the ceiling and munched on one of the cookies. He hated his father. Hated him. His mother was the only caring and kind person in Benjamin's life and his father hurt her again and again.

It was Friday and another miserable weekend home with his father. He never imagined that school would be an escape for him, but he longed for Monday to arrive. He had no idea how this weekend would change his life forever.

CHAPTER 56

Dinner consisted of two hot dogs, beans and some potato chips. Benjamin's mother was a caring person but cooking and housekeeping were not her forte. His father was not home, which was not unusual, especially on a Friday night. Benjamin was quite sure his father was at the local bar, drinking, laughing and arguing with his pals. The boy was happy not to have to share supper time with his father, but there was no way to know what kind of mood he would be in when he finally arrived home.

Benjamin was pretty confident his father would come home drunk but sometimes this merely meant he would be tired and collapse and fall quickly asleep - sometimes in his bed and sometimes he wouldn't make it past the living room couch. But the youngster quickly removed thoughts of his father from his mind, and, after supper, he walked outside and sat down on the steps at the front door.

It was a cool night. It was clear and the full moon brought a brightness to the trailer park. He could hear voices coming from nearby mobile homes since the walls were thin. Mostly they were muffled, unintelligible conversations, other than the one from the home next to theirs. He could hear Mr. and Mrs. Gaskins' voices. He was apparently attempting to fool around with his wife, and she was playing hard to get but not too hard to get. Sometimes she would squeal and say, "Stop!" but not too convincingly.

After about 15-20 minutes, it got quiet in their mobile home and Benjamin thought that Mr. Gaskins was receiving what he wanted.

Benjamin looked up at the star-filled sky and took several deep breaths. He wished that this night could be frozen in time. He didn't want school to end, indeed, he didn't want to grow up since the future frightened him. He had a few years of high school left but then what? College wasn't in his plans. He didn't have the grades for it and, certainly, his father wasn't in position or of a mind to pay for it. He didn't have any skill nor any interest to learn a trade. His father had already said on a number of occasions that he was anxious for Benjamin to pay for room and board or move out as soon as he completed high school.

He got up and went back inside. His mother was sitting in the living room watching the small screen television. He didn't know what program she was watching but there was canned laughter every few minutes so it must have been some sort of comedy program. His mother seemed to prefer these types of shows, maybe so that she would have something to laugh about. Certainly, her life was not filled with frivolity and happiness.

He went to the refrigerator and took the container of milk out and poured himself a glass. He squirted a long stream of chocolate syrup into it and grabbed a package of chocolate cupcakes. Taking his junk food supplies with him, he said good night to his mother and headed to his room. His mother looked up and smiled through her swollen lips.

"Good night, Benjie," she said.

"Good night, Mom," Benjamin replied.

Benjamin plopped down on his bed and turned on his small transistor radio. The tiny speaker played "Roses Are Red" by Bobby Vinton. He grabbed one of the cupcakes and ate it in three quick bites. Then he gulped down half the glass of chocolate milk. By the end of the next song, "Moon River" by Harry Mancini, he had finished the cupcakes and the glass of milk and was lying down on his bed, staring at the ceiling.

He was getting tired and knew he should get up and brush his teeth and change into his pajamas, but his legs felt heavy, and his eyelids began to drop. Soon, he was in a deep sleep.

CHAPTER 57

Benjamin awoke with a start. He could hear the tiny radio playing, "If I Had a Hammer" by Peter, Paul and Mary. He rolled over and turned it off. He looked at the round face of his alarm clock. The glow in the dark hands showed that it was 3:10 AM. He realized he had fallen asleep in his clothes and debated whether to get up and change or just go back to sleep. Then he heard it.

Voices. It took a minute for him to clear his head from the stupor of sleep. The voices became clearer. It was his mother and his father. His mother seemed to be whimpering and his father sounded angry, although he wasn't really raising his voice. As Benjamin's brain was able to focus, he heard his mother pleading, "Please, stop. Please." That was followed by a loud sound, like a crack which was immediately followed by his mother crying out.

Again, and again, the sound of a smack followed by a loud yelp penetrated Benjamin's senses. Then it began. The boy's eyes began to widen. His lips began to spread, and his yellowed teeth were exposed. That sound, not one that could possibly be human, yet it was, rose from deep within him. It was as if some mechanical part was out of alignment in his chest and continued to tick repeatedly and in time. Soon, a thick ooze of white spume formed in the corners of his mouth.

The young man rose from his bed robotically. He slowly and deliberately moved to his bedroom door and opened it into the dark living room. The sound of his mother's cries continued but now he no longer heard them as if he were no longer in control of any bodily functions. He dragged his shoeless feet to the kitchen and opened a cabinet drawer. There he pulled out a long, pointed slicing knife and then mechanically turned toward his parents' bedroom door.

Opening the door, he could see his mother lying on the bed wearing only a nightgown which was pulled up exposing her legs and panties. His father was kneeling on the bed next to her, holding a belt overhead which he quickly brought down over her legs and buttocks causing a loud slapping sound and another wail from his mother. Neither of his parents seemed to notice that he had entered the room.

Then the eerie sound erupted from Benjamin. It caused both his parents to take notice of his entrance. His father turned to him, and a malevolent smile broke out across his face, but he said nothing. His mother turned toward her son, "Benjie, get out! Get out, now! Please!"

His father spied the long blade of the knife in his son's hand. "Do you think you have the guts to do anything, you little shit? Do you think I'm afraid of you? C'mon, c'mon, I'll shove that knife up your ass."

"Please, Benjie, get back. Go back to your room. Please. Please!" his mother begged.

His father began to laugh. "No, don't chicken out, you little shit. Let's see if you have the balls to do anything," his father taunted.

Benjamin continued to move toward his father. The inhuman sound that the boy was making now sounded like a growl but not like anything anyone had ever heard. His movements were slow but steady as he proceeded toward his parents' bed.

Mr. McGrath's countenance suddenly changed. It was as if he realized that his son was actually a threat.

"Hey, Benjie, give me the knife. C'mon, I know you're upset. Just give me the knife. I promise I won't hit you. You know what? You and me, we'll have a beer together - man to man, father and son. What do you say?"

Benjamin said nothing. His eyes were focused on his father, and he just continued step by step toward his parents' bed. The knife protruded from his hand which was at his hip. The long blade caught the light from the lamp on the nightstand and reflected up onto the boy's face, illuminating his features and turning his glasses into opaque spheres which seemed to glow.

"Give me the fuckin' knife, you bastard!" his father finally screamed as his fear overtook him.

The portly boy was only a few feet from the side of the bed where his father was now facing. Suddenly, without warning, he moved with a swiftness that was unlike his normal gait. Before his father could react. Benjamin raced forward and plunged the knife deeply into the man's belly.

His father did not make a sound. He just looked surprised as his mouth opened, and his eyes showed an expression of disbelief. He looked down at the knife which was implanted into his abdomen right up to the wooden handle. His son then pulled the knife out and thrust it again and again and then again into the man's stomach.

Still no sound of any kind emanated from the man's mouth. It was as if his voice which was usually loud and boisterous was silenced. There was just a look of incredulity and amazement as he looked down at his ample paunch where a dark red stain was rapidly growing on his undershirt.

Benjamin stood back, looking at the result of his attack and stared at this father's potbelly and the ever-expanding crimson splotch on the white fabric of his undergarment. A clicking laugh began to come forth from the boy, starting slowly with a low volume and quickly getting louder and faster until it was a frenzied cacophony of the madness that was within this boy.

His father looked up from his stomach and into the eyes of his son. His mouth moved as if to speak but he fell over without a word. He was dead.

CHAPTER 58

The first reaction that Benjamin had after brutally stabbing and murdering his father was feeling the stickiness of the blood all over his hands. The long knife seemed stuck to his hand and after the initial euphoria of realizing that this beast of a man could no longer terrorize neither him nor his mother, he wanted only to get rid of the knife and wash his hands. Not that the blood itself bothered him, it was just so incredibly tacky.

He looked at his mother who appeared to still be in shock over what she had just witnessed. Her eyes went from her dead husband to her son who stood before her with blood dripping from his hand. Slowly, her conscious mind began to focus on the here and now.

"Benjamin, put the knife down. Put it down on the bed. Benjamin! Listen to me!" his mother said.

Benjamin upon hearing his mother's voice seemed to waken from a trance. His creepy, clipping laughter had now stopped. He looked down at the knife and slowly put it down on the bed, obeying his mother. He wiped the glop of saliva from the corners of his mouth, smearing blood across his cheeks. Overcome by the events that had just occurred, the boy began to weep. First his eyes filled with tears and then he hung his head and his shoulders jumped up and down without any accompanying sound. Soon, however, cries synchronized with his jerky shoulder movements.

With sudden quickness, his mother jumped up from the bed and took charge. She had always seemed so timid and weak but now she had to do whatever she could to save her son. She grabbed one of her husband's shirts from a dresser draw and picked up the knife.

"We have to work fast, Benjie. We must get everything set before we call the police, and we have to do that quickly. They can tell if we waited too long to call them." She seemed to be knowledgeable about what needed to be done. Watching all those late-night true crime shows was paying off.

"Okay, quickly, come to the door but just stay there and don't touch anything with those bloody hands," she instructed.

She put a pink terrycloth robe over her and went to the front of the mobile home. Benjamin followed his mother's directions carefully and zombie-like. He stood at the door while she poked her head out and looked about. The trailer park was quiet now, everyone was probably asleep. She then turned to Benjamin, "Okay, come with me but don't touch the doorknob or anything else."

They walked behind their double wide to where there was a green hose attached to a spigot. She held her finger up to her lips to signal for her son not to speak. Realizing that she needed to go back inside to get some things she instructed her boy.

"Stay here while I go in and get something I forgot. Don't move and don't touch anything. You hear? Don't make a sound," she said in a hushed tone.

She moved quickly around the home and Benjamin stood alone and looked up at the stars that he had looked at only a few hours earlier. He remembered how he thought how wonderful it would be if he could just stay in that time forever and now, only a few hours later, everything had changed. Oh, how things have changed!

His mother appeared with an empty laundry sack and some of Benjamin's clothes. She quickly dropped the fabric bag on the ground and told Benjamin to take his clothes off. At first, he was reluctant to undress in from of his mother.

"Hurry, Benjie. Don't worry, I have seen every part of you many times before. Hurry!" she whispered.

The boy obeyed his mother and began to strip off his clothes, first his button-down shirt and then his white t-shirt which were both heavily stained with his father's blood. He was embarrassed to show anyone his upper body with his bulging stomach and his chest which had the appearance of a young, developing girl. But he followed orders.

Then he removed his blue jeans and with a bit of hesitation, he dropped his underpants to the ground. His mother gathered up the clothing and jammed them into the laundry bag. Then she reluctantly picked up the bloody knife. She held it with only her thumb and index finger as if it were covered with a contagion. She dropped it into the sack.

She then led him over to the hose and began to hose him down. The water was ice cold, but Benjamin uttered no complaint. She then picked up a bar of soap she had brought outside and started to scrub him down. When she reached below his waist, the boy felt mortified that his mother would be washing him down there. Although she didn't actually touch his genital area, her touching near there produced a response. He did his best to think of anything but what was happening, but it did not help. Fortunately, his mother was rapid, and her perfunctory actions made it less stimulating.

She then picked up the hose again and sprayed the cold water over him, washing off the soap residue. With no other words, she took a towel she had brought and wiped him down. Then she grabbed the clean clothes and under her breath, told him to get dressed.

"Hurry, Benjie. We have little time. We have to call the police and give them a story," she said.

Benjamin still had not uttered a word since he killed his father. He had no idea what to do and had nothing to add to his mother's directives. He would just follow whatever she said. She was in total charge, and it was so different to see his mother act so assertively and he had to wonder what might have been different if she responded to her husband that way years ago. But whatever was is now the past and he had to prepare for the next few hours of his life.

After Benjamin was dressed, his mother took the hose and washed down the dirt area where she had cleaned up her son's deed. She stared at the muddy ground and then decided not to turn off the faucet completely but let it trickle a small amount. Grabbing her son's hand, she whispered, "Okay, let's go inside and get our story straight."

When they got back inside the house, they walked into the bedroom and they both suddenly stopped and froze as they saw his father lying dead and covered with blood. After a few seconds, Benjamin's mother went back into action.

"Benjie, this is what happened. Your father and I were sleeping, and a man came in. He appeared drunk and maybe he was someone your father had an argument with. He had been out drinking and could have gotten into a fight with someone. When he came home, we were both asleep. He came into my bed and I didn't wake up. The next thing I knew, there was this man stabbing him. I screamed and he ran out of the house. You woke up hearing me scream and came running into the room to see what happened. Then I called the police. You got it?" his mother said.

Benjamin was still mute. He nodded. His mother gave him a hug.

She added, "Now just don't say more than you have to. Remember, you woke up when you heard me scream and you came into my room. You never saw the man and you don't know anything more than that. Just say as little as you can."

His mother then spotted the laundry bag. She jumped up and grabbed it and put it up on a shelf in her closet behind some boxes. She knew this would be temporary, but she had to call the police fast or they would be suspicious as to why she waited so long. She could only hope that they wouldn't search for anything immediately.

She told Benjamin to go and wait in the living room and she went to the kitchen to make the phone call.

"Hello, I want to report a murder."

CHAPTER 59

"YES, a murder!" His mother yelled into the phone to the 911 operator. "It's my husband. He's been stabbed. I think he's dead. Hurry!"

Benjamin's mother seemed to change her entire demeanor. She sounded panicky and frightened. Benjamin was yet again shocked at his mother's ability to act. She was always timid and shy and hardly ever raised her voice either in anger or happiness. He felt a feeling of pride wash over him yet, he was confused as to why his mother never let this personality come out before.

She gave their address and responded to the person on the phone that the assailant had run out of the house after the attack and appeared to have gone.

"Yes, we'll stay right here. It's my son. Yes, I have one child and he is with me. Please, hurry! I'm afraid! Thank you. Yes, we'll stay in the room and wait for the police. But hurry! Please!" Mrs. McGrath sounded on the border of hysteria and her voice kept rising as she wanted to send the message that she was getting more and more horrified as the minutes passed.

Benjamin's mother hung up the phone. She looked at Benjamin and took a deep, drawn out breath, exhaling through her mouth.

"It will be okay, Benjie. Just do what I say. One more time. I woke up to see a man come into my bedroom. He stabbed your father and then ran from the house. You heard me scream and came into the room after it was all over. Do you understand?"

Benjamin still had not found his voice. He just nodded and looked down at his father's body. The blood was now creating a huge, dark beet red stain on the bed sheet. He was trying to understand that this was not just a dream but really happened. He had killed his father.

"Just make sure you don't say anything more than you are asked. The police will think you are in shock and won't expect you to say much. If you could cry, that would be fine but don't force it and make it look fake. Okay?" his mother instructed again.

Time moved very slowly and neither mother nor son said anything further until they heard the sirens and could see harsh white and blue lights send flashes into their mobile home. These jarring beacons seemed to wake the boy from his spell.

"Ma, I'm afraid," Benjamin was able to croak.

His mother grabbed him and hugged him hard. He could feel her strength transfer into him. She stood back a bit while still holding him and brushed his hair away from his eyes. Her mouth widened into a big smile and was like an injection of calmness.

"You'll be fine, Benjie, you'll be fine," his mother said.

A pounding on the door startled them both.

"Police! Coming in!" called on one of the cops as they entered the home.

"Police!" the cop yelled out again.

"In here!" called out Benjamin's mother.

Two cops entered the bedroom with guns drawn and their eyes moving quickly around the room.

One cop ran over to the bed and checked on Mr. McGrath. He looked up at the other uniformed cop and said, "He's dead."

"Ma'am, please state your name," said the tall, thin cop who was standing near both mother and son.

"Mrs. Helen McGrath," said Benjie's mother.

"And what's your name, son?" the cop asked Benjamin.

The boy was silent, his mouth opening slightly but no words came forth. His eyes began to well with tears but not enough for an overflow to stream down his cheeks.

"It's Benjamin - Benjamin McGrath. He's my son," said Mrs. McGrath. "He's all shook up."

The cop nodded as he wrote in a small notebook.

Just then, another uniformed cop entered the bedroom. His uniform looked a bit different than the two policemen who had entered minutes earlier. It was the police chief, Brian Faulkner. He was a familiar face and known to both Mrs. McGrath and Benjamin. He was a bit older than the other two cops and his hair was thick below his cap which had yellow strings on the visor that looked like glued on spaghetti.

He touched his cap and nodded to the woman. "Mrs. McGrath," he said.

He then looked over at Mr. McGrath's body and seemed to stare at it for a full minute.

"He's dead, chief," said the youngest of the two cops who was still standing next to the bed.

The chief pursed his lips and replied, "yeah," sarcastically.

"I'll take the Mrs. and the boy into the living room and get a statement," said the skinny cop with his notebook in hand.

"No, take the statement right here. I want to hear what they have to say as they say it," said Chief Faulkner. His eyes remained on the body, staring.

"Okay, Mrs. McGrath, can you tell me exactly what happened?" asked the officer.

"I was in bed asleep. My husband was out - drinking I guess - and I didn't wake up when he got home," said the woman.

With that, Chief Faulkner turned his stare to the wife as his blue eyes seemed to squint as if to focus and penetrate her thoughts. Mrs. McGrath could see the chief from the corner of her eyes but went on explaining how she was jolted out of her sleep by a ruckus and saw a man quickly run up to her husband who was now sitting up in bed and stab him in the stomach.

"How many times?" said the chief.

"I don't know. More than once, maybe three times?" said Mrs. McGrath.

"And then?"

"The man ran out of the house. I looked at my husband and then called the police," said Mrs. McGrath.

The chief turned to Benjamin. "And when did you come into the bedroom?"

Benjamin had been looking blankly at his mother the entire time and now turned to the policeman but before he could answer, his mother answered for him.

"He came in while I was on the phone to the police," said Mrs. McGrath.

"And what did you say when you came into the bedroom Benjamin?" said Faulkner.

At that moment, the officer moved between the boy and his mother, blocking their visual connection.

"Benjamin?"

"I . . . I yelled out, 'Mom, what happened? Are you alright?'"

"Uh, huh" said the policeman.

"Okay, take them into the living room and finish the interviews," said the chief.

"Mrs. McGrath, you and Benjamin will have to stay somewhere tonight. Do you have some relatives or friends to stay with?" the officer said.

"No, I don't have friends or any relations here," said Mrs. McGrath as her eyes looked down.

"Well, when Officer Ward is finished interviewing you, he'll take you to a motel. The forensic team will have to be called to go through the room and you might have to stay for a couple of nights so pack enough clothes and things because you won't be able to get back in until they are done," said the chief.

At that point, Mr. McGrath's body was being carried out in a dark gray plastic bag that was zipped up. A crowd had gathered outside - men in white undershirts, smoking and drinking beer from cans and women in bathrobes, a few were also drinking and smoking.

Both mother and son watched as the body was removed. Chief Faulkner kept his eyes on the two of them. Suddenly, several men entered the house carrying bags and equipment.

Faulkner turned to the woman and said, "Go get your things together as quickly as you can. I'll see you again tomorrow."

He took Mrs. McGrath's arm in his hand and gave it a quick squeeze and looked into her eyes with an almost imperceptible nod. With that, he turned and left.

Mrs. McGrath grabbed her son's face and turned it to so that their eyes were in direct contact. "It's going to be alright, Benjie. Everything will be alright," she said.

Benjamin began to cry.

CHAPTER 60

Early the next morning, the State Police Forensics Unit arrived at the mobile home park. When they drove up in their van, they observed the local chief of police who was already on the scene. They found him around the back of the trailer near a puddle of water where a spigot was located.

"Morning, chief," said one of the state troopers. He looked at Chief Faulkner with a bit of surprise since he was standing near the home and could have contaminated part of the crime scene. But he knew that Faulkner was a very experienced cop with a great reputation.

"Good morning, Russ," said Faulkner.

"You're here early this morning. I hope you're not trying to do our job for us," said Russ Gillman, the head of the forensics department in the area.

"Ha, ha, no problem, Russ. Just doing some last-minute checks. Couldn't see much last night in the dark. You know I'm careful not to mess up your work," said Chief Faulkner.

"I know you responded last night but if you want to follow us inside, just put on the plastic slippers and follow us in."

"Yeah, I would like to get another view in daylight if you don't mind," said the chief.

Russ led the way with his assistant close behind. Russ was sharp and detailed about his work. He graduated from the State University at Albany in New York with a bachelor's degree in Criminal Justice and a master's degree in Chemistry and had been in the forensics department for 15 years, the last three as head of the department.

The three men put on their plastic overshoes and gloves and walked into the double wide. As soon as they entered, Russ's assistant, Tom Donnelly, began photographing everything in sight. The flash went off so often that it soon was no longer noticeable, and this was in the living room before they even entered the bedroom.

After a thorough and painstakingly slow walk around the living room with Gillman, constantly speaking into his hand-held recorder, they entered the bedroom. All three men stopped upon entering and stared at the bed with a huge dark reddish-brown stain of Mr. McGrath's blood. The fixed gaze of Chief Faulkner and Officer Gillman was broken by the flash of the camera. Tom Donnelly began firing off shot after shot.

Gillman held up his hand to the chief, signaling him to stand his ground while he entered the room. He continued to talk into his digital recorder, relating every detail he noticed. Donnelly kept taking photos while Faulkner stood by the door feeling awkward.

After close to 20 minutes without moving a step, the chief said, "Hey, Russ, I'm going back to the station house. There's nothing further for me to do until you are through. Give me a call when you are done."

Gillman did not answer right away as he was scrutinizing every aspect of the room and was so focused, he didn't seem to hear the chief. After a few seconds, however, he replied, "Okay, Brian, I'll call you," barely turning to face the officer.

The forensic detective immediately went back to logging every element in his careful view and Chief Faulkner nodded to Officer Donnelly and walked out of the trailer to his car.

He sat in his car for several minutes reviewing what he had done before the forensic team showed up. Satisfied that his job was done, he bent over to remove the plastic booties on his shoes and threw them on the seat next to him on top of the gloves he had already removed.

An audible sigh blew out of his mouth, and he leaned over to start the engine of his cruiser. He clenched his lips and nodded to himself as if to affirm that he had done what he knew was the right thing to do. Now all he could do was wait for Gillman's call. Putting the car in gear, he slowly drove off.

CHAPTER 61

It took two days before Chief Faulkner got the call from Gillman. He could feel his stomach tense up when he heard the forensic officer's voice on the phone. He held his breath while he and Russ Gillman exchanged a quick greeting.

"Well, Brian, it looks like a murder committed by an intruder. There is just something bothering me," said Gillman.

Faulkner had trouble keeping his voice from cracking and the words came out with some shakiness as he asked, "What's bothering you?"

"There's something that just doesn't seem right in the back by that spigot where I saw you when I arrived there. We found traces of blood - Mr. McGrath's blood. Now, why would the killer take the time to wash off before running away?" said Gillman.

"Maybe he wanted to keep from getting blood in his car or being seen with blood all over him?" replied Faulkner. He felt a sense of pride that he was able to come up with a plausible explanation so quickly or at least it was plausible to him. But would Gillman accept it?

"Yeah, maybe you're right. Anyway, there isn't any other explanation that makes sense unless . . . How well do you know this family? Mrs. McGrath and the boy?" asked Gillman.

"Oh, I've been called there several times in the past when Mr. McGrath was drunk and loud and it looked like he had beaten his wife and son.

Neighbors always called. I never got a call from his wife, and she always denied he hit her but there wasn't much doubt. She's a nice lady."

"And the boy?" asked Gillman.

The query evoked a small chuckle from Chief Faulkner. "Benjamin? No, that kid is a bit strange but he's afraid of his own shadow. I don't think he could kill a bug."

Gillman hesitated a moment before replying.

"Well, that's it then. I am sending my report in - murder by an unknown assailant. The wife and boy can go back to their home now. You want me to call them?" said Gillman.

"No, I'll take them back. Thanks, Russ," said Faulkner.

After another minute of non-police chat, the two officers ended their call. Chief Faulkner leaned back in his chair and felt relief wash over him. He then picked up the phone again and called the motel where Mrs. McGrath and Benjamin were staying.

"Hello, Mrs. McGrath. I just wanted to let you know that you can go back home now. The forensic investigation has concluded. I can come by to pick you and Benjamin up and drive you back. When would you be ready?" said Faulkner.

"What did they say, the forensic police?" asked Mrs. McGrath.

"They concluded that it happened as you said. Now we will need you to come down to the station, maybe tomorrow and give us another description and have you look through some photos," said Faulkner.

"Is that necessary? I really didn't get a good look at him. I don't know if I would recognize him if I saw him on the street," said Mrs. McGrath.

"It's regular police procedure. We must get a report out to all the police agencies nearby to be on the lookout for anyone fitting the description you gave. If you can pick out a photo, so much the better," said the chief.

"Okay. I can be ready in an hour if that's okay," said Mrs. McGrath.

"That's fine, ma'am. I'll be there in an hour," said Faulkner.

The chief of police sat back and thought about the last few days. He had never protected anyone before who he was suspicious of. Certainly not someone who he knew was guilty. But he knew the woman and her son had suffered terribly from beatings from that animal. The last time he was called there, she was already black and blue, and her eye was swollen, and her mouth was puffed and bleeding.

She would not press charges no matter how hard he pressed her to do so. Mr. McGrath got in his face and his spittle had sprayed onto the officer's face as he yelled for him to get out of his home. Faulkner held his ground and hoped that the brute would just bump into him, and he would take him apart. But he had no choice but to leave the woman and her timid son and wonder if they received more pain after he left.

Now he was dead and, going against his value system, he was glad. The bastard deserved to die, and he was happy that this woman had defended herself.

Now he would go to bring her home and she could be safe at last. But first, he had a job to do. He had a package in the trunk of his car that he had to get rid of.

He had to get rid of the knife.

CHAPTER 62

It had been two days since Jimmy spoke to Father Loudin. Even though Jimmy realized that it might take some time for the priest to find out if his suspicions were accurate, he went to school each day with nothing on his mind but the thought that Father Loudin would be summoning him and tell him that he found out that Father Simmons was hurting his pal somehow.

Jimmy was on his way home with Ralph and the two priests on his mind. Ralph was acting worse than ever the past couple of days. He hardly spoke even when both he and Tony asked him simple questions. Tony had been kind of distant as well since the incident in the lunchroom when Jimmy had gone into a sort of trance. The trios lunch times were no longer the same.

After arriving home, Jimmy met with his buddy, Pete, and they headed to the park to play some stickball. Jimmy tried to put all the events with Ralph out of his mind, but his ability to hit Pete's pitches was lost. Pete was enjoying striking out Jimmy time and time again. When he pitched, Jimmy had trouble throwing strikes and he lost several games, mostly due to walking Pete so many times.

Pete didn't seem to recognize there was anything wrong, He just enjoyed his success as he won every game they played. Now it was after

5 pm and it was time for Jimmy to go home and walk his dog. After this dog walking chore, he showered before supper.

Dinner consisted of lamb chops, one of Jimmy's favorites, with potatoes and spinach. But Jimmy's appetite which was not great normally, was less than usual tonight. His parents were used to his picky eating, but his mother was disappointed that her lamb chop dinner wasn't being eaten.

His mother asked, "Is there something wrong with the meat, Jimmy? You always liked lamp chops."

"No, Mom, they are fine. I am just not real hungry tonight," replied Jimmy.

After supper, he helped clear the table with his sister while his father took the evening paper into the living room. Then he went into his room to watch the Knicks play basketball on TV. His dad had no interest in sports, but Jimmy watched basketball, baseball, hockey and football every chance he got. Jimmy had saved for a black and white TV for his room, and he spent many hours watching his favorite teams play.

Near the end of the game, his mother came in to say good night. His sister had already gone to her room and his father had retired to his bedroom to watch TV as well. Jimmy watched the Tonight Show where an actor from a western threw a tomahawk right between the legs of a cardboard target of a man. Everyone in the audience laughed hysterically. After the show Jimmy got up, brushed his teeth and went to bed.

In bed, he recalled the scene on TV and started to laugh to himself again. Both the basketball game and the Tonight Show gave Jimmy some needed time off from thinking about Ralph and Father Simmons but now his mind went back to the thought of the situation at school. He knew something very wrong was going on and he hoped that Father Loudin would have some information and solution tomorrow.

Eventually, he drifted off to that pre-sleep state. Before he would fall into a deep sleep, he entered that dream world where visions presented themselves to him. Soon he saw Ralph again standing at the end of a corridor in school. This time Ralph did not call to him but just looked at his friend with hopelessness. The man in the black cloak took the boy's hand and took him into a classroom. Jimmy followed them. He really didn't want to, but he moved as if floating and without free will.

He spotted his pal sitting at the teacher's desk and the man in black standing before him, hunched over the boy. The man's face was in the dark as the room was poorly lit and Jimmy could smell some kind of sweet scent that was familiar but yet, unidentifiable. The man's hand began to move toward little Ralph's crotch and slowly started to unzip his fly.

Jimmy wanted to scream out but, no matter how hard he pushed, no sound came forth. He opened his mouth and tensed his stomach and flexed his throat, but not even a squeak came past his lips. The hand continued to open his friend's pants, slowly, link by link. Then, out of the dark gray darkness. a light shined upon the hand. He could see the man's hand clearly.

He saw a ring. It was on the ring finger of his right hand. It had a large light blue stone. It was a ring he had just seen. Father Loudin's ring!

CHAPTER 63

It was Father Loudin all the time. There was no doubt about the ring. He remembered it quite clearly. He had been sure that Father Simmons was the one who was abusing his friend but now he realized that the "cool" Father Loudin, the priest that all the boys liked, and thought was different, was the abuser. Different? Yes, he was that and more.

And he had talked to Father Loudin about his suspicions! No wonder he told Jimmy not to speak to anyone about it. What would he do now? How could he face Father Loudin now that he knew who the guilty man was? How could he have been so wrong?

He often saw Ralph talking to Father Simmons and acting upset. He must have been talking to the priest about his abuse or maybe just that he was upset. Maybe Father Simmons noticed something was wrong and was trying to counsel Ralph. Jimmy noticed Father Simmons mannerisms in class and jumped to the conclusion that he was the abuser. He had been wrong and felt almost as badly for thinking that it was his music teacher as he did knowing it was his trusted Latin teacher all along.

Now the problem was what was the next step? Should he speak to Father Simmons now? No, how could he talk to the priest he had accused in his own mind? He would be too embarrassed. Should he just forget the whole thing and try to stay away from Father Loudin? That would be impossible as well. How could he drop this now knowing his friend was continuing to be abused? He had a major decision to make, and he knew he had to act soon. He would see Father Loudin tomorrow in class and just ignoring him would not be enough. These past couple of days were hard enough but he hadn't known about Father Loudin before now. Today he would face him with the knowledge that he was the molester.

During his entire bus ride to school, Jimmy could only think about his dilemma. What would he do? What could he do? As he entered the school building, his stomach was felt like a lead weight had somehow been swallowed and his breathing was rapid and shallow. As he walked into the main corridor and saw a few of the priests standing around talking, he felt nauseous and wondered if he would need to throw up.

He spotted Father McCormick, the stern assistant principal. He was a slight, short and bald man who wore frameless glasses. However, his demeanor completely overwhelmed his physical appearance. He was in a word - intimidating. No one had ever seen him smile. Students quaked in his presence. This was the last man on earth that Jimmy would speak to about his foreboding dreams. Yet, he found himself approaching him.

Jimmy nervously asked, "Father, can I speak with you?"

"Can you speak with me? Of course, you CAN. I think what you mean to say is, MAY you speak to me," replied the cold cleric.

Jimmy's mouth was suddenly very dry. He barely choked out, "Sorry, Father, may I speak with you?"

"What's this about?" asked the priest through tight, thin lips.

"It's about one of my friends," said Jimmy.

Then for some unexplainable reason, words flew from his mouth without any filter. "I think he's being hurt by one of his teachers. I saw Father Loudin, well, I saw his ring, so I think it's him. He was touching Ralph Thompson. I mean touching him in a bad way. I mean I didn't actually see him, I kind of dreamed it. But I'm sure it's true."

"Hold it right there, young man. No more of this here. Come to my office . . . right now."

Jimmy looked up at the assistant principal who seemed to grow in stature as his eyes glowered at the boy. He followed the priest who turned sharply and headed down the hall to his office. The boy wondered if this whole idea was a huge mistake. Now he had no way of turning back.

Suppose he was completely wrong, and it was just his imagination? No, he knew without any doubt that he was right and that his dreams were valid.

As they entered the office, Father McCormick said to his secretary, "Call Father Loudin and tell him I need to see him right away. Get Father Michaels to cover his homeroom."

Oh, no! Jimmy was overwhelmed with anxiety just telling his story to the assistant principal. Now he would have to face the priest who he was accusing! This was a gigantic mistake. He should never have talked to Father McCormick. He should never have pursued this whole idea. What was he thinking? His parents would be called. He would be in big trouble. He only wanted to help his friend. He only wanted to do what he thought was the right thing to do.

Father McCormick walked around his massive desk and sat down in a chair that seemed to make him appear taller. He pointed to a chair on the opposite side of his desk and told the boy to sit down. The chair was low, and Jimmy felt even smaller as he looked up at the scowling face of the assistant principal.

The priest looked down at the boy before him and with an icy stare said, "Tell me your story".

Jimmy swallowed and it hurt because there was no saliva in his mouth. There was no erasing the recent past and going back in time to when he entered the building. He had to go forward now.

He began, "I eat lunch with Ralph Thompson and Anthony Viscone. A while ago, Ralph started to act different, weird. He seemed sad. Then I started to dream about him. The first dream . . ."

CHAPTER 64

After explaining almost every facet of his dreams, suspicions and belief that Father Loudin was abusing his pal, Jimmy sat back in the chair and took a breath. It felt like the first breath he took since the very beginning of his tale to the assistant principal.

The cleric sat back and stared at the boy before him through his frameless spectacles. Jimmy didn't know what the priest was thinking as he sat motionless and in silence. There was no hint of how his account was received since the man before him was expressionless. The room was filled with dead air and a cloud of awkwardness descended upon the boy and enveloped him.

Jimmy wanted to break the stillness, but he couldn't. He just sat and waited for what seemed like several long minutes. Finally, the priest spoke.

"Go to your class now. Tell Mrs. Modell to give you a late pass," said Father McCormick. His voice was different somehow. It seemed weaker and without the usual sharpness that stung the listener.

Jimmy got up from the chair, using the arms to push himself up from the depths of the seat. He bent over to pick up his book bag and slowly walked toward the door.

"James," said Father McCormick, not using his usual manner of addressing students only by their last name. Jimmy turned around to face the priest.

"James, do not speak to Father Loudin as you leave. Just get your pass and go directly to class," said the priest.

'Yes, Father," said Jimmy.

He walked to the large wooden door that was heavy and dark and pulled it open. As soon as he looked into the outer office, his eyes fell on Father Loudin who was sitting in one of the chairs. He looked at Jimmy, but his familiar smile was gone. Instead, he sat with a blank expression and seemed pale and smaller as he slouched forward.

Jimmy turned quickly to the secretary and asked Mrs. Modell for a late pass. The friendly woman with jet black hair and glasses smiled as she reached for a pad and scribbled on it, tore the slip off and handed it to the boy.

"Thank you," said Jimmy and he moved hastily to the door to the corridor without even so much as a glance at Father Loudin. However, as he passed him, he could smell a familiar scent. It was Father Loudin's cologne. The same fragrance he smelled in his dream. When he got in the corridor, he turned back to look through the glass walls of the office to see the priest getting up and walking toward the assistant principal's now open door. He seemed to have a gait that was similar to one of the students who were called to meet with the administrator for unsatisfactory behavior. His head was down with his eyes on the ground and Jimmy stopped to watch him enter the inner office and slowly close the door behind him.

Jimmy's mind was racing as he walked to his classroom. Did he do the right thing? Is Father Loudin in trouble? Jimmy wondered if he would be in trouble for telling what he knew was true? Would his parents be called and how would they react? And maybe most importantly, how would this affect Ralph? Would his friend change back into the kid he knew before, or would he be forever turned into the somber and sad boy he had become?

Soon Jimmy found himself at the door to his first class which was just about to end. He opened the door and felt the eyes of the other boys upon him. Were they looking at him because he was late, and they were envious that he missed a boring period with Father Michaels substituting for Father Loudin or did they know what had just occurred?

He walked directly to the teacher's desk and gave Father Michaels the late pass. He barely glanced at it and told Jimmy to take his seat. The teacher then proceeded to finish his lecture about history in the Roman

Empire and how Latin was no longer used as a spoken language. He could see by the expressions of the faces of the other boys in class that they missed Father Loudin's dynamic teaching style. Little did they know that Jimmy was the cause of his absence that day and that the lives of several people would be dramatically changed by the meeting he had just had with Father McCormick.

CHAPTER 65

Several months later, much had changed for Jimmy. After his talk with Father McCormick, his parents were immediately called and asked to come to the school that evening. Jimmy was to stay at home and sat nervously in his room until they came home. Jimmy was too apprehensive to come out of this room when they came home hours later. He feared how his father would react to the meeting with the assistant principal. Strangely, his father went right into his parents' bedroom and his mother came into his room by herself.

"Jimmy, we had a long talk with Father McCormick, and he feels it would be best if you transferred to Holy Name High School," said his mother.

She continued, "Even though the school year is almost over, he feels it would be a problem for you to return for the rest of the semester. He has arranged for you to go to Holy Name next week."

"But mom, I don't know anyone there. What about my friends at the Sacred Heart? I will have all new teachers. I don't want to go there next week. Can't I wait until next September? There's only a few weeks left of school," Jimmy said.

"No, Father McCormick wants you to go right away, and your father and I agree," said his mother.

Jimmy thought about his father and wondered why he didn't join his mother in explaining the news of his transfer. He was uneasy thinking about his father and felt that it was better that he didn't have to face him.

"Besides," said his mother, "I am sure there are a few boys from St. Basil's there who you know."

Jimmy gave that some thought and remembered Peter Berger and Kenny Donohue who were boys from his class at St. Basil who went to Holy Name. There might be a few others as well. Anyway, it didn't look like he had much choice. Arguing with his mother might only bring his father into the discussion and he knew that the decision had been made anyway.

So, the following week he went to the new school. It was as awkward as he imagined it would be. There were actually three boys from St. Basil's School who were at Holy Name High School. He had forgotten about Leonard Moore who was in his class for eight years without ever having a conversation with Jimmy. The other two boys hung out together but were kind of tough guys who had never had much to do with Jimmy at St. Basil and even less now.

He pretty much kept to himself and made a few acquaintances with boys in his home room who were kind of dorks who didn't have any clique to which they belonged. He caught up rather quickly with his academics and was ready for his finals and his Regent Exams which were New York State Exams and given in several subjects. They were considered more difficult than teacher-made final exams, but Jimmy had little to distract him and studied hard for his tests.

A few weeks after he left the seminary, he got a call one night from his friend, Tony. He was surprised when Jimmy didn't show up for school for days and then there were rumors that he was kicked out of the school. He wanted to know what had happened. Jimmy told him he decided he didn't want to be a priest anymore and wanted to leave right away. He didn't want to go into his dreams and the accusation against Father Loudin, but he did want to know what happened with Ralph and the priest who abused him.

There was a pause before Tony continued. He told Jimmy that Ralph was in school for a little less than two weeks after Jimmy had left but he basically didn't speak. Tony said he acted even stranger than usual. Then one day, he also didn't come back. The grapevine said he was ill and would finish the year being tutored at home.

"Then one day, Father Simmons in music class asked us to say a prayer for Ralph. Jimmy, he died! All the guys were asking Father Simmons what happened, even though most of them never ever even talked to Ralph when he was here. He was a weirdo but I kind of liked him, you know?" Tony said.

Tony continued, "Father said he had no information about how he died but we all had heard he was sick, so I guess whatever he had, he died from."

Jimmy sat back. He knew how Ralph had died. The previous week he had a dream in which he watched Ralph swallow something in a bathroom with a glass of water. Then he turned toward Jimmy and sadly waved goodbye. He woke up at that point, but the dream wasn't frightening, and he didn't realize the significance of it. Actually, he kind of forgot about it. His friend had died of an overdose of some medicine, probably something from his parents' bathroom cabinet. He was sure of it.

"Hey, are you still there," said Tony when there was a minute of silence on the phone.

"Uh, how about our teachers, Tony? Anything interesting with any of them?" Jimmy asked.

"Well, it's mostly the same crap but Father Loudin is gone. We heard he got transferred to a boys' school in Pennsylvania. But man, it's great. The priest that took his place doesn't teach. He just assigns pages in the textbook and we kind of goof off. Father Loudin was cool but he made us work. Now Latin is my easiest class," said Tony.

Jimmy was upset at both knowing that Ralph had committed suicide and that Father Loudin was transferred to another boys' school where he might continue to hurt young boys. But there was nothing further he could do. He told those in authority about his suspicions and his dreams. It looked like he was ignored, and the priest was removed to another school so he couldn't make any more trouble.

It was the only time he heard from anyone from his old school. Tony never called again, and Jimmy realized that he had to move on. The following years at Holy Name were not as uncomfortable as those few weeks at the end of his freshman year. He still had some dreams that were disturbing but the dreams about Ralph and Father Loudin had ended. He would often wonder what happened to Father Loudin in the following years. He would never know.

CHAPTER 66

Over the next few years, there was an air of awkwardness between Benjamin and his mother. It's not that she didn't continue to love him, and she certainly didn't miss her abusive husband but there was an underlying tension between them. Perhaps deep down inside her was a fear of her son - justifiable since he was indeed a murderer.

High school was an uncomfortable, unhappy place as well. Although he was no longer openly teased by his fellow students, he had no friends and was terribly lonely. His few attempts at making connections with other students at school were met with either apathy or downright rudeness. Here, too, there seemed to be a latent apprehension toward Benjamin. Some had witnessed his vicious attack on his tormentors several years back in grade school and even those who went to a different elementary school seemed to give Benjamin a wider berth. Something had changed about this boy. It was hard to put a finger on it, but he was no longer the pathetic creature that everyone had made fun of when he started school at Poughkeepsie High School. Now there was a feeling of fear or at least trepidation when other students viewed Benjamin and it seemed like they all would rather just avoid him.

Now he was a senior and, while all the students seemed to be talking about graduation, college and the prom, Benjamin only thought about leaving this institution of isolation. Finally, as he turned 17, he made up his mind. He would leave school before he graduated and move away from this town where he only found torment and misery.

When he approached his mother about withdrawing from school without a diploma and moving away, he wasn't sure how she would react. After all, their relationship was cool, and conversations were limited. But he had made his mind up regardless of what his mother would say.

One day after a supper where words were few and far between, he took a deep breath and spoke up.

"Mom," said Benjamin, "I decided to leave school and move out of the house."

He waited for a response with some angst, but his apprehension was unnecessary.

"Have you decided where you would go?" his mother replied.

"Not exactly, but I want to get away from here. I don't mean away from here - this house - but away from school and this town," said Benjamin.

"Well, you have to have a job, pay rent, buy food. Have you thought about that?' asked his mother.

"Yeah, I will look at places and jobs first before I move out, but I can't stand another day at school. I want to start fresh and have a life," said the young man and then with a low voice, hardly loud enough to hear, "and find someone who likes me."

His mother did not hear his last words or chose to ignore them. He was disappointed that she made no comment about his lack of any relationships. Even though he spoke those words faintly, he had hoped she had heard him and would comfort him, but she continued.

"You will need to let the school know you are leaving so they don't send someone here to check up on you. You can stay until you find something elsewhere. Maybe you should pick up some newspapers to look at want ads," she said.

"Okay, I'll go to school tomorrow and tell them I am dropping out. Don't worry, I'll find something soon. I won't just sit here and stay," said Benjamin.

"You can stay until you find some work. I know that it won't be long," said his mother.

Benjamin wasn't sure if that last statement was confidence in his ability to find work or a veiled push out the door. The family of two now ate some ice cream for dessert and said no more. It was done now. Benjamin didn't know if he had expected more of a negative reaction from his mother, but he did feel some disappointment that she seemed almost eager for him to leave.

He brought his dish to the sink and went into his bedroom. At the door, he turned to say good night to his mother and closed the door behind him. He turned on his black and white small screen TV as he did every night after supper and jumped onto his bed. As his head sank into the pillow, he began to think about his future. Where was he going? Did he make the right decision? What kind of work would he do?

The most distressing thought, however, was that his mother, the only person in his entire life who cared for him, now appeared to be pleased to see him go. As this realization floated down from his mind into his heart, the young man's eyes began to fill with tears. An unintentional sob burst from his throat, but he immediately controlled himself and sat up in his bed.

He would find a new place to stay, a job and a person who would care for him like his mother used to. He was not afraid but determined that this would be a new beginning and he would show them all that he was a worthwhile person who someone could care for. Or he would show them that they underestimated him and that would be a terrible mistake.

CHAPTER 67

After withdrawing from school, Benjamin spent the days looking through want ads. Unfortunately, he found nothing that he was suited for. Jobs either needed an experienced worker or stated that they were looking for a high school graduate. Benjamin was neither.

One day when he walked to the nearby candy store which sold newspapers as well as cigarettes, soda and candy, he found a newspaper which printed jobs from areas further away. This publication served many areas in the country, but each edition was printed for a particular section of the nation. This one was for the northeast and included Pennsylvania, New Jersey, Connecticut, as well as New York. It had nothing but want ads for jobs as well as merchandise.

Benjamin purchased the newspaper and rushed home with excitement. He just knew that he was going to find his future in that folded up paper in his hand. As soon as he entered the mobile home, he sat down at the kitchen table. His mother was not home. She has been working at the local diner since his father's death. She worked long hours, starting in the late morning and working through the lunch and supper crowds. She would not be home until a little after eight that night.

Benjamin rushed to the refrigerator and took out a soda. Then he went to the pantry and grabbed a bag of chips and hurriedly opened both as he sat down in front of the newspaper. After munching a handful of potato chips and gulping down some of the cola, he took a deep breath and unfolded the paper. He saw that it was set up with merchandise listed first and then jobs. It was also organized by states within these two categories.

He turned the pages to the jobs/New York section first, but he hesitated before reading the first ad. He stopped and looked up at the front door of the double wide. He really wanted to get away - far away. He was looking for a completely new beginning and made the decision that, although New York was an immense state, he wanted to travel out of state. He had never been in another state. Indeed, he had never been out of the county. This was his chance.

His fingers grabbed a few pages and he turned to another section. It was the listings for Pennsylvania. He would look there first.

The first few jobs were the usual - experience or high school diploma required. Then he found the following:

"Factory workers needed. Ambitious, hardworking young men and women wanted. No experience needed. High school diploma suggested but not necessary. Base salary plus overtime available." There was a phone number listed but it did not state what town or city it was in.

Benjamin felt he found what he was looking for. He fit the description. He was ambitious, if only to get away from here. He would be hard working, he promised himself. No need for experience or that damn diploma. He just knew this was the right job. He was sure of it.

He ran over to the black phone on the small shelf next to the pantry. He was not allowed to ever make a long-distance call. Actually, he never used the phone because he had no one to call. But if he got the job, he could send his mother the money for the call. He realized his hands were shaking. He thought about forgetting the whole thing. Then he recalled the weeks of looking at ads with no possibilities. He thought about spending months in this house alone while his mother worked all day. He thought about the coldness he felt when his mother was home. He thought about having no friends, no one to hang out with, to laugh with, to share with.

He breathed deeply through his mouth and picked up the phone and dialed. A man answered the phone with a somewhat gruff voice.

"York Barbell Company."

"Uh, um, I saw your ad for a job and wanted to apply," said Benjamin.

"What skills do you have?" said the man's voice.

"Well, uh, I don't have any real skills. I just finished high school. I mean, I stopped going to high school and I want to work. I saw the ad and just wanted to ask about a job," said Benjamin.

'I see. Well, the pay for unskilled workers is the minimum wage of $1.25 an hour. Overtime is $1.50 an hour. There is no union. No dues, no insurance - just straight pay. We need people to pack up weights and equipment for shipping and we have plenty of openings. The work is hard but, as long as you do your job, you have a job. If you have potential, you could get a move up to the line and get a raise down the road. You interested?" said the man.

"Yes, yes," said Benjamin trying not to sound too excited and young.

"Okay, come in tomorrow after 8 am and see Mr. Schultz, that's me. You can start tomorrow night," said the man. "The shipping department works a night shift."

"Uh, well, I can't make it tomorrow. I have to travel there first," Benjamin nervously replied.

"Where are you comin' from?" said the man.

"Poughkeepsie, New York," said Benjamin.

"Paw what? New York? Man, kid you have a long way to go. Are you sure you want to do this? It's hard work and we're not here to play around," said the man.

"Yes, I am sure. I'll work hard, I promise. You won't be sorry. I can get there by Monday if that's alright," said Benjamin.

"Well, the job will be here next week. So be here at 8am next Monday and come and see me. Do you have a place to stay in town? There's a Motel 6 that some of the guys sometimes stay at. They have long term rates," said the man.

"That sounds good," said Benjamin. "I'll see you on Monday morning."

"Okay, kid, see you then," said the man.

The man on the phone gave Benjamin the address which he excitedly wrote on a pad by the phone.

Benjamin hung up the phone. He felt proud of himself. He found a job and it was far away from Poughkeepsie and all the terrible memories that this place held for him. It was Wednesday and he only had a few days to pack his things and find a way to his new hometown. He would work hard and find some friendly people. He might even find a girl who would like him.

As he thought about this new adventure and all the possibilities, his spirits rose to heights that he hadn't felt in a long, long time. Maybe he never ever felt this good at least not since that night in the train yard. He would move away from here and find a life that he deserved.

CHAPTER 68

That night he told his mother about the job offer in Pennsylvania. Before this she didn't seem to care much about Benjamin moving away but this time, she seemed hesitant.

"That's far away from here, Benjie. Are you sure you want to go so far away? We won't see each other, and I can't help you out," said his mother.

"I need to get away and start fresh, ma. And they offered me the job without needing a diploma. I can start on Monday, so I have to leave as soon as possible," said Benjamin.

"How will you get there?"

"I checked and there is a Trailways bus that goes to Philadelphia through New York City and in Philadelphia I take another bus to York. I called a motel this afternoon, too. They have vacancies so I can live there for now. I can leave on Friday and have the weekend to check out the area and see how far it is to work," said Benjamin.

His mother said. "Well, it looks like you have it all figured out."

She looked at her son and a sad smile formed on her face. Tears wet her eyes as she said, "I'll miss you, Benjie."

With that, Benjamin ran into his mother's arms and hugged her. He realized that it had been some time since he embraced his mother. Maybe the last time was the night he killed his father. It felt good. With that he realized that he would miss the only person he spoke to, although their conversations had been short and unemotional for some time.

But the young man knew that this was the right move and he had to begin his adult life without his mother. He needed to become a man on his own and this was the first step. He stepped back while still holding onto his mother and smiled back at her.

"It's going to be alright, ma. I'll be okay and work hard and make money and someday I'll buy a house and you can come and visit me," he said.

His mother's smile turned to one of pride and joy. Her boy had grown, and he would find his way in the world. She always was worried that he would never be strong enough to be on his own and would just live with her until she passed on. Now she felt he had a chance to make a place for himself and maybe, just maybe, he would have a family of his own someday. She never thought that she could see this day.

"You know what? Tomorrow is Thursday and since you are leaving on Friday, it will be our last day together. Why don't you come into the diner at supper time and I'll get some time off and we'll sit down and have supper together. It will be kind of a good-bye celebration. What do you say?" she said.

Benjamin smiled as he looked into his mother's eyes.

"Okay, ma. I'll come into the diner at 6. How's that?" said the young man.

"That will be perfect, Benjie. We'll have something special and you can have a big slice of that cheesecake you love," said his mother.

Benjamin felt warm inside. He wanted to tell his mother that he loved her, but he suddenly felt awkward and held back.

"Speaking of eating, I know you already had supper but how about I make some fried bologna and macaroni and cheese?" she said.

A big smile broke across Benjamin's face. It was one of his favorites.

"Sure, ma. Let's eat!" said the teen.

CHAPTER 69

The first day of work for Benjamin at York Barbell Company came quickly. When he had checked into his room at the motel his room had an odor of musty tobacco. But once he was inside, his sense of smell was numbed, and the smell was more like a damp sponge. Certainly not pleasant but he would get used to it.

When he arrived at the factory, the first thing that struck him was the noise. Describing it as loud was like saying a jet engine hummed. The office for the foreman was tiny and cluttered with papers spread all over his brown steel desk.

Although there was no sign on his desk, Benjamin took it for granted that the fat, bald man behind the desk was Mr. Schultz who he spoke to on the phone.

"Mr. Schultz? I'm Benjamin McGrath. We spoke on the phone and I am here to start work tonight," said Benjamin.

Mr. Schultz looked up peering over his glasses and said nothing for what seemed like a long minute. Benjamin became uncomfortable and started his introduction again.

"I'm Benjamin . . .," started the boy. Schultz interrupted, "Yeah, I remember. So, you made it here. Did you move into the motel?"

"Yeah, it's nice," said Benjamin.

"Nah, it's a shit hole but it's cheap and almost clean. Are you ready to work your ass off, kid?" said Schultz.

"Yes, sir! I'm here to work and ready to start," the chubby young man said.

The foreman again stared at the boy without saying a word or changing any expression. Benjamin became quite uncomfortable and didn't know if he was supposed to say anything further, but he just stood there and could feel wetness under his arms. His heartbeat began to race, and he noticed his mouth felt dry.

The rotund man in the white dress shirt with an open collar and no tie finally spoke.

"You're younger looking than I thought, and you look kind of soft and pasty. This is hard, heavy work, kid. You sure you want to do this?"

Benjamin tried to swallow to remove the wool sweater that seemed to now cover his tongue. But his saliva had dried up and he realized he had to push his chin up to just force down the dry air that now was all he could muster.

"Yes, sir. I want to work here. Please, give me a chance and I'll show you I can do the job," Benjamin pleaded.

"Okay, fill out these forms and come back this afternoon around 4:30. I'll show you what you have to do, and you clock in at 5. Quitting time is 2 am. You get an unpaid hour for dinner and a 15-minute break that is paid. Right now, there are three other guys you'll be working with. We need more but not many last long," said Schultz.

Benjamin forced a smile and looked out through the glass walls of the office where he saw big men hauling flats of black weights and huge pots pouring molten liquid metal into giant machines. They all wore white t-shirts wet with sweat and blackened by metal filings and paint. Their powerful arms glistened with perspiration as they pulled carts as the weights were pulled out of water in which they were submerged in to cool off after setting.

"Don't worry, you won't be working the floor with those guys," said the foreman. He chuckled, "They get paid more than the guys in shipping, but they work their asses off. You wouldn't last 5 minutes on the floor. The packing and shipping will be heavy enough for you, trust me."

Benjamin filled out the forms and handed them back to the foreman.

A smile forced its way onto the man's face as he looked at the boy in front of him who looked eager but scared as a rabbit being chased by a hound. He held out his hand to shake the boy's sweaty palm.

"See you at 4:30. Unless you chicken out."

"I'll be here," said the young man with conviction that was apparent in his voice but not in his mind. "See you at 4:30."

Benjamin walked back to the motel which was six blocks from the factory. He started out thinking that maybe this was a mistake. Maybe he should take what money he had left and buy a bus ticket home. But when he was within a block of the motel, he became more determined than ever. He would not fail. He would not go back home and disappoint his mother. He would be there this afternoon and he would do a good job. He would be a success.

CHAPTER 70

Benjamin had tried to nap but as he lay in bed, his mind raced about his upcoming night at the barbell plant. As he thought of what might be ahead, his anxiety grew. He was adamant to Mr. Schultz that he would not quit and would show him he could do the job but now, alone in his bed, he was not so sure. In fact, he strongly doubted he could keep up with the burly men he saw working in the factory.

Finally, around 3 pm he arose and put his pants back on, washed his face and checked himself out in the mirror. A rotund and tense face stared back at him. He realized his glasses were too large for his face and he thought that new glasses would be one of the first things he would buy with his paycheck. His paycheck. The idea that he would earn his first paycheck had a calming effect on him. He began to gain confidence and a smile formed on his countenance.

It was a bit before 4pm when Benjamin left the motel complex and started to walk toward the barbell plant. He arrived much too early, and he wasn't sure if he would appear to be too anxious to enter well before 4:30 or would it look like a sign that he had a good attitude. He decided to wait outside for a while but after only a few minutes which seemed like an hour, he entered the door of the employee entrance.

He walked directly to Mr. Schultz's office, but the foreman was not there. He looked around and wasn't sure if he should enter the office and wait there or stay outside. The noise was deafening and after a few minutes he decided to go inside and wait. There were only two chairs, one behind the desk and one in front of it. He thought it would be best if he stood.

Benjamin looked around the office while he waited for his new boss. The office was bare. The walls had no pictures or certificates and had black marks on the paint. The loud banging from the factory floor was muffled but still loud. His belly began to feel tight and he could feel his breathing start to increase. This was a mistake. He wished he had never left upstate New York and his mother's house. He could have found a job in town and just learned to deal with all his bad memories there. He was now almost panting.

"Rrrrrring!" The black phone on the desk rang with a shrill, drilling ring. It was a piercing blast and completely overwhelmed the racket from outside the office door. It startled the young man and he jumped and almost fell back.

"Rrrrrring!"

Benjamin stared at the phone which appeared at move and vibrate during each ring.

He froze and just kept looking at it and the ringing continued.

The door then burst open and Benjamin felt an arm push him aside. It was Mr. Schultz who just raced past the young man and grabbed the receiver.

"Yeah, Schultz," the large and sweaty man yelled into the phone. "What the hell are you telling me? Yeah? Well, don't bother coming back tomorrow." He slammed the phone down in its cradle.

"These good for nothin' bastards. They come in with a sob story, ask for a job and then have a million excuses to not show up. I hope to hell you're not one of them, boy."

Benjamin wished he could have somehow said something. But no words came out. His thoughts of leaving before he even began were now impossible to verbalize. He looked at Mr. Schultz with an open mouth and fear that was obvious to anyone.

"Alright, kid, it's time for you to show me you're better than most of the lazy bastards that come in here. Let's go. I'll show you what you have to do, get you a timecard and you'll meet the guys you are working with when they come in. Of course, they're not here yet. They punch in at 5 and won't be here a minute early."

As they walked through the cacophony in the factory, he saw huge men hauling weights and bars on big flats of wood. Their arms were black with metal filings and glistened with sweat. He hoped that his job would be much less physical because he knew he was not nearly strong enough to do their job.

He had to almost run to keep up with Mr. Schultz who moved quickly for a man who was significantly overweight. The foreman stopped at a wall that was filled with beige cards all lined up neatly in two large wooden racks. Benjamin almost ran into his boss who looked at him with disdain.

"These are the timecards. The left side is the day shift, and the right side is the night shift. You can see the left side is full but the right side in almost empty because the factory shuts down at night except for shipping and maintenance. Let's see . . . Yeah, here's your card," said Mr. Schultz as he handed Benjamin a card that was empty except for his name written in ink at the top.

The foreman grabbed the card back from the young man before he had much of a chance to look at it. He said, "You find it when you come in. They should be alphabetical, but it could be anywhere because these guys are too stupid to know the alphabet. Then you put it in this time clock slot here and the clock will print the time you arrived. Then you do the same when you leave. If you screw this up, you won't get paid. Got it?"

He put the card back in a slot in the cabinet. "You'll punch in later because you won't get paid for this tour," said Mr. Schultz.

He then began walking fast again. Benjamin noticed none of the men greeted the foreman when they passed. He thought that there was no love lost between the men and their foreman.

They went through a huge swinging metal door and arrived at the shipping dock. There were tables and wooden platforms piled high with weight training equipment, but the place was empty of employees. There were several massive garage doors which lead to the docks where the trucks would be loaded with the equipment.

"Okay, here's how it works. A guy will pull in a flat of weights or equipment and put paperwork taped to it. That paperwork is important. You read it, you can read, can't you?"

Benjamin still had trouble speaking and his boss spoke so fast he didn't know if the words would come out fast enough, so he nodded.

Mr. Schultz continued, "Okay, you read the paperwork and look at the chart on the wall. It tells you which truck gets a particular load. You match the depot on the paperwork and the chart and load the stuff into the truck on that dock. Get it? It's not rocket science, kid."

"I understand," Benjamin croaked out.

"Good," said Mr. Schultz. "There will be several guys working with you and they'll show you what to do. One guy already quit today so they'll be three of you."

Benjamin wondered if the guy who quit was the guy on the other end of that phone conversation. He looked around and saw many wooden flats of weights, bars and exercise equipment. They looked very heavy.

The foreman looked at his watch. "Okay, it's a little past 4:45. Let's go back and you can clock in and then come back here and wait for the two idiots you are working with," said Mr. Schultz.

They walked quickly back to the timecards. Mr. Schultz looked at Benjamin and waited for him to pull his card and put it in the slot of the time clock. Fortunately, he did it correctly and the clock made a loud click. The young man carefully placed his card back in the same slot he took it from.

"Okay, go back to the loading dock and wait for the other guys. I'll check on you later before I leave," said Schultz.

The foreman began to walk away quickly. Then he stopped and looked back at the young man who was walking in the opposite direction.

"Hey, kid! Good luck. See you later," said Mr. Schultz.

Benjamin was surprised by the man's statement. He smiled and waved back at this new boss. Mr. Schultz turned quickly and headed back to his office. Benjamin turned and began heading to his new workplace.

A smile began to grow on his face. He took a deep breath. He would be alright.

CHAPTER 71

At 5 pm a loud horn blew and startled Benjamin. He walked to the door of the shipping dock and opened it a bit and saw the men on the floor of the factory all moving quickly toward the time clock. The day shift was completed. Then he saw two young men heading his way against traffic. One was heavy set and the other was quite skinny. Both were laughing and shoving each other back and forth.

Benjamin quickly moved back into the loading dock and let the tall swinging door close. Just as he walked a few steps the door swung back open and the two young guys he saw entered, still laughing. Then they looked up and saw Benjamin and stopped laughing. The skinny guy walked up to Benjamin and held out his hand.

"Hey, I'm Lenny and this is Dick - Big Dick," With that, the skinny guy let out a hysterical, high pitched, staccato laugh that was a cross between a hyena and machine gun.

The overweight guy did not laugh. He first looked at Lenny and frowned and then turned to Benjamin and said, "I'm Richard but you can call me Rich. NOT Dick!" he said with emphasis.

Lenny seemed filled with energy and almost bounced over to a tall wooden desk that had a few scattered papers on it. Rich followed but his gait was much more deliberate.

Lenny said, "I guess Billy is gone. I knew he'd be fired when he said he wasn't coming in today. I told him but he said he didn't give a shit. Shultz hated him and I think he was going to fire him anyway. So, you're the new guy? Hey, what's your name anyway?"

The young man looked a bit bewildered by the sudden activity and hesitated for a moment. As he would find out, Lenny was hyperactive and had little to no patience.

"Well, cat's got your tongue? You can speak, can't you? What's your N A M E?" Lenny said saying the last word very slowly and with large movements of his rather oversized mouth.

"Benjamin," said the chubby lad who was somewhat overwhelmed by this wild-eyed co-worker.

"Don't mind, Lenny, kid. He's nuts and will drive you batty if you let him," said Rich. "Just ignore most of what he says."

"Hey, screw you, Dick! I'm just trying to introduce myself to our new partner in crime," said Lenny.

Rich moved toward the chart on the wall. He looked it over and said, "Okay, all five bays have trucks tonight. Let's get going before PIA shows up."

"What's PIA," said Benjamin.

Lenny jumped in. "That's Pain in the Ass as in Schultz, the foreman. But don't let him hear you call him that or you'll join Billy without a job," said Lenny.

Just then, as if by some eerie coincidence, Mr. Schultz burst through the door. His entrance surprised all three young men. It did indeed appear magical because it caused Lenny to stop talking and that didn't happen often.

Mr. Schultz said, "These two goof offs showing you how to hardly work and look busy? It's the only talent they have. But I am onto them. See all these pallets? Well, they better be unloaded and all this equipment on the right trucks by the end of your shift. You two numbskulls, show this kid what he needs to do and get to work."

With that, Mr. Schultz turned and left the shipping department. Rich and Lenny stood there for about a minute before Lenny said, "The PIA has spoken! Okay, let's start loading this shit onto the trucks."

Rich walked over to the flat nearest the first garage door and looked at the sheet of paper attached to it. He walked over to the chart and compared the information on the paper with the list of trucks. He then walked to the third garage door and pressed a large black button, and the garage door began to open with a loud bang. It slowly rose onto the tracks on the ceiling and exposed the back of a truck. Lenny walked over and climbed onto the bumper of the truck and pulled on a handle on the door of the truck and began to lift it up.

"Okay, kid, we'll pull this pallet over to the open truck and push it on. C'mon, give me a hand," said Rich.

Benjamin moved quickly to the flat of weight training equipment and pulled on the long handle attached to the front of it. It didn't move. Not an inch. He pulled again as hard as he could, Nothing.

A screaming shrill laugh broke the silence of the area which had become quiet now that the factory was closed. Benjamin turned to see Lenny bent over with his hands on his knees in uncontrollable laughter.

"I told you, don't pay any attention to that fool," said Rich. "He's a jackass. Here, look, we have to pull on this together. Hey, jackass, stop your laughing and get your ass over here and pull."

Lenny walked over and the three men pulled hard on the long black handle attached to the wooden pallet which had wheels below it. Slowly, it began to move and then faster and easier until the got to the truck and rolled it onto the dock and into the empty truck. From there they slowly lifted the bars and metal collars into the truck. The weights were very heavy - some were in boxes and some were separate. Benjamin soon learned to lift the separate weights one at a time and the boxes were moved by two men together.

It became apparent that both Rich and Lenny paced themselves. Rich spoke little and Lenny never stopped talking or laughing. Benjamin said as little as possible. At 9 pm they took a break for supper when they went to a room that had a couple of vending machines for soda and snacks and ate their supper. Benjamin didn't think that far ahead and didn't bring a sandwich.

"Hey, kid, didn't you bring anything to eat?" said Rich.

"No, I guess I forgot," said Benjamin.

Rich tore a small piece of his large hero sandwich and gave it to Benjamin. Lenny didn't look up and just kept tearing into his sandwich.

Benjamin had some money, so he bought several bags of chips, pretzels and cookies as well as a soda and wolfed the junk food down.

Rich said, "Tomorrow make sure you bring food, kid. There's a diner a block from the plant that has pretty good food and you can get a sandwich there to bring. You are coming back tomorrow, ain't you?"

With a mouth filled with pretzel mush, Benjamin replied, "I'll be here."

At 2 am, a loud buzzer went off and the men stopped working. There were still two pallets of equipment that were not yet loaded. Benjamin wondered what would happen since the foreman said they had to load them all onto the trucks.

"Uh, what happens now. We didn't get finished," said Benjamin.

Lenny said, "Don't worry, man. We never get it all packed. They'll send the four trucks off tomorrow, and we'll finish the last one tomorrow night."

The three men walked outside. There was a maintenance man still inside and he would lock up. Benjamin said good night to the other two men and walked in the opposite direction toward his motel. After a couple of minutes, he heard that wild laugh that he now recognized. It seemed to echo off the walls of the factory and went down the dark street. He smiled. He was totally exhausted but felt like he accomplished something important tonight. He got through his first night on his first job. He made it. He was now a man.

CHAPTER 72

Benjamin awoke at a little past 10am and was still feeling sleepy. However, hunger was more of a need than sleep right now. His supper of a small piece of Rich's sandwich and several bags of snacks were long ago digested and his stomach yearned for food. He got up, washed his face, put on a t-shirt and pants and walked outside to find the diner that Rich spoke about last night.

He walked past the plant where he could hear the noise outside as the barbells and equipment were being manufactured. When he got a block and a half past the plant, he saw a shiny silver diner with a flashing sign that read, "Open 24 hours."

Benjamin walked up the short stairway and pulled open the glass door. Inside was a counter with silver stools with red plastic coverings on the round tops. The counter was almost full, but he saw an empty stool next to a burly middle-aged man smoking a cigarette. He climbed up on the stool and sat waiting for the waitress to come over to him. There was a plastic enclosed container with pastries, turnovers and cupcakes blocking part of his view. The smoke from the guy next to him made his eyes burn.

He began to feel nervousness and realized he was swiveling back and forth on the round seat. He became self-conscious and stopped his joyride. He then began to cough and as much as he tried, the cigarette smoke was causing him to hack more and more. His eyes were now tearing as his convulsive coughing increased. He looked over at the man seated next to him and all he could see was a huge upper arm with a tattoo of a crucifix wrapped with yellow flowers.

The waitress behind the counter leaned over and asked, "What can I get you, honey??

Benjamin spotted her name on a card pinned to her uniform. It said, "Bernice."

"Uh . . ." the young man hesitated, trying to think of what he wanted to satisfy his hunger which was now lessened by the continued smoke that seemed to head directly into the lad's face. More coughing followed and his eyes now were ready to overflow and spill onto his cheeks.

Just then he felt a hand on his arm.

"I got him. He's going to sit in one of my booths."

Benjamin turned to look into the blue eyes of the most beautiful girl he had ever seen. She was young, maybe a couple of years older than Benjamin. She pulled gently at his arm and he walked with her, as if in a trance. She led him to a booth by a window and the youth sat down on a bench covered with the same red plastic as the counter stools.

"Hi, I'm Bonnie. Don't you just hate that smoke? I know I do. Now, what can I get for you?" she said smiling.

Benjamin was dumbfounded and, although his coughing had stopped, he could not speak. He just looked into her eyes and face. He noticed she had round, freckled cheeks and an amazing smile.

She said, "Hey, take your time. Check out the menu and I'll be back in a few minutes." With that, she winked at him and walked to another booth to ask the patrons if they wanted more coffee.

Benjamin could feel his heart racing. It felt like it had moved from his chest up into his throat. He couldn't take his eyes off of her. He just watched her as she went about her job and poured coffee and went from booth to booth.

Soon she returned to him and asked, "Well, did you decide what you want yet?"

The young man just stared at her. He hadn't even looked at the menu. He gave no thoughts to eating at all. He felt foolish and noticed that his face got warm, and he was sure he was turning red.

Bonnie leaned over and reached for a menu. As she did so, her chest touched Benjamin's arm and he inadvertently looked down her blouse. He quickly turned away before she might see him and get angry. Now his face was on fire. What if she would be revolted by him? All the girls he ever knew acted like Benjamin had a contagious disease. They would either act disgusted or laugh derisively at him.

The young waitress did neither. She smiled warmly as she handed him the menu. Benjamin took the menu and smiled back.

"Take your time. I'll be back in a while. You know, the waffles are really good here. Lots of calories so I can't eat them. I have to watch my figure, you know. But you can enjoy them," she said.

As he opened the menu, the youngster noticed that his hands were shaking. He had to get himself under control or Bonnie would probably start laughing at him like all the other girls did. When she returned, he still hadn't really thought about what he would order. He did read the menu, but it was only words, none of which penetrated his mind.

He stammered, "I guess I'll have those waffles you told me about."

The brown-haired young woman pleasantly said, "Oh, you'll love them. Do you want the works - strawberries and whipped cream? The strawberries aren't fresh. Their just strawberry preserves but they taste surprisingly good and it's real whipped cream."

Benjamin smiled and said, "That sounds good."

For the rest of the meal, he found his eyes kept going to the waitress as she worked her area. Whenever there was a chance she might look up at him, he diverted his eyes to the window and acted as if he had been looking outside the entire time.

When his meal was finished, Bonnie came back with the check.

"I guess you liked it, huh?" Bonnie said as she looked down at the plate which had only small evidence that it earlier contained food.

"It was really good," said Benjamin. "Thanks."

She smiled again at him and winked as she said, "You come back now, okay?"

"Okay," he barely got the word out as his throat seemed to close up.

He left a tip that was well in excess of the usual 15% and went to the register to pay. After he did, he looked back to see if he could see Bonnie. She was working at another table and was smiling at the new customers.

But Benjamin was sure the smile was not as bright as when she smiled at him.

He walked back to the motel room with a bounce in his step. As he walked past the barbell factory, he looked at it and smiled. You know, this is working out well. Really well.

CHAPTER 73

Jimmy awoke with a start. He sat up suddenly and felt damp and cold as the sweat on his face and t-shirt cooled his skin. He had one of those dreams again. That weird looking kid - round face, broad nose and big glasses - was the only thing he could remember from it but, for some reason, the visage disturbed him greatly.

Who was this kid? His face was appearing in more and more of his dreams. Even though this last dream left no memory of what event took place, it obviously was something sinister and there was something about that face that disturbed him. No, it frightened him. He had no idea who he was or where Jimmy had seen him before in real life.

Maybe it was in a photo in a newspaper? Maybe it was someone he passed on the street and for no good reason, he was imprinted on Jimmy's brain. Wherever he had come across that kid - he looked like a teenager around Jimmy's age - the face was burned into his subconscious. He wished there was some way he could keep him out of his dreams, but he had no control over the content of his nightmares.

It was a bit early for him to get out of bed, but he knew he would not be able to fall back to sleep nor did he want to because he had to get up in about half an hour and it would only make him more sleepy to wake up after such a short sleep. He also felt uncomfortable due to his wet shirt, so he decided just to get out of bed and get ready for school.

He was now a senior and school was close to the end. He would soon be graduating and moving onto college. He had done well on his SAT's and had a choice of several schools. Going away to college kind of made him uncomfortable so he had decided to stay home and go to St. John's University in Queens which was close to home. He could keep his boyhood friends and still meet new people at school.

He wasn't overly excited about the beginning of college once summer was over. It just seemed like another step, another school. Some of the guys at Holy Name were all eager about going to a college in September but, for whatever reason, Jimmy was not. He had been working part time in a department store for the past few months and that would continue. It just didn't seem to be much of a change. The biggest change would be taking a different set of city buses to school.

He got up and began to wash his face and brush his teeth. He stared into the bathroom mirror and looked at several new pimples that had popped up during the night. Fortunately, he didn't have to shave everyday so he could avoid the inevitable bleeding that took place when the razor took off the tops of some of his acne bumps. He put some colored pimple cream on the new ones as well as some of the bigger ones that had been there for a while. He wasn't sure if this paste did anything but bring more attention to the red blemishes which now were covered with the tan goop.

Jimmy got dressed and went downstairs for breakfast. His mother was at the sink where she seemed to spend so much time that her son often spoke to her back.

"Good morning! Aren't you up early?" said his mother without turning around. She had some kind of sense that seemed as if she could see from the back of her head.

"Good morning, mom. I just woke up a little early without my alarm this morning," said Jimmy.

"Would you like some hot farina or some eggs?" said his mother who perpetually tried to get Jimmy to eat a substantial breakfast which hardly ever worked.

"No, mom, I'll just have a piece of toast and some juice." said Jimmy.

His mother made another attempt to get Jimmy to eat a worthwhile breakfast, but it was a lost cause. After eating his toast and butter and drinking a big glass of orange juice, Jimmy carefully opened the back page of the newspaper to see last night's baseball scores. Since his father didn't want anyone to touch his newspaper before he read it Jimmy had become proficient at opening the back pages and reading the scores without any disturbance to the paper. His father had not yet entered the kitchen, so Jimmy was able to quickly read the sports information and put the paper back in its pristine condition.

Just then his father entered and grunted a good morning to Jimmy and his wife. Jimmy's sister, Ann, had not yet gotten up. Ann liked to sleep and had to be awakened several times before she got up. Since she didn't have to leave until after Jimmy had left, they often did not see each other in the mornings since Jimmy had started high school.

Jimmy took his time getting his book bag together, but he was still ready earlier than usual. There was nothing else to do so he said his goodbyes to his mother and father and headed for the public bus. It was about a three-block walk to the bus stop. When he got there the bus pulled up within a few minutes and Jimmy showed his pass, dropped in his nickel and went to the back of the almost empty bus. The bus would get very crowded about halfway on the forty-five-minute ride, but Jimmy always got a seat when he got on.

He sat back and looked out the window at the sidewalks and the hustle and bustle of the people heading to school and work. The sun caused his face to be reflected on the glass of the window and he began to look into the image that stared back at him. Suddenly, the face morphed into the face of that strange boy who had invaded his dreams so often. Jimmy continued to stare and could feel the tiny hairs on the back of his neck rise up like an army ready to do battle with his increasing anxiety.

His breathing increased and he could feel his chest rise and fall with each breath. The face in the window seemed to acknowledge Jimmy and a malevolent grin began to form - wider and wider. Jimmy saw oversized teeth that had large deposits of greenish plaque germinating down from the gums. The eyes were widening and a strange clicking laugh that was devoid of humor came forth from the glass.

A baleful moan escaped from Jimmy's mouth. He had no control over this woeful sound, and it became louder and louder. Finally, Jimmy forced his face from the window and broke the spell. He turned to see several people sitting around him gawking at him. A man sitting in the seat in front of him was turned around and asked him if he was alright. Jimmy just nodded and the man turned back to face front and slowly the others went back to their own reverie. In New York, people on public transportation were used to strange happenings with fellow passengers.

Jimmy's breathing slowly went back to normal but now he was afraid to look out of the window. For the rest of the ride to school he looked straight ahead and thought about who this terrifying face belonged to. He had no clue, but he realized that this would not be the last time this young man would enter his mind and somehow someway he would have to find out who this was and how he could be stopped.

CHAPTER 74

Soon high school ended for the year and forever. Jimmy had graduated and summer flew by. He was busy with his part time job at the department store during most nights and Saturdays and playing stick ball with his buddies most days. As the summer drew to a close, there was a melancholy that grew stronger with each passing day as he walked to the playground with a couple of his pals to play with a stick and a pink rubber ball. He didn't really understand it but deep down inside, he knew that this phase of his life was ending.

His life had been basically made up of going to school and playing some kind of ball in the streets or at the playground. Whether it was stick ball, punch ball, basketball, street hockey or touch football, sports and hanging out with the guys was his life. But, without actually thinking about it, he knew in his heart that these games would soon be ending as adulthood was beckoning.

He was nervous on his first day of college. He was still too young to drive so he had to take two city buses to St. John's University, a ride that took up to 2 hours depending upon how well he connected with the buses and adding a walk of about a mile from home to the first bus. The campus was crowded with young people rushing in all directions that first day. There were long lines in the registrar's office where they tried to resolve errors in class assignments. Fortunately, Jimmy had his schedule ready and headed for the building where his first class in college would take place.

The one thing that Jimmy noticed more than anything else was girls. He had spent four years in all-boys Catholic Schools and was not used to seeing girls at school. He hadn't even thought about it before but now that it was upon him, it was all he could think about. It was 1965 and girls wore skirts that stopped at mid-thigh or higher. It took concentration for the young man to keep from crashing into anyone in the crowded hall on his way to his first class.

This distraction only got worse or at least more intense as he sat in his first college class - French. Jimmy had only two years of French in high school but due to his extraordinary ability on entrance exams was placed in French Level 5. Not only were there mostly pretty girls in his class but the teacher was a young, beautiful blonde woman in her twenties who sat on the desk with her legs crossed. Jimmy was dumbstruck which was made even worse when the class was conducted completely in French, and he had absolutely no clue was to what was being said.

He sat for forty minutes staring at the teacher's smiling face and tried to keep his eyes from gawking at her long, shapely legs. The bell rang and Jimmy rose from his seat and then realized he had no idea what the assignment was. He turned to the young woman behind him and asked for help.

"Uh, I'm sorry but I missed what Miss Boucher gave us as an assignment," asked Jimmy.

The dark-haired girl who wore glasses and seemed a bit older than Jimmy replied, "She ran off copies of a few pages of Balzac's, "Le Pere Goriot," which we have to translate into English by Friday. They are on her desk."

Jimmy thanked the young woman, never thinking that it would be a good idea to ask her name. He would need her help many times in the next few months just finding out what the assignments were but Jimmy's lack of female contact up to this point made him very shy around girls.

He walked up to the front of the room where Miss Boucher remained seated on the edge of the desk, talking to several students in French. Jimmy saw a pile of papers on the desk and students were picking up copies. He smiled at the teacher who never looked at him and he glanced at the papers. They were all the same, so he took one and walked out of the classroom.

His first class in his college career was over. He hoped that American History which was next on his schedule would at least be in English!

CHAPTER 75

Most of Jimmy's other classes that first day were relatively mundane. The professors mostly talked about the syllabus and the assignments and goals of the class. By the end of the first day, he felt slightly overwhelmed but also confident that he would make it through. Academics were never particularly difficult for him. What was hardest was putting in the time and effort to get good grades.

As he rode the bus to his part time job at the department store, he realized that activities outside of school, homework and his job were going to be kept to a minimum. However, it didn't seem to bother him terribly. Although he was only seventeen years old, he was ready for this next step in his development to manhood.

As he began the third week of school, he began to feel somewhat isolated. He hadn't made any new friends in any of his classes. He ate alone in the cafeteria, and he hated that. He missed hanging with friends as he ate his lunch. He would sometimes reminisce about sitting in the cafeteria with Tony and Ralph at Sacred Heart. Thinking about Ralph would make Jimmy melancholy, but his mind often visited there. He would picture that sad face and realize that Ralph was no longer living, and his eyes would well with tears.

He finally decided to force himself to sit with some people during lunch to break this dismal lunch break. As he walked through the cafeteria, he saw a guy who was in his English class. He was sitting with three other guys, and they were talking and laughing. Jimmy walked over and asked if he could join them.

The fellow that was in Jimmy's class introduced the others but realized he didn't know Jimmy's name. Jimmy laughed and said he didn't know the other guy's name either. An awkward moment turned into one of amusement and, after the introductions, the new acquaintances shared some basic biographical information. As his college years continued, these four guys would be among his best friends. Finally, Jimmy could laugh, relax and talk about the present without drifting back into the sorrowful past.

College became much more than simply school as it had been in high school. The classes were much more interesting, although the work involved much more time and application. However, the best part was the social life. Drinking age in New York was eighteen and Jimmy was almost a full year away from his eighteenth birthday. But fake identification cards were available and checking them in local college bars was cursory to say the least.

The most popular hangout was Poor Richard's Pub right outside the St. John's campus. This became Jimmy's hangout after school on many days. He would only drink one beer because he had to get to work in a couple of hours, but it gave him a place to see his buddies and meet more people. Here they would share events of the day and exaggerate their lives to embellish stories. They not only knew most of the tales were more fantasy than reality but enjoyed the hyperbole of the narratives. It became almost a contest to see who could relate the most fantastic yarn that had some semblance of reality. It was usually the high point of the day.

Between classes, the pub and his part time job which lasted until almost 10 pm there was little time for homework. Even though Jimmy was bright, this lack of effort on assignments took its toll and his grades were barely passing. His parents were furious when his first semester report came home. It was worse when his second semester report arrived, and Jimmy's grades were lower than the first semester.

He did pass his courses, however, and after much shouting and threats of punishments, Jimmy was able to get through his first year in college without any scars. He was enjoying life, much more so than at any other time. High school was mostly painful and confusing. Although he really had no career goals yet, he was happy at school and with his new friends.

There was one flaw in his contentment with life. That was the continuing distress of his dreams. They didn't happen every night. Indeed, sometimes weeks would go by without the suffering caused by these nightmares and frightening daydreams. But they still occurred and, when they did, they would affect him for days. There was one character who appeared regularly, and Jimmy had no idea who he was. But his face was burned into Jimmy's brain and the countenance unnerved him. In reality, it terrified him.

CHAPTER 76

As these visages continued, they seemed to be developing. Slowly, they seemed to be adding to a storyline. At first, the face of the young man would just appear and then fade away. Then his presence would last longer and longer. Each time the manifestation would cause Jimmy to become upset and anxious.

Then the youth would be in a setting that was not recognizable. At times, Jimmy would only see the back of his head. Then it would slowly turn and face him. A spine-chilling grin would emerge on this face and a weird sound - like a clicking noise - would rise up from his throat. This reverberation would escalate the fear and panic in Jimmy and sometimes cause him to begin to moan. Even though he was in a dream state, he could hear and even feel his mournful cries. This, too, just heightened his dire dread.

Who was the young man? And why did the appearance of his face cause Jimmy to feel both fear and angst? As the dreams evolved, Jimmy soon found out why. The development of these visions accelerated with each event. At first, he only saw his face. Then the sound was added to the fantasy. The first time there was any actual activity, it was frightening.

One night as Jimmy began to fall asleep and was in that dreamy, pre-sleep state, the face appeared. This time, however, he saw him walking. Then he heard screaming - screaming that made his spine shiver with horror. In the youth's hand was a knife. Not a pocketknife or a small paring knife but it was what looked like a long and thick hunting knife.

The screams he heard seemed to be from more than one person, but he could not make out any clear speech - just horrific voices that sounded so terrified that they caused Jimmy to begin to moan. His arms became stiff and extended. His hands flexed furiously, first tightening into a fist and then his fingers stretched out until they felt like they would just burst from his hands. As this hand response continued back and forth, his legs began to stiffen, and both his feet and his head pushed down onto the bed and his pelvis began to rise up.

Then the vision focused on the young man's face which grew and grew until Jimmy was looking directly through the man's glasses into his eyes. Jimmy could actually smell his stale and putrid breath and the clicking sound got louder and louder. His moaning grew - Jimmy could hear himself. As he became conscious that he was in some kind of nightmare, he forced himself to awaken.

He jumped up in his bed. His pajamas were soaked through with perspiration. His breathing was short and rapid, and he quickly looked around the dark room, fearing he might see the face. He reached over for the lamp on his nightstand. He turned it on and slowly moved his head from left to right and looked around his room, fearing that the face would appear. But it was gone.

He then flopped back down on his bed and took a deep breath while looking up at the ceiling. He felt so cold as the sweat began to evaporate and his nerves reacted to what he had just gone through. His whole body began to shake, and he could feel his hands and legs ache as the muscles relaxed after the intense workout they had just gone through.

Why was he being tormented by this person? Who was he and what connection did he have to Jimmy? Was he just a nightmare or was he a real person? Deep down inside, Jimmy already knew the answer. But he was afraid to admit it, even to himself.

CHAPTER 77

Benjamin fell into a comfortable routine. His job was mundane and often physically exhausting, but he had adjusted well. In truth, he realized that he had gotten stronger as he spent the nights lifting heavy boxes which seemed less heavy as his strength increased. The constant jabbering by his co-workers became entertaining.

Lenny's talking was non-stop. It was like having a radio on. He and Rich went back and forth verbally but often Rich would just back off and let Lenny go on and on. Benjamin said little and just listened and went about his job. He had become a decent worker and he often let his thoughts go elsewhere - often he thought about Bonnie whom he saw almost daily at the diner.

Whenever he pictured her in his mind's eye, he could feel his heart begin to race and a stirring take place inside him. Lenny's voice was background noise as Bonnie's face appeared in his contemplations. Sometimes he would allow his imagination to portray a scenario with both Bonnie and he. At times, they might be at the diner and Bonnie would sit down with Benjamin and they would talk and laugh together. At other times, the drama would entail a venue outside of the diner. This time they are walking in a field and holding hands, looking into each other's eyes, their faces coming closer, lips about to touch . . .

"Hey, are you deaf or what?" Lenny yelled at Benjamin.

"I'm talking to you. Are you on another planet, man?"

Benjamin left Bonnie and blinked as he saw Lenny standing in front of him with a quizzical expression on his face.

"You had a weird look on your face, and you didn't move for a while. I thought maybe you were going to kiss that box on the flat," Lenny said. He started his staccato laughter that sounded like a lawn mower engine trying to start up.

"Hey, leave the kid alone, Lenny," said Rich. "I don't blame him for daydreaming. He gets to leave this place for a few minutes, and he doesn't have to listen to the constant sound of your annoying voice. Besides, it's almost quitting time. I'll be glad I don't have to listen to your bullshit anymore."

Benjamin said nothing. His mind went again to Bonnie. He could only hope that he could continue his daydream when he got back to his room. He did dream when he got back to his room but this time it was far from pleasant.

After falling asleep, Benjamin began to dream. He did see Bonnie and the dream was so similar to the reverie at the factory. Bonnie was walking in a field that looked just like the one in Benjamin's earlier daydream. She was walking hand in hand with him. She turned to face her companion. And this time, they kissed.

Benjamin could feel his heart flutter and he was filled with excitement and joy. He kissed his Bonnie! He realized that he loved her. Loved her like he never loved anyone before. They would be together. They would marry. They would have a family.

The kiss lasted for what seemed like an eternity. Finally, the kiss ended, and their lips slowly separated, a bit at a time. He saw Bonnie's smiling face. She loved him, too! He could see it in her eyes. All the pain, all the suffering, all the indignation he had felt throughout his young life - it was now going to change. The scene shifted from Bonnie's face and slowly turned to his face.

It was then that all his hopes and dreams, all his joy was stomped out and destroyed. He saw his face. But it wasn't his face. It was the face of another man. A handsome young man with dark, wavy hair and high cheekbones. He had deep blue eyes that seemed electric as they contrasted with this dark hair and tan skin.

He had seen this man before or, at least, he seemed familiar. He hated him, loathed him, wished him dead. Then the dream continued, and the couple walked off into a grassy field holding hands. And the clicking began. At first it was deep within his chest. Then it rose and became louder. Soon it was so powerful that Benjamin awoke from the turbulence that he was now producing.

He sat up, his chest heaving with a panting breath. His mouth was dry yet there was a sticky foam dripping from the corners of his mouth. He wiped the slime on the sleeve of his pajama top. When his breathing became close to normal, he arose from this bed and walked into the bathroom and turned on the light which consisted of a light bulb with a broken glass shade.

He looked at his reflection in the mirror. Without his glasses on, his face was out of focus so he moved closer to the mirror until he could make out the countenance staring back at him. The man in his dream was handsome and the face looking back at him was ugly. He had a broad, flat nose, thin lips and yellowed, discolored teeth.

Of course, Bonnie wouldn't find him attractive, never mind falling in love with him. What a fool he was! He became angrier and angrier. He was angry at the man in his dream. He was angry at Bonnie. But most of all, he was angry at himself. He allowed himself to feel love for another. That would never happen again.

Then he began to cry.

CHAPTER 78

Friday arrived and work was the same as usual. Lenny was excited that the weekend was upon them and Rich, too, seemed in a happier mood than usual. Benjamin was quiet, even more so than his customary taciturn self. Lenny tried to engage him several times but gave up and went into his jabbering mode for most of the night.

When work ended his co-workers made for the exit even quicker than usual, but Benjamin lagged behind, not being anxious to head to his motel room. The walk home was somber, and his feet seemed to drag on the pavement. When he arrived at his dismal room, he slowly unlocked the door and could smell the stale, musty odor that always greeted him.

After locking the door behind him, he moved carefully in the dark to his nightstand and switched on the small table lamp. The bulb propelled a harsh light that momentarily caused his eyes to squint and it took a moment for them to focus. The first sight he observed was a greasy stain on the faded wallpaper behind the bed. There was a matching stain above the headboard on the other side of the bed. He turned and plopped down on the bed, sitting on the mattress edge, his feet on the floor and his head and shoulders slumped over.

It was now Saturday. People were looking forward to a weekend of fun, spending time with those they loved. Benjamin was all alone in the world and the one person he had dreamed about having a relationship with was with someone else. He would never find someone who loved him, who cared for him.

He fell back onto the bed and without removing his shoes or his clothes, he curled up into a fetal position, closed his eyes and yearned for the escape of sleep. He did fall asleep but freedom from anguish was not to be. He soon began to dream but he did not dream about Bonnie. He did not dream about his job or the guys at work.

He saw a face. A young man's face. It was familiar. He realized he had dreamt of him before. But this time, the face spoke to him.

"I know what you have done, Benjamin," the voice said in a clear and not unpleasant tone.

"I know you killed those boys in the train yard. I know you killed your father. You are a murderer. And you will murder again," the young man stated with no emotion and without recrimination.

The man was in his late teens, had short light brown hair, blue eyes and a wistful expression on his countenance. He did not seem to judge Benjamin nor accuse him as much as he was stating a fact.

"You must be stopped. You must be stopped," the young man repeated this over and over, each time a bit quieter until Benjamin could no longer hear his words but only saw his face and his lips moving.

Benjamin awoke with a start. He quickly sat up in bed. His breathing was rapid, and he could feel his heart beating in his chest. Who was this? He looked somewhat familiar. How did he know about the murders? Would he report Benjamin to the police? He said that Benjamin had to be stopped. No, this young man, he had to be stopped. Somehow, someway, Benjamin would find him and put an end to this. No, he, the young man, he would be stopped.

Chapter 79

Benjamin fell back asleep. This time, however, he didn't dream, or at least, he didn't remember any dreams. His sleep was deep and continued until almost three in the afternoon. When he awoke, he still felt tired and not even hungry, although he usually would have eaten by now. He turned on the TV and watched several boring children's programs, followed by an old black and white movie about aliens that looked like gorillas wearing diving helmets. It was worse than bad, but it fit his mood.

He was bored, sad and felt sorry for himself. Then he got up and went to the bathroom. He looked into the mirror and when he saw himself, his thoughts went to Bonnie and his eyes welled up with tears. But they were tears of anger and his face grew red and puffed up and finally the fury reached his right arm and without thought, he punched the mirror with his fist. The mirror which was the door of the medicine cabinet instantly cracked in all directions from the impact. Benjamin looked down at his fist and smiled. He felt power. His chest swelled as his head leaned back and laughter emerged from his lips.

They would pay for his pain. Bonnie and that man she was with in his dream. Benjamin would return the pain they inflicted upon him. He would find out who that guy was and return the favor. The pretty young woman who he felt love for only yesterday, was now an enemy, a hated enemy. And he would show them both that he was not to be made a fool of. He began to plan.

This idea excited him. He had been lethargic and felt weak. Now his veins pulsed with his power. He sat on the edge of his bed and took a pad of paper that was on his nightstand and, with a dull pointed pencil he began to write his course of action. First, he would have to follow Bonnie home and see where she lived. Then he would hide and wait for the boyfriend to show up. It was Saturday and tonight surely, he would be taking his lover out on a date. Then he would . . . What would he do next? He couldn't follow them. They would certainly be driving in a car. He had no car. He couldn't follow on foot. His plan was not complete, but Benjamin was not about to let it die.

He suddenly realized he was hungry. Yes, hungry and what better way to satisfy his hunger than go to the diner? She worked on Saturday afternoon. He would see her, and she would act like she liked him. But he saw through that now. The bitch would serve him his lunch and then he could follow her to her home to see where she lived.

What he would do after that he didn't know yet. But he felt confident that the plan would come together. She cheated on him. He would take care of her and her boyfriend. Take care of them good. Benjamin felt rejuvenated. Alive. Excited. And incredibly determined.

CHAPTER 80

Benjamin changed his clothes, not bothering to shower. He smelled under his armpits and yes, they stunk. Normally, he would shower and use a deodorant before seeing Bonnie at the diner but today he didn't care. No, he did. He wanted her to smell him. Smell him as he really is. The odor was raw, manly, powerful. It was how he felt, and it wanted her to feel it as well.

He went to his nightstand and took out the hunting knife that he had purchased weeks ago in a pawn shop. He wanted to have protection in his room because the lock on his door was weak and the neighborhood where the motel was had a reputation for violence. The knife was razor sharp on one side of the blade and had a serrated edge with deep notches on the opposite side of the blade. He pulled it from its sheath to examine it and gingerly felt the sharp edge with his thumb. A smile spread across his face as he slowly slid the weapon back into its scabbard and threaded his belt through the loop of the leather case.

He left his room and walked briskly toward the diner. Since the dream of his love cheating on him, his walk appeared as if he were almost skating, his sneakers barely above the pavement. But now, he walked proudly and with confidence. Soon he arrived at the diner and with no hesitation, opened the glass door and walked over to his usual booth. The diner was not too busy for a Saturday and having his regular booth available just added to his feeling of determination and sureness.

Soon, as if by design, Bonnie arrived at his table with her wide smile and bright blue eyes. Her perfectly formed white teeth almost shone as she said, "Hey, Benjamin, how are you today?"

Benjamin slowly looked up at her and he returned her smile with his own. "Oh, I am just fine. Just fine."

Something about his reply must have given Bonnie some kind of awareness that Benjamin's manner was not normal since her wide smile diminished ever so slightly, her eyebrows drooped a scintilla, and her eyes lost a shade of their sparkle. However, she continued brightly, "What's your pleasure today."

Benjamin, staring into her eyes, said, "Oh, what I want is not on your menu, but I'll have a grilled cheese sandwich and a large Pepsi."

Bonnie had a notion that something was different today about this strange young man who she always had felt somewhat sorry for. He seemed so alone and had so little going for him. He was so unattractive and had shared a bit about his life and his job. She didn't want to put it in those terms, but he was a loser. There was no pretense she could think of. Yet, she did feel badly that anyone had to live such a lonely and pathetic life. As a result, she always tried to be extra friendly since he probably had no friends.

She said, "I'll bring your Pepsi and get that sandwich going for you right away." Her smile returned to its full effect.

Benjamin said nothing. He just stared at her with his weird smile that was more of a grin. His stained teeth with yellowed tartar covering them gave him a ghoulish expression. Bonnie stood there for a moment unable to move. For the first time in all her many dealings with Benjamin, she was frightened. Finally, she forced some words out.

"I'll go get that Pepsi now," said Bonnie and she broke the spell and almost ran from the table.

She put in the order and then went to the soda fountain and filled a large glass with ice and Pepsi. She stopped and took a deep breath, feeling the need to compose herself before returning to that peculiar young man. She didn't know why but she felt personally threatened by that look in his eyes. She thought about it while holding the now frosting glass in her hand and then shook her head and smiled to herself. How foolish she was being.

She carried the glass to the table and placed it in front of Benjamin. She had intended to say something pleasant, but her throat seemed to close up and she gave him a quick smile and walked away. She could feel her spine tingle and the hair on her neck rise. Why was she allowing herself to be upset? She told herself she was being silly and went back to serving her other customers.

Benjamin sat sipping his cola slowly through a straw. He was in control. He looked out the window but did not see the parking lot or people walking by. He only could focus on revenge on those who hurt him and, as it had in the past, it made him feel strong and significant. He would show them. He would show them all.

CHAPTER 81

Benjamin finished his lunch and left his usual generous tip. Even though he was now filled with hatred for Bonnie, he didn't want her to be suspicious of any change in his demeanor. He went to the cashier and paid his bill and walked out without looking back to glance at the young woman whom he had loved only yesterday.

He walked back to his room and waited until close to 8 pm which was the time that Bonnie would end her shift. He wasn't even hungry which was surprising for him since he seemed to be in a constant state of hunger. But now his appetite was not for food but for vengeance.

He went straight to the eatery and waited across the street. He stared into the hardware store window, but his focus was on the reflection of the diner in the glass, not the tools and equipment that were displayed. He could see the two doors and watched patiently. The diner was busy as a number of people were entering for a late supper. Then finally, she emerged. Dressed in a simple pink dress, his former sweetheart began to head home.

She walked with a bounce in her step as if she were feeling lighter than air. Her arm which carried her pocketbook swung back and forth as if it were a pendulum that was in a fast forward mode. She was apparently in a happy mood and this just darkened Benjamin's temperament even more so. His breathing became more rapid, as if each sprightly step she took synchronized with his hyperventilation.

He trailed about a block behind her, stopping occasionally to keep the distance from dwindling. They soon left the main avenue and walked several blocks in a residential area. She suddenly turned and opened a gate to a short picket fence and walked up the steps to a modest house.

Benjamin froze and watched as she took a key from her pocketbook and opened the door and entered. For a moment he felt awkward and obvious. It was beginning to get dark, but the twilight exposed him to anyone who might be watching. So, he observed the address and the house and continued to walk. As he passed the white house with blue shutters, he spied upon a tall hedge in the adjoining yard and made a mental note of it.

He then continued to walk down the street, not sure of what his next move might be. The sky continued to darken and soon night was falling. He was now several blocks past Bonnie's house and turned around and began to walk back.

By the time he reached her house again, night had fallen. There was only a sliver of a moon, so darkness had enveloped the neighborhood. He passed the white house without even looking at it. He felt nervous and was fearful that some nosy neighbor might be seeing him going by again. Once he reached the end of the block, he stopped and looked back. The street was dead quiet. All he could hear was the chirping of crickets. He took a deep breath and turned around and headed back.

This time he walked past her house and quickly spun behind the tall bank of shrubs. There was a huge tree on the property next door that blocked anyone from that house seeing him, so he positioned himself between the hedges and the tree. He wedged himself into the bushes and could clearly see the front door of the house of his prey. Now he would wait.

After a while he tired of standing and sat down deep within the tall greenery, but he could still see the front door. The bed of pine needles was soft but slightly damp and he could feel his pants getting wet. But he didn't care. If his pants were wet and looked like he peed in his pants, why would he be embarrassed? The only person he cared about scorned him, humiliated him. He hated her. Hated her.

Soon a car drove up and parked right in front of her house. It was that guy. He was dressed in a casual button-down blue shirt and light beige chino pants. He walked with an air of joyousness and strolled up to the front door. Soon it opened and Bonnie leapt into his arms, and they kissed. For a long time. She turned and locked the door and they sauntered to the car. He opened the door for her, and she smiled at him. Benjamin could see her smile from where he sat. It was different than the smile she bestowed upon him at the diner. He had never seen her look so radiant and jubilant.

The car drove off and Benjamin sat, wet and deeply miserable. He leaned over toward the trunk of the nearest bush and curled up into a fetal position. He began to sob - quietly at first - and then louder. The cries came from deep within him. From his heart. No, from his very soul. There was no one. He was completely alone. Feeling a pain deep within him, he fell asleep.

Chapter 82

Benjamin began to dream. There he was again. That same young man. He was staring right at Benjamin and spoke with a low but powerful and serious voice, "I know what you did. I know you murdered those people." He wasn't physically imposing yet he frightened Benjamin. Frightened him intensely.

Who was he? What did he want from him? Benjamin didn't know the answers, but he did know that in some way he must find him and stop him from telling what he somehow knew. He was dangerous. He had to be dealt with.

Suddenly, he awoke all wet and sticky. He wasn't sure if it was from the wed shrubs and grass or sweat from the nightmare he just had. He was confused at first, not sure where he was or why he was lying within bushes outdoors. Then he remembered. He was watching Bonnie leave with her new boyfriend and, as his memory sharpened, he heard voices. He jerked his head and there they were. The car doors slamming shut must have awakened him. It was Bonnie and that guy.

The boyfriend walked around the car and put his arm around Bonnie's waist. They walked slowly up toward the door to her house. Bonnie leaned over and began whispering into the young man's ear. Then they both laughed as they slowly began to go up the steps to her front door. Benjamin jumped to his feet, contradicting his weight and lack of athleticism. He felt the knife in its sheath. He let the ridges of the handle rub his palm which somehow soothed him. He watched them ascend the steps, Bonnie giggling gently.

Benjamin rapidly moved from his fern lair. He began to walk briskly to the house, through the gate and up the steps. He pulled the knife from its scabbard as he approached the unsuspecting couple. Bonnie was the first to see Benjamin and she had a look of puzzlement on her face which quickly turned to horror as she saw the evil in his eyes.

The young man turned to see what had made Bonnie so fearful and immediately, Benjamin struck. He rammed the knife deep into the unsuspecting suitor's abdomen. The beau's eyes bulged, and his face showed an expression, not of pain but of bewilderment. He looked down at the hand which was up against his stomach. Then watched as Benjamin pulled out the long hunting knife and plunged it again and again and again into his belly.

Blood began to flood out onto Benjamin's hand and arm and all over the entryway. The young man fell to the concrete mortally wounded. Bonnie stood dumbfounded and opened her mouth to scream but no sound would emerge. She could only look at this pathetic creature whom she had tried to be cordial to at the diner.

A gruesome visage was before her. Benjamin began to drool, and his yellowed teeth were bared. A weird and inhuman clicking began to rise from his throat. Bonnie tried again and again to scream but only a slight squeak could be heard. Certainly, not enough to draw attention from behind the darkened windows of any houses in the neighborhood.

This monster in front of her seemed to pause and stand frozen before her. Seconds passed. Long seconds when decisions are made that change lives or, in some cases, end them. Then with suddenness and viciousness, the fiend struck. He forced the blade deep within the woman he had worshipped. He hated her now. His eyes glowed. The clicking sound intensified and became more rapid. He pulled the knife out and jammed it into her soft abdomen again. This time he ripped it upward hard and fast until her breastbone halted its ascent.

Bonnie began to fall, being held up only by the shaft within her. She looked up at her killer and with questioning in her eyes, softly spoke, "Benjamin?"

He pulled out the knife and the dead woman fell to the ground. He stood for a short time over the bodies and saw blood everywhere. Bonnie had fallen on top of her beau, and it seemed as if she was embracing him. Benjamin bent down and pushed her away from him and she rolled over onto her back. Her eyes were open, and she looked as if she were alive. Benjamin could almost hear her ask him what he wanted to order. But she was dead, and he knew it. And he was glad.

He glanced around and the street was quiet and dark. He had no idea that it was past 2 am and everyone was probably asleep. He stood over the woman he had given his heart to and felt, not sad, but satisfied that she could never love another.

With that he turned and began to walk home. He didn't care if someone saw the blood covering his shirt and pants. He returned the knife to its sheath and sauntered back to his room. He encountered no one on his way back and when he got to the motel he quickly showered and put all his clothes into a big, black plastic bag. He then went outside and threw the bag into a dumpster that was behind the Chinese restaurant next to the motel.

He went to bed and looked at the clock. It was 3:43 am. It was some night. He turned over onto his other side and said to himself, "Don't mess with Benjamin." A smile was on his face as he fell asleep.

CHAPTER 83

For Jimmy, his college years seemed to pass quickly. The four friends he met in the cafeteria, not only became closer as time passed but the five amigos decided to join a fraternity together and soon, they expanded their circle greatly. Several cliques combined to start a new frat on campus since none of the present ones seemed to fit into their personalities. They received permission from the university and became a chapter of a national fraternity.

Now the fun began. There were parties almost monthly at someone's parents' house. Usually, there was a finished basement and lots of alcohol available. Although some brothers arrived at these events without dates most would come with a girlfriend or a date for the night.

Jimmy felt pressured during the week before a scheduled party to bring a date. He didn't want to be one of the guys who showed up stag and sat around talking to other unattached guys all night. He would watch his frat brother, Paul, go up to a girl that he had never met before in the cafeteria and ask her to the weekend party. If he were turned down, he would just ask the next attractive girl who walked in. Jimmy couldn't be that bold and self-confident. No way. So, he would work on getting a date for an upcoming party for weeks and, if he failed, he would usually make an excuse and stay home.

Then it happened. During his junior year in college, he was out on a

Friday night two weeks before an upcoming party. He went to a club with one of his frat brothers. He really didn't want to go but felt he needed to try to find a date for the frat party. This would be another opportunity and time was running out. He was in a glum mood for some reason and told his buddy to pick out any girl he wanted to dance with, and he would dance with her friend.

Mike, Jimmy's frat brother, eyed a pair of girls dancing with each other. Mike had his eyes on the one girl who appeared to be Hispanic and had a large bust. Jimmy paid no attention to anyone on the dance floor but just stared into his glass on the bar.

Mike said, "Hey, how about those two?"

Jimmy didn't even look up and said, "Listen I am just not into it tonight. Pick out the one you like, and I'll dance with the other one."

Mike didn't need any further conversation. He jumped up and almost ran onto the dance floor. He asked the girl with the large bosom that was stretching out the fabric of her blouse to dance. She smiled and said okay. The other girl stood there for a moment alone and then began to walk off the dance floor.

Jimmy had been slow to move, not really wanting to dance with this girl or anyone tonight. But he felt sorry for her as she looked around self-consciously and headed back to her table. Jimmy came up to her just as she was about to sit down and asked her to dance.

She looked around a bit as if to see if a better offer was coming and then smiled and said, "All right."

The song that was playing ended almost as soon as they arrived, and they both laughed and began to dance when the next song started. Jimmy barely looked at the girl in front of him, dancing mindlessly. Several times he looked over at Mike who had a huge smile on his face and was gabbing away.

When the song ended, Jimmy said, "Do you mind if we sit this one out? I really am not in a dancing mood tonight."

The girl smiled and followed him to a table further away from the dance floor. Jimmy asked her what she was drinking and went to the bar to get drinks for both of them. When he returned, he put the drinks down and looked over at this girl closely for the first time. She lifted the glass and slowly sucked on the straw. When she finished, she looked up at Jimmy and smiled.

A jolt went through him. He never felt anything quite like it before. She had dark hair, a small nose, soft lips and green eyes. As he looked into her eyes, he was mesmerized. No words came forth. He could only stare.

Finally, she spoke. "My name is Jennifer, but most people call me Jenny." She seemed to wait for a response, but none was coming. Jimmy just stared.

"What's your name?' Jenny said.

A warm smile spread on Jenny's face as she waited for an answer. It seemed like time was frozen as the young man continued to gape at this beautiful girl before him.

"Hello! Anyone home?" said the girl.

Jimmy woke from his trance and blurted out, "Uh, Jimmy. Jimmy."

Then Jenny's smile grew, and she laughed. A laugh that was like a medicine for his stupor. Jimmy laughed as well. And he immediately knew. He knew he found her. The girl he would spend the rest of his life with. His forever love.

CHAPTER 84

The last two years of Jimmy's college experience flew by. The parties with his fraternity continued at least monthly. The academics became easier as he was able to take classes in his major which was English Literature. Finally, in mid senior year he was filling out his final semester schedule card and the course he and his frat brother, Mike, were taking as an elective-introduction to criminal justice-was closed. So, they sat at the frat table trying to find another elective that fit into that time slot.

Just then a couple of the girls who hung around the frat came over. They were elementary education majors and talked the guys into taking a health education class. They assured them that the class was easy, and a bunch of the girls were in the class and would help the two guys with assignments. This seemingly insignificant interaction became a life altering event. They signed up and eventually, while taking this class, Jimmy realized that this was what he wanted to do. He wanted to teach.

His relationship with Jenny continued and strengthened as time went on. They saw each other on Friday and Saturday nights and talked almost daily on the phone. Jenny even came to Jimmy's college when she had a day off from her job in Manhattan. There was little doubt that they were meant for each other.

Finally, in the early spring of his senior year, Jimmy made up his mind. He would bring Jenny to a special place and ask her to be his wife. He wanted this event to be extraordinary and felt, for some reason, that he had to make it some place that would be both memorable and demonstrated his love for her. Although his extreme fear of heights could paralyze him, after much research and deliberation, he decided that the Empire State Building in New York City would be the place.

He called Jenny and asked her if she would like to go with him on the upcoming Saturday to New York city and visit the Empire State Building. Jenny knew about Jimmy's phobia, but she did not understand the extent of it. She readily agreed. Saturday arrived and Jimmy picked her up at her house and drove to the subway station nearer to his home. Jenny lived right near the elevated train, but Jimmy knew that would be a problem for him. Every time he took the elevated train, he had a panic attack. Jenny thought that he wanted to take the subway because he was more familiar with its routes.

When they arrived in Manhattan, they had to walk several blocks to the Empire State Building. When it is close by, you cannot really appreciate the enormous height of this landmark of the city. They entered the huge lobby and got on the line to buy tickets to the top. Entering the elevator, Jimmy began to finger the small jewelry case in his pocket. He felt for it many times on the trip to the city but now the big moment was close to arriving and his hands were sweating as he rubbed the soft velvet box. The elevator rose with a speed that he had never experienced. They could feel the pressure of gravity pushing them toward the floor as the large enclosure sped upward. After some time, it stopped, and they realized they were only part of the way up! They had to enter yet another elevator to reach the top of the building.

They were on the 86th floor which is where the observation deck was. They could take another elevator to the 102nd floor to the top which had been Jimmy's original plan. But now he was already feeling an overwhelming sense of panic and made the decision that this would have to do. Most of the people seemed to get off here anyway so he said to Jenny, "Let's check out the view here."

Jenny was always agreeable, and she took her boyfriend's hand which felt cold and wet.

"Sure, let's see the city from above all the noise and traffic," said Jenny.

Jimmy began to breathe faster as they opened a door to the observation deck. There was a small walkway with gray cobblestones and then there was the view all around the top. It was open with a crisscross type of fencing to keep anyone from falling or jumping over the railing. The wind which didn't seem to exist in the city streets below was quite strong. It was a cool day, but the wind made it feel very cold. It didn't help that Jimmy's heart was racing and his breathing became more and more rapid.

Jenny let go of Jimmy's hand and ran to the wall and peered out with excitement. Jimmy was frozen to the spot where she left him and no matter how much he tried, his feet would not obey and take another step. He began to flip the little jewelry box around and around in his hand. He wanted so badly to run over and join his love. This was the time he had rehearsed in his mind over and over. He would go up to Jenny and then kneel before her and present the ring and ask her to marry him.

No way. He could not move. Jenny was so enthralled with the view at first, she didn't realize she had left Jimmy behind her. Then she turned to speak to him and finally realized he wasn't next to her. She turned around confused and saw her boyfriend standing frozen in place where she left him.

"Come here, silly. Look at this incredible view! I can see Central Park and the brochure said we can see the Statue of Liberty and the Brooklyn Bridge. I don't see them from this spot but if we walk around . . . ."

She stopped. Something was wrong. Jimmy looked ill - no, scared. His face seemed to be pleading with her. She slowly walked toward him with concern. She never saw this look before. It worried her. When she reached him, he seemed stiff and wide eyed.

"Jimmy, wants wrong, honey?"

No response.

"Jimmy, are you okay? What's the matter?" Jenny was becoming frightened.

"I . . . I can't go over there. I can't handle the height. I can't. Sorry, I . . . can't." Jimmy's eyes began to fill, and it looked as if he might start to cry.

"It's okay, honey. Let's go inside," Jenny said as she gently took his arm.

"No! I have to do something. It's important. I have to. Out here. Have to." pleaded Jimmy.

"What? It's okay. Let's go inside." said Jenny.

She pulled Jimmy's arm and tried to lead him to the entry to the gallery inside. But he wouldn't budge. He seemed nailed to the concrete tiles. Finally, he looked at her with imploring eyes. Jenny leaned over and kissed his cheek.

"I love you! Do you know that? I do. Let's go inside. I'm cold out here anyway. Please, Jimmy, for me?" Jenny said gently.

Jimmy looked one more time at the fencing on the edge of the observation deck, took a deep breath, hesitated, turned again toward Jenny and slowly nodded his head. He knew there was no way he could take even one step closer to the perimeter. With Jenny holding his arm tightly to her side with her head on his shoulder, they walked through a glass door and into the inside mezzanine.

They found a bench and sat down. Jimmy shook his head as his breathing began to slow down. He turned to Jenny and smiled with his eyebrows raised.

"I'm sorry, Jenny. I had this whole day planned and I blew it," said Jimmy.

"What do you mean? It's no big deal, honey," said Jenny.

"Oh, yes, it is, babe, But I am going to do something that I intended to do out there so it would be memorable," Jimmy said as he reached into his pocket.

He got up from the bench and knelt down before his girlfriend. He pulled out the little navy-blue box and, with shaking hands opened it and presented the ring to his love. Before he could say the words, Jenny screamed, "Yes! Yes! I love you!"

Without taking a second look at the ring, she grabbed Jimmy and kissed him. She then hugged him around his neck real hard.

She leaned back and looked at his beaming face and said, "Memorable? We'll never forget it. Never!"

When they returned home, they told Jenny's parents who loved Jimmy and then drove to his house to tell his mother. His father was still at work, but they couldn't wait. They then retreated to his room and began to make plans. They would get married the week after Jimmy graduated from college and since funds were quite low, they would honeymoon in eastern Long Island.

The life ahead was beginning to form, and dreams were becoming a reality.

However, there were other dreams that would not end. Jimmy continued to have dreams about that strange and frightening young man who seemed to murder and enjoy it. No monster in the movies could come close to comparing with the monster of his dreams. They were on a screen and were the product of fiction. This monster was personal and was real - very real. Jimmy had no doubt that this was not just a product of his imagination. No, this evil, soul-less being was alive and somehow, Jimmy knew deep within himself that eventually the two would meet.

The violence and evil of these nightmares seemed to grow in intensity. The most recent series were of this fiend murdering two young people - a man and a woman. The details of the murders became more and more clear with each ensuing apparition. The first one presented the vile young man coming upon the two young people and pulling out a knife. They progressed to project the unwary couple facing their stalker and being stabbed repeatedly. The blood - like a dark red spreading lake - covered the two bodies as they lay on what appeared to be a cement platform in front of a door.

The face of the demon also became clearer with each new vision. Soon he would turn toward Jimmy after completing the repulsive rampage and smile. And, always, there was that spine-chilling sound. The anomaly would reverberate a kind of clicking sound. It would begin slowly and with little volume. Then it would gain speed and power until it became as if it were a growl. It was inhuman and animal-like. No, it was not like any animal Jimmy had ever heard. It made his entire body freeze with unmitigated fear.

Although the ultimate fear that Jimmy felt each time one of these dreams took place, he knew that somehow, sometime, someway, he would be forced to face this demon and only one of them might survive.

CHAPTER 85

Graduation from college took place a week ago and today was Jimmy and Jenny's wedding day. They surprised their families and friends when they first arranged for the date. Being it was so soon after graduation, Jimmy didn't even have a job yet.

However, nothing was going to spoil or interfere with the celebration of their wedding. Jimmy had a small family and therefore was able to invite many cousins and friends. Jenny, on the other hand, had a large family with seven brothers and sisters. Her cousins were also from large families, so Jenny's side of the family dominated the guest list.

These kinds of details meant little to the couple whose only thoughts were about each other and how wonderful it would be to be man and wife and live happily ever after. The preparation for the wedding and reception went quickly and smoothly since neither of the young people spent much time anguishing minutiae that so many of their friends seemed to be caught up in. For them, the ceremony and party following were events to be remembered but the true meaning of the wedding was their commitment to each other. And that commitment was absolute.

The church that the wedding was held in was the Catholic parish that Jenny and her family had belonged to all her life. It was a small church in Brooklyn but, since neither Jenny nor Jimmy were regular attendees at Sunday Mass, the ceremony was merely something that was expected.

As was the custom, the groom was not to see his bride in her wedding dress prior to the wedding. Jimmy stood nervously at the altar with his best man, Mike, and waiting for his future spouse to appear. The organ was powerfully playing Handel's Wedding March and Jimmy took a deep breath as the rear door of the church opened.

There she was. She was the most beautiful sight Jimmy had ever seen. Glowing in her white dress with her dark, long hair in curls draped down each side of her face, Jennifer was beyond description. Icy goose bumps raced down the sides of Jimmy's neck and his spine shook. It was if an electric shock shot down from the top of his head through every vertebra of his back. His coolness that he had nurtured up to this point was totally gone. His mouth opened to allow for his rapid breathing and his eyes filled with moisture to the point of overflowing.

As Jenny walked up the aisle with her father, every eye in the church was on this radiant young woman. As she entered the sanctuary, her father kissed her cheek and presented her hand to her future husband. Jimmy now froze as if before him was an angel, his angel. Finally, Jenny gently guided Jimmy toward the priest while she giggled at his stupor. The young couple now stood before the cleric as he began the reciting of the marriage troth. He then turned to Jimmy and asked him to repeat the vows after him. Suddenly, Jimmy's eyes lost focus. He stared at Jenny but appeared to be looking right through her. This trance was something that Jenny had witnessed a number of times while dating him. She never could understand it but recognized the symptoms. This was different than his previous short-lived reverie when she first arrived at the altar. Jenny knew this was one of his frightening visions.

Jimmy began to perspire. Jenny shook his hand, lightly at first and then more vigorously. The priest at first did not notice anything different about the groom's expression since he was focusing on reading the vows aloud from his well-worn book of rituals. Finally, when the groom did not respond, the clergyman glanced at the young man and soon the priest's smile faded a bit as he noticed something was amiss.

"James?". the robed man said softly. When he received no response, he said his name again but a bit louder, "James "? Jenny began to show concern and called out to her future husband, "Jimmy!". The congregation slowly became aware of Jimmy's daze and most of them were smiling thinking it was merely stage fright or fear of marriage. However, a growing number began to show concern as Jimmy was not awakening from this frozen state.

His face now a combination of sweat and paleness continued to just stare into space. Then he began to moan. At first, it was barely audible. But with each passing moment, the lamentation grew in intensity. As the people in attendance could hear these woeful cries, concern spread. Just as Jimmy's father stood up, his son blinked once and then repeatedly. Jimmy smiled at his Jenny and then turned to the priest and said, "Father, could you repeat that?"

The break in tension and the understanding that all was returning to normal caused an almost discernible sigh of relief as Jimmy's father turned around smiling and shaking his head as he sat back in the pew. A few in the crowd felt the need to release some tension with mild snickering.

The priest repeated the groom's vows and the balance of the ceremony continued without a hitch. Jimmy kissed his new bride and looked deeply into her eyes. All was well now. The new husband and wife walked smiling down the aisle, nodding to friends and family as they exited the church. The reception followed without any further difficulties, although a few of Jimmy's friends teased him about freezing up on the altar.

"Hey, you almost chickened out up there, pal," said one of Jimmy's neighborhood buddies. Jimmy just smiled at these barbs and didn't explain how wrong they all were. He knew most everyone recognized that something occurred on the altar and presumed he just froze up. Only Jimmy knew that there was an uninvited guest at the wedding. That ugly monster had appeared to Jimmy and told him that he was not rid of him. Indeed, he would be moving in with him and his new bride.

CHAPTER 86

The first few weeks after the double murder of the young waitress and her beau were the talk of the town. Nothing like this had ever happened in this small Pennsylvania town. People began locking doors that were never locked. Women only went out in groups when walking alone at night when previously going out alone was not given a second thought.

However, as time went on, the story of the two young victims slowly disappeared from the nightly news on television and the local newspaper which was filled with details of the grisly murder and photos of the two young lovers went from front page news to a small column on page ten. Soon, it was not even a daily report since nothing new was discovered and repeating the same story over and over did not help sell newspapers.

The police investigated day and night for the first several weeks. However, as time went on, overtime for the small detective squad was cut back and the four plain clothes cops were back to investigating simple breaking and entering and the regular vandalism that took place almost every weekend. A dual murder such as this was something that no one on the force had worked on previously. In fact, the veteran pair of detectives had only one homicide in their experience and that one was when Charlie White shot his wife in a drunken rage over a leftover dinner six years ago.

Benjamin's first instinct after the murder was to quit his job and leave town as fast as possible. But, although he didn't like his job much, it was a regular paycheck, and he had a routine that he felt comfortable with. He was afraid that the police would soon be knocking on his door at the motel since he was sure diners recognized the crush he had on Bonnie. However, he soon realized that no one paid much attention to the quiet, fat young man who ate by himself and spoke to no one.

A few days after the murders, he began to relax and almost enjoy reading the accounts in the paper and watching the clueless reporters on the television news. He found himself yelling at the television and laughing aloud at their suppositions which were always way off the mark. One night a reporter would presuppose that the young couple were victims of a robbery gone bad. Another time the account was that it had been a case of mistaken identity. The idea that it was a jealous lover was dismissed early on by the police when, after questioning Bonnie's parents and the young man's family and acquaintances, it was obvious that neither had any previous relationships that would bring about such a violent reaction. Indeed, Bonnie had hardly even dated and hadn't gone out with a man since high school. And those dates were casual and never led to a relationship of any kind.

No, as each day passed, Benjamin felt more and more confident that he would not become a suspect. His reluctance to converse was working in his favor. He never spoke to anyone outside of work unless it was absolutely necessary. Even at work, he would listen to his two co-workers go on and on about the murders for the first couple of weeks afterward. He was tempted a few times to defend Bonnie when Lenny would make some off-color comments about her, but he kept his mouth shut. Soon the conversation at work moved onto other areas. It seemed like the entire town had completely forgotten about the young couple after a few months. Doors were soon left unlocked again. Women began to go out to stores alone in the evening.

One morning after he came back to his room after work as Benjamin sat on his bed and watched the early morning news on television, he realized there was no mention of the murders nor had there been for a couple of weeks. It was old news. He became conscious that the general public had the same sense as he did that murder wasn't such an unforgettable act. You think about it when it first happens. You concern yourself with it for a short period of time. But then you move on with life. Someone is dead. It happens every day. It's really not a big deal, is it?

CHAPTER 87

As the news returned from a commercial and began the sports report, Benjamin's eyes became heavy, and he fell into a deep slumber. Soon his snoring roared from his throat and would have awoken his neighbors if any of them would have been in their rooms at this time.

On one side of his room was Margarita, a middle-aged Hispanic woman who worked as a housekeeper for a much larger hotel in town. On the other side was Robert who may have been called by another name, but Benjamin never spoke to the man. He only knew his name because his mail occasionally was delivered to Benjamin's room. Since all three of them were long term renters, they used the hotel address to receive mail. Robert worked as a plumber's helper. Benjamin only knew that because he had seen the white van with "York Plumbing" painted on the side pick him up. Other than a simple nod of the head, the two men had no interaction. Since both Margarita and Robert worked the day shift and Benjamin worked at night, they seldom even saw one another.

Benjamin rolled over onto his side and his snoring stopped. Within a few minutes, his eyes began to flutter and within his sleep he found himself in an unfamiliar neighborhood. He was walking down a quiet tree lined street that had a cement sidewalk and tall multifamily houses on both sides of a wide roadway. The houses had different shades of light-colored brick and black metal fencing and railings on colored cement steps.

He stopped in front of one house and saw the number of building, 1610, in bright, brass-colored numerals. As his eyes focused on the integers the light brown door suddenly opened. A young man emerged from the building and Benjamin recognized him right away. It was that guy, the one who Benjamin had dreamed about many times. The guy who somehow knew that Benjamin was a killer.

The young man walked down the steps with a spring in his step, that is until he saw Benjamin. As their eyes met, his light, jaunted step changed to a slow and deliberate gait. He walked right up to the chubby, unkempt man and looked deep into his eyes as the space between them was a mere foot or less.

"I know what you have done," said the clean-cut young man in a slow and deliberate voice. His tone changed to a deep and foreboding modulation, "You are a murderer."

Benjamin felt a chill that racked his bones. Somehow, this man, this person who he had never met, somehow, he knew. He knew about the murders. He would reveal Benjamin's secrets. He would report the carnage he has carried out to the police. Benjamin would be jailed or maybe even executed. This young man had to be dealt with before he could notify the authorities. And he would. Benjamin knew he would go to the police.

He didn't know how this guy who he had never met had this knowledge. What he did know, without the slightest doubt, was that this good looking, dapper man before him, knew everything. He knew of the two boys that Benjamin killed. He knew that he had murdered his own father. He knew that he had butchered Bonnie and her boyfriend.

The young man slowly walked away and moved in a deliberate gait down the concrete sidewalk to the corner of the street and then slowly turned back to stare at him. Benjamin felt a chill go up his spine and his body shook. A car that was traveling down the street suddenly screeched to a stop when a child ran in front of it to retrieve a ball that had bounced into the roadway. Benjamin glanced at the car and saw the license plate which was orange and black and had "New York" on large letters across the top. His eyes again fixed upon the young man who was standing next to a tall, silver streetlamp. He saw the street sign. Seneca Avenue was in bold, black letters.

A slamming door startled Benjamin out of his deep sleep. He was covered in sweat and felt severely shaken. He walked to the window and looked out to see what the sound was. There was a big Pepsi truck coming to reload the soda machine in the hotel lobby.

As Benjamin turned from the window, his hands began to shake. Soon, his entire body quivered and trembled. He stumbled over to the bed and sat down to try to regain his composure. But he felt worse. Nausea soon overcame him, and he ran to the sink and vomited what was left of his dinner. But it wasn't enough. His stomach retched again and again. There was no food left but a yellow-green bile was regurgitated into the sink. Finally, after several dry heaves during which he felt like his stomach, itself, would be expelled, he began to recover. He moistened a towel to wipe his lips and remove the spew and saliva that remained.

He turned on the water faucet to rinse the vomit down the drain and then staggered back to his bed. He grabbed a scrap of paper that was part of an ad for a pizza shop nearby. He took a tiny pencil that had been sharpened down to a tiny fragment. Quickly, he wrote "1610 Seneca Avenue, New York". He then collapsed face down onto his bed and buried his face into the pillow. His breathing slowed down to normal, and his thoughts went back to that guy. This time he didn't fear him. This time he wasn't terrified. This time his anxiety was replaced with anger. Blazing outrage. He made a decision. One in which he had no doubt whatsoever. Now he would have to take this young man's life before he destroyed his own. How he would do it, he wasn't quite sure, but he would. He will kill him.

Chapter 88

Jimmy spent the summer desperate to find a job. He had decided in senior year that he would become a teacher. However, he had not taken the necessary courses for his New York State certification, so he went back to night school at St. John's to get the needed credits while working during the day and weekends at a series of jobs that were difficult to say the least. He worked delivering newspapers to high rise apartment buildings with an adult route, pumped gas during the day and on weekend nights, even tried selling pots and pans door to door. Between the jobs, classes at night and studying in between, Jimmy was incredibly busy, but he had a goal-he would become a teacher.

Finally, the semester ended, and Jimmy applied for his certification. However, teaching openings in the public sector were as rare as a white elephant. Jimmy and Jenny filled out applications everyday with either no response or a "There are no openings at the present time. Your application will be on file in case there is an opening in your field." That was a gentle way of saying, "Forget about it." The war in Vietnam was raging and, since teachers received a deferment, many young men became teachers in order to avoid the draft.

Then Jimmy saw an ad for an opening in a Catholic School in a tough section of Queens. When he called, he was told that it was for a sixth grade opening where the new teacher suddenly quit. He went for the interview and quickly saw several reasons why the new teacher had left. The area was run down with debris both trash and human on the streets and steps of broken-down houses. But it was a job and he would be teaching! Jimmy was quickly offered the position by the nun who was the principal and came home on cloud nine even though the pay was barely enough to survive on. He shared his news with Jenny who, as always, was enthusiastically supportive.

As they celebrated that night by splurging with a meal of Chinese take-out, Jenny had news of her own. Between bites of roast pork fried rice, she said she had something to tell Jimmy. She looked at her husband with some trepidation in her eyes. Jimmy could feel her anxiousness.

"What? What is it?" Jimmy exclaimed.

He looked into her eyes and Jenny hesitated.

"C'mon. Tell me! What? Are you okay?" Jimmy began to worry.

Jenny took a breath.

"We're going to have a baby!" she blurted out.

At first, there was no response from Jimmy. He just sat there looking at her. Jenny began to feel upset. Maybe Jimmy didn't want a baby, at least not yet. Maybe Jimmy didn't want a child at all. Maybe . . .

Then Jimmy's face exploded into a huge smile as he jumped up from his seat and hugged his wife so hard, she felt like he would crush her. After a few moments, Jimmy realized he was squeezing too hard and quickly released his wife.

"Oh, sorry. Did I hurt you?" Jimmy said. "I have to be more careful now," Jimmy said as he held his hands up as if to surrender.

Jenny laughed.

"Well, you did overdo it a bit, but you don't have to treat me like fine China now, you know," Jenny chuckled.

Jimmy sat back in his chair and looked at his beautiful wife. He loved her so much that it almost hurt. And now they would become a family of three. He thought about how his meager salary would have to be stretched even further. Then he realized that Jenny would have to quit her job sometime soon. The whole concept of this new addition was making Jimmy think about all the new responsibilities that would be thrust upon them. His elation began to turn into overwhelming concern.

Jenny saw the change in Jimmy's countenance and had her own sense of concern.

"What's wrong, Jimmy? Are you having second thoughts?" asked Jenny.

"Oh, no! I am just thinking about how the baby will change things. I am not going to make much money and you'll have to stop working soon and the baby will need clothes and furniture and there will be doctor bills and . . ."

Jenny cut him off.

"Stop! We'll have to take it one day at a time. Right now, let's be happy and finish our Chinese food before it gets cold. You know we might not be able to afford take out for some time after this," she said somewhat jokingly.

Jimmy took a deep breath and looked at the woman he loved. She was always the voice of reason. She could calm him down and bring his feet back onto the ground. And she was going to be a mommy! And he was going to be a daddy! Of course, that would mean everything could change for them. Maybe he could find a part time job after teaching. Maybe . . . He was doing it again but this time he caught himself. He laughed to himself as he scooped up some roast pork fried rice onto his fork.

He looked up at Jenny. Man, he sure loved that woman! She was his world.

CHAPTER 89

Jimmy absolutely loved his new job. The school was run down, and their budget was bare bones. There was no paper or mimeograph machine. However, the public school had to send a remedial teacher there once a week and she had a copying machine and allowed the classroom teachers to use it. Of course, there was still the paper problem.

The teachers found out that the church bulletin was run off every Saturday and there were stacks left over each Sunday. So, Jimmy would go into the church on Monday morning and pick up the bulletins which were printed on one side of a sheet of paper. He would bring them back to the school and share them with the two other lay teachers who were both young women. Then he could run off tests on the back of the bulletin. The only problem was the church was in a former Polish neighborhood which had now changed to about 90% African American. So, his tests were on one side and there was the week's Mass schedule on the other side – in Polish.

He enjoyed sixth grade because the children were old enough to have discussions and had more developed personalities. He loved working with some of the troubled boys who had no father figure at home. He would play basketball and soccer with them during recess which was supposed to be a "free" period for him. Playing with his kids was more enjoyable than sitting around listening to other staff members' complaints.

One day he gave a social studies test and saw one of the girls who was particularly weak in school concentrating hard and circling her answers on the multiple-choice test. He walked around the room and when he approached her desk, he peered down to see if she was getting the correct answers. He felt pride swelling in his heart since this girl was one of his worse students. He had gotten through to her. She must have really studied last night. His eyes focused on the paper in front of her. He was hoping she would pass this test and gain confidence in herself. When he looked at her paper, he realized that . . . she was circling the names of the dead parishioners who the Masses were being said for. She was looking at the church bulletin and couldn't tell the difference between that and the social studies test! And the bulletin was written in Polish! This young black girl sure didn't understand Polish.

His pay was terrible. The working conditions were bad. The neighborhood was dangerous. But Jimmy loved teaching so much that he looked forward to each day at work. When there was a school holiday, he wished it would pass because he wanted to be back in his classroom with his children. The students loved him. Soon, his reputation grew, and everyone wished he would be their teacher next year.

Jenny was beginning to show her pregnancy and Jimmy was so proud to be married to this wonderful woman and to soon be a father. Although it was difficult to make ends meet, Jenny never complained nor put any pressure on Jimmy to find a better paying job. Having enough money to buy food for the week became a challenge rather than quarrel. Jimmy would cash his check and hand over the money to Jenny. She, somehow, made it all work.

Life was good. For now.

CHAPTER 90

Benjamin had made up his mind. He must somehow find this guy who knew about his murdering ways. It's not like any of the victims were innocent. They all deserved to die. Those two boys in high school were nasty and mean and would certainly grow up to hurt other people. His father was a drunken and violent man who beat both him and his mother. Bonnie? Well, at first, he thought Bonnie was a sweet young woman who cared for him. But he came to realize that she was a phony who just strung him along. She probably hated him and just acted nice because it was her job and she wanted a good tip. Her boyfriend also deserved to die because she chose him over Benjamin and maybe she would have cared for him if this guy hadn't showed up.

Now, there was another person who deserved to die - the man in his dreams who knows all about these deaths. Yes, they were justified but he knew that others wouldn't understand. Although he could stay in Pennsylvania and continue living there, he had to move on to New York and find this man and get rid of him. Otherwise, he would be discovered and face unjust punishment for his actions.

He began to plan for his trip to New York. He went to the Greyhound Station and inquired about the cost of a bus ticket to New York. Benjamin had never been to a big city before and wondered what it would be like. He had heard all kinds of third hand information about New York. Most of it not good. The people were unfriendly. There were an incredible number of crimes daily. It was dirty. It was crowded. How would he find this guy? He knew the number of the address where he lived. He knew what the neighborhood looked like but how many neighborhoods looked like that in New York? He had no idea. But somehow, he would track him down.

He had to put some money away first and this was difficult because, although his expenses were minimal, his salary did not allow for much savings. He realized he would not be able work while he was tracking down the whereabouts of this man so, he would have to have enough money to survive for a few weeks. He heard that living in New York, even in the manner that he was accustomed to, would be costly. Saving a few dollars a week wasn't going to be enough. How would he get the money he needed?

He stood by the window of his room and thought about his problem. There was no doubt that this person had to be dealt with. He had to go to New York and find him and take care of him. He had to. There was no choice. He must get some money and quickly before the guy went to the police and reported what he knew. Time was not an option. Yes, he had no choice. He had to go out and get the funds he needed and, if that meant someone had to be hurt, it wasn't his fault. Why should someone else have the money that he needed?

Today was Saturday and he was off from work. Tonight, there would be people out enjoying the weekend and would be spending money – the money he needed. His money. Why should they have funds to waste going to bars and drinking and taking girls out on dates when he worked hard and had to get to New York to save himself? These bastards were out having fun tonight with his money. He'll just go out and get what he needed and do what was necessary. Whatever was necessary.

CHAPTER 91

It was 8pm and Benjamin was in his room finishing his supper of a fast food hamburger, fries and a soda. He crumpled up the greasy papers and stuffed them into the paper bag. He was still a bit hungry, so he grabbed a package of cupcakes he had bought earlier and swallowed each in three huge bites. He wiped his slippery hands on his t-shirt and sat up in his bed, thinking. It was almost time to leave and go hunting for his trip money. He went to the night table drawer and took out his wallet and his hunting knife.

He had given thought to where he would go and who he would kill to rob. He was not at all sure how much money he would need for traveling and living for a while in New York. He didn't want to be forced to find more money there.

When he arrived in New York he knew he had to concentrate on his task - eliminating his enemy. He had decided to take a bus to an area that had high end clubs where people with means went to party. The bars near where he lived certainly were not going to have customers that had lots of cash on them.

He walked the three blocks to the bus stop and waited for a bus. After a forty-minute ride, he got off in an area that he had heard about but never had gone to before. It was now almost 9:30pm and it seemed like activity was just beginning to happen. The street was filling up with couples and singles who were hustling and entering bars where loud music erupted whenever a door opened. Benjamin nervously went up to one of the bars and slowly began to open a door. He hesitated entering and this pause caused two young men to bump him out of the way as they rushed into the bistro. One in particular seemed to sneer at Benjamin as he pushed his elbow into the side of his head.

A decision was made.

Benjamin walked up to the bar and tried to buy a drink. The wooden counter was dark and sticky. People were packed and in places, they were three deep. There were women sitting on stools and men crowded around them. Several were calling for the bartender to serve them. Benjamin stood there for a length of time before a bartender approached him.

"Hey, buddy, you want something?"

Benjamin was somewhat startled since he was standing there being ignored for so long.

"Uh, yeah, I'll have a ginger ale."

The bartender looked at him for a few moments, made a smirk and said, "Yeah, right."

He returned in a minute and put down the soda on the bar and said, "That will be a buck, buddy."

Benjamin took out his worn-out wallet and looked through his bills and gave the guy a dollar bill.

The barman looked at the bill, frowned, raised his eyebrows, grabbed the dollar and walked away.

Benjamin was being crowded out from the bar and was tired of being shoved from every side. He took his glass of ginger ale and began walking amongst the crowd. He spotted the two men who shoved him at the door. They were holding drinks, talking and laughing with two young women. His heart began to beat faster, and anger rose up from his belly. He stared at the two guys who seemed to be having a great time, probably bragging as their heads bobbed up and down.

The two women appeared both impressed and quite intoxicated as they convulsed with laughter frequently. One of the men kept his arm around the woman with long dark hair. The other woman who was blond and wore a particularly tight dress, often put her hand on the other guy's chest and went on her toes to speak into his ear. It was obvious that they had paired off.

Then after another whisper into his ear, the one man tapped the other and nodded toward the door. Quickly, all four put their drinks down on someone's table and headed for the door. Putting his glass down as well, Benjamin followed them outside.

As the two couples began walking down the street, it was most obvious that the two women were totally drunk. They could hardly stand, and the men were holding them up as both women laughed uncontrollably. After walking with much difficulty for almost three blocks, the couples walked down an alley way between a clothes shop and a hair salon – both of which were closed. It was quite dark and none of the party noticed the fat man following them.

After walking deeply into the alley, the men stopped and held the women up against a brick building amongst debris and a dumpster. Soon their hands were inside the women's clothes and unbuttoning and unsnapping whatever held the clothing closed. Within a couple of minutes, both women were wearing nothing, but bras and panties and it appeared those two remaining garments were soon to follow to the ground. Mouths were all attached, and all four participants were oblivious to their surroundings, including the chubby young man who was approaching, slowly and deliberately. Not even the loud clicking that was closing in, caused any hesitation from either of the young men in their pursuit of sexual satisfaction.

Not until the cold steel blade of Benjamin's knife plunged into the side of one of the men did any of the physical activity stop. And it only interrupted one couple. The young man who was stabbed grunted and turned to look at his attacker. The young woman he was making out with, slid down the side of the building with her mouth open and appeared to have no apparent recognition that her sexual partner had been wounded. Benjamin then rammed his blade into the stomach of his prey as the man turned to face him, still silent other than another grunt. The victim then looked down at the knife that was protruding from his midsection as Benjamin ripped it out and stabbed him several more times. Before he hit the ground, he was a fatality.

At this point the other couple both turned to see the carnage that was happening right next to them. Before a word could be uttered, Benjamin went into action. His knife wielding hand now warm with his first victim's blood, thrust the dagger forward into the stomach of his second victim but, this time, after it entered his abdomen, Benjamin pulled it upward until bone stopped its ascent. Finding strength that was beyond what this chubby young man seemed to have, he lifted his quarry off his feet as the knife became a tool to elevate him several feet in the air. He held him there as his face, distorted in incredible pain, pitched forward and touched his assailant's head. A long dribble of spittle hung from his lower lip and dripped down on Benjamin's chin.

The second woman, realizing that they were being viciously attacked, began to scream. Her partner was still sitting on the ground and appeared to have passed out. As the woman screamed, Benjamin turned his attention to her. He jammed his forearm across her throat, pinning her against the wall and took his knife wielding hand and stabbed her stomach again and again and again. Her screams became merely a whimper and she fell dead to the ground.

Now, he turned his attention to the woman who had passed out. She did not witness the butchery and sat on the ground in her underwear with her legs spread apart in a pathetic yet seductive pose. Benjamin stared at her and felt his penis hardening. He knew he had to finish what he started but hesitated as his arousal forced his eyes to view her breasts which were squeezed together and pushed up by her black bra. Then the clicking began again. White, sticky globs of spit formed in each corner of his mouth. He longed to rip off her lingerie and ravish her. He looked over at the slaughter he had consummated. Three bodies bloodied and lifeless, his hand and arm sticky with blood of his victims. A voice spoke within him - "finish!"

He reached down and grabbed the unconscious woman's hair and pulled her head back, took his bloodstained knife and tore it across her throat. She made a gurgling sound but never opened her eyes. He took the knife again and pushed hard and deep across her throat and almost decapitated her. He felt the muscles of her neck release as her head hung back and almost touched her upper back.

It was done.

He quickly remembered why he was out on this night and went into the pockets of the two men, removing their wallets and, without looking at the denominations, stuffed the bills into his front pocket. Then he opened the two handbags of the dead women and looked for cash there as well. He found money in wallets in both pocketbooks and added it to his loot.

Only then did he become cognizant of his surroundings and look toward the street to see if anyone was watching. He could see people rushing past, never looking into the alley. He picked up one of the dresses that was lying on the ground and wiped his knife and hand as best he could. There was blood everywhere, but he had no time to worry about it. He put his blood-stained hand in his pocket and started toward the street.

He entered the street and began walking toward the bus stop. Although no one made notice of him as he walked, he looked down on his clothing and saw blood stains on his shirt and pants leg. He realized that he would be much more noticeable taking the bus than when he was walking on a crowded street where everyone is busy heading somewhere or talking to their companions. After standing at the bus stop for a few minutes, he knew he would be unable to get on the bus without being looked at by at least the driver. So, he began to walk.

As he left the busy commercial area where there were crowds of people bar hopping, he entered an industrial area. He saw a few men standing on street corners, smoking cigarettes and looking at passing cars. He noticed a few cars stopping and talking to a few of these men. He paid it little mind and just kept walking. He had a long walk ahead of him. The hand he used for murdering was bothering him because it was so sticky from the dried blood. He had it in his pocket up to this point. He took it out and looked at it and studied the dried blood. He then began to laugh out loud. That idiot looked at him with disdain when he entered the bar. Now, how does he feel? He reached his motel room at this point and took out his key. Looking at his hand again, he laughed even harder.

CHAPTER 92

After taking a long shower, Benjamin fell onto his bed and quickly went to sleep. When he awoke, he had a vague remembrance of a dream involving that bastard who was going to report him to the police and it made him only the more determined to kill him. He tried to recollect the details of the dream but all he could recall was the face of the young man who was accusing him. He knew that traveling to New York, finding him and removing his threat was what he had to do.

Then it dawned on him to look at the money he acquired last night. He had been so exhausted last night, he just dumped the money on his dresser, removed his clothes and went into the shower as if he were a zombie. Killing can really tire you out, he thought with a chuckle.

He walked over to the dresser and found a ball of bills, crumpled together. Some had dried blood on them, and a few were stuck together. He peeled them apart and started to count his bounty. When he was through, he went over to his bed and plopped down. The four murders had rewarded him with a total of $118. It was certainly more money than he earned in a week at his job at the barbell foundry. But he realized that amount of money would not last long in an expensive city like New York. He really had no idea how much money he would need to survive there and how long he would have to be there to accomplish his goal, but he understood that a little over one hundred dollars would certainly not be enough.

So, he had to go out and get more money. But how? It was Sunday and the bar scene would probably be much more quiet tonight. It also didn't bring him the money he expected. He got up from the bed and began to pace around the small room. He really had no ideas. After a few minutes of marching back and forth in the small space, he still had no clue as to what he would do to get much more money for his trip.

Finally, he went back to sitting on his bed and hung his head in despair. He suddenly realized something else. He was hungry. He hadn't eaten in some time and satisfying his hunger was most important to Benjamin. Maybe he would think more clearly if he had something to eat. So, he got up, put on his shoes and went to the dresser to get some cash. He took a $10 bill that had a small blood stain on it and jammed it into his pocket.

He headed to the diner with the thought that one of those smart-asses from last night would be paying for his breakfast. The knowledge that the money he took would fill his belly brought a smile to his face and an accompanying snicker. The concern about finding another plan took a back seat to eating. He walked to the diner with a carefree step in his gait and a wide grin on his face.

CHAPTER 93

When he got to the diner, he picked up a newspaper at the entrance and told the cashier to add it to his bill since he didn't have any change. He quickly found a booth by a window and slid into the seat. The tables were bolted to the floor, and they obviously didn't consider people who had a sizable waistline. His stomach pressed against the side of the table, and he considered moving to a table in the open area. However, he always felt more tucked away and, well, safe in a booth so he decided to deal with the mild discomfort. A waitress came over and asked if he was ready to order. Of course, he was since he always ordered the same first meal of the day. He looked at the middle-aged woman who had hair wrapped up in a beehive and a pencil stuck in the middle of it. She sure didn't look like Bonnie. That was probably just as well. No need to go down that road in his mind right now. There was enough going on.

"I'll have a cheeseburger, rare, a double order of fries and a large chocolate shake," he said.

"Sure, sweetie," was the reply.

"Sweetie!" thought Benjamin. Yeah, she wouldn't think so if she knew who I was. He giggled to himself as a smirk moved across his lips.

Benjamin looked at the front of the newspaper. There, right on page one, was a description of last night's murder of the two young couples. There were little details since the paper was printed only a couple of hours after it occurred, but it stated that it was a particularly violent stabbing and appeared to be a robbery.

He read the short article several times. It pleased him to know that he understood exactly what really happened and was, indeed, the only person who had this knowledge. He began to recall the specifics of last night and he went slowly step by step through the events of the previous evening, enjoying his retrospection.

Then his eyes fell upon an article on the right column of the first page. It was about the arrest of several drug dealers that took place last night as well. Benjamin quickly realized that this was in the very area that he walked through! He now understood what those guys were doing going up to cars that stopped along the curbs. One particular item in the article caught his attention.

Just then the waitress arrived with his food.

"Here ya go, sweetie," she said as she placed two plates in front of Benjamin. One had the burger on it. The other was overloaded with fried potatoes. A huge glass followed filled with a thick, brown goo topped with a dollop of whipped cream.

"Anything else, honey?" the woman sang.

At this point, Benjamin was deep into the article about the drug dealers and didn't respond.

"Sweetie?" the waitress again asked.

"Do you want anything else?"

The young man moved his eyes from the newspaper and slowly raised them to meet the eyes of the forty something woman. She never felt such coldness and a chill ran through her. For several seconds, no words were spoken. She would later think back and wonder why she felt a terrible fright, but she did.

Finally, the young man replied, "No." It was said with no emotion or inflection.

Usually, the overly chummy woman would attempt to make some small talk but with this customer, all she wanted was to leave his stare. So, saying nothing further, she moved away and told her waitress partner that she was taking a cigarette break.

Benjamin went back to reading the article about the drug dealers' arrests. It said that besides finding plastic bags of heroin in their possession, they also found large amounts of cash. This was most interesting. A new idea was forming. This might be his ticket to New York.

He picked up his burger as the grease dripped on the plate and took a hefty bite. Ketchup dripped from his mouth which he wiped off with the back of his hand. He nodded as he thought about his next move. A broad smile broke out across his face as he raised the glass of thick chocolate liquid and sucked hard on the straws.

CHAPTER 94

After his brunch meal, he left the diner and began walking in the opposite direction from where he came. He thought he could think clearer while walking and really didn't want to just hang out in his room all day on the last day of the weekend. It was a pleasant day and Benjamin felt particularly upbeat. His usual gait was kind of a waddling step where every move seemed to be awkward and painful. But today was different. His plan was taking shape and working well.

After walking about twenty blocks, he realized that he had to walk back as well so he was about to turn and head to the motel. He spotted a hot dog cart. Actually, he smelled it first. He had a hamburger platter just about an hour ago but that never stopped him before. He went up to the cart where an elderly man with a huge white mustache was wiping down the stainless-steel cart.

Benjamin stood in front of the man who said, "What can I get you, young fella?"

Without hesitation, Benjamin said, "Two hot dogs with everything."

The vendor wiped his hands on his white apron and said, "You know they're three for a dollar."

"Okay, give me three then," said Benjamin.

He finished the first one before the guy could prepare the next two.

"That will be one dollar," said the old man.

Benjamin reached into his pocket and pulled out a wad of bills. He looked past a $10 dollar bill and found a single which he unfurled and handed to the peddler. After passing it over, he realized that it had a couple of blood stains on it. The old man didn't seem to notice.

"Hey, you're a big spender, huh?"

Benjamin said nothing but just looked at the man. Something about his eyes made the man look away. They appeared cold and dead. No further words were spoken by either man.

The walk back took more time than the original trek. Maybe it was because his stride became less jaunty and more like his usual dull gait. Also, he felt really bloated since he ate the three hot dogs only a short time after his burger and fries meal.

When he got back to his room, he fell onto his bed face first and quickly went to sleep. It didn't take long for a dream to take over his subconscious mind.

He was in a long, dark corridor of some sort. He was agitated and felt frightened. He kept going forward but each step brought more and more anxiety. Soon, a familiar face appeared. There was no body, just a face and it quickly floated toward him, getting larger and larger. It was that bastard. The guy who knew.

When the bodiless head was huge and just about on top of him, it spoke.

"You are a murderer. I know who you are, and I will get justice for all the innocent people you have killed," said the voice in a deep and foreboding tone.

Benjamin began to shake in his bed. Acid refluxed up his throat and into his mouth and the extreme burning sensation bolted him awake. He leap up and began coughing violently. This caused even more of the fiery liquid to shoot up into his mouth and the coughing became worse. His eyes teared as he ran to the sink to drink some water to attempt to expunge the blaze within his throat.

He finally got control and sat on the edge of his bed trying to catch his breath. After a couple of minutes, he regained his composure and wiped away the moisture from his eyes. He got up and walked back over to the sink and looked at himself in the dirty, broken mirror.

He had already decided that he must go to New York and kill this squealer. This latest encounter only confirmed that he really had no choice. It must be done, and nothing will stop him.

CHAPTER 95

Benjamin waited in his room until it became dark outside. He had watched some TV and ate a large bag of chips and drank two sodas. However, since a few hours had now passed since he had his snack, he was now hungry and decided to stop by the diner for a quick bite before heading to his final task in Pennsylvania.

When he arrived at the diner, he went right to the same booth as this morning but there was a different waitress. This one gave him a bland greeting and handed him a menu. He already knew what he wanted so he ordered a pastrami sandwich, fries and a soda. The waitress said nothing but took the menu back and walked away.

In a short time, she returned with his food and asked him if he wanted anything else. She left his check right then and thanked him with an expressionless tone. She was quite unfriendly and that's just the way Benjamin liked it. He hated phony amiableness. Just give me my damn food.

After quickly wolfing down his sandwich and fries, he left a small tip, paid the bill at the cashier and began his journey to the industrial area of town. He walked quickly as he started getting excited, even though he was quite anxious. When he got to the area he saw the night before, he was at first surprised that it appeared empty. Of course, all the buildings were closed for business but last night there were quite a few men standing around smoking cigarettes and making transactions at the curb.

He then realized that the arrests last night kept the drug dealers away, at least for now. Damn! He needed the money and he needed it now. The dream earlier only made it more certain that he had to deal with the guy in New York as soon as possible or he would be found out and put in prison-or worse.

He continued to walk, and it was eerily quiet and creepy dark. He walked several blocks and saw no one on the street. Then he eyed a skinny, black man smoking a cigarette and leaning up against a building that had a metal gate covering the entrance. He slowed down to get a better look at the guy.

"Hey, man, you want a bag? It's good shit, man," said the dark-skinned man.

Benjamin stopped and stood there saying nothing and looking at him.

"Show me some cash, man. Hey, I'm telling, this is good shit," the guy drawled out.

He sounded like he had just used some of his product himself. He appeared stoned and unsteady on his feet. Benjamin looked around and there was no one in sight. Indeed, during the entire time in this area of town, he had seen no one other than this guy who looked like he might fall over if he didn't lean against the metal fencing.

"C'mon, I ain't got all night, man. Show me some cash," droned the gaunt black man.

Benjamin said nothing but reached into his pocket as he began to move toward the guy. It looked like a transaction was about to take place. The man steadied himself as he waited to see the cash. Instead, he saw something else - a long-bladed knife!

"Wha!" was all he could utter before the knife plunged into his gut. The knife ripped into his stomach and was then pulled out and, as the drug dealer tried to turn away, was violently driven into his side, tearing into both his liver and kidney on the right side of his abdomen.

Blood shot out of the second wound and the drug pusher began to sink to the ground, his mouth open but no words were coming forth. Benjamin pulled his weapon out just as the vendor of death crumpled to the ground.

Blood was quickly forming a pool on the sidewalk. The other incidents never seemed to cause this much blood to gush out so rapidly.

Benjamin stood there for a moment staring at the enlarging red puddle and then caught himself and put his hands into the tight pockets of the man's jeans. His hand emerged with a handful of small plastic bags filled with white powder. He dumped them on the ground and pulled the man over onto his other side. His entire right side was crimson, and the vital fluid continued to envelop his shirt and pants.

There was no time to ponder and analyze his handiwork. He reached into his other pocket. His fat fingers were barely able to get into the cramped and tight pocket that was bulging at the bottom. However, he wiggled his hand down and stretched his fingers around a ball of paper of some kind. He pulled it out, tearing the pocket of the jeans. And there it was - his ticket to New York.

It was a hefty roll of money. It looked like there were no singles – just twenties, fifties and hundred-dollar bills. It was hard to imagine that this emaciated loser would be carrying so much money. Benjamin then thought maybe he worked for a mob. He finally looked around to see if anyone was watching. The streets were as empty as they had been when he walked up. There was no one to be seen in any direction.

He stuffed the money into his own pockets. There was so much that some of it fell on the sidewalk. He picked up the dropped bills and jammed them into his pants. He then saw his knife on the ground where he dropped it when he started to retrieve his money. He wiped the knife on the shirt of the dead man and placed it back into the scabbard in his back pocket.

He began his long walk back to his motel room. He saw that this time there was only a small bit of blood on his left pants' leg. Since it was now the middle of the night and no one was out, he got back to his room without crossing the path of a single person.

When he entered his room, he immediately went to his night table and, pushing the small lamp to the side, he dumped his earnings from both pockets onto the table. It was more money than he had ever seen in his entire life. He began to count it but lost count several times before he stopped in frustration.

It didn't matter how much was there. He now had enough. Enough to leave York, Pennsylvania and travel to New York and remove the final problem. He went over to the mirror and looked at himself. His eyes clouded over and the clicking began. Soon, however, the weird sound was replaced by laughter. Soft at first but the intensity got stronger and stronger until his face was distorted by an enormous grin and the uproar almost caused the walls to quake.

CHAPTER 96

Although Jimmy and Jenny were settling into a daily routine, there was something unsettled in Jimmy's mind. He tried to disguise it, but Jenny felt something wasn't right. She would ask him about work, about how he was feeling, if anything was bothering him, but Jimmy's answers were always positive, and he would force a happy expression, but Jenny knew it was a false smile. Something was wrong but she didn't know what it was. Jimmy, himself, knew that his countenance was false and that his Jenny could see through it, but he would smile and deny any problems regardless of her questioning.

This lack of honesty was troubling to Jenny, and she began to wonder if their marriage was in jeopardy. Maybe Jimmy no longer found her attractive, especially in her state of pregnancy. Maybe he was disappointed in the life they were having, after all, they had to struggle financially day to day. Maybe he just fell out of love with her. That premise was the worse one to face. Jenny often cried when she was alone. She knew that Jimmy was hurting but so was she. If only he would be honest with her and share his heartache and sorrow.

When Jimmy was at school and working with his kids, his mind was no longer preoccupied with that evil person in his dreams. He dove into his lesson plans and exuberantly taught and moved about the room incessantly. His students, many of whom had difficult home lives, adored their teacher. His salary made it almost impossible to pay his bills and shop for healthy food for him and Jenny, but those worries were dismissed from his thoughts when he engaged his students.

There was no gym class for the children in the school, so Jimmy acquired a portable basketball backboard from the local YMCA who only used it in the summer. One period a day was unassigned so that each teacher had a forty-minute break in addition to lunch. Rather than relax and have some refreshments, Jimmy used this time to teach a gym class to sixth, seventh and eighth grade students. Sometimes it was basketball. Sometimes it was soccer. Sometimes it was track activities. The kids returned to class all sweaty but re-energized.

The affection for their teacher seemed to drive most of the children to do their best in their academics so as not to disappoint him. Before Jimmy arrived, this class was dreadful in both their study habits and their behavior. In fact, their conduct was the main reason the previous teacher resigned. Now, this class was by far the best-behaved grade in the school even though most of the other classes were taught by nuns who were less than gentle in their classroom management techniques. Corporal punishment was not something that Jimmy utilized. A stern lecture or even a cold stare was all that was needed to bring a student back in line.

On one day a week, Jimmy held a math workshop after school. He demonstrated methods to make math more enjoyable and turned computation into a competitive game situation. Soon, about a dozen students stayed after school to attend his math lessons. It was a way to improve the students' abilities in mathematics but, also, extended Jimmy's time away from allowing his mind to revisit the vile young man of his reverie.

On his drive home, invariably, the horrid face of the young man who haunted both his waking hours and his sleep would appear. At times, the visage would speak and threaten him. At other times, the mere appearance of the head of this creature would cause Jimmy to be sickened. Once he was so involved in looking transfixed at the countenance that he almost had an accident.

That time, the floating head first appeared in the distance but slowly advanced and grew larger. As the head became enormous, Jimmy could see a slimy strand of slopper begin to form and grow on one corner of the mouth. That clicking sound that had become so familiar to him was now beginning and getting louder, louder. The eyes were not visible because the lens of the glasses it wore were all clouded over. Soon, he could smell the foul breath of the creature as it continued to move closer and closer, almost touching nose to nose.

"Hey, you, buddy, are you okay?" said a voice from beyond.

Someone was shaking him and again said, "Hey, should I call for help?"

Jimmy turned to see an older man who was wearing a cap and had gray stubble on his face. The man was kind looking and appeared concerned. Jimmy was breathing heavily and just then realized he was in his car. The car had been driven into the sidewalk and stopped diagonally at the curb. A couple of people came over to see what was going on. Jimmy was fortunate that no car was parked where he lost control of this car and coasted into the sidewalk.

"Uh, yeah, I'm okay now. Just had a kind of a blackout or something," said Jimmy to the gentleman whose face showed apprehension.

"I don't think you should drive your car right now. It could happen again. Maybe you should call someone to come and get you," said the kind stranger.

Jimmy realized that he couldn't just drive off and certainly couldn't explain to anyone, let alone someone he didn't even know, that he was having a nightmare while he was driving.

"Yes, I'll call someone. I'll just straighten my car out first and sit here awhile. Thanks, but I'll be fine. I appreciate your concern," said Jimmy.

The man didn't look convinced but stood up straight from his leaning position, waited a moment and then walked away slowly, looking back several times. Jimmy put the car in reverse and maneuvered the car into the parking spot. The other folks who were stopped to see what was happening now walked off. Jimmy sat in his car for about fifteen minutes. He realized he was damp with perspiration around his neck and on his back as his shirt stuck to the back of the car seat. Finally, he started the car back up and continued his drive home.

He knew that somehow, someway, he would have to deal with this monster. He knew he was real, and he was getting closer. The day of reckoning was fast approaching.

CHAPTER 97

When Jimmy arrived home, he was greeted by a smiling Jenny. But her smile hid her worry that something was wrong with Jimmy. Was he ill? Was he tired of the stress of financial difficulties? Or was he tired of being married? She had to know what was wrong. What was going on?

"Jimmy, we need to talk," said Jenny.

Jimmy could see the seriousness of the look on her face. His stomach jumped into his throat. Was she sick? Was something wrong with the baby?

He took her hand in his and asked, "What's the matter, honey?"

"Nothing is wrong with me, Jimmy, but I am worried about you. You haven't been yourself for some time now and I need to know what's bothering you," said Jenny.

Jimmy realized it was time to tell his wife, the woman he adored, everything that has gone on. He had never shared his past dreams that predicted a future event. He never told anyone about his ability to know the future. It was so weird that he felt that others would think he was deranged. But this was Jenny. She was his world and she deserved to know and if she thought he was a wacko, well, he had to take that chance.

"Jenny, I have to tell you something. I should have told you about this a long time ago, but I just couldn't," said Jimmy.

Now, Jenny was really scared. What in the world was her husband who she loved with all her heart, going to tell her?

"Sit down, please. I hope you don't think I'm a nut job or anything but since I was a kid, I sometimes would have a dream that came true," said Jimmy.

"What? Is that it? Jimmy, we all have dreams that come true sometimes. You scared me and it's nothing," said Jenny.

"No, it's much more than that. It's not just a dream you have when you are asleep. It's more of a . . . well, kind of a vision and these dreams or visions or, well, apparitions are usually about someone dying. And they then happen," said Jimmy.

He went on to give her details about all his nightmarish phantasms from the first one involving Sister Anastasia when he was a little boy up to the frightening series that have been occurring now that feature the ugly, foul-breathing monster who has murdered time and time again.

"And now he's coming. I know it. He's close to us right now and I don't know how to protect us," said Jimmy.

Jenny loved her man and trusted him completely. She believed him totally and felt his fear. She wanted to reassure him that all would be alright, but she knew that it would not be convincing. She needed to be strong both for him and for herself.

"We need to make a plan. Do you think we should go to the police?" she asked.

"No," said Jimmy. "I already dismissed that. They would never believe me, and I don't know his name or anything about him really. They'll think I'm a lunatic and probably laugh at me."

"Well, then, we'll just have to deal with this ourselves," said Jenny.

Jimmy looked at his love. She was not only beautiful but courageous. And she believed in him. That was more important than anything.

CHAPTER 98

Benjamin got off the bus at the Greyhound Depot in Manhattan. He left York, Pennsylvania quickly with little fanfare. He was kind of surprised that his two co-workers seemed to accept his leaving with almost no reaction. After all, he had worked with them for a while, and they seemed to get along well. Sure, they weren't close friends and didn't socialize outside of work, but he expected more of a good-bye from them. They just shook his hand and wished him luck and went back to work. Well, screw them! They were no different than all the other people he met throughout his life. No one really cared.

If only they realized the power he had over life and death. If only they knew he could decide if they would have had their last breath. In his mind he dismissed their apathy but deep inside, it hurt. He thought back to his own mother and how little she seemed to care about his leaving. He killed his father to protect her from constant abuse and she appeared to be almost happy for him to leave and never return. His entire life was one of disappointment in humanity. If only one person had shown care. Only Bonnie demonstrated any kindness toward him and that was only to get a good tip. She didn't really have any interest or affection for him. Well, he took care of that.

Now, he had to find this person who was the only one who could go to the police and have him arrested. He knew the address, but he now had to find it. The bus depot was crowded. He never saw so many people in one place. New York was going to be overpowering. He stood back and watched for a while. People were moving fast and, although they didn't seem to look up, they never collided. It was if they had some kind of radar and avoided contact at the last second.

His two immediate goals were to find a place to stay and then to find out where the address for his enemy was. He picked up his large duffel bag which contained all his worldly possessions. He was apprehensive about getting robbed of his money which was wrapped in a rubber band and kept deep within his jeans pocket. He had heard about pickpockets in New York and read that a rubber band helped make it harder to remove cash from a pocket. In addition, his blue jeans' pants legs were tight, and the pockets were hard to reach into. He carried his duffel bag in his right hand so that his arm protected the right pocket where he kept the stash. His knife was in its sheath and kept inside his waistband in his back, hidden by his shirt hanging over his belt.

As he began walking toward one of the exits to the depot, his mind concentrated on his pocket, his arm and his knife. He was on high alert and could feel his heart beating in this strange and unfamiliar place. Once he was on the street, he had to stop to allow his eyes to adjust to the bright sunlight. Once his vision was restored, he marveled again at the sheer number of people walking rapidly on the sidewalk. Never had there been so many people walking at one time in York, Pennsylvania.

He began walking in one direction with no plan in mind. After traveling a few blocks, he came to a hotel that was several stories high. It was well below the buildings adjacent to it and, although it would be quite tall for where he came from, it was small in comparison to the rest of the block. He entered the lobby and walked up to the long counter. He asked for a room and the clerk stated the price per night which was much more than he paid for a week in York. The older man looked at this disheveled young man before him and a smirk began to appear on his lips.

"Maybe you're looking for something a bit more reasonable?" said the uniformed gentleman.

"Uh, yeah, is there anything for 10, uh, 20 or 25 dollars a night?" said Benjamin.

"Well, son, you're not going to find much in Manhattan for that amount. Why don't you take a subway over to Brooklyn or Queens and look there?" said the hotel staff member.

"Uh, how do I get there?" said Benjamin.

"Go down three blocks and you'll see the subway entrance and you go down there and take the train downtown to 14th Street and then take the L train to Brooklyn. Take it to the last stop which is Canarsie. I used to live there, and you'll find a couple of hotels that are pretty clean and in your price range," said the clerk.

Benjamin thanked the man and headed to the train. He had never been on a subway, and it made him anxious to think about it. He had heard horror stories on muggings on the subways of New York. But he had his mission and had no choice but to follow through. He also had his knife and certainly knew how to use it.

He found the black iron railing at the entrance to the subway. There were concrete steps going down into a dark hole lighted by only a small electric lantern. It was frightening but he must go on. However, he hesitated at the top of the stars and held onto the banister with his left hand. He was shoved by a couple of people – one man and one woman as he stopped to gather his nerve. Finally, taking a deep breath, he began to descend into the cavity and heard the loud rumble of a train entering the station.

Once he arrived at the bottom of the stairway, he saw a train on the opposite side of the tracks and walked up to the booth to inquire about buying a fare. The elderly black man who was behind a caged window looked up at him and waited. Benjamin asked for a ticket for the subway to Canarsie.

The man slowly spoke.

"You mean you want a token, son. One way or round trip?" said the man in the blue uniform shirt.

"Uh, one way, I guess," said Benjamin.

"That will be 20 cents."

Benjamin reached into his left side pocket where he kept some change. He pulled out a quarter and handed it to the subway agent. The man took the quarter and handed him a gold-colored coin and a nickel came rolling down a stainless-steel chute. Benjamin took the two coins and stood there for a moment not knowing what to do with the token. By now, there were two more people on line behind him.

The man in the cage saw that the young man before him had no idea what to do next. He told Benjamin to take the token and go over to the entrance and put the token in the slot. The young man walked over to the entrance way but stood there mystified as to how to operate the turnstile. So, he waited for the man who was behind him in line to enter and watched what he did. He then put the token in the slot and pushed the turnstile and walked up to the platform. Just as he did so, a train came roaring into the station. The sound was deafening. The brakes squealed with a high-pitched screech that made Benjamin want to cover his ears.

Once the train stopped, the doors opened, and a few passengers exited. One thing Benjamin had noticed in his short time in New York was that nobody made eye contact, and no one ever seemed to smile. That was fine with him. He could get used to this city. He entered the train and found a seat. He took his duffel bag and place it on his lap with both his arms over it. He mentally felt his knife and, knowing it was there, it helped make him feel secure.

He understood that, in this city, people do not look at one another so he looked down at his shoes until he got to the next station and read the black and white signs on the metal poles that said, "23rd Street". He had to get off at 14th Street so it would be soon. He had to pay attention. Sure enough, the next stop was 14th Street and he jumped up to get ready to disembark. He almost fell as the train stopped and had to grab onto a white pole to keep from crashing to the floor.

The doors opened and he walked onto the platform. Now, he had to find the next train. He went to another token booth and asked where the L train was. The man who was white and considerable younger than the token seller at the last station was said, "The Canarsie Line. That's up the stairs and to your left."

Benjamin walked up the stairs and saw a sign over another set of stairs leading down that said, "L Train."

He walked down the stairs and there were two tracks – one sign said, "local" and the other said, "express". Benjamin wasn't sure which one to take but the local train came in first and he just got on it. It took a long ride but, finally, he came to the last stop which was Canarsie. He got off and walked up the stairway to the street.

He did it! He made it from Manhattan to this place called Canarsie.

It looked much less hectic than Manhattan. He walked several blocks and found a small building that said, "Hotel Savoy." He went in and could smell pine disinfectant as soon as he entered the lobby. He went up to the woman at the counter and asked about a room. She said it would be $18 a day or $110 dollars a week.

Benjamin stood there for a moment deciding what to do. The price was probably as good as he would find, and he was exhausted. Should he pay for a day or a week? He decided to pay for three nights and add to it if he needed more time.

He was given a key and a room number. It was on the first floor and when he found the room, he entered it and immediately jumped on the bed. He was beyond tired. Almost immediately he fell asleep. Within minutes, he was dreaming.

There was the young man that Benjamin had seen so many times before in his dreams. He was with a young, pretty woman who appeared to be pregnant. They were holding hands as they looked into each other's eyes and smiled. Their affection for each other only made Benjamin feel anger. They were happy and in love and Benjamin had no one on this earth to love or be loved by.

Then the young man slowly turned to face him and said, "I know you have killed many people and you must pay for your crimes."

Although it was said calmly and without malice, it frightened Benjamin. He knew he must kill the young man. He knew he must kill them both. And it was time to set a plan. A murderous plan. It was the only way.

CHAPTER 99

Jimmy had left for school earlier in the morning and Jenny was getting herself ready to go out to get a few groceries for supper tonight. She felt so huge and awkward, and she had pain in her lower chest which the doctor said was a gas pocket and not unusual for a woman this far along in pregnancy. Even getting dressed and walking down the stairs in the hallway of the apartment house was a major chore.

But after the conversation with Jimmy yesterday, she wanted to make something a bit special for dinner tonight. It would be difficult with her tight budget, but she had produced miracles regularly balancing tasty and nutritious meals with so little money to work with.

When she thought about what Jimmy had told her, as fantastic as it was, she completely believed him. Jimmy was as honest and truthful as anyone could ever be. If he said he was clairvoyant, well, then he was. Strange, how something like this would seem to be a wonderful gift. Who would have thought it was such a painful burden for Jimmy all his life? She was so glad that he finally shared it with her so she could do whatever she could to make it less torturous for her husband.

She still wished that they could go to someone in authority to ask for help but she realized that Jimmy was right. The police would laugh at them and reject any plea for help. Somehow, someway, they must take care of this problem themselves.

She locked the door to the apartment and slowly made her way down the two flights of stairs in the hallway. She held tightly onto the bannister because her balance wasn't too good. Her protruding belly and the weight of the baby threw her equilibrium off.

When she got outside, the fresh air felt good as she took a couple of deep breaths before descending the concrete steps leading to the sidewalk. She walked over to her car which was parked a few doors down. When she returned, she would have to park across the street since the city had rules for alternate side parking each day of the work week. If you didn't park the car on the opposite side early in the day, it would be almost impossible to find a spot in the morning.

She unlocked the passenger side of the car first and put her large pocketbook on the seat. She then waddled around to the driver's side and unlocked the door and slowly maneuvered herself and flopped down into the seat. She then reached out to grab the handle of the door in order to close it. She had to stretch as she struggled to reach the handgrip. Everything was a chore in her present condition. While reaching and wiggling her fingers as she tried to extend her arm further, she didn't notice the unattractive and homely looking man who was quickly approaching her car. Her hand finally reached the door handle and, as she shut the car door, the passenger side door opened, and a man jumped into the seat.

Jenny was startled as she looked over at this invader. She was unable to speak for a moment but just looked at his moon face, with round glasses atop his flattened nose. Then she saw him pull a long knife from under his coat and he pressed it into the side of her stomach. He reached behind him with his other hand and pulled out her handbag and threw it into the back seat.

"What . . . what do you want?" stammered Jenny.

"Just start the car and begin driving. Slowly," said the stranger.

Jenny looked around, hoping to see a neighbor, anyone who might be walking by. Of course, there was no one around in mid-morning.

"Please, I don't have much money and you can have all I've got," cried Jenny.

"I don't want your money. I want you," growled the ugly man whose yellow teeth appeared in his scowl.

"Now, drive!"

Jenny started the car and slowly pulled out of the parking spot. Suddenly, she knew. This was the man that Jimmy had dreamed about. This was the monster who murdered all those people in Jimmy's dreams. There was no longer time to discuss and come up with a plan. He was real and he was here.

CHAPTER 100

Jimmy sat down for lunch in the school basement where the lay teachers ate. There were mostly nuns teaching in the Catholic School, but their numbers had been dwindling and as the years went by, more and more lay teachers had to be hired. Now there were three of them – two young women and Jimmy.

Often Jimmy would skip lunch to spend time with the kids and supervise some basketball or soccer games during their recess. But today he decided to sit down, rest and eat. He hadn't slept well for days and felt empty and exhausted.

The two women were talking about some television show they were interested in. Jimmy mostly watched sports programs at home and the show they were talking about, The Mary Tyler Moore Show, was one that Jimmy had never watched. His mind wandered as he unwrapped his ham sandwich and took a bite.

Suddenly, he froze with the ham sandwich suspended halfway between the table and his mouth. His eyes glazed over and there he was – the monster that had been stalking his dreams. His face was close to his. He looked into his almost black eyes. He could smell his foul breath. He wanted to escape and return to the school basement.

"I have her. I have your pretty wife. And unless you come here, I will kill her, and you know I will. Don't call the police because if I see anyone other than you are approaching, I will throw her off the tower."

Tower? Tower? What tower?

Slowly, the scene pulled back and Jimmy saw what looked like a water tower. Yes, as his vision went further back, he could see it was a water tower and then he saw his Jenny. The fiend held her arm and in his other hand Jimmy could see a knife being held against her swollen belly.

The image continued moving further away until Jimmy could read the side of the water tower - "Ridgewood". He knew this place, having seen it in the distance often. It was an old landmark for his neighborhood, probably not utilized for many years. Cold and gray with black lettering, looking more ominous than usual. It always kind of spooked Jimmy, especially at night when there were lights on it, blinking to warn low flying aircraft of its presence.

Now, it was a monument to all his fears – huge and tall and containing his nemesis. But he must conquer this enemy and his paralyzing fear of heights to save his love and his unborn child. Somehow, he must.

The two women who were sharing the table with Jimmy stopped discussing their favorite television program when they noticed their fellow teacher rigid and making slight moaning sounds. His eyes seemed distant, and his face was distorted and appeared to be experiencing terror.

"Jimmy?" questioned Cathy, a dark-haired 3rd grade teacher. "Jimmy!" she shouted with a more forceful voice.

The other teacher, Barbara, grabbed his forearm and tried to shake him awake. There was no result.

The two women looked at each other and grimaced showing their bewilderment.

Then, Jimmy blinked and put his sandwich down, glanced at each of his colleagues, and without saying a word, jumped up and ran out of the basement room.

He ran up the stairs and went into the nuns' break room where they were finishing their lunch. There was Sister Edward, the principal. She was a stern and unpleasant person who seemed to instill fear in the nuns, as well as the two lay women teachers.

Jimmy blurted out, "Sister, I am sick and have to leave."

The nun was about to object both to his sudden and uninvited entrance and to the possibility of his leaving early, but Jimmy did not even give her a chance to respond. He immediately turned and ran out the door. He didn't stop to go back to his classroom for his jacket or to leave any instructions for his class. He raced to his car in the parking lot and his tires squealed as he began his trip to both his and Jenny's destiny.

Chapter 101

Jimmy drove like a maniac. He was concerned that he might be stopped for speeding, but he had no choice. The drive from Jamaica, Queens to Ridgewood would take about 20 minutes at this time of day but Jimmy arrived at the water tower in 12 minutes.

There it was. The ominous tower stood tall dressed in its drab gray. There was a chain link fence surrounding the small yard that contained the structure. However, as is the case for many fences in New York, kids had cut several holes in the chain link in order to gain access to an area that would be dark and private at night. Jimmy looked up at the imposing edifice and his entire body shuddered.

He jumped out of this car and ran through one of the openings in the fence. He looked up as he approached the water tower and froze in place. His head slowly bent back and back as his eyes focused on the ladder that went up and up. When his head went back as far as it physically could, he felt dizzy and stumbled back a couple of steps.

No one can understand the intense and paralyzing fear that any heights caused in Jimmy. He could not take an elevated train. He had trouble looking out of an open window in his third-floor apartment. He couldn't even climb up to the top of a small ladder to change a light bulb. How could he possibly climb up this open ladder to the top to reach the water tower and his beloved Jenny?

There was no way he could do it. No way.

But he must.

He walked up to the metal ladder that was attached to metal beams that led to the water tower above. He grabbed onto the cold railing on each side of the ladder and took a step. Then another. Then a third. He looked up and viewed the seemingly endless steps above and got lightheaded. He almost lost his grip and had to stop.

He could feel his heart racing. His chest rose and fell rapidly as his breathing increased in intensity. He could not go on. It was impossible to overcome the fear that incapacitated him. He took the three steps back and stood on the ground again. He held onto the railings and hung his head in shame. This embarrassing terror that had plagued him all his life was now going to allow this monster to kill his wife and unborn child.

Then he heard Jenny scream.

Jimmy's eyes bulged and he heard himself growl. His head rose up and he began again to climb. One step. Then another. Five steps. Twenty. Fifty. He just kept looking straight ahead – not up and, certainly, not down. He stopped counting and just kept ascending. Higher and higher. It seemed endless but he was now on a mission. His fear was replaced by anger. An anger so intense that he could overcome a phobia that had caused him so much torment throughout his life.

Finally, he reached the top of the ladder and climbed onto the platform that surrounded the swollen metallic belly. There was another smaller ladder that went up the side of the water tank. Was Jenny and the murderous fiend on top of the cistern?

Then he heard it. The sound he had heard many times before in his horrific dreams. A strange clicking sound. It was unlike an insect or animal but certainly not human sounding. It was the degenerate miscreant that he watched murder over and over and now had Jenny.

He slowly walked around the tank on the platform, holding on the thin metal railing that was about waist high. He couldn't bear to look down or even straight ahead because his eyes would see nothing but sky. So, he focused on the silvery vessel to his right that was covered with soot.

His hands were covered with black grime from the railings on the steps, the handrail around the catwalk and the water tank, itself, which he placed his right hand on for balance and security.

He again heard the fearsome clicking, louder and louder. Dread rose in his heart, but his overwhelming anger won the battle between terror and the absolute desperation to save his family.

Then, he appeared. The monster. The beast. The devil. The being that has haunted his life for years. There was Jenny. Red faced from crying. Swollen with their child. And looking incredibly beautiful. And vulnerable.

Benjamin stood partially beside her and partially behind her. In his hand was a large knife which he held against her protruding stomach. His other arm was around her neck.

The two men stared at each other. It was the final scene in their dreams.

CHAPTER 102

The two men stood silently and felt both fear and anger. For one, his adversary was his enemy who would have him stopped and arrested for murder. For the other, this monster was a violent killer who was now threatening his beloved wife and unborn child.

Jimmy suddenly became aware that he was standing at a railing over 150 feet in the air. His right hand grasped the metal railing, and the cold grimy steel sent a shiver through his body. He dared not look down but, yet, he had to. He glanced over the edge and his eyes focused on the ground below for an instant. He then looked back at the beast who was holding a knife at the stomach of his mate.

Jimmy did not have to decide what to do. He was frozen in place. A statue, rigid and unable to move.

Then, the infernal clicking began. The eyes of the demon appeared to glow yellow beneath the lens of his round, oversized glasses. Then, suddenly, it all happened.

Benjamin shoved Jenny aside and rushed at Jimmy who had no time to react. His hand was still locked onto the bar at the top of the railing. The fiend came at him with his knife held in front of him. It all transpired in a split second. Jimmy moved to his right slightly while still holding onto the railing. The knife missed its mark, but Benjamin's shoulder collided with Jimmy's shoulder and the young man stumbled backward and his hip slammed into the top of the railing and Jimmy catapulted over the low barrier and plunged into space.

Jenny screamed as she watched her lover, best friend and father of her unborn child sail over the low fence and disappear.

Benjamin looked over the brink and viewed the result of his confrontation with his enemy. Now, he turned to Jenny to finish the task of taking care of those who would harm him. He took a step but stopped. He looked at this young woman with her protruding belly and saw how beautiful she was.

Tears were streaming down her cheeks and gulps of sobs erupted from her open mouth. She was helpless to stop this maniac and protect her child. But she knew she would do whatever she could to stop him.

Benjamin took several careful steps toward her but then appeared to hesitate. He slowly turned around and looked back at the railing where he ended the life of his antagonist. To his utter amazement, there was Jimmy! How could that be? He saw him go over the railing. He saw him on the ground below. He was dead but, yet there he was, standing there ready to fight for his bride.

Benjamin began emitting those spine - shuttering metallic sounds that were now accompanied by a low-pitched growl. Foaming saliva began to emerge from the corners of his mouth.

With a burst of quickness that belied his physical appearance, Benjamin rushed at his archenemy. But, when he was only inches from him, Jimmy disappeared. Benjamin crashed into the short fencing and went headfirst over into the expanse.

He was gone.

Jenny stood shocked and unable to move. What had just happened? This evil being who was responsible for the death of many, including Jimmy, had just ran up to the railing and dived over to his death. Why? Was he committing suicide? He seemed to see something that drove him to the edge.

With shaking hands, Jenny slowly approached the precipice but could not bear to look down. She began to walk around the footway to the ladder and, taking a deep breath, started to descend to the ground.

Once she reached the earth, she haltingly walked around to the place where the two young men had met their fate.

There was the bulky body of the devil lying face down with his arms trapped beneath him. A huge pool of blood encircled his head.

And then she looked at Jimmy. He was lying face up with his arms extended. His pose was not unlike the crucified Christ. Strangely, his countenance had a gentle smile on it. He looked as if he was pleased and satisfied. He saved the love of his life and his unborn baby. He stopped the vile murderer from any further killing. He overcame his paralyzing fear of heights which he never thought he could do. Maybe he did die contented.

Jenny knelt next to her hero. She buried her sobbing face into Jimmy's chest.

"Thank you, Jimmy, for saving us. I love you forever."

Epilogue

She sat on the wooden bench with green painted two by fours held up by concrete stanchions. The warm spring sun brought a sense of both comfort and relaxation to her. Spring was Jenny's favorite time of the year and May was her most cherished month. Flowers were blooming, the air was scented, and birds were chirping.

She watched her young son, Jaime, as he climbed the monkey bars in the playground. He was only eight years old but already looked like his dad – blue eyes and the light blond hair that Jimmy had when he was Jamie's age. He had the same crooked smile of the dad he never knew. She thought about how things like expressions and personality were inherited rather than learned.

One thing that Jamie did not inherit was Jimmy's overwhelming fear of heights. Jamie was fearless. This trait often caused Jenny trepidation as it did now while she watched him climb to the very top of the monkey bars. She knew that if they had additional levels he would continue to climb until he reached the summit, regardless of how high that might be.

Jamie already showed high intelligence. His second-grade teacher just yesterday met with Jenny and told her that he could move up to fourth grade and skip third grade and wouldn't miss a step. She said his vocabulary and reading skills already surpassed most beginning fourth graders. He was also exceedingly popular and most of the other children in his class wanted to be his friend.

Yes, she was proud of her little boy, but she was also proud of herself. It hadn't been easy being a single mother these past eight years, raising her son by herself while she had to work to pay the bills. Her mother was a godsend. She babysat every day when Jamie came home from school so Jenny could go to work and her mom prepared supper for Jenny's dad, Jenny and Jamie every weekday.

But today was Friday and it was the start of the Memorial Day Weekend. Both Jenny and Jamie were off from work and school, and it was a time Jenny spent with just Jamie. In a month school would be finished for the year and Jamie would be spending his whole day with grandma. It bothered Jenny that she would not be able to be with her little boy every day during the summer, but she appreciated that her mother was more than willing to take care of Jaime while Jenny worked.

As the thoughts of the approaching summer left her mind, Jenny looked over at the monkey bars and saw Jaime still at the very top, but he appeared rigid and was staring off into the sky. She began to walk toward the jungle gym and, as concern turned into alarm, her pace quickened into a trot.

When she arrived at the base of the unit, she looked up and saw Jamie who appeared frozen in place. His hands were gripping the bar in front of him, and his eyes were transfixed into space.

"Jamie! Jamie!", Jenny called out loudly.

When there was no response, she called out his name frantically over and over.

Other parents who were sitting nearby looked over, first casually and then, with more intent.

"Jamie, it's mommy. Come down! Please, come down now!", Jenny pleaded.

A father of one of the other children came over and asked, "What's wrong"?

"It's my son. Something is wrong and he won't come down. I am afraid he's going to fall", cried Jenny.

Without another word, the man began to climb up the jungle gym. He moved quickly and was at the top in a few moments.

He looked at Jamie who appeared to be in a trance-like state.

"Hey, sonny, your mom wants you to come down," said the man.

There was no reaction from Jaime. The man gently touched his arm, and it startled the child. Jamie looked over at the man and began to lose his grip on the bar. He teetered and the stranger grabbed him as he was about to fall.

Jamie looked into the man's eyes and asked, "Where am I? Did you see the fire and smoke on the airplane?"

The man had no idea what Jamie was speaking about and told him they need to climb down.

With one arm around the boy's waist and the other on the monkey bars, the two slowly descended. By now, a crowd of concerned parents, mostly women, had gathered at the base of the playground unit. A few applauded as the man and his human bundle touched down on the ground below.

Jenny grabbed Jaime from the man's grip and hugged him desperately, sobbing into his neck.

She looked at the man and choked out, "Thank you."

The man just nodded with teary eyes.

Jenny quickly went to the bench to pick up the pocketbook she had left there and rushed home.

When they arrived home, she put Jamie in bed since he fell asleep in the car on the short ride home. He immediately fell back asleep and slept for over 2 hours.

When he awoke, Jenny wanted to find out what happened, but she didn't want to further upset him. She made an effort to speak to him in a casual manner.

"Jamie, what happened today when you were on the monkey bars?", asked Jenny.

"Mom, didn't you see the fire and smoke when the airplane crashed?", asked Jamie.

"Jamie, I didn't see any airplane on fire," said his mother.

"I saw it, mom! When I got to the top of the monkey bars, I could see an airplane and the engine fell off and it crashed and blew up into flames," exclaimed Jamie.

"I saw people inside the plane, and they were screaming and crying. It was scary, mom!", said Jamie.

Jenny hugged her son and told him it was a bad dream and to try to forget about it. No one was hurt and there was nothing to worry about.

Before she prepared supper while Jamie was in his room reading, Jenny turned on the TV news. There was a video of an airplane in flames and the reporter explained that the plane had been taking off at O'Hare Airport in Chicago at a little before 3 PM Central Time. The engine apparently had broken off the wing as the plane was beginning its takeoff. The plane flipped over and exploded into flames, killing everyone on board. Over 270 people were killed, making it the worse aircraft accident in history.

Jenny felt weak and plopped down into a chair. Her hand covered her mouth, and her body shook. She then thought about the time. The plane crashed at 2:50 PM Central Time. That would be almost 4 PM Eastern Time – just about when Jaime said he saw the plane crash and burn.

She walked over to Jaime's room. She looked at him from the hallway as he sat up in his bed, quietly reading. Her head leaned over and rested on the door jam. She began to softly cry.

Printed in the United States
by Baker & Taylor Publisher Services